TUMBLING HEADLONG
INTO LOVE—OR UNSEEN DANGER . . .

The wind tore at her hair where it hung below the motorcycle helmet, and made tears stream from her eyes. Allie felt at the edge of control, more vulnerable than she'd felt flying in the glider with nothing beneath her but sky.

Rafe felt strong, warm, and solid. Under her, the Harley roared like a wild, untamed beast. It was like riding in the eye of a great storm. In a way, this, too, was like flying.

The steady stroke of the motor hummed along every nerve ending, and created a wild, restless energy that coalesced into a hard knot of desire. It was a ride of the senses as the cold air tore at them from the outside, and the heat built inside their tightly molded bodies.

Finally they arrived at his house, and Rafe took Allie's hand as they slid off the cycle. She hesitated at the doorway, remembering her earlier uneasiness, but it was just a dim memory—or was it?

"It's only you and me," Rafe said in a low voice. "No one else here. No ghosts." Then he pulled her into the circle of his arms, and touched her lips with wildfire. . . .

Books by Pamela Simpson

Fortune's Child
Mirror, Mirror
Partners in Time

MIRROR, MIRROR

PAMELA SIMPSON

BANTAM BOOKS

NEW YORK · TORONTO · LONDON · SYDNEY · AUCKLAND

MIRROR, MIRROR
A Bantam Fanfare Book / May 1993

FANFARE *and the portrayal of a boxed "ff" are trademarks of Bantam Books, a division of Bantam Doubleday Dell Publishing Group, Inc.*

All rights reserved.
Copyright © 1993 by Pamela Wallace and Carla Simpson.
Cover art copyright © 1993 by Alan Ayers.
No part of this book may be reproduced or transmitted in any form or by any means, electronic or mechanical, including photocopying, recording, or by any information storage and retrieval system, without permission in writing from the publisher.
For information address: Bantam Books.

If you purchased this book without a cover you should be aware that this book is stolen property. It was reported as "unsold and destroyed" to the publisher and neither the author nor the publisher has received any payment for this "stripped book."

ISBN 0-553-56200-2

Published simultaneously in the United States and Canada

Bantam Books are published by Bantam Books, a division of Bantam Doubleday Dell Publishing Group, Inc. Its trademark, consisting of the words "Bantam Books" and the portrayal of a rooster, is Registered in U.S. Patent and Trademark Office and in other countries. Marca Registrada. Bantam Books, 1540 Broadway, New York, New York 10036.

PRINTED IN THE UNITED STATES OF AMERICA

RAD 0 9 8 7 6 5 4 3 2 1

Mirror, Mirror

I

ALEXANDRA WYATT WALKED SLOWLY up to the open doors of the Church of the Wayfarer in Carmel and stopped dead still at the threshold. A dark-suited usher stared at her. The memorial service was about to begin, and everyone else had already been seated. In a moment the doors would be closed. Still, Allie hesitated, standing there in the bright sunlight of a remarkably clear, warm day, staring into the cool dimness of the old adobe church.

I have to do this, she told herself. For Mac.

She stepped inside and the usher showed her to one of the few remaining empty spaces in the very last pew. The small, unpretentious church was full; some people even stood in the side aisles. Allie sat down next to an elderly woman who had the stoic expression of someone who'd lived long enough to have attended many of these sad events. She smiled gently at Allie and asked, "Friend or family, my dear?"

For a moment Allie couldn't respond. The answer should have been simple—*family*. But somehow that word, with all its profound meaning, was difficult to speak. I *am* family, Allie reminded herself determinedly, even if I don't feel like it. Finally, she murmured, "Family," and the woman nodded in commiseration.

A distinguished-looking white-haired minister walked up to the podium and began the memorial service. Allie paid scant attention. Her gaze was riveted on the Sloans, sitting together in the two front pews, their backs straight, their expressions unemotional. If they felt anything, they wouldn't dare let it show, for they were, after all, the Sloans of Pebble Beach, sixth-generation Californians, power brokers and members of the social elite of the state. They had an image to maintain. Filling the other pews, like vassals surrounding a ruling family, were their wealthy, powerful, socially prominent friends and business associates. Allie realized there was probably an enemy or two here as well. But they were all there to honor the man who lay in the casket. Mackenzie "Mac" Sloan was dead at eighty-six.

As the minister turned the podium over to the man who would deliver the eulogy, Allie quietly got up and made her way down a side aisle until she could see the faces of the Sloans. As she looked at each profile, it amazed her that she could identify them from the old newspaper photographs she'd pored over. They had changed remarkably little in the twenty-five years since the photos were taken. But then, Allie realized, their privileged lives had been comfortable and secure. There had been no hardship or tragedy during those years to add lines of character or suffering. For the older members of the family there had merely been the softening of their faces and bodies, and the graying of their hair, as they gently aged. In the younger ones the youthful promise of physical beauty had been fulfilled, and they were now extremely attractive in their maturity. A handsome family, Allie thought.

"Mackenzie Sloan was a man beloved by all who knew him," intoned Grant Samuels, a state senator and an old friend of Mac's. "He was the patriarch of a great family, and that family meant everything to him."

Gavin Sloan stifled a yawn of boredom. Patriarch, he thought, was simply another word for boss. As the eldest male Sloan, and holder of a controlling interest in the Sloan Land Company, "Uncle Mac" had bossed them all around, telling Gavin how to run the company, telling them all how to run their lives. Well, no more. With Mac's death, his money would be divided up among the family, and control of the company would go to Gavin. And just in time too. If Mac had stubbornly clung to life much longer, he would have blown the biggest deal Gavin had ever put together, a deal that everyone in the family wanted desperately—everyone except Mac.

Senator Samuels went on. "He was a throwback to another age, when traditions were honored . . ."

Erica Sloan shifted in her seat, next to her husband. Mac had advised her not to marry Gavin. He told her that he didn't believe Gavin loved her nearly as much as she loved him. In a marriage, he said, it was always better if the man loved the woman just a little bit more than the woman loved the man. Marriage meant more to women than it did to men, and there were so many temptations to lure a man away from a marriage that wasn't really solid. She glanced at Gavin, sitting rigidly beside her, and realized how absolutely right Mac had been.

Samuels was saying, "Mac was a good friend, and will be sorely missed . . ."

I won't miss him, thought Charlotte Sloan Benedict coldly. He kept me on a pitifully inadequate allowance, as if I were a teenager. I'm middle-aged, for God's sake, and I've never had financial freedom. Well, now I will. And I'm glad.

Her husband, David, sitting next to her, glanced at his wife, then guiltily looked away. Charlotte knew exactly what he was thinking. He was every bit as glad as she was that finally he wouldn't have to be an indentured servant to the Sloan family.

". . . and his determination to maintain his family's illustrious heritage . . ."

Heritage, hell, thought Nicholas Benedict, Charlotte and David's son. Who gives a damn about that nowadays? The old man was out of it. He'd forgotten what it was like to be young, and to want to enjoy the things a great deal of money could buy. After all, what was the point of being rich if you hardly spent a dime?

Next to him, his sister, Valentina, gave him a sly grin, as if reading his thoughts. Leaning over, she whispered in his ear, "I've already spent my part of the inheritance. How about you?"

Nicky smiled. "Oh, yeah. Every penny."

"Mac Sloan didn't let anything stand in his way when he was convinced he was right," Samuels went on.

Rafael Sloan, sitting at the end of the pew, putting as much distance from his family as was seemly, smiled grimly to himself in agreement. Mac definitely hadn't let anything or anyone stand in his way once he'd decided on a course of action. He hadn't let Rafe's anger and bitter resentment prevent him from persuading Rafe to return to Pebble Beach. When Mac first approached him about returning to the family he'd long-since cut himself off from, Rafe told Mac to go to hell. But Mac refused to take no for an answer. And one day, to his amazement, Rafe found himself doing the one thing he'd sworn he would never do—returning to the area where he was born and raised, and taking his rightful place in the Sloan Land Company.

Mac Sloan was a tough old guy, Rafe thought with grudging admiration. There was a hint of affection in his feelings for his great-uncle, but he refused to acknowledge it. There was no way he would ever admit, even to himself, that he felt anything but cold dislike for any of the Sloans.

Samuels paused in his lengthy speech, and during that brief moment of silence there suddenly came the sound of something hitting the wooden floor. It was only a small black leather clutch that had fallen, but in the stillness of the church the sound seemed unnaturally loud. Looking at his sister-in-law, Erica, who had dropped the purse, Rafe found her staring almost in horror toward the aisle of the church. Erica had turned deathly pale, and looked as if she'd seen a ghost, Rafe thought. Following Erica's frozen gaze, Rafe saw a beautiful young woman with dark gold hair and gray-blue eyes, and an aura of almost heartbreaking vulnerability.

Rafe frowned, puzzled by Erica's response to this stranger. He stared at the young woman, and then, suddenly, he felt as if he'd been punched in the gut. He recognized that oval face, those delicate features, that air of fragility.

Barbara.

No wonder Erica looked as if she'd seen a ghost. This wasn't possible! Barbara had died twenty-five years ago. She couldn't be standing there now, looking as young and breathtakingly lovely as she'd looked then.

One by one the other Sloans noticed Erica's fixed gaze and

turned to look. One by one their expressions showed first blank confusion, then utter shock.

"Oh, my God," Valentina whispered out loud.

"What is it?" Nicky asked in a low voice. Then, seeing where she looked, his mouth fell open. "What the hell . . ."

Beside him, his mother turned to whisper a rebuke. But when she saw the person her son and daughter were staring at, she caught her breath in amazement. Nudging her husband, she whispered violently, "David . . . look!"

"What is it?" he snapped in a voice that carried beyond their pew, causing people to look at them in surprise. Looking toward the side aisle, he studied the people standing there, recognizing and dismissing most of them. Then he saw the young blond woman in the simple dove-gray suit, and he nearly fell off the pew. It can't be, he thought desperately. It *can't*.

In the pews immediately behind them, someone murmured, "What is it? What are they staring at?"

Sensing that he was losing his audience's attention, Samuels quickly brought his eulogy to a close. "We'll all miss Mac Sloan," he said. "We'll never see his like again."

Picking up his notes, he returned to his seat in the front pew with the Sloans. He glared at Gavin in silent but pointed rebuke for Gavin's lapse in attention.

As the minister returned to the pulpit to end the service, the whispers continued:

"They're staring at that girl. Who is she?"

"I don't know, but she looks familiar somehow."

"A member of the family?"

"I don't think so—"

"Wait a minute, I've got it. You know who she looks like?"

"Who?"

"Remember the Sloan girl who was murdered by her husband?"

"But that was twenty, maybe twenty-five years ago."

"I know, but that's who she looks like."

The minister finished. "The family has asked me to say there will be a gathering at Mr. Sloan's house . . ."

Erica Sloan whispered in an agonized voice, "It can't be . . ."

Her husband pulled himself together. "Of course not," he said in a tight voice. "She just happens to look like Barbara." He paused, then finished determinedly, "Whoever she is, she's nobody."

But Rafe, catching Gavin's words, knew better. He didn't believe in ghosts, and he knew who the woman must be.

Alexandra.

What the hell was she doing here? he wondered. Why had she come back? And, most important, how much did she remember?

2

TWO WEEKS EARLIER, ALLIE had sat in a hypnotherapist's office in Seattle, and had just been put in a deep trance.

"Open your eyes, Allie!" the therapist, Janice Moore, ordered.

Slowly, Allie's heavy-lidded eyes obeyed the command and she looked into Janice's kind face. She had consulted Janice in desperation, plagued by a sudden onslaught of terrifying nightmares and feelings of inexplicable anxiety. Now she felt incredibly relaxed, almost as if she were floating.

Janice, a comfortably plump, middle-aged woman with short, fading brown hair, smiled reassuringly at her. "You're still in a trance, but you're completely conscious and aware of your surroundings."

Allie nodded briefly. The brilliant morning sunlight streaming through the window gilded her dark blond hair with a golden sheen. Her pale skin looked almost translucent. A softness about her gently rounded features—her doe eyes, upturned nose, and full mouth—gave her an aura of girlish vulnerability that made her look far younger than her thirty-two years.

Janice continued in her gentle, soothing voice. "I want you

to focus on something that you see through the window, Allie.'' She gave her a moment to look at the view, then went on. ''Tell me what you see.''

The bank of windows in the fourth-story office in downtown Seattle looked out on Elliott Bay, the sapphire-blue expanse of Puget Sound beyond, and the jagged blue-gray outline of Bainbridge Island across the water. Allie's attention was riveted on the water, an intense blue beneath a misty haze of sky, and the dozens of sailboats dotting it. The striking juxtaposition of deep blue water, pale blue sky, and boldly colored sailboats nearly made her eyes ache with the sheer beauty of it all.

''What do you see?'' Janice prompted her gently.

''Sailboats, dozens of them. Daysailers, Santanas, a yacht. And Hobie Cats.''

The twin-hulled Hobie Cats with their multihued sails skimmed and danced across the water like water skeeters.

''I want you to select one particular boat, Allie. Describe it to me.''

Her eyes went to a small boat in the distance. She said carefully, ''The pontoons are silver. The sails are purple and orange.''

''Concentrate on the orange and purple sails.'' Janice gave Allie a moment until she was satisfied that Allie was completely focused. ''Now, tell me about this paralyzing fear that's been troubling you lately. When does it usually come over you?''

Allie's gray-blue eyes followed the Hobie Cat as it cut across the shimmering bay. Her body tensed, and she answered haltingly, ''The water.''

''What about the water? Tell me exactly what you see, Allie.''

Allie struggled with vaguely frightening images. ''Water . . . on the ground. There's something reflected in it.''

''Can you see what it is?''

Allie shook her head adamantly, her voice high with fear. ''No! I don't want to!''

Janice quickly reassured her. ''It's all right, Allie. You don't have to.'' She waited until Allie's rigid body began to relax.

Then she said, "Tell me about another time when you felt this fear."

Allie drew a deep, ragged breath. "The mirror . . . in my bedroom."

Making a brief note on her pad, Janice prompted Allie, "Yes?" clearly expecting her to go into greater detail.

Suddenly intensely uncomfortable, Allie sat erect in the overstuffed chintz-covered chair. "Sometimes I catch my reflection in the mirror as I'm walking past . . . and I have to look away."

Now her breathing became more rapid, and her mouth tightened in a frown. She shook her head in frustration as she struggled to find the right words. "Nothing is real in the mirror. I'm not *me* anymore. . . . It's as if I'm someplace in between. I'm afraid. I have to get away. I'm running—" Her voice came to a shuddering halt, her fingers clutching the arms of the chair.

"What are you running from, Allie?" Janice asked quickly.

Allie's breathing was hard and labored now, as if she were actually running. Her voice sharp with terror, she answered frantically, "I don't know!"

"Tell me what comes into your mind at these times. Is it an image, a sound?" Janice's voice was firm.

Allie's entire body shook convulsively as she struggled to remember, to peel back the protective layers she'd hidden behind for so long. She'd never before allowed herself to feel this depth of emotion.

"Allie?" Janice prodded her.

Tears filled her soft gray-blue eyes and her lips quivered as she whispered, "*Mirror, mirror, on the wall, who is the fairest one of all?*"

Janice leaned toward Allie as if trying to physically hold on to the subconscious memory that had broken through. "What does that mean, Allie?"

Allie shook her head from side to side, fighting the memory. "I don't know . . . I can't remember."

"Yes, you can, Allie. You must *let* yourself remember."

"No!" It was a cry of frantic denial.

Janice was insistent. "It's the only way to understand the

fear. Once you confront it, it will end. Now, who said those words to you?"

Conflicting emotions shadowed Allie's delicate face as she struggled to deny the long-repressed memory. Her hands clutched at the front of her oversize sweater as a drowning child might frantically grab at something, *anything,* holding on for dear life.

"Who said the words, Allie?" Janice repeated.

Slowly, her fingers loosened their hold on the sweater. Her expression softened, and her eyes were heartbreakingly sad. In a small, helpless child's voice, she answered, "My mother."

"Was it a story she read to you?" Janice asked, thinking of the familiar lines from the Snow White fairy tale.

Allie shook her head. Now the barest hint of a smile played about her lips. "It was a game we played."

In a soothing voice Janice went on. "Tell me about the game, Allie. Why does it frighten you?"

She shook her head. "I don't know."

Sensing the powerful denial within Allie, Janice persisted. "How does it make you feel when you look in the mirror?"

"Sad and . . . scared." Allie's smile was gone. She cried out, "*It's* there, in the mirror! I can't get away from it!"

Janice saw the battle of feelings in Allie's face. But she couldn't let her give in to the fear. She had to lead Allie back to the memory that haunted her. "What do you see in the mirror?"

Allie resisted. "I . . . I can't do this!"

"Yes, you can. Tell me what you see in the mirror."

Slowly, painfully, Allie said, "It's . . . a monster. It's looking at me in the mirror. . . ."

There was utter silence in the room for a moment. Then Allie said in a tormented whisper, "I can't go on!"

"The monster can't hurt you, Allie," Janice replied. "We need to find out where that monster comes from. I'm going to count down from ten to one. Ten—you're growing smaller, Allie. Your arms and legs are shrinking . . . four . . . three . . . two . . . one."

There was a moment of silence, then Janice said, "I'm going to take you back to the time you first saw the monster. Where are you now, Allie?"

"Inside my house." Her voice was that of a child.

"Is it day or night?"

"Night."

"What's going on?"

"I'm upstairs. I'm all alone . . . I don't like being alone. I go to Mommy and Daddy's room, but they're not there. Then I go downstairs, and I hear it."

"What do you hear?" Janice asked.

"Shouting . . . arguing."

"Who is shouting? Do you recognize the voices?

"I don't know," Allie insisted.

"Is it a man or a woman?"

Allie's eyelids fluttered as the images played back through her memory like the frames of a home movie. Her hands clutched her sweater again, the knuckles white. "I don't know," she answered. "It's a loud voice. Angry. I don't like it . . . I don't like that person . . ."

Janice leaned toward her and urged quietly, "Go down the stairs, Allie. Tell me what you see."

Tentatively, Allie's head came around, as if she were walking down those remembered stairs and turning at the bottom landing.

"What do you see?"

"The mirror in the hallway . . ."

"What do you see in the mirror?"

Allie answered slowly, "A door . . . it's open. I can see inside the room. It's Daddy's den."

"Who do you see, Allie?"

Allie's slender body instinctively reacted to the profound fear she had felt as a child. She grew even more agitated, twisting in the chair, as if she were were trying to get away from something.

"Who do you see, Allie?" Janice repeated.

"The monster!"

"What is the monster doing?"

Allie's childlike voice was filled terror. "There's something in its hand! It's big and heavy!"

Breathing in deep, painful gasps, she fought the terror back down into her subconscious. But it would never go back into the dark again.

Janice insisted, "What's happening, Allie?! You *must* tell me!"

Allie curled onto her side in the large chair and drew her knees up against her chest. Wrapping her arms tight about her legs, she rested her face on top of her knees. Tears streamed down her cheeks.

"It's hitting her!" she sobbed. "It won't stop!" And then in a desperately pleading voice, "It's hurting her! Please, make it stop!"

"Who, Allie? Who is the monster hitting?"

Curled tight within herself, Allie struggled to protect herself against the terror and brutality of what she had refused to see for twenty-five years.

Finally, unable to hold back the memory, she said in her little-girl voice—*"Mommy."*

3

LATER THAT AFTERNOON ALLIE stood before the wide expanse of windows in her sixth-floor office at Winslow Architectural in the historic Bon Marché building. It was classic turn-of-the-century style, six stories of red brick, with wrought iron exterior fire escapes and window ornamentation, and a copper roof. It had once been a warehouse filled with imported silks from China, cotton from India and Egypt, grains, tea, coffee, pumps, engines, and machinery, all of it arriving on clippers and steamships from New England, the Far East, and Europe.

Allie loved the building, and had felt at home in it from the first moment she stepped inside. But at the moment she was oblivious of its charm, as she stared out across the bay and Puget Sound. Instead of focusing on some distant sailboat as she had in Janice's office that morning, her gaze wandered beyond the bay to the expanse of deep blue ocean. It seemed to go on forever, like the endless darkness that surrounded deeply buried memories.

She still couldn't quite take it all in. In a matter of a few minutes her life had been changed profoundly, irrevocably, forever. Everything she had ever believed about her family, about her own history, was a lie.

"Your mommy and daddy died in a car accident, Allie. They're in heaven now. Whatever else you remember is just a bad dream. It's not real."

Her grandparents had repeated the lie often when she first came to live with them, until they were certain she'd accepted it. She could have told them not to worry. She didn't remember anything about the tragic night her mother, Barbara, died. Her memories of her parents, and her life with them, were blacked out completely. It was as if a shutter had closed, tightly blocking out the sunlight. For Allie, her childhood memories began after coming to live with her grandparents on their small farm outside Seattle.

She knew only that for some reason, mirrors, water, anything that showed a reflection, frightened her. When she shied away from them, and her grandmother asked her why, she said, "There are monsters in there." Her grandmother would hug her tightly, promise her that everything was all right and assure her there were no monsters.

Now the safe, secure, insular world her overprotective grandparents had created for her had been shattered. And she had no idea how to begin picking up the pieces. Because of her session with Janice, Allie had remembered what she'd spent twenty-five years successfully forgetting—that she'd witnessed her mother's brutal murder at the hands of someone who had looked to her then like a monster. Now, as an adult, she knew it had been no monster. A cold-blooded killer had looked up to find a little girl watching in horror, and had still continued to beat her mother to death.

Until that morning in Janice's office, Allie had managed to repress all memories of her mother and father. Her grandparents had numerous photographs of their only child, Barbara, and often Allie would look at them, trying to force herself to remember the woman in the photos. But no matter how hard she tried, no memories would come.

There were no photos of her father, and her grandparents made it clear they didn't want to discuss him. Allie felt frustrated, but she soon realized it was pointless to ask about him. As she grew older, she simply assumed that they'd disapproved of him.

She still remembered nothing of her father. But now

memories of her mother had begun flashing across her mind faster than she could process them . . . a lovely, gentle, soft-spoken woman, warm and affectionate with her child. A woman who laughed easily and often, who taught Allie the names of trees and flowers, as her own father had taught her when she was small. A woman who read bedtime stories to Allie every night when she put her to bed.

A particularly vivid memory filled Allie's mind, of her mother reading "Snow White" to her. Allie recalled asking if the love inside the princess died when she ate the poisoned apple and fell into a deep sleep. Her mother had replied, "The love inside her didn't die, it just fell asleep, like she did. Then the prince came, and his kiss awakened her. In fairy tales, the prince always comes just when all hope is lost."

"Snow White" had been Allie's favorite fairy tale. *Mirror, mirror, on the wall, who's the fairest one of all?* Allie and her mother had repeated the phrase to each other often, laughing together, playfully arguing over who was the prettier.

Barbara was a breathtakingly beautiful woman, with fair coloring and a perfect symmetry about her features that could have made her a fortune as a model or an actress. To the young Allie, her mother was the most beautiful woman in the world, more beautiful than the queens and princesses in the fairy tales she read to her daughter.

Barbara always insisted that Allie was the fairest one of all. Remembering now, Allie could hear her mother saying in a voice warm with love, "When you were born, I told the doctor you were the most beautiful thing I'd ever seen. You always will be, Allie."

How could I have forgotten that? Allie wondered helplessly.

All that love and beauty and joy had been senselessly, viciously, destroyed, and Allie's sense of loss was so acute, it was nearly unbearable. It was easier when she hadn't realized what she'd lost. Now that she remembered, it was devastating. At least, in a sense her mother had been returned to her through these memories. Why couldn't she remember her father too? she wondered. What kept her memories of him in the darkness of her subconscious, out of reach?

Since returning from her session with Janice, Allie had been unable to concentrate on her work. Her mind was too full of the knowledge of all she'd lost, and her heart was too heavy with an overwhelming sense of sadness.

A voice from her open office door startled her out of her reverie. "I suppose when Charlie Abbott asks why the final changes on the Edgewater project weren't delivered this afternoon, I can chalk it up to the eccentricities of creative genius."

Allie looked up sharply. The smile she gave the woman standing in the doorway was apologetic. Julia Winslow, her boss, leaned a shoulder into the doorjamb. She was sixty-eight, and looked fifteen years younger. Her short, sculpted brown hair, naturally frosted with silver, had the stylish look of a very expensive salon technique. Barely medium height, she always wore high heels to give herself a more authoritative presence.

The expression in her brown eyes was warm, open, shrewdly assessing without being unkind. Her features were even, if rather unremarkable, and she wore little makeup to enhance them. Those eyes, like the no-nonsense clothes she wore, and the open smile, could be deceptive. For underneath the casual appearance was an accomplished, assertive businesswoman who'd refused to accept the limitations imposed on the women of her generation, and had made her first love—architecture—a lifetime obsession.

She'd been an architect for nearly fifty years and had a vision of precisely how people should coexist with the land. She'd devoted her life and her career to creating architecture that preserved the environment, didn't plunder or destroy it.

Her greatest achievement was a development in the San Juan Islands called Edgewater. It embodied the achievements of an entire career. Ten years in the planning, five years under construction, it was a complete urban development that preserved the environmental integrity of a fragile ecosystem and magnificent coastline.

Allie felt fortunate and honored to be part of it. The project was critically important. Allie shared Julia's fervent conviction that architecture should protect and enhance the environment. She had inherited from her grandfather a deep and abiding love of the land, and through her work with Julia she was able to express that love.

Julia had been Allie's employer and mentor for eight years,

since Allie graduated from the University of Washington and passed her state licensing boards. She'd been a close and trusted friend for almost as long. As an architect, Julia scrutinized the smallest detail. As a friend, she looked even deeper, with compassion and caring.

"I wasn't aware you'd started smoking again," Julia commented from her relaxed post at the doorway. She'd kicked off her heels and stood with one stocking foot crossed over the other.

Allie glanced somewhat guiltily at the slender cigarette in her fingers. She's started smoking in college, a nervous habit left over from frantic group study sessions and cramming for finals. But she hadn't smoked in years. "I smoke only every once in a while," she said, aware that the hand holding the cigarette trembled. She didn't remember purchasing the pack, or lighting the cigarette.

"Are the changes on the Edgewater project that complicated?"

"What?" Allie asked, slowly making the shift of mental gears. Suddenly realizing what Julia was talking about, she shook her head. "No, not really. It shouldn't take more than a couple of hours work." She dragged her other hand back through her straight, shoulder-length hair. "I'll get it out this evening. I promise."

"Forget it for tonight," Julia said. "Charlie Abbott can wait until morning."

Allie frowned. She hated not getting something done when she'd promised. She prided herself on being responsible, reliable, and accurate. She'd always had an almost obsessive need not to let anyone down. Finally, she understood why. As a child, she had watched helplessly while her mother was murdered. The feeling that she should have somehow saved her mother, that she had failed her, had haunted her subconscious.

Now, looking guiltily at Julia, she asked, "Did Charlie call?"

Julia cut a glance down to the stack of pink message slips piled on Allie's desk and grinned good-naturedly. "Maybe a couple of times." There was no censure in her voice.

She hesitated, then came into Allie's office and closed the door behind her. "Want to talk about it?"

Allie tried to shrug it off. "It's just been a little hectic lately." But she still felt disoriented and profoundly disturbed by the session with Janice.

"You thrive on a hectic schedule. Actually, frantic is more your normal pace," Julia remarked thoughtfully. "Look, I like my privacy as well as anyone," she went on, "but if something is bothering you . . ."

Allie had turned back to the windows. The sudden reflection of the inside of her office on the paned glass was startling, bringing back the events of that morning with painful clarity. She hesitated, then the word burst out from her need to understand what was happening to her. "Families!"

Before Julia could respond, Allie went on. "Tell me about your family—please."

Julia sat in a chair across from the desk. She made a dismissive gesture. "I've got the usual number of aunts, uncles, cousins. Some likeable, others" —she shrugged, then finished ruefully—"not so likable. There are lawyers, doctors, maybe even an Indian chief, if my grandmother was right about there being Cherokee blood in the family. An eccentric or two, a war hero in the Second World War, and a couple of draft dodgers during the war in Vietnam. The usual mixed bag."

In her usual no-nonsense, pragmatic way, she made it all sound so simple and ordinary. Unusual for a woman who was anything but simple.

"But how well do you actually *know* your family?" Allie persisted.

Julia's smile flattened. "I know some of them better than I'd like. Actually, I probably don't know any of them as well as I think I do."

Allie shook her head in frustration. "What I mean is—do you *really* know them? What if you discovered that someone in your family, someone very close to you, had lied to you about something in order to protect your feelings?"

Julia answered without hesitation. "If it was important, I'd want to know the truth, no matter how painful."

Running a hand through her baby-fine hair unconsciously, Allie frowned, even more troubled now. "What if you were terrified of the truth?"

Julia gave the question thoughtful consideration for a moment. Then she said carefully, "I've always believed that no matter how painful it is, the truth can be dealt with. Our imagination usually conjures up much worse scenarios than the truth turns out to be."

Gravely considering Julia's response, Allie looked out the window again, and saw the late afternoon shadows slipping up the sides of the building. Traffic, already heavy well before five o'clock, edged slowly along the Baywater freeway.

Julia's words had helped Allie to reach a decision. She turned back to her. "I need to go out to Lake Stevens."

Her grandmother lived in Lake Stevens. The answers she needed were there, or at least some of them were. At any rate, it was a place to start.

To her intense relief, Julia didn't question her further. She simply said, "Take a couple of days off. You've earned it. Call me when you get back."

Allie flashed a grateful smile. "Thanks, Julia." She added quickly, "Don't worry, I'll get these changes done before I leave."

"Forget the changes, I'll do them myself." When Allie started to protest, she waved her off. "I'm so busy running this office and reassuring nervous clients, I don't get the opportunity to sit down and play architect much anymore. I miss it. It'll be fun to push a pencil around again." She wrapped an arm around Allie's shoulders. "Go to Lake Stevens. Do what you need to do. I'll see you when you get back."

"I feel like I'm abandoning you."

"Don't be silly. I ran this office single-handed for many years. Besides, I have Arnie and Stan in the drafting room. They can pinch-hit."

Julia's expression softened as she finished. "I know you, Allie. Something is bothering you. You wouldn't ask for the time off unless it was important. Go do what you need to do. I only hope it all works out well."

I hope so too, Allie thought soberly.

It was little more than an hour's drive to Lake Stevens from Seattle, but the transformation from concrete and steel to rolling green hills and wooded parklands was like a journey to a distant world. Allie turned the white Mustang convertible onto the familiar Lake Stevens road she'd taken so many times before. The small village of Lake Stevens had originally been a mill town, before the mill closed down. Now the idyllic setting drew residents of Seattle looking for a quiet country life-style. She passed small farms, with horses and cattle grazing in lush green pastures, and drove over wooden bridges across narrow creeks that meandered through the area. So tranquil, so utterly peaceful and perfect.

Today Allie saw it as somehow cruelly deceptive because she knew she would never again feel at peace until she learned the truth about her parents. She was terrified of that truth—but even more terrified of not knowing it.

Raised by her maternal grandparents, she had grown up here, playing hide-and-seek in forests of magnificent trees, exploring caves, balancing on stepping stones that crossed creeks and streams, hiking into the high country with her grandfather. It had seemed idyllic.

And even though Seattle had beckoned with its theaters, social life, high-rise office complexes, and high-rise possibilities—an enticing place for someone who dreamed of making her mark in the world—Lake Stevens had always been a place she was eager to come home to. It grounded her, and defined who she really was inside. Beneath the Armani suits and talk of exciting, prestigious projects, she was still the same girl who loved to run barefoot in the summer, felt a special affinity for animals, especially wounded ones, and despised pretense.

Now she was no longer certain who Allie Wyatt was. She knew only that she hadn't lost her parents in an automobile accident as her grandparents had told her. She had lost them in some kind of terrible tragedy that had now come back to haunt her.

She slowed as she drove past the small, picturesque lake. On this brisk autumn afternoon there were only a few sailboats on the lake, skimming across the shimmering water.

Mirror, mirror, on the wall . . . She couldn't get the haunting phrase out of her mind.

"What's happening to me?" she had asked Janice after she came out of the trance, still terrified by the awful memory that had surfaced.

"A repressed memory is a defense mechanism," Janice had patiently explained. "Like a shield to protect you against the pain of what you saw. Children often forbid themselves to think about things that are too painful. They forget what they saw in order to survive emotionally."

She had sat in Janice's office, unable to speak, almost unable to grasp what was being said. Janice made it all sound so matter-of-fact. But for Allie it was explosive. The memory was so vivid that even now, thinking of it, she once more felt the violence in the air, and her terror at seeing her mother bludgeoned to death. The sight of the bloody mass that had been her mother's head, and later, the even greater terror of being alone with her mother's lifeless body, were images she knew she would never again be able to erase from her mind.

"Why did it take so long for me to remember?" she had asked Janice, wishing desperately she could once more bury the memory.

"It's common for a repressed memory to come back in the late twenties or early thirties. You no longer see yourself as a vulnerable, helpless child. You're an adult, finally strong enough to accept the truth of the forbidden memory."

"But what made it come back *now*?"

Janice explained carefully. "There must have been a mental trigger—something similar to the original event—that set the memory in motion. It could be almost anything; something that happened, a person you met, a place, something you saw on television. But it somehow connects back to the events of the memory."

Now, driving past the lake, Allie realized what it was that had triggered the memory. A few weeks earlier she had gone to a carnival with her friend, Sherry, and her son, Brett. He was five, rambunctious, and fearless, and had dragged his mother and Allie into the fun house.

There, she had abruptly come face-to-face with her distorted reflection in a wall of mirrors. The images shimmered and wavered, almost normal one moment, grotesquely misshapen the next, with unnaturally long legs, a short torso, and pinhead in one image; long skinny legs, no torso, and enormous head in another. But one image was more frightening than all the others. A man had stood beside her. His image was completely shrunken so that it was very small, except for the hands—huge, grasping, brutal hands—*monster hands*.

The image had filled her with crippling, mind-numbing terror, and she'd rushed out of the fun house ahead of Sherry and Brett. That night the nightmares began, and the unreasoning jolt of fear every time she saw a reflection. Now she understood why.

At Old Hartford Road she turned left, and a few minutes later pulled up in front of her grandmother's small white-frame house with its faded blue shutters and sagging front porch. For a moment she sat in the car and looked at the place that had been her home from the time she was seven years old.

Her grandfather, Ethan Wyatt, had built the house on land he inherited from his parents, who were farmers. He had a natural talent as an artist, and loved to hike through the nearby mountains, drawing and painting the animals and scenery. From his Indian grandmother he inherited a deep love of the land and a fierce sense of protectiveness toward it. He was a true environmentalist before it became "in" to be one.

"How can people destroy the land?" Allie recalled his words. "Don't they realize we all have an obligation to nurture it so that it will be here to nurture the future generations? If we destroy the land, what will we have left? You must always remember, Alexandra, the land does not truly belong to us. We are merely the caretakers. If we abuse it, it will be lost forever."

From her grandfather Allie inherited a talent for drawing that eventually led her to architecture, and a love of the land that focused her interest on preserving the environment.

She adored him, and when he died shortly after her twelfth birthday, she felt devastated and abandoned. Losing the only male influence in her life, especially at a time when she was growing from a girl into a young woman, had affected her deeply. She was painfully aware that she had lost half of the only family she had ever known. Always a shy child, she became even more shy and withdrawn after that. She couldn't help envying friends who had big, happy families with mothers, fathers, brothers, sisters, and the extended family of aunts, uncles, and cousins.

She especially felt awkward around boys, and never had a date in high school. When she went away to college, to the University of Washington at Seattle, she was surprised that young men were attracted to her. Her friend, Sherry, whom she'd grown up with in Lake Stevens, had tried to tell her that she'd always been really pretty and it was only her extreme shyness that put off boys. But Allie, who felt awkward and unsophisticated, found that hard to believe.

In college she'd had a few dates, but never gotten seriously involved, preferring to focus on her studies. Her grandfather's death had left her grandmother, Anna, with a very limited income, and Allie was a scholarship student. She didn't want to risk losing her scholarship by goofing off. And besides, none of her relationships could compete with her driving ambition to become an architect.

Shortly after she achieved her goal, she became engaged, briefly, to a fellow architect named Dennis, who was everything she felt she wasn't—outgoing, confident, and so handsome he took her breath away. She couldn't believe how lucky she was that out of all the girls he might have had, he chose her. Then she discovered that he had never given up all those girls, and had no intention of doing so.

She broke off the engagement when he said to her matter-of-factly, "You don't really believe there's any reason to limit yourself to *one* person for the rest of your life, do you?" She answered in a voice trembling on the verge of tears that she fought to contain, "My grandparents did, and they were happy together until the day my grandfather died. I want what they had, Dennis. I won't settle for anything less."

His betrayal had been devastating. It reinforced her deep-seated conviction that she wasn't particularly attractive or worthwhile. After that she buried herself in her work and tried to tell herself it was enough. But the truth was, she hated sleeping in her big, empty bed alone, hated coming in late at night to a silent apartment, and especially hated the thought that she might never have children. Unlike some women she knew, she couldn't see having a child on her own. She knew all too well what it was like growing up without the requisite set of parents, and she didn't want to do that to a child. She wanted the kind of family she had missed, and she was afraid she would never have it.

Now, sitting in her car, looking at her grandmother's home, Allie felt an even deeper and more devastating kind of betrayal than she had experienced with Dennis.

The last thing Janice had said to her was, "The killer's identity is there in your memory. But the terror and pain broke something inside you, and you buried the truth in an unreachable part of your subconscious. Now that you're no longer a child, the adult in you is ready to deal with what happened. That's the reason the memories have started to come back."

"Will I remember more?"

"Perhaps. Perhaps not. There's no way of knowing for certain. We can continue with hypnosis, and it might help. But a more effective way to retrieve all your memories could be to go back to the place where it all happened."

Allie didn't know where it all happened. But her grandmother did. Her grandmother, who had lied to her all these years. Why? Allie asked herself over and over, trying to understand. And what happened to her father?

She knew she couldn't put off the confrontation with her grandmother any longer. She got out of her car and slowly walked to the front door. As usual, it was unlocked. She went inside, calling out to her grandmother as she made her way through the house. There was no answer. On this cool, clear autumn day, Allie knew where she would find her.

She walked through the small, cozy living room cluttered with the accumulation of a long lifetime, things that had no financial worth but great sentimental value—framed drawings and paintings done by her grandfather hanging side by side with Allie's efforts to copy him; pillows embroidered by her grandmother; an antique pewter collection in a small curio cabinet with a gracefully curving teapot holding pride of place; and built-in bookshelves filled to overflowing with the nature books her grandfather had loved, and the gardening books and catalogues her grandmother loved to pore over.

As Allie moved past the rock fireplace her grandfather had

made with small boulders dragged up from the nearby creek, her attention was drawn to the photographs of her mother on the mantel. There were several, beginning when she was a baby, up through college.

Barbara Wyatt had been an adorable baby and a beautiful young woman. Allie's grandparents had adored their only child and were devastated by her death. For years Allie had lived with their reluctance to talk about her mother except on rare occasions. Now, for the first time, it occurred to her that there were no wedding photos of her mother and father. Why wouldn't they have a picture of their daughter on her wedding day? If there hadn't been a formal wedding, at least they should have had a picture of their daughter and son-in-law together.

Allie paused to look at the last photo of her mother, taken shortly before Allie's seventh birthday. Barbara posed with her daughter, smiling down at her lovingly. As always, Allie felt plain compared to her exquisitely lovely mother. Tears came to her eyes. She fought them back and forced herself to move on through the narrow galley kitchen and out the back door.

At the end of the large backyard Anna Wyatt knelt by a flower bed, weeding vigorously. She was so intent on her work that she didn't hear Allie.

Allie stood at the top of the back steps, watching her grandmother for a moment. Her garden was her passion. For as long as Allie could remember, this was where she could always find her grandmother—when she ran in from school, excitedly waving a test paper that she'd gotten an A on; seeking her out to talk about arguments with Sherry; working their way together through the long, difficult teenage years filled with wildly fluctuating emotions. Her grandmother had always been there for her, always kind, always understanding.

All that, too, seemed like a sort of betrayal now. Allie had relied on and believed in the love and security her grandparents had always given her. They had been her solid foundation. Now that foundation had been eroded by the shock of a discovered lie.

"Allie?" Anna Wyatt stood up from her gardening and brushed the dirt from her work gloves. She was tall, like all the women in their family, although not as tall as either Allie, or

Barbara had been. She smiled with delight, and her bright blue eyes crinkled at the corners. Anna Wyatt was seventy-five years old, but she moved with an energy and spryness that belied the years. Her hair, which had once been deep gold like Allie's, had gradually faded over the years, until now it was pure silver. She wore it in a short cap that emphasized her still-lovely heart-shaped face.

She had forced herself to adjust quickly to being a widow after Allie's grandfather died, saying she didn't have time to be a sad recluse when she had a teenager to raise.

Thinking of it now, Allie realized how completely she had been the focus of her grandmother's life. Anna had given her so much and asked for so little. Even now there was no reprimand in her voice because it had been several weeks since Allie had last been home. There was simply that warm, unconditional welcoming love.

"What a surprise! It's not like you to take off in the middle of the week." Anna beamed as she crossed the neatly manicured lawn toward Allie.

As she came closer, her expression changed. "There's nothing wrong, is there?" Before Allie could respond, Anna answered the question herself as she drew off her gloves, "Of course not. There I go, worrying too much." She cupped Allie's face lovingly in her hands. "But you do look a bit tired. You're probably working too hard."

Allie shook her head. "Work is fine, Gram. I've just finished up the Edgewater project."

Anna linked her arm through Allie's as they turned toward the house. "Your grandfather would have been so proud of you," she said as they went in through the back service porch to the kitchen. "I'll pour us some tall glasses of iced tea." Glancing through the open archway into the living room, she asked, "Where is your bag?"

"I didn't bring one."

Anna looked disappointed. "You're not planning on staying over?"

"No. I . . . I need to talk to you, Gram." Allie moved into the living room and stood in front of the fireplace, staring at the photographs of her mother.

Her voice must have betrayed her inner turmoil, for her grandmother frowned. "What is it? What's wrong?" she asked, following Allie into the living room, still clutching the hand towel she'd grabbed to wipe her hands on.

Allie didn't know how to begin, didn't want to begin. But she had no choice. She turned to face her grandmother, and in a voice filled with pain, said, "I've remembered the night my mother was killed."

A stunned silence stretched out between them for what seemed like an eternity. Finally, Anna sat down heavily in the large chair by the fireplace. In an instant she had aged terribly, and suddenly seemed very old and very frail, all her strength and vitality drained from her.

Allie asked, "Why did you and Grandpa lie to me?" She hadn't meant to sound so accusing, but she couldn't help it. She felt betrayed by the two people she had trusted most in the world.

Her grandmother started to answer, then stopped. After a moment she tried again. "You were in shock, you didn't seem to remember anything that happened that night, and we didn't encourage you to. We thought it was a blessing that you had forgotten. As you grew older and still didn't remember, I was convinced the decision your grandfather and I made was the right one."

She looked helplessly at Allie. "I hoped you'd *never* remember that night."

"You made sure I didn't remember," Allie said angrily. "You lied about everything. Do you know how that makes me feel? To suddenly discover that everything I've believed my whole life is a lie?"

"It wasn't *all* a lie, Allie," her grandmother insisted. "We loved you! You were all we had. We were desperate to protect you."

"Protect me? How have you protected me? Did you really think it would remain forgotten forever?"

Allie paced across the small living room. Her gestures were frantic, like those of a caged animal desperate to be set free. "What else did you lie to me about? What happened to my father?"

"Oh, Allie . . ." Her grandmother gestured helplessly, "You don't want to know."

"Yes, I do! I need to know the whole truth! Tell me!" Allie insisted.

"Oh, sweetheart . . ." Anna's eyes filled with tears, and her voice shook as she tried to speak. She struggled to pull herself together. Finally, she said in a barely audible whisper, "Your father killed your mother."

4

For several empty seconds there was no sound in the room but the ticking of the ancient grandfather clock in the corner. Allie stood there, unable to respond, shattered by her grandmother's devastating words.

Anna explained reluctantly. "He . . . he was tried and convicted. He was executed one year later."

Allie felt a jolt as another piece of memory emerged. "He was in jail. You took me to see him."

Anna nodded. "He wanted badly to see you one last time. We had kept you away from him during the trial, and afterward. Your grandfather didn't want you to go, but I felt it was important for you to say good-bye to each other. I couldn't face Alan, so I arranged for his attorney to take you into the visiting room at the prison."

It all came back now—being in a small, bare room with her father. She clearly recalled everything about him. He was tall and handsome, but haggard-looking. She clung to him, and he hugged her fiercely. Then she felt hands pulling her back, tearing her away from her father's arms. She experienced again all the aching loneliness of the child who had cried out and tried to fight off those hands that were so much stronger than she was.

As she was lifted, kicking and screaming, and carried from the room, she reached out to her father with both arms. Tears were streaming down her cheeks. *"Daddy, please! Don't let them take me away!"*

He had tried to go to her. But two men wearing uniforms had stopped him. He had reached out, as if he could span the growing distance between them. *"Always remember that I love you, Allie!"* he had cried out after her. *"And I loved your mother!"*

She could still hear her own frantic screams echoing down the void of years, could see the tears that glistened on his cheeks, and hear the door as it slammed between them.

"Oh, God." Allie squeezed her eyes shut and wrapped her arms tightly around herself, as if trying to physically keep out the devastating memory. She couldn't bear it. Why had she forced her grandmother to tell her the truth? She would have been better off not knowing.

Hastily, she gathered her purse and car keys. "I have to go," she said through her tears.

"Allie, wait!" her grandmother begged, frantic to stop her. "Don't go back to Seattle tonight. You're too upset, you shouldn't be driving. Stay the night, and we'll talk."

Allie shook her head. "I can't stay here. I have to go someplace where I can think."

Anna's voice was a ragged whisper. "Please don't hate me."

Allie felt her heart constrict with pain. "I don't hate you, Gram. I could *never* hate you. I know you and Grandpa were only trying to protect me. But I can't stay here. I don't belong here—I don't know where I belong anymore."

"Allie!"

"I'll call you," she said, fighting to hold on to what precious little composure she had left. She ran to the convertible and slid into the leather seat. Dust and gravel churned under the tires as she hurriedly pulled out of the driveway.

It was a little after seven when she got back to Seattle. Instead of going directly to her apartment, she went to the main branch of the city library. An assistant librarian pulled all the microfiche for the Seattle newspaper from twenty-five years earlier.

For the next two hours Allie sat in a small, enclosed cubicle, scrolling through edition after edition. Headlines focused on the war in Vietnam; Johnson's decision not to run for reelection against the Republican nominee, Nixon; the rise of "the women's movement"; and black power.

Finally, Allie found what she was searching for. PROMINENT SOCIALITE FOUND DEAD, the headline blared.

It was all there, a lengthy article and photographs. The story chronicled the seemingly fabled marriage of Barbara Wyatt, a small-town girl from a middle-class family in Lake Stevens, to Alan Sloan, scion of the wealthy, politically powerful Sloans of Pebble Beach, California. The Sloans were at the pinnacle of California society, and Barbara's marriage to Alan had been seen as something of a Cinderella story.

There was a brief history of the Sloan ranch, called El Sureno, which had been established in the Big Sur area over a hundred and fifty years earlier with the marriage of cattleman Ben Sloan to Spanish heiress Elena Marin. Her family land grant established El Sureno—the last original Spanish land grant to remain intact. Simon Sloan, Allie's grandfather, had continued cattle ranching until his death in 1963. At that time, control of the ranch, and Sloan Enterprises, passed to her father, Alan.

The article mentioned Barbara's busy social life, and her devotion to her only child. There was a photograph of Allie as she was being taken from the Sloan ranch by a middle-aged couple that she recognized as her grandparents, with the accompanying headline: YOUNG HEIRESS GOES INTO SECLUSION.

The newspaper had covered the investigation thoroughly. Barbara Sloan had been a local girl, and it was a notorious case. There were articles about it in practically every issue. The murder, and subsequent trial, had rocked Pebble Beach, an exclusive community that boasted some of the wealthiest and most famous people in the state.

Some of the articles profiled other members of the family. There was a picture of Gavin Sloan and his wife, Erica. Gavin was Alan's cousin, and one of the principal heirs of the Sloan estate. He looked to be in his late twenties, and bore a marked resemblance to Alan. When asked about the violent argument he had witnessed between Barbara and Alan only a few hours before her death, he answered tersely, "No comment."

Erica Sloan was sleek and sophisticated, always dressed in clothes by Oscar de la Renta, and her name was connected with every prominent charity on the Monterey peninsula. Asked the same question that had been asked of her husband, she had replied, "It was a minor disagreement, nothing more."

Charlotte Sloan Benedict, Gavin's sister, had a passion for horses and was involved in the international horse set that loved to congregate at Pebble Beach. There was a picture of her riding at the Sloan ranch with her two small children. Her husband, David Benedict, corporate attorney for the Sloan Land Company, when asked to give his opinion about the case, said, "My wife and her family are stunned by these tragic events. Naturally, I will give whatever support I can. But it would be unethical for me to involve myself in the case."

There were other cousins. Nicholas Sloan was several years younger than Gavin. He'd just returned from college in the East, and was shown standing beside a shiny new Porsche. There was a lengthy account of his athletic accomplishments at college, and a brief mention of a run-in with local authorities over a young woman who had accused him of rape. The student had quickly recanted her story, and left the college.

Valentina Sloan, in her early teens, had been expelled from St. Joachim's, a parochial school, the year before. She was pictured arriving home from the private school that she currently attended in Switzerland. She frowned into the camera, a typical sullen adolescent. The one comment she had made to the press was expressed with that same sullenness. When asked if she'd overheard the argument between Alan and Barbara, she answered, "Well, sure. It was the family Christmas party, for Christ sake! Everyone was there. We all heard them arguing like crazy."

There was a picture of Mackenzie Sloan, first cousin to Allie's grandfather, Simon. He was of medium height and slender, with the aquiline features of his Spanish ancestors. At fifty-seven, his silvery-gray hair and mustache were a stark contrast to his darkly tanned skin. Reading about him now, twenty-five years later, Allie had no memory of him, just as she had no memory of any other members of the Sloan family. But looking at his picture, she had a sense that he was someone she had once liked very much.

Mac had been interviewed briefly on the steps of the courthouse at the beginning of the trial. "Alan is innocent. He couldn't have killed anyone, certainly not Barbara. I'll never believe otherwise. This is a travesty of justice."

Allie scrolled through the next few weeks. There were more articles and photographs of the Sloan family . . . Gavin and Erica attending the trial, Charlotte Benedict putting on a brave front as she chaired the annual Cascarones Ball put on each year for charity by descendents of the original Californios, and David Benedict's somber countenance as the trial wore on.

Then suddenly Allie stopped. She stared intently at a particular photograph. She had no memory of the other people she was reading about, but this person was different. She recognized Rafael Sloan. He was tall with dark hair and eyes, and the sort of lean, tensile lankiness of youth. His picture both fascinated and disturbed her. There was something familiar about his angry expression, the tight mouth and blazing eyes . . .

Her stomach churned. There was something . . . something that she tried to remember but couldn't. She stared at the photograph of him entering the courthouse. He had been seventeen at the time of the murder, yet there was none of the typical teenage sullenness that had been so apparent with Valentina Sloan. He looked older than his years, and already had a smoldering sensuality that would have undoubtedly later developed into a potent attraction for women.

According to the article, he was Gavin Sloan's half brother. At the time of the murder he was living at the ranch house at El Sureno with Allie's parents. After the trial Rafe Sloan had disappeared.

Allie racked her brain for a specific memory of him, but none came. Yet he, of all these people, looked familiar. Why did she remember him, and none of the others? she wondered. And why did she feel this inexplicable sense of fear when she looked at him?

Allie shook her head in frustration, angry at her inability to put it all together.

Then she found the final headlines: SLOAN CONVICTED

IN WIFE'S DEATH . . . ALL APPEALS EXHAUSTED IN SLOAN CASE . . . SLOAN DIES IN GAS CHAMBER.

Afterward, Allie had no idea how long she sat there, staring at that last headline, too devastated to move. The dark place inside her that had kept everything hidden away all these years had suddenly been exposed to the harsh glare of daylight. She felt as if she were choking. Her throat was so tight that she could hardly breathe.

"Oh, God!" she whispered. "Daddy . . ." Tears blurred her eyes.

"Miss? Are you all right? Miss?"

She looked up to see the middle-aged librarian looking at her uncertainly. The woman went on. "We close in five minutes. I have to put away the microfiche. Do you want copies of anything?"

Allie shook her head. "*No.*" She didn't ever want to look at any of this again. Gathering up her sweater and purse, and the small notepad on which she'd written a single name, she left the library.

An hour later she sat in the living room of her small apartment in one of the modern high rises that dominated the Seattle skyline. The simply furnished room, with its sofa and chair in off-white Haitian cotton and cream-colored walls bare save for a few treasured paintings done by her grandfather, was dimly lit by the one lamp she'd turned on when she'd come in earlier. She'd been thinking hard, going over everything, trying unsuccessfully to remember more about the night her mother was killed.

Most important, she tried to remember if it was her father's face she had seen in the mirror. But try as she might, it wouldn't come clear. She kept seeing the scene from a child's perspective, and the face of her mother's killer was that of a monster, not a person. Her mind was stuck. In only a few hours she'd remembered so much, but now it seemed her ability to remember had come to a crashing halt.

Fragments of things she'd heard and read came back to her. *"Alan is innocent"* . . . *"We all heard them arguing like crazy"* . . . And then Janice's voice—"The only way to know what happened is to go back. . . ."

She knew what she had to do. Before she could change her

mind, she got up and went to the telephone sitting on a small oak desk in a corner. Picking up the receiver, she quickly dialed information for Pebble Beach, California. She was relieved to learn there was a listing for the person she sought. He might very well have died over the intervening years. Or had an unlisted number.

With a shaking hand she dialed the number the operator had given her. She let the phone on the other end ring several times, and was about to hang up when a gruff male voice finally answered. "Yes? Who on earth is this at such an ungodly hour!"

Allie glanced at the small crystal clock on the desk. It was only eleven, but to an elderly person that must seem very late. "Is this Mackenzie Sloan?"

"Of course it is. What do you want?"

Nervousness made Allie stutter. "Th-this is Alexandra Wyatt." Quickly, she corrected herself. "I mean, Alexandra Sloan."

There was dead silence at the other end. What if he didn't remember her? she thought worriedly. He was very old. And even if he did remember, what if he didn't want to have anything to do with her?

"I'm . . . Alan and Barbara's daughter," she explained hesitatingly, feeling more and more like a fool.

Again there was only silence. She bit down hard on her lip, certain she had made a stupid mistake. She was about to apologize for disturbing him and hang up when there came a terse response. "I'm not senile, for God's sake. Of course I know who you are."

The gruff voice thickened and wavered with emotion. "Little Allie . . . I've waited so long to hear from you. Thank God you've finally called. I have so much to tell you."

5

THE SMALL COMMUTER JET from San Francisco touched down at Monterey Municipal Airport. Allie had called Mackenzie Sloan—"Uncle Mac" as he asked her to call him—from the airport in San Francisco, telling him of her arrival time.

"I'll send the car for you," he had insisted in that gruff yet somehow gentle voice that now seemed so familiar. It was a voice out of the past, tied to the life she'd once shared with her parents.

"No, thanks. I'd rather rent a car. I'll need something to get around in."

He argued with her for a bit, then gave in, but insisted that she come to his house as soon as she arrived.

In the cold light of day, after a sleepless night, she was even more determined to find all the pieces of her past. She had called Julia first thing in the morning and said simply, "I need to take more than a few days. It's a . . . *family* matter."

As she said the word, she realized that her concept of family had consisted of herself and her grandmother, and her grandfather before his death. Now she knew she had another family, whose existence she'd been unaware of. She didn't know if they were people she could care about or who could care about her. But she had to find out the truth about her parents. She had to confront the nightmare.

"I need an open-ended leave of absence," she had explained to Julia. "I can't explain right now. I don't entirely understand it all myself yet. I realize how unsatisfactory that sounds, and if you tell me not to bother coming back, I won't blame you."

Realistically, she knew she couldn't expect Julia to hold her job for an indefinite period, and she had no idea how long she might be gone.

The voice at the other end was as caring and supportive as it had always been through eight years of close collaboration and friendship. "Don't be ridiculous. I'm not about to lose the best damn architect I've ever worked with. You've hardly taken off more than a few days in all the time we've been together. You have some time off coming. I sometimes forget that unlike myself, most people have other things in their life besides work."

As she had occasionally done before, Allie wondered if Julia ever regretted the choice she made to make her work her entire life. But it was far too personal a question. And, besides, Allie was certain that Julia was the kind of person who never second-guessed herself once she'd chosen a particular path.

"Thank you," Allie said quietly. They seemed such simple words, but she meant it from the bottom of her heart. She was about to leave the life she'd known and explore another that was fraught with uncertainty. She needed the security of knowing her job would still be there when she came back, and she was deeply grateful to Julia for being so understanding.

Julia responded with real affection in her voice. "I'll miss you terribly, my dear. Who else will I argue so creatively with? But you go do whatever it is you have to do. We're in between big projects for the next few months, and the boys can take care of the little ones."

"I'll call you as soon as I know when I can return," she promised Julia. She added hesitantly, "I . . . I just need to find out who I am."

Julia said firmly, "I know *who* Alexandra Wyatt is. And no matter what she has to deal with, I know she'll be just fine."

Before Allie could respond with heartfelt gratitude for

Julia's support, the line went dead. Julia wasn't one for maudlin conversations or long good-byes.

Allie waited to call her grandmother until she arrived at the airport in San Francisco, right after she talked to Uncle Mac.

"Oh, Allie. I've been so worried," Anna said quickly. "I've been calling your apartment and the office. Where are you?"

"I'm in San Francisco." There had been a stunned silence on the other end of the phone.

"Gram, I have to do this. I've remembered more."

"Have you considered that it might be best not to remember?" her grandmother suggested hesitantly.

"No," Allie had replied firmly. "I need to know the truth about my parents, whether it's good or bad. For as long as I could remember, I've felt incomplete somehow. I'm just beginning to understand why. I need to fill in the missing blanks in my life. No matter how hard it may be, somehow I'll just have to deal with it."

She hesitated, unsure whether to mention the next thing to her grandmother. Finally, she said slowly, "There's something else—about my father. It's just a vague feeling now, but I sense somehow that it's important. I have to find out what it is."

There had been tears in her grandmother's voice. "Oh, Allie, I love you so much. You're all I have left. Please, please be careful. And come back soon."

"I will, Gram. I promise." Before her grandmother could say anything further, Allie finished. "I have to go now, Gram. They've called my flight. I love you." And she quickly hung up.

Now Allie carried the one piece of luggage she had brought to the Monterey airport car rental counter. A half hour later she pulled out of the rental parking area, and cut over to Highway 68. She crossed over at the Highway 1 interchange according to the directions the rental attendant had given her, drove a short distance farther, and found herself at the toll gate to the exclusive Seventeen-Mile Drive area where Mac lived.

Somehow reluctant to use Uncle Mac's name as her entree to the area, she paid the five-dollar fee that everyone except the residents, who had a sticker attached to the front window of their automobiles, had to pay. The residents were quickly waved through by the security guards.

From the moment she first entered Del Monte Forest, Allie was struck by its magnificent beauty. It was green and lush, and each bend in the road revealed a breathtaking ocean view. Seventeen-Mile Drive, a two-lane residential road, meandered through some of the most exclusive real estate in the world: past Pebble Beach golf course, Cypress Point Club, Spyglass Hill. To golfers they were some of the most challenging names in the world. And they surrounded some of the most luxurious homes in the world. The elaborate gated residences reflected every architectural style imaginable: Greek revival, Mediterranean, colonial, Cape Cod, and in some instances a modern blend of several.

There were no sidewalks. The streets spread to high rock walls that surrounded seaside estates. Over those walls Allie glimpsed houses built of rough-hewn redwood that had weathered to silver-gray, and others built of stucco, and rock. Many of them were topped by Spanish-tiled roofs, and all were set among the wooded splendor of pines, redwoods, eucalyptus, and the fabled gnarled Mediterranean cypress trees.

It was like entering a private woodland. A canopy of trees spread over the road, spraying dappled sunshine down on the hood of the car as she passed underneath.

In circular driveways behind wrought-iron gates she saw the other accoutrements of wealth; countless Mercedeses, Range Rovers for the more rugged types, sleek Jaguars, an occasional Rolls or Bentley, several Porsches and BMWs. The few cheaper cars clearly belonged to the hired help.

Allie drove slowly, looking at everything intently, trying to find some essence of memory. She had spent time there as a child, undoubtedly riding along this same road with her parents, on their way to visit Uncle Mac, who had lived there his entire life.

To her disappointment, she didn't feel the slightest sense of recognition. She felt frustration threaten to overwhelm her, and she fought it back, telling herself it was silly to expect to arrive here and suddenly remember everything. Janice had said it could take a while. She remembered unhappily that Janice had also said she might not ever remember anything more than she had already. That was a possibility she refused to consider. She *had* to remember.

Mac's house was on Seventeen-Mile Drive itself. Allie drove another couple of miles along the winding road through the forest of cypress before she finally found it. The name was emblazoned in wrought-iron letters above the massive iron double gate—CASA SURENO. There was no number, simply the name. No one who expected to get through that gate needed to know anything more.

The name had been taken from the ranch at Big Sur, Rancho Sureno, or southern ranch. According to the brief history of the area that she'd picked up in the newspaper accounts of twenty-five years ago, the Big Sur area took its name from Rancho Sureno. It was a little daunting to realize that she was intimately bound to so much California history.

She pulled just inside the entrance to the driveway and stopped the car. Casa Sureno lay sprawled across a rocky bluff, perched between a turn in the road of Seventeen-Mile Drive and the churning Pacific Ocean. It was a plaster and tile Mediterranean legacy to the Spanish ancestors who had first come to California, with an inner courtyard at one end and a turreted garret at the other.

It looked like a Spanish villa, gleaming in the bright sunlight, set amid Mediterranean cypress that looked like bent sentries. Brilliantly colored geraniums and creeping crimson bougainvillea spilled from enormous red clay bowls along the driveway that was set with red clay tiles.

According to Mac, she had spent a great deal of time here as a child. During their brief conversation the night before, he'd told her that his only child, a son, had died very young. He and his wife had been very close to Allie's father, who had been more like a son to them than a nephew. Many family celebrations were held here, including the reception after her parents were married.

Now Allie rolled down the car window. Sunlight sparkled off the ocean, visible through the trees that surrounded the house. She closed her eyes and tried to remember—something, *anything*.

A cool breeze stirred off the water, blowing a strand of hair across her cheek. She brushed it back, and let herself relax as she had in Janice's office, mentally going through the meditation exercise Janice had taught her to remove everything else from her mind—everything except this place.

Like the sunlight that had filtered down through the canopy of trees, dappling the hood of her car, images danced across her mind fleetingly, as if struggling to break through . . . a tall man crouching down beside her on the tiled steps so that he was at eye level with her . . . handing her a basket . . . *"Find the Easter eggs, Allie. There's a special one with a surprise in it" . . . "Is it a baby chick, Daddy?" . . . "You have to find it, to see what's inside, Princess . . ."*

Then the fleeting memory was gone, like those elusive patterns of sunlight on the car. There was nothing more except a lingering sense of complete and unconditional love from her father. The feeling warmed her.

"My past is here, somewhere. I have to reclaim it," Allie whispered to herself fervently. Until she did so, she knew she could never get on with her life.

She put the car in gear and slowly drove toward the magnificent sprawling mansion.

As she pulled up in front of the main entrance, one of the tall, hand-carved wooden doors opened. An elderly man stepped out onto the tiled steps. He was thin and stooped, with flowing white hair and mustache, and a patrician bearing—the last surviving grandson of Ben Sloan and Elena Marin, whose marriage had united two worlds in old California and founded a family dynasty.

Though he had aged a great deal in the intervening years, she still recognized him from the photographs in the newspaper. He must be close to eighty-five years old, she knew. He was frail and stood shakily with the aid of a cane. But his dark eyes—the legacy of his Spanish grandmother—burned bright with excitement, and his smile welcomed her.

As she got out and slowly walked around the car, he carefully made his way down the steps, as if he couldn't wait for her to come to him. His expression sharpened with surprise, and then a slow, expanding pleasure. "*Allie.*"

The sound of her name in that gruff but gentle voice stirred distant memories. She'd heard that voice before.

He cleared his throat as he extended a thin hand that trembled slightly, and reached for hers. "Forgive me, my dear, for being startled. You look so much like your mother. It's almost like seeing Barbara again."

"Uncle Mac," she said, letting him take her hand. The tentativeness and uncertainty she'd felt while talking to him the night before melted away with the warmth of his hand about hers.

"Welcome home, my dear," he said, emotion thick in his throat and his eyes brimming over with tears. "It's been a long time—too long." He chuckled then. "I'm afraid I'm being embarrassingly emotional, something my father, a rather fierce man, wouldn't have approved of."

Then he reached out to her, encircling her shoulders with an arm that felt unbearably thin through the immaculate suit he wore. "Come inside, Allie. There's so much to talk about. I want to know *everything* about you."

They sat in a courtyard that opened out onto a beautiful manicured lawn. Beyond it, a sheer cliff dropped away to jagged rocks and the restless ocean. Occasionally, sea spray jetted over the rocks from the water below, sending misty plumes into the air that hung suspended like millions of crystals catching the sunlight in refracted rainbows before scattering in the wind.

On a small marble-topped table between them there was a pitcher of lemonade for Allie. Mac drank from a goblet of wine.

"My physician recommends it," he had told her with a wink as his housekeeper served them. "And who am I to argue with that?" The housekeeper, Inez, a plump, placid woman, gave him a rueful look that suggested he was fabricating the statement about his doctor, then left them to talk in private.

"Now then," Mac said, "tell me everything about yourself."

Hesitant at first, then put at ease by his warmth, Allie told him about her life in Washington, focusing on her career, and speaking fondly of Julia. "She has such an extraordinary vision, and such passion to preserve the land. My grandfather was like that. I suppose I got my own feelings about the land from him. It seemed natural to become an architect. But in all honesty, I don't think I could have worked for anyone else but Julia. We feel the same way about so many things."

"She sounds like a remarkable woman."

Allie smiled. "She is."

"And what will happen to this exciting job while you're gone?" Mac asked pointedly.

"I've taken an indefinite leave of absence." Allie frowned slightly. "I didn't know how long I would need to stay here. I don't want to leave here until I've remembered—"

She stopped, unsure how to go on. Mac gave her a shrewd look, but said nothing. She resumed carefully. "Until I've remembered all that I need to remember."

"You are referring, of course, to what happened that night," he murmured sadly.

He seemed to age before her eyes, and his voice fell to a whisper. "Such tragedy, such sadness. I loved them both so very much." His moist eyes fixed on her. "Your father was like a son to me after my own son died as a child. Alan lost his own father quite young. He was a fine young man, principled, ambitious, talented in so many ways."

His voice quavered as he went on. "But he never forgot who he was—his heritage—the gift of the land from Ben Sloan and Elena Marin."

"Uncle Mac, how did he feel about my mother?" Allie asked, afraid of the answer she might get but desperate to know.

Mac answered readily. "He loved your mother from the first minute he set eyes on her. I never knew two people more in love with each other, except perhaps for myself and my dear Joanna. We were blessed with a love that could endure many tragedies, including the loss of a child. Your father and mother loved like that."

Allie leaned toward him and said intently, "In one of the newspaper articles you said you could never believe that he killed her."

"I'll *never* believe it!" Mac said adamantly. "It wasn't in him to kill anyone, much less someone that he loved that deeply and completely. He would sooner kill himself."

"I saw something that night—someone in my father's

study . . ." she began. "Somehow I can't believe it was him."

Mac's expression was achingly sad. He shook his head slowly. "You were in the house that night, but before they took you away with them, your grandparents told the authorities that you'd seen nothing of what happened. I never believed them."

He went on. "You were traumatized. In a very real sense you had just lost both your parents." He reached over and touched her hand then. "I know they were trying to protect you. I wanted to keep you here with me at Casa Sureno, but they were determined to take you away. They made me promise that none of us would attempt to contact you. In many ways, I suppose they were right. You needed to get away from everything that had happened. And the scandal of it went on for years."

Allie rose and restlessly paced the courtyard that was sheltered from the wind and overspray at the seawall. So much had happened over the past twenty-four hours, it was impossible to relax. She said slowly, "My father told me that he loved me, and that he loved my mother."

Mac brightened. "You remember that?"

"My grandmother told me that she took me to see him in prison. I remember being with my father in a gray room. There were uniformed men there. They wouldn't let me stay with him. I kicked and screamed, but they took me away."

Mac said with passionate conviction, "I am absolutely convinced they executed an innocent man."

"How could they convict him if he was innocent?" she cried, desperate to believe that her father was a good, loving man who couldn't possibly have done such a monstrous thing.

The fire seemed to go out of Mac. He answered unhappily, "There was a great deal of circumstantial evidence."

"More than just the argument that everyone overheard?" Allie asked.

"Yes. One of the servants found Alan bending over Barbara's lifeless body. His fingerprints were on the murder weapon, a small statue. It didn't help that Alan didn't put up much of a defense for himself. He seemed to have lost all desire to live, totally shattered by Barbara's death. And he knew he'd lost you too." He shook his head sadly. "Taken all together, the evidence and his apathetic attitude, it was enough to convince the jury."

For a moment neither Mac nor Allie spoke. There was only the rustle of the breeze through the trees and the roar of the ocean below.

"I need to know the truth about what happened that night," Allie told him. "I want to believe in my father, in his love for my mother and for me. But—" Her voice caught in her throat, and it took all her strength to continue. "Whatever the truth turns out to be, even if it's bad, I can't hide from it anymore."

"You're right, of course. Running away from the truth doesn't work. Eventually it catches up with you." He looked at her appraisingly. "I think you're strong enough to deal with it, Allie. You were a very brave little girl when your entire world was shattered. You're a very brave young woman now."

Allie sat down across from him. She laid her hand across his, drawn to him by those elusive memories that still remained unseen, and by the gentleness and unconditional acceptance she'd sensed from the first moment. "What is the whole truth about my parents?"

Mac began carefully. "The truth isn't simple, Allie. There are many facets to it. As I said, I've never seen two people more in love with each other. But that depth of emotion can lead to problems."

"You mean the rumors that my mother was having an affair?" Allie asked frankly. Some of the newspaper articles had hinted that this was what her parents were arguing about the night her mother died.

"That's all it was—idle rumors," Mac said adamantly. "I knew Barbara well, and I'm absolutely certain there was no foundation to those rumors at all. But vicious gossip like that wounds, and it caused problems between them."

"Why would people say such things about her?"

His angry expression softened. "You must understand, your mother was one of the most beautiful women I've ever known. But it was more than just physical beauty. She had a genuine sweetness and innocence about her that attracted men to her. She was kind to everyone she knew. Most people aren't that kind, or so very innocent. I suspect that most of the young men who met her fell a little bit in love with her. Perhaps some more than others. But she seemed truly unaffected by any of it. For her, there was only one man, your father. They were both practicing Catholics and were married in the church. For both of them, marriage was sacred. Barbara would *never* have committed adultery.''

Allie winced. ''Was it true that she was pregnant when she was . . . when it happened?''

''Yes,'' he said sadly. ''That's what they quarreled over that night. Your father had been gone on an overseas business trip for several weeks. He was drinking that night. He said some terrible things . . .''

Unhappily, Allie could imagine what had been said that night. Memories of the ugly shouting, the child's fear, went through her with a shudder.

Mac went on reluctantly. ''He accused her of having an affair—saying that the child couldn't possibly be his. God help him, he believed the rumors might be true. He stormed out of the house and was gone for several hours, but once his head cleared, he realized how wrong he was. That's why he went back. To apologize. And he found her body . . .''

''But why would he think the child might not be his?'' Allie asked.

''After you were born, Barbara had trouble conceiving again. She and your father wanted more children very badly. Then while he was gone, she discovered that she was pregnant.''

''And everyone was more than willing to believe the child was the result of an affair,'' Allie said angrily.

''Yes, I'm afraid so. You see, as much as men were attracted to your mother, some women were bitterly jealous of her.''

''What about the rest of the family? Did they believe the rumors?''

''Those who knew Barbara well, and truly cared about her, never believed the rumors for an instant, nor did they believe it was possible that your father killed her. But there were some who were perhaps less certain.''

Allie thought of the newspaper articles about the trial. Her father's cousin, Valentina, had spoken frankly about the argument that night, suggesting that she believed he was guilty. David Benedict was a respected member of the legal community and his attitude was suitably circumspect. Still, he had seemed less than absolutely supportive of her father's innocence. As for the rest of the family, she had no idea what they felt.

Thinking of the others reminded her of Rafe Sloan. It made no sense that she should single him out, yet his picture had had a profound effect on her. There was no clear-cut memory of him, but there *was* something—that vague sense of recognition, and something more. *Fear.*

Mac took her hand and held it tightly. "Allie, it was all a very long time ago. All that matters now is that you're finally back here, where you belong."

She didn't argue, but she knew Mac was wrong. Her reunion with her family wasn't all that mattered. What mattered was finding out if her mother had committed adultery and if her father was a murderer. With every fiber of her being, she resisted believing this could be so. But, ugly as those thoughts were, they had to be faced if she was ever to know any peace in her life again.

Mac looked past her and frowned. "My nursemaid," he said as Inez returned. "It must be my nap time. She always seems to think I need her help," he grumbled good-naturedly. "Well, I'll show her that I don't."

He struggled to rise from the deep chair, finally pulling himself upright with great effort. Allie slipped an arm beneath his and gently held his hand as she helped steady him.

He laid a hand against her cheek. "So like your mother, so kind and so beautiful."

Then he seemed to shake off the bittersweet memory. "I can still find my way about, my dear. Even if Inez doesn't think so." He leaned over and whispered to Allie, "I think she's just making certain she has job security."

"*Bebió mucho vino,*" Inez retorted with a smile.

Allie had taken high school Spanish, and she knew that Inez had accused Mac of drinking too much wine.

He took exaggerated offense. "I have not had too much wine. Only what the doctor prescribes. Now, then, madame, *ayúdame por favor*!"

Inez took his arm. He turned and winked at Allie, then leaned over and gently kissed her on the cheek. "Make yourself at home, Allie, and feel free to wander around. I'll see you later. You're staying for dinner, of course. When you're ready, I'll arrange for you to meet the rest of the family."

At her look of nervousness, he smiled and went on. "Don't worry, I won't impose them on you just yet. I realize you need some time to get acclimated. And besides, I'm a selfish old man. I want to keep you to myself for a while, and give us a chance to get to know each other first. In the meantime, Inez will come back and show you around. If you need anything, you have only to ask her. By the way, she does speak English. She just likes to get my goat, thinks that I can't remember the Spanish language—that I won't know what she's talking about. But I understand every impudent word."

Inez said nothing, but her eyes twinkled mischievously.

Mac left then, leaning heavily on Inez's arm.

While Inez made certain that Mac was resting comfortably, Allie walked through the house, familiarizing herself with rooms and furnishings that she knew must once have been very familiar to her. In the large formal living room with its cathedral ceiling and French doors leading out to the terrace, there was a grand piano. She ran her fingers lightly across the polished keys as a vague memory of an impressive-looking older woman sitting at the piano stirred in her thoughts.

"Aunt Joanna," she whispered to herself with certainty, remembering Mac's wife. Instinctively, she picked out the keys to a favorite childhood tune that had become lost, like so much else, the night her mother died. She smiled faintly at the pleasant awareness that she had spent many happy hours here with Aunt Joanna.

Then she looked up from the keys across the expanse of polished ebony wood at the array of pictures that sat atop the piano. They were pictures of the family, most of them familiar from the newspaper photographs. All the Sloans were there, at various stages in their lives, dressed in graduation gowns or wedding attire, posing formally in family groups, or informally alone. There was a beautiful young woman with flowing auburn hair—Valentina, Allie guessed. And a handsome, slightly older man who must be her brother, Nicholas.

Many of the photos were very old—tintypes or daguerreotypes. One was of a small boy posing formally in a studio, staring straight ahead into the camera as he had undoubtedly been ordered to do. Because of its prominence and the fact that there were no more recent photographs of the boy as he grew older, Allie realized this must be Uncle Mac's son, who had died very young.

"My cousin, Stephen," she whispered as a piece of memory fell into place. She felt a small thrill of delight. Janice had been right after all. Just being here was helping her to remember.

Then she discovered pictures of her mother and father, and herself. There were several of them, taken separately, and together as a family. There was a photograph of her mother gazing lovingly down at the newborn Allie, and an almost identical photograph that included her father.

Allie gazed in wonder at the happy family pictured there—mother, father, child. Just as it was meant to be. Until that moment she'd only *thought* she realized what she missed by losing her parents. Now she fully understood, and the enormity of the pain and loss were nearly overwhelming.

I should have been able to grow up, safe and loved by my parents, she thought desolately. I should have been able to turn to my mother with all the questions I had when I stopped being a child and became a woman. I should have been able to feel my father's arms around me when I was hurt.

She knew if she thought about it for one more moment, she would break down and sob uncontrollably. So she forced herself to focus on the other photographs. They were from every phase of her life as she grew up. The team picture taken the year she was ten and her softball team won the pennant for their age division; her confirmation picture; graduation from parochial school; her high school graduation picture and another when she graduated from college. All were in black and white, and looked grainy, slightly unclear. Looking at them closely, Allie realized they were newspaper photographs.

"Your uncle used to sit and stare at those pictures as if he were trying to bring them to life, or something."

Allie whirled around, her college graduation picture still in her hand.

Inez smiled gently. "He's resting comfortably now. He must take a nap each afternoon or he becomes too tired."

"Where did he get these?"

"From the newspaper." At Allie's confused look, she explained. "He has always taken the Seattle newspaper, and the small one from Lake Stevens too."

Allie put the picture back. "I don't understand."

"He promised your grandparents that he wouldn't try to contact you. This was the only way he knew anything about you. He would sit for hours, going through all the newspapers, looking for information about you. He told me when you were named valedictorian of your class, and when you designed a wonderful new building. He is very proud of you, Miss Allie. And he always said that you would come back someday."

"How could he possibly know?"

Inez laid her hand across her heart. "He believed it here. He prayed he would live long enough to see you again."

Allie suddenly felt a twinge of alarm. "He's not well, is he?"

Inez answered frankly, "He is very old, and there is the problem with his heart. Some days are better than others. Today is a very good day."

"I hope my visit hasn't overtired him."

"Oh, no, it has made him very happy."

Allie said, "I think I'll just wander around for a while, if that's okay."

"Of course."

Allie left the house and headed for the small stretch of private beach at the bottom of the rock steps that descended from the seawall. Out on the water she saw fishing boats, or an occasional sail cutting along the horizon. Farther down was a stretch of state beach. Die-hard surfers challenged the cold water in wetsuits; children scampered among the rocks exposed at low tide, exploring tide pools; and cars mingled with bicycles on Seventeen-Mile Drive as it curved along the exposed coastline heading toward the small suburb of Pacific Grove around the curve of the bay.

Allie had put on a white cotton cardigan over her white slacks and pink silk shirt, and now she wrapped it close about her. The wind was brisk down by the water. Her mind raced, alternately trying to find some essence of memory in surroundings that should have been familiar, and wondering about the family she was about to meet after twenty-five years.

She thought of Rafe Sloan. More than any of the others, his photograph had evoked, if not a direct memory, then a sort of sensory recognition. She knew him in a way that she didn't know the others. That left her feeling uneasy.

Why? she wondered. Was it because he had lived at the ranch house with her mother and father until her mother's death? That must be it, she thought. But it didn't explain her unreasoning fear of him.

6

OVER DINNER THAT NIGHT Mac tried to persuade Allie to stay with him instead of at the La Playa Hotel where she'd booked a room. She politely turned down the offer, telling him she didn't want to impose. The truth was, she was afraid to sleep in this house, where she had occasionally slept as a child. She believed the nightmares would be even worse here than they'd been in Seattle.

He said to Allie, "Come into the library, my dear. I want to show you something."

They went into the large, book-lined library, and Mac took an old leather-bound book from a glass case. He held the book reverently, almost as if it were holy, and gently handed it to Allie. "Elena Marin Sloan's journal," he said proudly. "Very few families are lucky enough to have such a personal record of their ancestors. This is the most valuable possession the Sloan family will ever have. Please take it with you, my dear, and read it. It will put you in touch with your heritage as nothing else possibly could."

Touched by this indication of his acceptance, Allie took the book, feeling the roughness of the cracked leather cover, and smelling the unmistakable mustiness of old paper. "I'll be very careful with it."

He smiled at her affectionately. "I know you will, my dear. Now then, I'd best be off to bed before Inez comes looking for me."

Allie helped Mac up the stairs. He was completely exhausted, but pleased with himself. "I can't wait for you to meet the others." He chuckled. "It will come as quite a surprise to them."

"What are they like?" Allie asked.

Mac thought for a moment, then answered carefully. "Being rich and powerful doesn't always bring out the best in people. Some of them are all right. And some—aren't. But that's true of any family. And the fact is, we can't choose who we're related to."

At the door to his room he gave Allie a warm hug and a good-night kiss. "Will you join me for breakfast?"

She nodded. "I'd love to."

"Good. Perhaps we could go out to the ranch. Would you like that?"

Allie hesitated. The ranch—the place where she'd lived for the first seven years of her life, the place where her mother had been brutally killed. She wasn't sure she was ready to face it, but she reminded herself that the purpose of this trip was to stop running away from her past. She forced herself to say, "Yes, that would be nice."

"Good. Sleep well, my dear. I'll see you in the morning."

"Good night, Uncle Mac."

For the next few days Allie spent every waking moment at Casa Sureno with Mac, getting to know him again, hearing his stories about the family. It was very frustrating, listening to Mac talk about her parents yet remembering almost nothing.

She had been so confident that just by coming here it would all come back. But it hadn't. There were only glimmers of memory every once in a while that peeked out from the dark corners, like a child teasing her, always fragmented—a name, the description of a place, or an event.

And then there were the dreams—always the dreams. Sleeping in the hotel instead of staying with Mac hadn't kept them away. They haunted her nights, playing over and over.

One afternoon she sat out on the patio, reading the journal

while Mac took his daily nap. Inez brought a pitcher of iced tea, and set it down on the table next to Allie. Glancing at the journal, Inez said, "Are you having difficulty translating it?"

Allie grinned ruefully. "Yes. I took Spanish in high school, but that was a long time ago, and I've forgotten much of it."

Then Inez said something that stunned Allie. "You spoke it fluently when you were a little girl. I have heard Mac speak of how proud he was that your father felt so strongly that you should not lose your Spanish heritage."

"My father spoke Spanish?"

"Yes, but not very well. He could never get the accent right. You spoke it fluently. It was your first language. You were taught by the old woman, Consuelo, who lived at the ranch and took care of you after you were born."

"My God," Allie said with growing sadness. "I don't remember any of that. I don't remember Consuelo."

"Perhaps now that you have begun to remember, the language will come back to you," Inez suggested hopefully.

"I hope so," Allie said.

Inez left, and Allie turned her attention once more to the journal:

Elena's Journal, May 17, 1852.

Today Papa and I rode with the vaqueros to Monterey. Papa has a buyer for the cattle, and will meet him at the stockyards near the wharf. While in Monterey we are staying with Don Santiago de la Torre and his family at their home.

I don't like Dona de la Torre. She is always staring at me with fish eyes. And when she speaks, it is always to compliment her son, Antonio: what a fine vaquero he is, how handsome he is, how the young girls from the best families look favorably upon him. I listen without speaking because I want to please Papa.

He is always sad since Francisco's death. It is as if he died when his only son died. He speaks mournfully about how everything is changing since the Anglos discovered gold at a place called Sutter's Mill. He worries that they will come in even greater numbers and take away all the land, as so many already have done. What will become of Rancho Sureno, he wonders.

I have told him that I will take care of the rancho. No one will take it from us. It was granted to our family by the provisional governor over twenty years ago. We will raise and sell our cattle. Rancho Sureno will always be our home.

But today in Monterey something very strange happened. When we arrived, Papa insisted that I go straight to Dona de la Torre's house, but I begged him to allow me to stay with him and the vaqueros until the cattle were sold. I met the buyer and I was very surprised, for he is an Anglo. His name is Ben Sloan.

After the business was finished, Mr. Sloan invited us to eat with him at the inn. Over supper he explained that the hardy Mexican cattle he bought from Papa will be bred with the heavier brown and white cattle he has brought from a place called Virginia.

I listened very carefully. Ben Sloan is very young, no older than Antonio. It seemed strange for him to be talking of such things as land management, water rights, and cattle breeding. Antonio appears much older. Yet all he and his friends ever talk about are the bets they place on horse racing at the Presidio, or the bear and bull fights at the neighboring haciendas.

Ben Sloan is a very serious young man. I think Papa likes him very much. He is also very handsome. He has deep blue eyes, and a gentle smile that makes me feel very strange inside whenever he looks at me. I have never felt this way before. It makes me feel good, yet at the same time it somehow frightens me.

An hour later Allie put down the journal and took a long, grateful drink of the iced tea Inez had left. Translating the journal had been painstaking and slow at first. She was able to pick out only the most common words. But after she read about the first time Elena Marin met Ben Sloan, she realized that she understood far more than what she had learned in her high school Spanish class. Spanish, her first language, had started to come back to her.

A few minutes later Mac joined her, looking refreshed from his nap. He smiled at Allie. "I thought we might go out to the ranch today—if you feel you're ready."

She considered the suggestion soberly. She wasn't entirely certain she was ready to face the ghosts that she knew must haunt that place. But she couldn't back out now. She'd come too far just by returning here.

She took a deep breath. "I'd like very much to go out to the ranch today."

Mac patted her on the hand. "Good. We'll leave immediately."

Allie drove Uncle Mac's large Mercedes sedan. It was more comfortable for him than the much smaller car she'd rented at the Monterey airport. Inez watched with a worried expression as they swung out of the long driveway and turned onto Seventeen-Mile Drive. Allie knew that Inez was concerned about Mac leaving the house, something he rarely did nowadays.

Over the past three days since she'd arrived in Pebble Beach, Allie had become increasingly aware just how fragile Mac's health was. He was over eighty years old, and along with the natural deterioration of time, there had been a heart bypass surgery a few years earlier that Inez said he'd barely survived. He always took an afternoon nap—his siesta, as he called it—and Inez made certain he was in bed no later than eight o'clock.

Inez was just as careful with his diet and the medications he took. He complained that he hated to have her hovering over him like a mother hen, as he put it. But Allie realized that was just a reflection of his stubborn desire for independence rather than a resentment of Inez. She was more than a devoted employee. She was a devoted friend. And though Mac would never admit how much he needed her, Allie sensed that he deeply appreciated her concern and loyalty.

Inez had been with Mac for over thirty years, but, as with everyone else, Allie didn't remember her. Inez had been widowed young, and left with four children. Mac and his wife, Joanna, saw to it that she not only had a well-paying job with them, they also made sure that each of her children was well educated.

Allie and Mac kept up an easy dialogue during the forty-five-minute drive south along Highway 1 to Big Sur. He explained more about the family, throwing in a bit of local history that he said she would find in the journal. Then he fell silent and she thought that he must have dozed off. When she glanced over at him, she found him watching her intently.

"What is it? Are you all right?" she asked apprehensively.

He reached across and patted her arm as his expression eased into a gentle smile. "You remind me so much of your mother. At times I almost forget that you're not Barbara."

He hesitated, then went on. "I try to understand how difficult all this must be for you . . . how frightening, in a way. At the end of life, all we have are our memories. You know, Thomas Campbell said that to live in the hearts we leave behind is not to die. To have lost that connection to the past, and to the people we've loved and lost, must be very nearly unbearable."

"I'm determined to get those memories back," Allie responded soberly. "That's why I'm here. I won't leave until I've accomplished that."

Mac smiled affectionately. "I hope you won't leave at all."

Before she could respond, he went on. "We are your family. This was once your home. It could be again, Allie."

Rightfully interpreting her sad look, he said, his lips quavering beneath the bristle of silvery-white mustache, "I can only imagine the pain you must have felt as a little girl. The death of your mother and father nearly destroyed this family. But I hope you won't let the tragedy of the past keep you from taking your rightful place here with us."

Keeping her eyes on the winding road ahead, she laid her hand over his. "I can't think about the future right now, Uncle Mac. I have to figure out the past first."

"I understand, my dear. I'm just glad you came back."

A few minutes later he indicated the turn off Highway 1. The road was paved several miles back in as it wound through trees, across a creek, and then split. The left fork cut back to the northeast, and passed the neighboring village of Big Sur that had taken its name from Rancho Sureno. The right fork angled southwest, following the rocky coastline.

"Take the right fork, slowly," Mac instructed. "The pavement ends shortly and there will be a gate."

They soon came upon the gate to the northernmost entrance of the ranch property. It was like taking a step back in time. Dual pillars of adobe brick stood at least ten feet tall on either side of the gate, which was made of wood with a sliding wood latch. Cross beams extended overhead from one pillar to the other. A sign hung in the middle. It read:

RANCHO SURENO

ESTABLISHED 1832

Allie got out and opened the gate. As she laid her hand on the peg, big enough for a man's hand, there was a flash of recognition.

"Let me do it, Daddy. Let me open the gate."

"Are you sure you're strong enough to slide it open, Princess?"

"I can do it. Look, Daddy!"

She remembered wearing faded jeans and a cotton shirt. The boots on her feet were new and too big. She experienced all over again the sensation of her feet sliding in them. She ran toward that gate in her memory, her long, golden braids slapping at her shoulders.

The memory was so unexpected and sharp, like a flash of brilliant light in the dark void of her forgotten childhood, that for a moment it took her breath away. She stood there, holding on to the gate with white-knuckled fingers, as if she could hold on to the memory, and more would follow. But there was only that much, no more.

Mac finally called out to her from the car. "Allie? Are you all right?"

"I'm fine," she called out to him, then returned to the car. "I remembered something," she explained.

He sat quietly beside her, listening intently as she told him what she'd recalled. He didn't push, just as he hadn't pushed over the past three days. He was simply there for her, a gentle, comforting presence, so like her grandfather in many ways.

When she finished, Mac told her, "Your father gave you those boots for your seventh birthday. They were specially hand-tooled and made in Spain. He brought them back from a trip he and Barbara made to the old country." He sat looking out the windshield with her. His voice had gone gravelly with emotion.

"They were too big for you. European sizing is different, I suppose. But he had to have those boots for you. He said that if you were a true Sloan, you would want to ride over every inch of this ranch just as your ancestors had done before you. And in order to do that, you had to have a good pair of boots."

Tears welled up in Allie's eyes as Mac continued. "Your father, more than Gavin, Charlotte, or any of the other cousins, understood the legacy of Rancho Sureno handed down from Ben Sloan and Elena Marin. I think that's why he was so set on having those damned boots for you—a kid no bigger than a mite. They had to come from Spain because the dream began there."

"The dream?" Allie asked, holding tight to his heavily veined hand.

He gestured expansively, beginning at the gate that opened onto the vast open beauty of Rancho Sureno in a wide arc to the glistening blue Pacific Ocean. "Rancho Sureno was the dream for Rafael del Santiago de Marin. And he handed it down to his daughter, Elena. When Ben Sloan married Elena, it became his dream as well. But you'll find out about it as you read the journal."

"Rafael," Allie commented thoughtfully. "He was Elena's father?"

"Yes, and she named her firstborn son for him, your great-grandfather."

Obviously, her half cousin, Rafe Sloan, had been named for their very distant ancestor. She found it disturbing to think about him but somehow couldn't get him out of her mind. There had been only that glimpse of him in the old newspaper photo, yet there was something about him—like one of those echoes of memory, that lay unformed at the edge of her consciousness.

Setting aside thoughts of Rafe Sloan, Allie squeezed Mac's hand. "Are you certain you feel up to this?"

"Absolutely," he responded emphatically. "Drive on, my dear. It's time you became reacquainted with the Sloan legacy."

And my past, she thought as they drove through the gate.

They drove along the gently curving gravel road that meandered along the breathtaking California coastline for almost three miles. Bare hillsides gave way to watersheds of dense forest, creeks, ravines, then fanned out unexpectedly across a large plateau above the rocky cliffs that plummeted down to the ocean and Highway 1 below. In the distance, nestled into the forested protection of the hillside behind it, was the actual ranch house itself.

Her first impression was of rolling pastures, rough-hewn fence corrals, weathered outbuildings, including a barn, stables, paddocks, and finally, some distance beyond, the hacienda.

Allie drove slowly past the outbuildings and then up a gently rising slope where an overgrown lawn fanned out from the main house. At one side were the rusting remains of an old swing set. The walkway was made of square adobe blocks set into the ground. There was a heavy-beamed arbor along the entire front of the long, low house. It was overgrown with long, trailing vines of brilliant bougainvillea in stunning disarray, draped like showers. It surprised her that the house seemed to be made of stucco.

She helped Mac out of the car and they slowly walked toward the house. Partway up the front walk he called out for Miguel, the caretaker, who lived at the ranch just as his parents had before him. There was no answer. The front door was unlocked.

"He's probably out with the vaqueros," Mac informed her as he led the way into the house.

She looked at him with some amusement. "Vaqueros?"

He smiled. "The ranch employs twenty experienced hands full-time. Twice that many during the spring and fall roundup. This is still a working cattle ranch."

Then his expression saddened. "At least until Gavin and the others sell it off."

Allie didn't know what to say. She hadn't heard about the ranch being sold. Now that she had seen it, she found the thought disturbing.

She followed Mac inside the main entrance of the hacienda. The gate sign with the year the ranch was established had been a reminder of the age of the ranch, the last original land grant dating back over one hundred fifty years. But the hacienda, built by Elena Marin's father when he was a young man, was a reminder of a far older heritage—the dreams of people in the New World, the hopes of a young Californio girl whose way of life was rapidly disappearing.

And yet, here, at Rancho Sureno, that way of life had somehow survived and endured because of Ben Sloan.

Fascinated, Allie looked at the house with an architect's eyes as well. Now that they were inside the house, she saw that the arbors that lined the front of the house and provided afternoon shade shielded rows of arched windows set along the entire front of the house to take advantage of the ocean breezes.

The interior walls were whitewashed stucco of the Mediterranean style. The ceilings were low and yet the rooms were spacious, several leading off the tiled central hall that led back to the other side of the house like an open breezeway.

By contrast, the wood-frame window openings were stained dark. The glass panes, although not original to the house, were very old. Instead of being perfectly clear, they contained ripples and swirls from uneven heating usually found in windows of the mid- to late-nineteenth century.

The hall table in the entry looked as if it might once have been a sideboard for serving in the dining room. It was also made of dark wood, its surface smoothed by many years of wear. Glass-paned double doors stood open to what would have passed for a living room in most houses. She glanced inside.

The floor was smooth wood, gleaming in the muted light from partially draped windows. A large rug covered the floor, along with leather-covered chairs and a long couch.

Mac followed her gaze. "The furnishings in this room are original to the hacienda. Elena's father had the chairs and couch made in Monterey from hides provided by the rancho. It's all in the original ranch records. Contrary to most of his compadres, he was very careful with his money. He didn't waste it on gambling or lavish living.

"This hacienda was his one extravagance. He built it for Elena's mother, and the family they hoped to have."

"There was an older brother," Allie remembered from the journal.

Mac nodded. "He was thrown from his horse and killed. By then Elena's mother was dead. He had only his daughter left, and the rancho. But you'll read about that."

"Where does the hallway lead?" Allie asked, trying to find something familiar in the house where she had once lived with her parents.

"To the room that later became the den. In the old days, the gentlemen used to retire there to smoke cigars and drink Madeira wine. It was your father who turned it into a combination office and den. He ran the entire ranch from that room. It's quite a magnificent room with a huge adobe fireplace and several very valuable artifacts from the old days."

He stopped and stared at her as she went rigid and her face turned white. "Allie?"

"That's the room where my mother died."

"Yes. Gavin wanted to have it sealed off afterward, but I wouldn't allow it."

She looked at him, puzzled.

"This house is over one hundred and fifty years old. People have been born and died here, some tragically. Elena's brother, Francisco, died in one of the upstairs bedrooms after that fall. Her father died here, as well as both Ben and Elena in their own time. As tragic as Barbara's death was, I felt that it was wrong to close off any part of the house."

Allie had walked partway down the hallway toward the stairway leading to the second floor, a newer addition to the house built in 1882 to accommodate the growing Sloan family. The stairway, with its turned-wood railing and Spanish decorative carving, were to her right. She reached out tentatively, her fingers trembling as she struggled with an uncertain memory of herself coming down those stairs countless times, swinging around that same post, hopping over the last two steps and landing surefooted at the bottom, eager to be off somewhere, too impatient to take each step. But there was another memory that peered out of dark corners—a memory that had come in horrible nightmares and exploded from those dark recesses that day in Janice's office.

Her fingers trembled as she touched the newel post, as if she could feel the memory of that other time. She was little once more, carefully slipping down those stairs, terrified of the shouting and angry words.

Allie turned and glanced across the wide hall, as she had that night, and her gaze fastened on the large, framed wall mirror. Immediately, she turned away. She didn't want to look at it—couldn't look at it. Yet, even as she turned away, she felt the terror build low as it came from that dark, subconscious fear buried deep inside her. And even as she closed her eyes and tried to block out the images, the memory came back. She was a child again, reliving all the terror she'd experienced the night she saw her mother killed. . . .

"Allie?"

Her name came from very far away.

Then, closer, "Allie!"

She didn't immediately recognize the voice. Then she realized it was Uncle Mac.

"Take her to the sofa in the study."

Someone lifted her and carried her a few feet, then gently lay her down.

Mac said, "She's coming around."

Allie recognized the emotion in his voice—it was the aftermath of fear. Over the past weeks, since the dreams first began, she'd learned to live with that same kind of fear.

He went on. "Bring her a glass of water."

Light began to return, chasing back the dark void of terrifying half-formed memories. Allie opened her eyes and looked up to find Mac sitting on the edge of the leather sofa beside her, looking extremely concerned. She heard but didn't see someone leave the room, then quickly return with a glass of water.

Mac took it and handed it to her. "You gave us quite a scare, my dear," he said with real concern in his voice.

Allie drank the water slowly, and felt her dizziness gradually dissolve. "I'm sorry," she began hesitantly. "I don't know what happened."

It was a lie. She knew exactly what had happened. She had looked into the mirror at the end of the hallway . . . the same mirror she had stared into as a seven-year-old child and seen the reflection of her mother's brutal murder.

Mac's frown suggested he didn't believe her for a moment. But he merely asked, "Are you feeling better now, my dear?"

"Yes, much better."

She sat up, and aside from a momentary dizziness, knew that she was all right now. "I'm sorry if I worried you, Uncle Mac, but I'm fine now. I'd like to see the rest of the house."

"Are you sure?" he asked worriedly.

"I'm sure."

"Well . . . all right. Actually, we need to take advantage of this opportunity, for I'm not certain how much longer Rancho Sureno will belong to the Sloan family. If Gavin has his way, it'll be sold off to a group of Japanese developers, who will pour concrete over every square inch."

"Why?" Allie asked in dismay.

"In a word, taxes," Mac answered tersely.

"But isn't there anything that can be done?"

Mac responded defiantly, "I've fought this as long as I can. But I'm afraid I've lost." He shook his head sadly. "That's why I wanted you to see the ranch as soon as possible. Your legacy is here, the legacy of every member of this family. But it may be gone soon."

Before Allie could respond, he went on. "Ah, well, enough of this gloom and doom. Let me show you around your old home."

They walked through room after room, going slowly because of Mac and because Allie wanted to take the time to look at everything carefully. She felt as if she were touring her own personal museum filled with the artifacts of her early life. Most of her parents' personal possessions had been packed up and put away, but the furniture and paintings were exactly the same. Allie recognized the big old oak four-poster in her parents' bedroom. She remembered swinging around those posts, holding tightly to the pineapple-shaped tops.

Then Mac led her into her old bedroom, and suddenly her

childhood came back to her in a rush. She remembered everything about it as if she'd left it only yesterday—the pale yellow walls and white shutters on the windows, the paintings of teddy bears and clowns, and the white French provincial bedroom set with the canopied bed. While Mac stood in the doorway, watching, Allie slowly made her way around the room, lightly touching the familiar objects. In this room her mother had read bedtime stories to her, including the "Snow White" fairy tale. In this room her father had come up to tuck her in and kiss her good night. In this room she had awakened late on that fateful night to hear the sound of shouting coming from downstairs. . . .

Turning, she looked at Mac, and there were tears in her eyes.

"Oh, my dear," he said worriedly, "I didn't mean to make you unhappy. I shouldn't have brought you here."

"No," she said shakily, "you don't understand. I remember this room, these things. I'm starting to put the pieces of the puzzle back together again. And it feels wonderful."

Walking slowly over to her, he put his frail arms around her and held her tightly. "Welcome home, Allie," he whispered.

Later they sat out on the central patio, sipping the hot tea Miguel had brought out to them. Allie learned that it was Miguel who had carried her to the sofa when she fainted earlier, and who brought her a glass of water.

Mac said, "Miguel has lived his entire life here at the ranch. He and his wife, Cathy, take care of the place. Just as his parents took care of it when your parents lived here."

Miguel smiled broadly, exclaiming that he remembered Allie. He looked to be in his early forties. She wondered if he had been at the ranch that night, and decided to come right out and ask.

He shook his head, and his expression sobered. "Regrettably, no. I'd gotten into some trouble over in Salinas. My father had to come get me."

"He's trying to gloss over the fact that he was arrested for going joyriding with some of his friends," Mac explained with a gruff snort.

"I *was* a bit wild," Miguel admitted with a sheepish expression. Excusing himself, he went back into the house.

It was so peaceful there and pleasantly warm within the sheltering walls of the courtyard. Allie thought what a beautiful, serene haven it must have been when Elena Marin was a young woman. She found herself wondering if Elena might have sat just where they were sitting, surrounded by her family.

Mac turned to Allie. "I'm going to arrange a dinner party so you can meet the rest of the family. Is that all right, my dear?"

Allie nodded. She had been nervous at the thought of meeting these long-lost relatives, but now she felt up to doing so.

Mac went on. "Is there anything you'd like to know about them before then?"

Allie asked curiously, "Tell me about Rafe."

Mac hesitated, then answered slowly, "He was the illegitimate son of Paul Sloan and Amelia Estrada. Paul was married when Rafe was born, and because he and his wife were both Catholic, there was no question of a divorce. Rafe was raised by his mother in Monterey. A sort of open secret. I can only imagine how he must have felt, reading about us in the paper, knowing we were his family but never being acknowledged as one of us. His mother was a very proud woman, and refused to accept any financial help from Paul. She felt he'd lied to her about his feelings for her, and taken advantage of her. She was angry and bitter. I know because I tried to help her financially, and she gave me a tongue-lashing I'll never forget. She said, 'You Sloans think you can ruin people, then make it all right by writing out a check.' I hate to admit it, but in a way she was right."

He paused, then went on. "They lived in poverty. After she died when Rafe was thirteen, there was no one to take care of him. Paul felt it was time to bring his son into the family. God knows he'd wanted to do so for a very long time. But there were Gavin and Charlotte to think of. They both took their mother's death very hard, and he knew there would be hell to pay if he forced Rafe on them."

Mac was silent for a moment, then went on thoughtfully. "I suppose Gavin's resentment was understandable. He was always his father's favorite—the fair-haired son, the heir apparent, and all that nonsense. But Charlotte was younger. As far as I know, she wasn't aware of her father's affair with

Rafe's mother. Yet she took it far worse than Gavin when their father brought Rafe to live with them.

Allie said with feeling, "It must have been miserable for Rafe, being forced to live with people who bitterly resented him."

Mac sighed heavily. "Yes. It hasn't been easy for him, always living on the edge of this family. The only ones he got along with were your mother and father. They felt sorry for him, and tried to help him. I think that's why Rafe ran away when he did. With Alan gone, there was no one here he felt he could turn to."

"When did he come back?"

"I persuaded him to come back two years ago. We may have treated him shamefully, in a way, but we are still his family. His place is here, among us. Whether some of us like it or not."

But her thoughts kept returning to Rafe. Finally, she turned to Mac. "Where was Rafe when you persuaded him to return?"

"Los Angeles," he explained with a disgusted snort. "It always was a disreputable town, from its very beginning. Not like the north coast. Makes one wonder why they called it the City of Angels. They must have been hoping for salvation."

Allie couldn't quite hide a smile at Mac's disdain for Los Angeles, the typical attitude of someone who'd been born and raised in northern California. She knew the northern part of the state prided itself on being morally, culturally, and intellectually superior to the south.

Mac gave her a curious look. "Of all your relatives, why do you ask about him?"

"I . . . I'm not sure," she lied. Somehow she couldn't tell Mac that Rafe's photo was the only one that had elicited any response in her.

Looking at Mac as he sat slouched over in an old black wrought-iron patio chair, Allie was reminded of the fact that he wasn't strong. She worried that this long, full day might be too much for him, and was trying to figure out a polite way of suggesting they forego the tour of the ranch and go home, when he spoke again.

"He'd been in the service by the time I caught up with him,

went to Vietnam in the last days before that fiasco ended. Somewhere along the way he managed to build an extremely successful contracting business without ever bothering to go to college."

Somehow Allie was surprized. "Construction?"

Mac nodded proudly. "A self-made man, just like his great-great-great grandfather Ben Sloan. Started with nothing but his hands, a dream, and enough ambition to make certain that nothing stood in his way. He called his company Marin Construction—wouldn't associate it with the Sloan name. For a while he even went by his mother's name, Estrada. I suppose that was his way of getting back at the Sloans for the way he and his mother were treated. I don't think he ever understood that his mother was as responsible for the way things worked out as his father was."

"But he uses the Sloan name now," Allie said.

"Yes. Like I said, Rafe is ambitious. He realized the name meant a lot—opened a lot of doors. So he began using it. I suppose, in his way of thinking, that, too, was a way of getting back at the Sloans."

"What happened to his company?"

"He sold it. Like I said, he made a big success of it, and made himself rich at the same time. But money wasn't important to him. It never was."

"How did you persuade him to come back, Uncle Mac?"

"I didn't really persuade him. It was very much his decision. I think he was searching for something." He looked at her. "Not unlike you, Alexandra." He went on. "I believe he came back because he needed to figure out who he was, so to speak. He didn't do it in Vietnam, or Los Angeles, or any of the countless other places he lived before that. His identity is here, in this area, and specifically on this ranch."

Allie said, "I take it he wants to develop the ranch property?"

"Yes." There was intense disapproval in Mac's voice.

The disapproval was still there as they drove away from the ranch house a few minutes later in Miguel's truck, with Miguel driving. They rode for several miles across open grazing land dotted with white-faced cattle. The cattle's lineage was carefully traced back one hundred fifty years to the original record books that Ben Sloan had meticulously kept about every aspect of ranch life. There were no fences on this part of the ranch. None were necessary, for the boundaries were natural—a steep canyon to the south, a deep river at the north, the Santa Lucia mountain range on the east, and the Pacific Ocean with its rocky cliffs on the west.

Miguel drove carefully over deeply rutted dirt roads that all but disappeared completely where seasonal creeks flowed strongly in the winter and left shallow washes the rest of the year. Mac pointed out sights of interest along the way, including a slope of hillside that rolled gently to a stretch of beach across a highway that hadn't existed a century and a half earlier.

At one end of the beach Allie could see the remains of ancient pilings that protruded through the water's surface even after all this time—the original boat landing for Rancho El Sureno, where ships dropped off supplies that the ranch couldn't provide for itself. Mac explained that at one time the landing served the entire area and all the surrounding ranchos. Now all that was left were those ghostly pilings.

The countryside was wild, primitive, breathtakingly beautiful with its stark contrasts of forest and sea, steep cliffs that plunged down to white sand beaches, green grassy hillsides, gurgling creeks that sped on their way to the ocean, towering pines and spreading oaks that had been there since Elena Marin was a girl. It seemed to go on forever, from horizon to horizon.

It was almost incomprehensible that this much land remained unspoiled, almost pristine in its natural beauty. Allie tried to imagine what it would look like developed out for maximum density that would include houses, condos, shopping malls, office complexes, gas stations, and ugly electrical towers crisscrossing the landscape, along with the requisite uncontrolled landfills that always moved in with society, leaving their own toxic scars on the land.

She shuddered at the knowledge of what rampant development might mean in the hands of people who cared nothing about the land and even less about its legacy. She knew that Elena Marin had once looked out on it as she was looking out at it now. Elena couldn't possibly have conceived of such a fate for the land she loved.

"Well," Mac said. "What do you think of what you've seen so far?"

"It's beautiful. And it's terribly sad knowing what's bound to happen to it," Allie responded with feeling. Everything she believed in as an architect, everything she'd been trained for by Julia Winslow, raged at the knowledge of what would happen to this rare and special place.

She looked out the window at the magnificent cliffs that dropped to the pounding ocean below. "It's so sad that man has to put his mark on it. We don't leave a very good legacy in what we do to the land."

"And what would you do with it, madame architect? If it were yours to do with as you please?"

The what-if game. Allie and Julia often sat across an enormous drafting table and played that game, throwing out ideas, some of them preposterous. "What if you had an enormous parcel of land to do with as you pleased, what would you do?" they would ask each other.

Now Allie answered Mac's question without hesitation. "I'd leave it unchanged, just the way it is, forever."

Beside her she felt the intensity of his scrutiny. After a moment's silence he said sadly, "Until very recently I assumed I would be able to do just that—leave this place unchanged, practically untouched. But I've come to realize that nothing remains unchanged forever. Even if the state hadn't stepped in and changed the tax status, I'm afraid that sooner or later the other members of the family would have forced the sale. This paradise is doomed, just as the biblical one was."

He murmured, almost to himself, "If only I had more time . . ."

Allie assumed that Mac felt frustrated because he was no longer strong enough to fight a younger generation of Sloans who didn't feel as he did about the ranch.

She said, "There's no way of holding back progress. Julia and I have faced this same situation countless times with projects we've worked on. But there are ways to preserve the integrity of the land, to make certain that it isn't sacrificed for wholesale development."

"And how would you do that?" Mac asked with real interest.

Allie gave her imagination free rein. "There would be no high rises, extremely low density, the rural atmosphere would be preserved and controlled in a way that enhances the land."

"Could it be done?" Mac asked quickly.

"It's been done before. I worked on a project in the San Juan Islands very much like that, but never on a scale like this." She grinned. "It just makes it more challenging when the dreams are a little bigger."

"But it *could* be done?" Mac repeated.

"Yes, in the hands of the right person, and with the time and money to spend on it." Her grin dissolved into a frown. "But as you pointed out, there isn't time. Or, for that matter, the right person to do it. Unless you think Rafe might be that person?"

"He has enough single-minded determination. He *could* be the right person—but he lacks the heart."

Before Allie could question that surprising statement, Mac turned to Miguel and told him to drive on. Clearly, he didn't want to talk for a while; he wanted to be left to his thoughts. Allie could only imagine what those thoughts must be as Mac faced the destruction of a place that he deeply loved.

The next morning, as Allie got dressed to go to Mac's, she thought about what she'd learned in the past few days. Mac had told her endless stories about her family, trying to help her get to know them before she met them. But they still felt like total strangers, people she couldn't relate to. Except for Elena.

Allie picked up the journal from her bedside table. She felt a bond between her and her great-great-grandmother. Elena was a kindred spirit. Like Allie, Elena had suffered the loss of family. And like Allie, she had been faced with momentous changes in her life. Allie was eager to read more of the journal, to find out how Elena handled those challenges.

At Casa Sureno she joined Mac out on the small patio that opened off the breakfast room. He was wrapped up warmly in a heavy sweater to ward off the brisk breeze that came in off the ocean. His thin, frail body was all but swallowed up by the oversized sweater.

His eyes were closed and his head leaned against the high back of the black wrought-iron patio chair. He didn't acknowledge her or make any indication that he was even aware of her presence. In the past several days she had grown used to his prolonged silences. At those times she was uncertain whether he dozed or was merely lost in thought.

They sat in companionable silence for a while, and Allie watched the early morning sun glinting off the water, exposing its blue depths.

Abruptly, Mac opened his eyes, looked at her, and broke the silence. "It was a damnably hard voyage," he said. "They came from Vera Cruz, in Mexico, and the province of Castille before that."

"Elena's ancestors," Allie guessed.

Mac nodded. "Pure Spanish blood. Old family friends of the appointed governor. The Mexican government was desperate to settle this land. Offered them as much land as they could ride over on horseback in a week."

He turned to her, his sunken blue eyes watching her keenly. "I'll bet you didn't know that."

Smiling, she admitted, "No, I didn't. Who made the ride?"

"Elena's father. He was a hot-blooded, adventurous young man eager to explore this vast wilderness. The Marin family had already established themselves in Monterey, where his father was first counsel to the governor. Rafael rode the land from Yankee Point south."

He went on, growing more animated as he spoke. "He spent his own money on a fine Andalusian stallion. Not the fastest horses in the world, but very possibly the strongest. While his compadres rode their horses into the ground the first two days, trying to cover as much land as possible, Rafael was smarter and set a steady pace. He rode almost nonstop for those seven days, pausing only briefly to rest his horse. He ate cold meals in the saddle, and drank from the streams his horse drank from. By the time he finished, he had ridden the three boundaries of the ranch as it is today. The fourth boundary was the eastern ridge of the Santa Lucia Mountains. The last point of his journey was the southern point—El Sureno. That's where he built the hacienda."

Allie felt a thrill of pride in her distant ancestor. What a strong, single-minded young man he must have been. Then she remembered that the land he had claimed by his determination and fortitude was about to be sold. She asked unhappily,

"What will happen to the hacienda when the ranch is sold?"

Frowning, Mac made a gesture through the air with a heavily veined hand. "It will probably be razed to make room for a clubhouse or a grocery store!"

"What about Rafe's plans to develop the ranch?"

Mac snorted. "Not quite as bad as the Japanese, but nearly."

"Do you think he could succeed?"

Mac nodded. "He's qualified, all right. It's the other he lacks."

"Heart?" she asked, recalling what he'd said the day before.

Mac sighed heavily. "Rafe's feelings for the land are all confused with his feelings about the past."

Allie said gently, "The same could be said of you."

He gave her a sharp look that immediately softened. "Very true. But I care about the land and want to keep it as it is. He wants to control it, to prove he can take something away from this family. There's a great deal of anger inside him, my dear. Used in a positive way, anger can be a great catalyst, but used in a negative way . . . it can destroy."

"And yet you brought him back to Monterey and involved him in the Sloan Land Company," Allie pointed out.

"Yes, and I'd do it all over again. I saw something in him as a boy—a fire, a spirit that no one could stop." He added wistfully, "Perhaps I saw some of my own son in him—the man Stephen would have become had he lived."

For the first time since Allie had been here, she sensed the full extent of Mac's sadness over the loss of his son. She felt a rush of compassion for him, and wished she could soften his pain. But she knew no one could do that. She couldn't lessen his loss any more than he could lessen her loss of her parents. All they could do was be there for each other.

Mac asked, "What are your plans for today?"

She smiled. "I thought I'd hang out with you, listen to some more stories. You're quite a storyteller, you know."

He smiled in return. "You're humoring me, young lady. I know you must be getting tired of me by now. Why don't you go do some shopping this morning?"

"I could do that this afternoon," Allie replied, thinking that he'd be napping then, and wouldn't miss her. Somehow, she felt reluctant to leave him. On the drive over she'd felt an unreasoning fear that now that she'd finally found him again, she could lose him. He was, after all, quite old and not in good health. She wanted to take advantage of every moment she could spend with him.

Mac snorted. "I've already got one nursemaid, young lady, I don't need another," he chided her with mock gruffness. "You take care of your business and leave me to take care of mine. I have things to do this morning, and won't have time for you anyway."

"Are you trying to get rid of me?" she teased.

He reached out and covered her hand with his. "Quite the contrary, dearest Alexandra. I'm going to do everything in my power to keep you right here for as long as I can. But you don't need to spend all your time keeping an old man company. You're young and lovely, and you should be out living your life. There are a lot of memories out there for you to rediscover."

She grinned. "In other words, get lost."

He winked at her. "Something like that."

She stood up. "I can take a hint. I'll make a few telephone calls and then I'll get out of your way for a few hours."

Allie stood up. Then, impulsively, and without quite understanding why she felt the sudden need to do so, she leaned over and hugged Mac. "Thank you," she said with heartfelt gratitude.

"For what?"

"For inviting me here and making me feel welcome. But mostly, for believing in my parents."

"I'll go to my grave believing in them," Mac said soberly. Then, before she could respond, he added, "Off with you now, and leave me to my business."

Back at her hotel room, Allie made several phone calls, the first one to her grandmother. She had put off calling sooner because she knew there would be countless questions for which she still had no answers. And she knew her grandmother would plead with her to come home. She was relieved when, instead of the barrage of questions she was expecting, her grandmother merely asked, "Are you all right?"

"I'm fine. Mac Sloan has been very kind. He's going to introduce me to my other relatives."

She sensed that it took every ounce of control her grandmother possessed to restrain herself from commenting on the Sloans.

Allie went on hesitantly. "I'm not sure how much longer I'll be staying."

Her grandmother sighed heavily. "Then you haven't found what you were looking for."

"Not yet, but I've begun to remember things from when I was a child. I was told it could happen all at once, or very slowly over a period of time. It seems to be happening slowly."

Her grandmother could no longer contain herself. "Oh, Allie, how long will you go on searching for answers that aren't there?"

"The answers *are* here, Gram," she insisted.

"But they're not the answers you want, child. I'm so afraid you'll be deeply hurt when you realize that."

"Gram, please!" She tried to cut her off as gently as possible as she felt the conversation going in the familiar, frustrating direction. "I've remembered something important from that night."

There was a tense silence on the other end of the phone.

Allie went on fervently. "I *know* the murderer wasn't my father. He *didn't* do it."

"Allie, I understand why you want to believe that, why you need to believe it—"

"Gram, it isn't just wishful thinking. I'm certain he was innocent."

"Then there's nothing I can say."

"No, there isn't."

Her grandmother's voice was gentle. "I love you, Allie. If you need me, I'll be here for you."

"Oh, Gram." Allie's voice broke with emotion. "I love you too."

After she hung up, she sat for a moment, composing herself. Then she called Julia and told her she still wasn't sure when she would return. To her relief, Julia was as supportive as she'd been when Allie left. She said simply, "Stay as long as you need to, Allie. And if there's anything I can do for you, just let me know."

When Allie hung up, she was overwhelmed with profound gratitude toward Julia. Deciding that the least she could do was find a special gift for Julia, she went out to explore the shops and art galleries of Carmel.

She drove down Ocean Avenue, the main street of Carmel. The village was a blend of old California and English country with quaint shops, restaurants, art galleries, and bakeries connected by meandering gardens, overflowing flower boxes, and cobbled walkways. There were no traffic lights, neon signs, or tacky billboards. None were allowed in the small seaside town that was more like an English country village plunked down at the edge of the Pacific Ocean.

As always, the village was packed with tourists, and parking places were at a premium. Allie took the first one she could find, on a side street, then got out and began exploring on foot. She discovered that Carmel was a blend of Old World charm and contemporary chic, from the Mediterranean Market that had every sort of cheese and wine available, and the Scotch Shop with its tartans, to the Crystal Fox accessory store, Lady Fingers jewelers, and the Peppercorn gourmet store.

She wandered through narrow shops that measured hardly more than ten by twenty feet, only to discover other shops and artists' galleries in the back, across small courtyards. Brick steps and wrought-iron stairs led to more charming little hideaways, always discreetly marked by a single, small sign.

The aroma of fresh-ground coffee beans from a shop specializing in coffee and tea blended with the ocean air and the pungent fragrance of pine trees. The sun was warm, the air was crisp, filled with the last remnants of morning mist. Planters and flower boxes overflowed with dark blue lobelia, soft pink cyclamen, and lazy purple cosmos. Allie felt like an explorer as she meandered through shops in stone cottages and made her way down brick-paved paths.

In an art gallery tucked away off San Carlos Street, at the back of a brick courtyard filled with a profusion of colorful flowers, Allie found the perfect gift for Julia. It was a series of lithographs of old Victorian houses in San Francisco. It was exactly the sort of thing Julia would love, and while it stretched Allie's budget, she felt it was the least she could do.

In another shop she found a gift for her grandmother, a marvelous book of English country gardens, with lovely full-page color photographs. By the time she returned to her hotel room to deposit her parcels, she felt very proud of herself.

Picking up the phone, she dialed Mac's house to ask what time she should return. The phone rang more times than usual, and she thought she must have dialed the wrong number. She was about to hang up and dial again, when Inez finally answered. Realizing who it was, Inez said in a broken voice, "Oh, Miss Allie, I was just about to call you."

Allie immediately felt a rush of fear. "What is it, Inez? What's happened?"

There was a momentary silence, and in that moment Allie knew what Inez was going to say. Even so, the words were devastating.

"Señor Sloan was having trouble breathing. He didn't want me to call an ambulance, but I did anyway." Her voice broke into a sob. "There wasn't anything they could do. Oh, Miss Allie, I'm so sorry."

7

RAFE'S PIERCING GAZE SENT Allie hurrying out of the church ahead of the others. One by one she'd watched her relatives turn to stare at her in utter amazement. Then Rafe noticed her, and his look seemed to cut through all her defenses. She'd recognized him immediately. The rebellious teenage boy glaring into the camera on the front page of a twenty-five-year-old Seattle newspaper was evident in the mature man whose look was so intimidating.

His even features were strong, patrician, his skin a deep burnished gold. Black hair fell across his forehead, above straight dark brows and equally dark eyes. He was lean, with a sort of animal restlessness. And he was looking directly at her.

Watching him now, she was every bit as affected as she'd been when she'd first seen his picture in the paper. For some reason, he frightened her. She had no idea why, she knew only that she couldn't fight her gut reaction to him.

She fled outside to the light and warmth, hurrying to her car. She got in and drove away before any of the Sloans, especially Rafe, could come after her. This wasn't the happy reunion Mac had planned, she thought miserably. Nothing in her relatives' looks suggested they were pleased to see her.

She drove down Ocean Boulevard the few blocks to the beach, parked her car, and sat there, staring out at the ocean. She was filled with an almost unbearable sense of loss. Every man she'd ever cared deeply about—her father, her grandfather, now Mac—had died. She felt utterly alone, and her first impulse was to leave this place, to go home where there were people who cared about her. Julia would welcome her back, and encourage her to bury her problems in work. Her grandmother would envelop her in a warm embrace and reassure her that she was loved.

You can't run away, she told herself firmly. You have to face the Sloans. They've seen you, they know you're here.

She had no idea why she was so nervous about meeting them. After all, she reminded herself, they were her family, just as Mac had been. She hadn't sensed the same welcoming warmth in their first response to her, but she told herself they were just unprepared. Mac himself had been caught off guard when she first called him.

She knew what she had to do. She had to go to Casa Sureno, where the mourners were gathering, and officially introduce herself to her family, as Mac would have wished.

By the time Allie arrived at Casa Sureno, the driveway was filled with cars. She parked behind a large black Bentley, then got out and slowly walked to the door. She had barely touched the doorbell, when the door was opened by Inez, who had clearly been waiting for her.

Impulsively, Allie reached out to hug the older woman, who responded with real warmth. When Allie finally pulled back, the tears she'd been fighting all morning threatened to spill from her eyes. "Oh, Inez, I should've been here with him."

"It wouldn't have made any difference, miss. He was very ill. I honestly believe he clung to life as long as he did only because he hoped to see you." Inez smiled through the tears that glistened in her dark eyes. "You made him so happy at the end."

"He made me happy too. He accepted me, and he gave me a chance to reclaim my childhood." Allie sighed heavily. "Are . . . the others here?"

Inez nodded. "In there," she said, pointing to the formal living room. Behind the huge double doors that closed off the room from the entryway, Allie could hear the low rumble of conversation and the tinkle of glasses as people drank to the memory of Mac Sloan.

"I'd like to freshen up before I have to face them," Allie said.

"Of course."

Inez led Allie upstairs to a small guest bedroom and adjoining bathroom, with French doors leading out onto a small balcony, then returned downstairs to greet the people who were still arriving.

In the bathroom Allie splashed cold water on her face, then dried it and repaired the minimal makeup she wore. Quickly, she ran a comb through her straight, baby-fine hair, and she was done. Leaving the bathroom, she started to cross the bedroom, when she stopped to take one final look at herself in the mirror over the dresser. At that moment through the open French doors came the deep-throated rumble of something that didn't sound like a car. Curious, Allie went out onto the balcony to look.

The rumble was much more distinct outside, and Allie thought she recognized the unmistakable growl of a motorcycle. Her guess was confirmed as she saw a motorcycle—long, low, and black—pull up in front of the house. The sun glinted off ebony fenders and tank, and long chrome side pipes. Allie stared in surprise, wondering half seriously if some member of a motorcycle gang had somehow lost his way on Seventeen-Mile Drive. But she knew the security guards posted at either toll gate to the forest made that unlikely.

Then she saw the rider more clearly as he rolled to a stop at the main entrance. He was dressed in jeans, boots, black leather blazer, and white shirt, the color stark against a dark throat where the collar lay open. His black helmet looked like a race car driver's, except that the face shield had been removed, and he wore glasses with reflective lenses that looked like the chrome side pipes.

He cut the engine with a last loud rumble, then released the kickstand with his right boot, and the large motorcycle set heavily into place. He removed the glasses and tucked them inside his jacket pocket, then reached for the helmet. He pulled it off and set it on the handlebars, then combed restless fingers through thick hair as dark as the motorcycle he'd ridden in on.

Allie leaned over the railing at the edge of the terrace, hoping for a glimpse of his face. She had no idea who he might be, but he acted as if he belonged there. It was something in the confident angle of his shoulders, and the slow, unhurried way he removed the glasses and helmet. Not as if he were reluctant to go inside, but rather that he would go inside when he chose to. There was something distinctly uncompromising in his attitude, almost defiant. Yes, she thought, definitely defiant. After all, he'd ridden a motorcycle instead of arriving in an expensive luxury car like everyone else, and he wore jeans and boots rather than a formal suit.

Allie's foot brushed against the small wrought-iron table on the balcony, causing it to grate against the tile. The man heard the sound and looked up, tilting his head back so that his face was in the light.

Rafe Sloan.

Allie immediately stepped back from the railing and went back into the room. She pressed a hand against her stomach, which suddenly seemed tied up in knots. You're being stupid, she chastised herself. There is no reason to be afraid of that man. Or any of them, for that matter.

She decided it was time to meet them, *all* of them, and get it over with. Taking a deep breath, she straightened her shoulders, opened the door, and left the room. She quickly descended the stairs. The doors out onto the courtyard had been left open, and a gentle breeze stirred the elegant floral arrangements decorating the tiled entry.

She didn't see Rafe in the foyer. Perhaps he had already come in and joined the rest of the family, she thought. The tightness in her stomach had become a knot that choked off any hope of drawing another deep breath.

Calling up all her strength, she started to cross the foyer toward the living room. Suddenly she froze. Across the entry hall she glimpsed her reflection in a large, gold-framed mirror. She'd seen the mirror before when she'd been there, but it hadn't affected her. Now, in a state of heightened emotion, she felt herself being drawn into a frightening memory. . . .

"I can't bear to look in the mirror . . . I'm afraid of what I'll see."

"What do you see, Allie?"

"The monster—the monster is in the mirror!"

She hadn't experienced this terror when she'd been here before, but now she felt a desperate desire to run and hide from the monster. Forcing herself to resist the panic that threatened to overwhelm her, she struggled back from the pain of that childhood memory. She wasn't going to be frightened away any longer. Turning her back on the mirror, she strode to the living room doors and opened them.

The large, high-ceilinged room was crowded with many of the mourners who'd been at the church. They sipped wine and nibbled on hors d'oeuvres passed out by white-coated waiters. As Allie entered the room, she saw the Sloans standing in a group in a far corner, formally accepting condolences. Rafe wasn't there, and for a split second Allie wondered what had become of him. Then her relatives noticed her, and she had no more time to think about Rafe. Meeting their openly curious stares, she forced herself to make her way through the crowd to them.

The man she recognized as Gavin Sloan stepped forward to meet her. "You're Alexandra, aren't you?" he asked in a firm tone that betrayed none of the shock she'd seen on his face in church.

"Yes, I am."

"I'm your father's cousin, Gavin Sloan." He went on in a deceptively even voice. "You bear an uncanny resemblance to your mother. We were all . . . quite surprised at your unexpected appearance after all these years."

In his fifties, he was athletic with light hair that hadn't yet started to go gray, and a well-honed physique that suggested a private gym and personal trainer.

"I'm sorry if I distressed you in any way," Allie apologized. "I didn't mean to."

A tall, attractive woman with chin-length blunt-cut hair in an expensive shade of blond stared intently at Allie. She had blue eyes and the patrician Sloan features. She appeared to be in her early sixties. From the newspaper photographs, Allie recognized her distant cousin, Charlotte Sloan Benedict. "You're Alan and Barbara's daughter?"

"Yes," Allie responded. "I . . . that is, I'm sorry to intrude . . ."

"Of course you're not intruding, Alexandra," Charlotte said quickly. "After all, you're one of the family. It's just that it really is quite a shock, seeing you again after all these years."

A strikingly attractive woman stood slightly behind Gavin. Her hair was a rich sable brown, pulled back in an elegant chignon. Her dark, luminous eyes were utterly blank, as if she'd erased all emotion and felt nothing. But Allie knew better. This was, after all, the same woman who'd dropped her purse in surprise when she'd seen Allie in the church.

Reaching out, the woman took Gavin's arm, as if to remind him of her presence. Glancing back at her, he said stiffly, "Alexandra, this is my wife, Erica."

Allie said, "It's very nice to meet you."

Erica murmured a polite but cold response.

Allie told herself she should feel at ease with these people, who were, after all, her relatives. Instead, she felt intensely uncomfortable under their polite but curious scrutiny. Erica's fixed gaze was especially unnerving.

Gavin went on. "How did you hear of Mac's death?"

Allie carefully chose her words. "I . . . happened to talk to Mac recently, and he invited me to visit. I arrived a few days ago. He was about to introduce me to all of you when . . . he died."

A gorgeous woman with waist-length auburn hair, wearing a tight black dress that was far more sexy than somber, slipped smoothly in beside her and into the conversation. "What fortunate timing. No one hears a word from you in twenty-five years, and you just happen to show up when there's an inheritance to be divided up."

Before Allie could defend herself, Gavin snapped, "That's enough, Valentina! Remember the occasion, and try to act appropriately."

Valentina merely smiled defiantly at him, then turned back to Allie. "By the way, I'm your cousin, Val. Uncle Gavin's right about one thing—you look just like your mother. It's eerie as hell."

Val was a classic beauty, with dark almond-shaped eyes, magnificent high cheekbones, and flawless skin. The skin-tight dress hugged slender hips and stopped several inches short of her knees, revealing incredibly long legs. It was a dress meant to be noticed, along with the woman in it.

At that moment a man with dark hair flecked with silver intervened. His gray eyes held a speculative expression. "This is absolutely amazing," he said in a voice filled with incredulity. "After all these years . . ."

He stopped, hesitated for a moment, then went on. "Forgive me, you probably don't remember me. David Benedict. I'm legal counsel for the Sloan Land Company. I'm also a member of the family."

Allie smiled. "Yes, I know. You're married to my cousin Charlotte."

Val interrupted rudely. "You could be Barbara's ghost."

"Good heavens, Val," Charlotte exclaimed. "What a dreadful thing to say."

"Well, why not?" Val retorted. "After everything that happened, maybe Barbara's ghost *has* come back to haunt the Sloan family. I hear people sometimes do that, especially if they were murdered."

Allie was so stunned by Val's incredible rudeness and insensitivity, she was speechless.

Gavin said in a voice that was clearly accustomed to giving orders and being obeyed, "I won't tell you again, Valentina. Behave yourself, or you'll be sent home."

Val leaned close to Allie and said dryly, "Are you certain coming back was a good idea? You know what they say about families—they're like company and bad fish, after a few days, they all start to stink." She laughed at her own little variation on the old saying.

Seizing another drink from the tray of a passing waiter, she took a sip and grimaced. "We really must get them to open something better than this mediocre stuff." She smiled wickedly. "After all, now we're celebrating Cousin Allie's joyous return."

"Why don't you see to it, Valentina. It will give you something useful to do," Gavin suggested.

Val didn't argue. Without another word she disappeared in the direction of the kitchen.

David gave Charlotte a pointed look and she immediately

went after her daughter. He turned to Allie. "It's good to have you back after all this time."

It was said with a genuine warmth that helped ease some of the tightness in Allie's stomach. Out of everyone that she had met so far that evening, it was ironic that David Benedict—not one of her blood relatives—made her feel the most welcome. Perhaps he, too, felt just a bit like an outsider.

Beside her, a woman was saying, "I'm not family, but Mac was one of my dearest friends."

Allie turned to look at an attractive older woman in a dark brown dress. Her shoulder-length hair was the most striking shade of pale silver Allie had ever seen, held back from her face with a wide brown velvet headband. Her skin was surprisingly smooth and unlined for someone who Allie guessed must be in her sixties, and she had lovely lavender-blue eyes.

"You're as close as anyone could be without being family," David Benedict was saying. "Alexandra, this is Elizabeth DiMaggio. She owns a very successful art gallery in Carmel—the Sobrante Gallery."

Elizabeth said gently, "Your mother was one of my dearest friends." She went on with a rush of emotion. "It's true, you know, you look just like Barbara. When I first saw you come into the room—" She stopped, and tears glistened in her magnificent eyes. She finished with a catch in her voice. "It was like seeing Barbara again."

"How did you know my mother?" Allie asked curiously, eager to get information from someone outside the family.

Elizabeth answered easily, "Barbara and I had a great deal in common. We were both more or less outcasts. I earned it, by marrying the wrong man—several of them, actually," she added with an impish grin. "And running off to Paris when my family wanted me to marry someone suitable and have a family. Your mother was an outcast because she wasn't old California. We bonded like blood sisters."

She cocked her lovely head at an angle. Her clear crystal drop earrings twinkled in the light of a huge chandelier that hung suspended from the center of the tall ceiling. "Val was right, crude as she was. But then, that's Val. It *is* like seeing your mother again. Although I see a little of your father in you too. Alan had that same way of standing back and watching everything go on around him—assessing everything and everyone. Not an impulsive man. Except when he married Barbara."

"Was their marriage impulsive?" Allie asked. She liked Elizabeth instantly, and felt comfortable questioning her about her parents.

Elizabeth grinned. "She was the one impulsive thing in his life. And he loved her madly."

Her smile was warm, comforting. Her eyes and her smile offered a friendship for which Allie suddenly felt a desperate need. Leaning forward, she gently patted Allie's arm. "Welcome home, my dear. I'm only sorry you had to return under such sad circumstances. I want you to know, my door is always open."

"Thank you," Allie said with heartfelt appreciation, her eyes stinging.

Val had returned. She carried a bottle of champagne in one hand, and hooked the other through the arm of the only other member of the family Allie hadn't been introduced to. Her sultry voice carried a distinct edge as she made the introductions. "My brother, Nicky. Nicky, this is our long-lost cousin, Alexandra." She made a grand gesture through the air with her free hand, and several inches of loose gold bangle bracelets of varying design jangled along a slender length of arm.

Judging by Val's behavior, Allie realized that the bottle tucked under her arm wasn't the first one she'd opened that day.

Val went on. "Isn't it amazing that she just *happened* to show up now."

"Val . . ." There was a distinct warning in Gavin's voice that suggested he had every intention of carrying out his earlier threat.

Nicholas Benedict stared unabashedly at Allie. "Val's just a little keyed up," he explained. "There's a race in three days, and she hasn't yet qualified her car."

At forty, Nicky was as handsome as he had been at eighteen, Allie thought. Like Gavin, he had a well-honed athleticism. He was deeply tanned like his sister, and had his mother's dark blue eyes. Unlike his mother, his hair was dark, a legacy of Elena Marin. He had a devastating smile and he knew it. A scar curved at the edge of his chin, somehow making him all the more attractive.

All in all, he looked surprisingly unchanged from his photo of twenty-five years earlier. The only thing missing was the Porsche. Allie suspected she might find one if she glanced out the window at the driveway. She'd met many men like her cousin—real estate developers, builders, and contractors. She ran across them constantly in her work. Multi-million-dollar architectural projects attracted them. Men with Nicky's sort of charm and looks would always have a Porsche, a dark tan, and a sexually charged smile that promised so much to more than one woman.

Val interjected herself back into the conversation. "Nicky, you know I can't qualify my car without an engine! And I can't get an engine unless I can pay for it." Her lovely mouth curved in a self-satisfied smile. "Of course, that shouldn't be a problem now."

David Benedict gently rebuked his daughter. "This isn't the time to discuss money, Valentina."

"Why not? It's on everyone's mind," she retorted.

While everyone reacted to her stunningly blunt statement, she looked across the room and her expression changed abruptly. "He's here," she whispered. As quickly as a summer storm blows over, her attitude changed from combative to sultry. She disengaged herself from her father's grasp and moved across the room toward the double doors that Allie had just come through.

"I suppose he *had* to come," Charlotte snapped, clearly displeased.

Nicky tossed back the drink he'd been holding. "I was wondering if he'd show up here." He thrust the empty glass at a passing waiter and seized another from the tray.

Allie had met every member of her family except the man entering the room now. She wondered what had kept him lingering out in the driveway. Had he been as reluctant to join this gathering as she had been?

She heard Nicky's sardonic comment. "Fashionably late. I suppose we should be flattered that he decided to show up at all." Then he added, "Allie, there's one last relative you haven't met yet. Our rebel *with* a cause."

There was no need for introductions. If there had been any doubt who the last member of the family might be, it would have been eliminated as Val rushed to the doorway to greet the man who'd arrived on the motorcycle. "Rafe!" she said in that smoky, seductive voice, slipping her arms about his waist and hugging him. "Thank God, you came. This is such a dreary gathering. You'll never guess who's here."

As he looked across the room, she took advantage of his momentary surprise. Unexpectedly, she kissed him fully, hungrily, running her tongue along his upper lip before plunging it teasingly inside his mouth in an attempt at blatant seduction.

But his fingers closed over her upper arms and he set her from him so abruptly that the hunger inside her was obvious even after the contact was broken. "Still up to your old tricks, Valentina?" His gaze crossed the room to the stranger standing with the other Sloans.

"Of course. You know I can be very persistent." Val ran a hand down the inside of his jacket, her fingers slipping to the front of his shirt.

He caught her fingers. "Be careful, Val. You could get burned."

She leaned into him, her magnificent hair spilling across his sleeve. "I like to burn, Rafe. Hot and fast."

Her words didn't have the desired effect. He was still watching the woman across the room.

She went on. "Come on, I'll introduce you." She seized his hand and drew him with her across the room. "You're the last to meet our dear cousin, Alexandra," she said to him in an introduction of sorts.

She turned to Allie. "This is our *half* cousin, Rafe Sloan," she announced to Allie. "Remember, he lived with your family out at the old ranch before your father murdered your mother."

"That's enough, Valentina!" Gavin said in a hard voice. "I think you'd better go now."

"Gavin's right!" David exclaimed. "If you can't behave yourself, perhaps you should leave." He turned to Charlotte. "Do something with your daughter," he ordered her.

"No, it's all right," Allie said quickly. It was obvious Val had had far too much to drink. She continued in a tight voice.

"I came back to face what happened. I can't run away from it every time someone mentions it."

"No, but you damn well don't have to have it thrown in your face either," David exclaimed.

Allie turned to Val. "Let's go into the kitchen and see if Inez can make us some coffee."

Val giggled as Allie started to lead her away. "You really are too nice to be a Sloan. Watch out! If you aren't careful, they'll have you put on the rack, like the Grand Inquisitor used to do to heretics. Our ancestors were part of that, you know."

Rafe joined them and took Val's arm. Covertly, Allie appraised him, from the dark, overlong hair that waved about his collar, to the casual jacket and the restless energy that seemed to fill it. When she'd seen his face in the church, then when she'd watched him from the balcony, she'd felt the same shock of recognition and feeling of unease she'd experienced when she'd first seen his photograph in the newspaper. It took all her self-control not to visibly shy away from him as he watched her. His eyes were dark, appraising, as if he, too, were remembering something. In that, he had the advantage, for she didn't know *why* she remembered him.

"I'll go with you," he insisted, leaving no room for argument. "She can be a handful."

Allie smiled grimly. "So I noticed."

They got her into the kitchen and left her in Inez's capable hands. Val's pointed and cruel remarks had made Allie reluctant to go back into the living room and face her family.

Rafe seemed to sense her unease. "Let's get some fresh air," he suggested, and she reluctantly agreed.

Which was more nerve-racking, she wondered—exposing herself once more to the intense scrutiny of her family, who clearly questioned her motives in returning here, or being alone with him.

"You're staring at me," Allie said as she and Rafe walked out to the courtyard. "Just like you were staring at me in the church."

"Of course. It was quite a shock for all of us."

"I didn't plan it that way, you know. It didn't occur to me you would all recognize me."

"We all remember your mother, and you look just like her."

"So I've been told," Allie replied curtly, remembering Val's painful comments.

Rafe went on. "You were watching me when I arrived."

"You saw that?" Allie asked in surprise, and was dismayed to feel herself blushing furiously.

He asked, "Why did you stare at me like that?"

"I was a little surprised, that's all."

"About what?"

Unsure of his reaction, she replied hesitantly, "I think it was the motorcycle, after everyone else arrived in cars. It was—out of character for a Sloan."

"I'm not a real Sloan," he replied harshly.

This wasn't the time to question him about that revealing remark. Instead, she said, "Nicholas called you a rebel *with* a cause. What is your cause?"

Again he avoided giving her a direct answer. "The last time he called me that, he accused me of trying to destroy the family."

Her startled look met his. "How could you possibly do that?"

His eyes narrowed. They were as dark as the night that surrounded them, and just as secretive. "By being one of the last holdouts, along with Uncle Mac. He was a bit of a rebel himself."

"What were you and Uncle Mac holding out against?"

"Our family's greed," he replied bluntly.

"At least you have a family," she reminded him. "A lot of people don't."

"And that's what you want?"

"Of course, doesn't everyone?"

He laughed then, a hard, brittle sound that hung suspended in the cool night air. But when he spoke, his voice was edged with old pain. "Be careful, Alexandra. This family destroys people they don't want to accept. They could destroy you."

She looked at him. "They don't seem to have destroyed you."

"No, but they tried." Before she could pursue that, he went on. "Why did you come after all this time?"

She was tempted to say it was none of his business. After all, he wasn't even a close relative, just a half cousin, twice removed. But somehow she felt compelled to explain herself, to justify her presence among these people who she'd already begun to sense were convinced she'd come back only for what she could get financially.

She answered carefully. "I grew up without knowing my father's family. I didn't remember them, or my parents, or anything about the first seven years of my life. When I finally began to remember some things about my childhood, I felt this family might fill a void I've always felt in my life. Does that make sense?"

Instead of answering, he said harshly, "Go home, Alexandra."

She was completely taken aback. "What?"

"Go back to wherever it is you come from, back to your life there. There's nothing for you here now that Mac's dead. He was the only member of this family who was worth anything, the only one who actually wanted you here."

Anger surged through her at his arrogant presumption that he could tell her what to do, and that she didn't belong here. Her blue eyes glinted furiously. "This is *my* family, dammit! I have a place here, and I won't be run off—by you or anyone! I still have a lot of questions to find the answers to, and I intend to do it!"

She stopped to catch her breath, and before she could go on, he said, "Some questions are better left unanswered."

With that Rafe turned on his heel and strode away, leaving her standing there alone.

8

IN HER ROOM AT the old Spanish-style La Playa Hotel in Carmel, Allie stirred in her sleep. Her dreams made her as restless as the cool breeze that moved the floor-length draperies at the French doors opening out onto a balcony. She was a little girl again, standing at the top of a staircase. Below her there were shouting voices. She called out, "Mommy!" but there was no answer. She walked downstairs, holding tight to the heavy wood banister. The tile steps were cool under her tiny bare feet. The shouting grew louder. She didn't like it, but she had to go toward it because she knew her mother was there.

She reached the foot of the stairs. The glow of a dim light drew her gaze down the broad entryway. It reflected in the large mirror with its intricately carved oak frame. Suddenly the shouting stopped. Allie saw a movement reflected in the mirror. She started to walk toward it. Then she saw it—the monster. It was gesturing wildly, its arm lifting and falling over and over again. It seemed to have huge hands that kept pounding and pounding—ugly, terrifying monster hands.

She could hear sounds—horrible sounds— as the monster growled and grunted. She covered her ears with her small hands, trying to block out the sounds.

She turned and ran back up the stairs, tripping over her nightgown, crawling, sobbing as she fought to reach the safety of her room. She screamed, *"Daddy! Where are you? You have to help Mommy! A monster is hurting her!"*

"Daddy!" Allie cried out. She jerked upright in bed, and stared wild-eyed around the unfamiliar room. She was breathing heavily, her body drenched in perspiration, yet her skin was cold as ice.

Slowly, the horror of the dream receded. She shoved her tangled hair back and closed her eyes against the ache of remembered terror that settled in her chest.

Then she opened her eyes in amazement as she realized the importance of the dream. That awful long-ago night she had fled upstairs, desperate to find her father so that he could help her mother. She wouldn't have gone in search of him if she had been terrified of him . . . if *he* were the one she had seen in the mirror that night.

"I love you, Allie. Always remember that I loved your mother."

Allie laid her head on top of the knees she'd pulled up to her chest. Heartfelt relief mingled with the pain deep within her. She whispered, "It wasn't you, Daddy."

Now she knew beyond any doubt that her father had been innocent. He had been executed for a crime he didn't commit.

And then came a new, stunning thought. The person who had killed her mother had gotten away with murder. The monster might still be out there right now. She might even have met him at Mac's funeral. . . .

The moon was full and flat, illuminating inky water that moved uneasily along the rocky shoreline, tumbling tiny sea creatures beneath pounding waves, and strewing seaweed along the beach like the torn tendrils of a woman's hair. Shadows made everything seem distorted and misshapen in the pale silvery light. Especially the hands that moved restlessly, clenching and unclenching, hands that almost resembled the hands of a monster. A low voice muttered.

"Why has she come back? How much does she know?"

And then, "How much will she remember?"

9

RAFE DROVE SOUTH FROM Carmel, down the California coastline. It was late morning. The fog rolled out from the shore, leaving behind sparkling blue water and the imposing cliffs and craggy promontories of one of the most dramatic coastlines in the world. The water was deep blue, shaded with midnight shadows in underwater canyons and deep gorges, aquamarine in shallow tidal pools, coves, and inlets, endless, unchanged for thousands of years, yet forever changing.

From Marin Bay, named for his Spanish great-great-grandmother, a few miles south of Carmel, to the southernmost point, almost ten miles away at Point Sur, then sweeping inland into the Santa Lucia Mountains and the Ventana Wilderness like a huge, defiant, spreading hand—this was El Sureno.

It was mountains, valleys, creeks, rivers, and canyons. It was generations of the Spanish Marin and Anglo Sloan families, their blood, dreams, and ambitions entertwined. It was also the last original Spanish land grant.

The wind swept up a rocky cliff, across the narrow two-lane Highway 1, and pinned Rafe in the seat of the open jeep. In spite of the warm sun, the wind was cold, the damp air stinging his face and neck. He slammed the transmission into a lower gear and swung the vehicle out around a plodding tourist, camera lenses protruding from front and rear windows of a rental car.

He was dressed even more casually this morning than he had been the day before at Mac's funeral. The leather bomber jacket was old and worn, suggesting it might be the real thing instead of an expensive knockoff. Faded jeans covered his long legs and lean hips. The boots were like the jacket—scuffed, unpretentious, with a history of their own.

At Sloan Point, named for his great-great-grandfather, Benjamin Sloan, he slowed the jeep only marginally, and swept off Highway 1 in a controlled sideways slide that churned dirt and gravel in his wake. He should have been concentrating on the road. Instead, he was thinking of Alexandra Wyatt Sloan.

He'd thought about Allie a great deal through the sleepless hours until dawn. The resemblance of Barbara was startling, almost unbelievable—the same fragile features, that soft voice that reached out across the void of years, and those blue-gray eyes that looked deep inside a man, their expression revealing a complete absence of artifice or guile.

Barbara had been the reason he'd been accepted by the Sloan family when he was a rebellious thirteen-year-old. She was the reason he stayed, and in the end the reason he fled. He'd been a seventeen-year-old kid whose dreams of love and family ended tragically one night in a pool of blood.

Jamming the shift lever into second, he barely controlled the four-wheel-drive vehicle as it sped along the ungraded mountain road. Now Barbara's daughter had come back, with only fragments of memory of that night, hoping to find the missing pieces. He smiled bitterly at the irony—he'd been trying to forget that night for twenty-five years.

His mood was reckless, just beyond the edge of control, and he drove the same way. The jeep bucked and lunged up what had been labeled a road at the turnoff from the highway, but was in fact nothing more than a slash up the side of the hill, often narrowing between rocks hardly wide enough to pass through.

The memory of the night Barbara died drove him as it had for twenty-five years. Over the years he'd learned to live with what had happened that night, forcing the memory back into a dark corner of his mind. Now Allie brought it all back. He'd read once that the past is never over. Now he realized how true that was.

There was so much of the past he wanted to forget—the rundown farmworker's shack where he lived with his mother and grandparents; the nights he went to bed hungry; the degrading names his mother was called in Spanish because of her half-Anglo bastard child; the hope she lived on even when she knew Paul Sloan would never marry her; the later years when he lived with Alan and Barbara and attended high school with rich white kids who didn't accept him; then the horror of Vietnam, and afterward, years of aimless drifting, until he found himself in Los Angeles.

His lips curved in a barely perceptible smile. There was one memory he valued, one that brought him pleasure, and even a measure of happiness. *Julianne*. Even now, after almost twenty years, he could still picture her vividly, a petite woman with red-gold hair and skin that seemed to glow. God, she was beautiful. Next to Barbara, she was the most beautiful woman he'd ever known.

They met when he was working at a construction job in the La Costa Beach area of Malibu. He'd been hired by a company that built houses to do rough carpentry. He was so broke, he slept in his car, a battered old Chevy truck, at the site. Julianne lived in the house next door to the construction site, and every day she watched the men work, then leave in the late afternoon. But Rafe didn't leave. He got food from a nearby market, and sat in the empty shell of the house, eating it alone and looking out at the magnificent ocean view. He knew he would never be able to afford a house as expensive as this multi-million-dollar one he was building, nor a view as marvelous.

Then one evening Julianne came over, carrying a bottle of wine and two glasses. "I'm tired of watching you sit here alone every night while I sit alone in my house. We might as well keep each other company."

He was in his early twenties, she was in her early thirties. He couldn't believe a woman as beautiful, as rich, as sophisticated as she was could possibly be interested in him. He assumed her life was the opposite of his—happy, secure, perfect. He quickly learned differently. Her husband, a wealthy producer of television series, was never home. He told her he was working, but Julianne knew better. She didn't flinch from facing the truth.

When Rafe asked her why she put up with such treatment, she said matter-of-factly, "Because I don't have the guts to try to make it on my own. I'm like all the rest of the women in this town. I'm convinced I'm nothing without my husband."

They didn't make love at first. They simply talked. Julianne was starved for companionship, and to his surprise, Rafe realized that for the first time since 'Nam, he wanted to connect with someone, to get to know someone and let them get to know him. By the time they made love for the first time, just before the house was completed, they had come to care for each other deeply.

Julianne asked him what he wanted to do with his life. When he answered that he had no plans, and besides, it didn't matter, because he couldn't do much anyway, she told him how wrong he was. She told him he was bright and talented and strong, and could make his life whatever he wanted it to be. She believed in him, and the miracle of their relationship was that she made him believe in himself.

By the time the house was finished and his job was over, he had the courage to ask her to leave her husband and come with him. She smiled tenderly at him, and said, "Oh, Rafe, you're the strong one, not me. I'm trapped in the life I've made for myself. But you can do anything, be anything."

It hurt like hell to leave her. But he didn't forget what she said. He clung to the strength that her confidence in him gave him, and eventually he proved her right.

One day, when he'd taken over the construction company that he'd once worked for in the lowliest, most menial position, and was a rich and successful man, he went back to Julianne's house. He wanted to thank her, and maybe even persuade her to come away with him if she was still unhappy in her marriage.

He was stunned to learn that she'd committed suicide only months earlier, shortly after her husband left her for a much younger woman. For the first time in years Rafe got drunk, so drunk that it took days for him to entirely sober up.

There had been other women over the years, some of whom he desired as much as he'd desired Julianne. But not one of them made him feel as good as she had made him feel. He told himself he would never feel that way again.

Now, remembering Julianne, his smile was bittersweet. He wished he could have saved her. But he couldn't save her any more than he could have saved Barbara.

But he wouldn't think of that. He couldn't.

Near the summit he downshifted, sending the jeep over ruts and washes at a dangerous speed. He traversed several switchbacks and bone-jarring cuts that ran water in a spiderweb of seasonal streams during wet months.

The Pacific Ocean, a brilliant blue jewel according to the Spaniards who had sailed it, fanned out to the horizon at his back. But the golden crown was El Sureno, the legacy of the Sloan family—over one hundred thousand acres of original Spanish land grant spreading out before him.

The road flattened deceptively for almost a hundred yards and then suddenly shot up an incline. He floored the accelerator, crested the hill in a burst of dirt and gravel, then ground the jeep to a hard, sudden stop.

There were no doors to crawl out. The jeep was almost fifty years old, a relic of World War II, bought from army surplus. He'd picked it up, used, fifteen years before to use on construction sites. He loved it, because he loved to salvage things that other people had considered useless and had discarded. He made all the necessary repairs himself. He'd added the requisite lights and seat belts that made it street legal, and installed a modified V-8 Chevy engine and transmission. It was as solid as the day it was built, although that was hardly apparent by the original dull army green color that had faded to drab. Old and ugly, it could run the wheels off its shiny new counterparts.

"Is there anything left of that road?"

The criticism was direct and blunt, as blunt as the man who gave it. For the first time that day, Rafe grinned as Jim Collier came toward him, beating the dust from his clothes with the brown felt fedora he always wore. Jim had a neatly trimmed beard lightly streaked with gray, and sported a pipe clenched between his teeth. He usually forgot to light it. He had a paunch he'd been trying to lose for as long as Rafe had known him, which was more than fifteen years. And he was the best damned civil engineer in the business.

Rafe responded to the good-natured ribbing. "I left a little road for next time. You can ride with me."

"That's very generous, boss," Jim said easily. He was old enough to be Rafe's father, but was completely comfortable with having a much younger man for a boss. He'd worked for Rafe for almost fifteen years, first in southern California and now for the Sloan Land Company. He respected Rafe for working his way up, building a small hammer-and-nail outfit into a successful development company, then selling it for several million dollars.

Rafe hired him away from the new owners and lured him north with the enticement of working with the Sloan Land Company, one of the oldest family enterprises in California. Only then Jim realized for the first time just who Rafe Sloan was. And he respected him even more for not relying on his family's name and money to get ahead.

In response to Rafe's offer of a ride in the old jeep, Jim said with a grin, "How big a fool do you think I am?"

"No bigger fool than I am," Rafe answered easily. The attitude underscored Rafe's feelings—it was all a gamble, anyway, with everything from the past on the table.

Two years ago Mac had located him and urged him to come back. "You're a Sloan as much as any of us. Your father may not have married your mother, but he made certain you had his name. Alan and Barbara took you to live with them because you *are* one of the family. There's a legacy that goes with the name. It's time you quit running away and accepted it."

He'd asked Mac the same question that day; "Just how big a fool do you think I am?"

"Big enough to want what is rightfully yours, and strong enough to take it."

Mac was right. Rafe had spent a lot of years running away from his heritage. When Mac called, he knew it was time to stop running. The timing was right—after selling his company, he could return to the Sloan fold as someone with his own money. He didn't need theirs.

He'd told Mac, "It will have to be on *my* terms. I want to be a legitimate part of the Sloan Land Company."

Legitimate was a word that meant a lot to him, and Mac knew it. Mac agreed to his demand, and Rafe returned. His welcome was even less warm than Allie's had been, but he hadn't cared. He'd spent his entire life reassuring himself that he didn't care what the almighty Sloans thought of him. Now he found himself wondering if Allie cared what they thought of her.

He forced his thoughts back to the matter at hand, and reached for the long anodized steel tube behind the seat. It was approximately three feet long, and four inches in diameter, and held the first-draft site plan for the proposed project.

"You took that road like the devil was riding your tail," Jim commented. He added quietly, "I'm sorry to hear about Mac. He was a hell of a guy."

Instead of responding, Rafe quickly changed the subject. "Did you verify that adjacent land?" he asked, glancing into the distance where two men were working with a tripod and levels.

"We just finished shooting the grades on this section. Needless to say, there've been substantial changes over the past two hundred years." Jim referred to the original parchment grant maps, written in Spanish, that set out the land gradations when El Sureno still belonged to Rafael Domingo de la Marin.

Rafe had already had several meetings with an investment group over the past months, and while his past business relationship with them had been successful it wasn't enough to get them to commit to the El Sureno project. Rafe's own money, while substantial, wasn't nearly enough to fund a project of this scope. Even the Sloans didn't have that kind of money.

"You don't control the property," the potential investors had pointed out. "You are only a minority owner. And it is our understanding that those who hold controlling interest won't commit to this project."

He had tried to override their doubts as he had in the past. "Give me a commitment for financing of the first phase of development, and I'll get their commitment on the land—in writing."

"These are hard economic times," they responded as if he weren't aware of that. "Investors are taking a more conservative posture. We're no longer funding projects of this magnitude.''

''That conservative posture over a prolonged period of time will kill economic growth, and you know it,'' Rafe had insisted.

But they refused to commit to the project.

Time was against him. Six months earlier the state had forced through a zone change on the property from rural-agricultural designation to commercial, a lucrative move for the state that stood to collect escalated tax revenues, and a potentially disastrous change for Rancho El Sureno. The taxes had been forced sky high, beyond the ability of any single owner to pay them and leave the land as it had been for more than one hundred fifty years—open cattle land, quiet inlets and bays, vast rolling hillsides.

Rafe continued to argue as persuasively as he could with the investment group, but the answer was still the same. It was a catch-22 situation. Without control of the property they wouldn't commit the financing. Without the commitment for financing, he couldn't get control of the land.

''What happens now?'' Jim asked.

Rafe was adamant. ''I'll find someone who will finance it. Even if I have to sell off my portion of the land to do it.''

Rafe's gaze scanned the expanse of privately owned California coastline, and the endless horizon of ocean beyond. ''I am going to build this project,'' he repeated. ''It's the only way to keep this land from being completely raped. No one in my family is going to stop me.''

Then Rafe added grimly, ''I'll do whatever it takes.''

10

ERICA LANDIS SLOAN HAD been born to wealth. Her father, Amory Landis, was one of the original ''four''—the group of private investors who, at the end of World War II, established the company that developed four square blocks of what became known as one of the most exclusive shopping and art enclaves in the world—Carmel, California. Their original investment of ten thousand dollars each multiplied by millions.

She went to private schools in Monterey, then Mills College in the north. Her family belonged to the Pebble Beach Association and the Del Monte Country Club. Her father served on the boards of several pro-am golf committees. Her mother, Joan Avery Landis, was an avid golfer who'd chummed through college with Babe Didrickson Zaharias in the thirties and forties. The ''Babe,'' along with other professional golf legends and celebrities such as Bing Crosby, had established the mystique of one of the most challenging golf courses in the world—Pebble Beach.

Erica belonged to that privileged inner circle of peninsula society that included many of the oldest families in California, including the Sloans.

Her first memory of Gavin Sloan was when she was six

years old. She and her parents were guests at the Sloan ranch, the old hacienda at Big Sur. At that time no one in the Sloan family actually lived at the ranch. They lived in charming Carmel "cottages" or on vast Pebble Beach estates. The hacienda was a weekend retreat, a place for horseback riding and elaborate barbecues where, more often than not, the guest of honor was a visiting dignitary from the worlds of politics or the arts. Ex-presidents, opera singers, and movie stars mingled there. The Sloans were important people, and they liked to socialize with people who were just as important.

It was still a working cattle ranch, but a foreman ran it. Gavin and Charlotte's father, Paul Sloan, had long before abandoned life at the ranch for an office in the financial center of San Francisco to the north. There he oversaw the worldwide interests of the company.

Gavin was nine when Erica first saw him. He perched confidently astride one of the cutting horses used to work the cattle—not one of the well-bred ponies that were kept for the children. Even then he was tall for his age. His fair hair and blue eyes contrasted with the sharp, patrician features of his aristocratic forebears on the Marin side of the family. He handled the horse, a big bay gelding that stood at least sixteen hands, with a confidence that bordered on arrogance as he openly showed off for Erica.

She fell in love with him instantly, and never seriously looked at another boy.

As they grew older, both families felt it was a perfect match. They made a striking couple—Gavin, with his fair looks, and Erica, with her auburn hair and dark eyes. They began dating when Erica turned sixteen, and from then on neither dated anyone else. He took her to charity fund-raisers, country club dances, the celebrated annual Cascarones Ball, tennis and golf tournaments, and sailing in the regattas.

Gavin had already graduated from college and joined his father in the family business when Erica went off to Mills. They began sleeping together during the fall of her freshman year. She'd had to seduce him, for Gavin's sense of morality was deeply ingrained. On the weekends when she wasn't home, he drove up to see her. They were a perfect blend of looks, background, and wealth. Their eventual marriage was discussed between their families as a foregone conclusion.

Their unofficial engagement was so taken for granted that Erica didn't worry when his letters and phone calls became less frequent, and he was gone more and more often as the diversified company business took him to Seattle, Texas, and Australia. Erica didn't know that on one such trip to Seattle, Gavin had met Barbara Wyatt, and for the first time in his life fell passionately in love. But as Christmas grew near, Erica realized that it had been nearly a month since Gavin had returned her calls or responded to her letters. When she returned home for the holidays, intent on having it out with him, she was brought face-to-face with Barbara.

They were as different as two women could possibly be. Barbara was fair, like Gavin, with thick blond hair, soft gray-blue eyes, and delicate, fragile features. She had an unpretentiousness and reserve that bordered on shyness. But that shyness disappeared with the warmth of her smile and her easy laughter.

When Erica was finally able to get Gavin alone, and tearfully demanded an explanation, he said with genuine confusion and guilt, "God, Erica, I'm so sorry. I can't explain what happened. I know I'm treating you badly, but I can't help it. Barbara's different from anyone I've ever known. . . . What I feel for her is different . . ."

Stunned, Erica barely managed to ask, "Are you saying you're in love with her?"

Unable to meet her accusing look, he glanced away and nodded unhappily. "I . . . I'm going to ask her to marry me."

Disbelief and shock mingled with almost unbearable pain. She couldn't bear it. This couldn't be happening. She stammered through the tears coursing down her cheeks, "You only just met. How could you possibly think you're in love with her? You don't know anything about her."

"I know how she makes me feel," Gavin answered stubbornly.

"What about *us*?" Erica demanded.

All he could do was to keep repeating, "I'm so sorry, Erica. I know I'm treating you badly, but I can't help it."

Erica couldn't believe this was happening. Choking back her tears, she shouted furiously, "She's not one of us! She's just some little nobody, a gold digger out for what she can get! Your parents will never accept her!"

She heard the rising hysteria in her voice, and didn't care. For the first time in her life she was rocked by emotions so powerful that they obliterated any concern for the rigid standards of correct behavior that had been drummed into her all her life.

Gavin's expression hardened. "Don't talk about Barbara like that. She doesn't care about money. It isn't important to her."

Erica snorted disdainfully. "Oh, of course!" She went on desperately. "Gavin, I can accept that you were tempted to have an affair with her. These things happen, I know that. But we've spent years planning a future together . . ."

Gavin said in a weary voice, "I know that everyone always assumed we would get married. But no one asked if it was what *we* wanted. Admit it, Erica, we went along with it because it was expected."

"I love you. I thought you loved me."

"I did . . . I still do, in a way." Awkwardly, he tried to explain. "I care for you a great deal, but it's just not . . . not what I feel for Barbara."

"Is she in love with you?" She was tormenting herself more with each question, but she had to know.

"We haven't discussed it, but I'm certain she feels the same way." It was said with the same self-assuredness that had always been so much a part of Gavin, as if everything would naturally be the way he wanted it simply because he wanted it to be that way.

Of course she loves him, Erica thought miserably. She couldn't imagine any woman not loving Gavin. At that moment she felt a cold hatred for Barbara lodge somewhere deep in her heart. It would remain there forever.

"I hate you!" she cried. But she didn't, really. She hated Barbara.

"Don't do this, Erica," Gavin said impatiently, as if she were a petulant child making a big deal about nothing.

She gave in to her rising hysteria then, dissolving into loud sobs as she ran from the room. She left the Christmas party at Mac's house, too wounded and humiliated to keep up the pretense of holiday spirit for the sake of their families.

She spent New Year's in Hawaii with friends from college, then returned early to Mills. She didn't hear anything from Gavin again until she returned home for spring break. Then she learned that Barbara's feelings for Gavin weren't the same as his for her. The engagement had never materialized, and Barbara was seeing someone else—Gavin's cousin, Alan Sloan, whom she'd met the night of the Christmas party.

Alan and Barbara were married in April of that year. Barbara Wyatt returned to Carmel for the first time since that Christmas visit not as Gavin's wife, but as Alan's. She looked radiantly happy and was clearly deeply in love. By June, when Erica graduated from Mills and returned home for the summer, Barbara was pregnant, and she and Alan were living at the old family hacienda in Big Sur.

At a tennis party Erica saw Gavin for the first time in over six months. She made a point of being friendly to him, and letting him know that she harbored no lingering resentment over their broken engagement. The truth was, she'd never blamed Gavin for what had happened. It was all that bitch Barbara's fault. While Erica could forgive Gavin, she would *never* forgive Barbara for coming between them and spoiling their utterly perfect relationship.

They began seeing each other again that summer. The following Christmas, exactly one year after Gavin had told her that he was in love with Barbara, they officially announced their engagement at an extravagant party at Casa Sureno. Their lavish wedding, one of the high points of the social calendar that year, took place in February. They honeymooned in Puerta Vallarta, and returned to Carmel two days after Barbara gave birth to a little girl, Alexandra.

Erica wanted badly to give Gavin a son. A son would have put her one up on Barbara, for male heirs were all that mattered in the Sloan dynasty. But after four miscarriages, the specialist warned her it would be dangerous to get pregnant again. Her inability to give Gavin a child somehow intensified her feelings of failure and inadequacy in comparison to Barbara. Erica was privately happy that Alan and Barbara had no more children. If

Barbara had provided a male heir, it would have killed Erica.

Living within the public spotlight that went along with the Sloan name, the two couples maintained a façade of congeniality. Erica knew that Barbara's attempts at friendship were sincere, and she pretended to feel nothing but familial closeness to Barbara. But she continued to hate her with a cold, unforgiving passion that never abated. Each time she and Gavin made love, she sensed that he wished she were Barbara. The thought tormented her, but she could never bring herself to confront Gavin with her suspicion because he might admit it was true.

Then Barbara was brutally murdered. The tragedy, and the scandal of the trial that followed, devastated the Sloan family. Newspaper articles hinted at rumors that Barbara had been having an affair. The rumors became all the more sensational as it was learned that she was two and a half months pregnant at the time of her death. She and Alan had argued publicly about the affair the night she died.

Was it Gavin? Erica wondered. She could tell by the way he looked at Barbara whenever they were together that he'd never stopped loving her. But as with her other suspicions, Erica couldn't confront Gavin about this. Because if he said yes, he was having an affair with Barbara and had gotten her pregnant, Erica simply wouldn't be able to bear it. The carefully nurtured illusion of her marriage as a happy and solid one would be shattered forever.

So she didn't ask Gavin any of the questions that haunted her. And both of them pretended that everything was perfectly fine.

"Good morning," Erica greeted Gavin as he came into the dining room.

It was early, barely past seven o'clock in the morning, but he was already dressed for work in a conservative, very expensive suit. He frowned slightly as he went to the marble-topped sideboard and served himself from the dishes set on warming trays. "Aren't you up a bit early?" he asked, taking his chair at the opposite end of the table.

The maid, a Filipino woman, appeared from the kitchen and poured coffee from the silver server.

"I like getting up early," Erica said, smiling radiantly as Tia poured her coffee.

"Since when?" Gavin asked as he sliced through a homemade bran muffin.

She laughed but didn't reply.

"Since Mac's funeral," he suggested pointedly.

She ignored the barbed comment. "It gives me a chance to see you. You keep such long hours."

"You know what it's been like lately. There's a great deal of work to be done—meetings with the bankers, the coastal commission, real estate agents, the advertising people. It's not like trying to sell a farm in Salinas. There are thousands of critical details involved in a project of this size."

Normally, he didn't bother discussing his work with her. The fact that he chose to share these brief details encouraged her to ask, "Do you think the sale will go through?"

His expression hardened. "It *has* to go through. There's no choice. The taxes have made it impossible to keep the land."

"Rafe seems to think otherwise."

He looked at her sharply. "Since when have you been talking to *him*?"

"He believes we can develop it ourselves. He says it's just a matter of finding the right financial backing."

Gavin said angrily, "What he's proposing would take years to develop! We don't have years. In less than eight months the state is going to want next year's taxes. Our only hope is to sell off most of the ranch."

"Mac didn't want it sold," Erica reminded him.

"Mac is dead. Anyway, he was living in the past, in the days of the old dons, for Christ's sake. His desire to keep the original land grant in one piece just wasn't possible."

Nibbling on a piece of toast, Erica asked with deceptive casualness, "Did you know that Alexandra's an architect?"

Gavin had turned his attention to the morning paper. His concentration never wavered, nor was there any other indication that he had heard what she said.

"She's been working for a very reputable firm in Seattle for the past several years," Erica went on. "My God, can you believe it? All this time—almost twenty-five years . . . and I understand she doesn't remember anything that happened before her grandparents took her away. Do you suppose she's . . . unbalanced?"

Gavin set his cup down hard, spilling coffee onto the pristine white tablecloth. "It's too bad the rest of us can't forget what happened. That's what this is all about, isn't it?"

Erica's careful composure crumbled as she struggled with the ragged emotions she'd fought ever since Mac had called to tell them that Allie was back. "She looks just like *her*."

Gavin's fist slammed down, rattling the dishes on the table. "Don't start this, Erica!"

"Do you know what it felt like, seeing her?" she asked, ignoring the warning edge of his voice. "After all these years? Except for her hair, she looks exactly like Barbara. It was as if Barbara had come back, looking exactly as she looked that night."

"Stop it!"

He rose from the table, shoving back his chair, which scraped across the Florentine marble floor. He threw the newspaper down and turned to walk away.

"You can't bear to talk about her, can you!" she cried, unable to hold back the old pain and the jealous rage that went with it. "Barbara, always Barbara! My God, she's been dead for twenty-five years, and she still comes between us!"

"I'm not listening to this!"

Gavin stormed out of the room, picking up his briefcase from the hall table and slamming the front door behind him.

Erica went after him, following him out the front door and down the steps to the driveway, where his car, a large silver Mercedes, was parked.

"You never got over Barbara, did you? Not even when she died!" Tears spilled down her cheeks. "After all these years it's still Barbara! You're still in love with her!"

Unable to stop, she went on. "I was glad when Barbara died! I thought you couldn't love her anymore if she was dead, and the rumors would finally end. Were the rumors true?" she demanded. "Were you the father of her unborn child?"

Gavin tossed his briefcase into the backseat of the car, and without turning to look at Erica, said firmly, "Stop it!"

But twenty-five years of repressed jealousy and anger were finally coming to the surface in a eruption of volcanic intensity, and Erica couldn't stop. She went on recklessly. "*Was* it your child—the child you always wanted and I could never give you?"

She grabbed his arm, pulling him around. "Don't lie to me, Gavin!"

Slowly, he disengaged her fingers, then flung her hand away from him as if he couldn't bear her touch. His words cut deeper than the suspicion she'd lived with for so long. "I have never lied to you, Erica."

Then he turned, got into the car, and drove off.

She stood in the driveway, tears of rage and humiliation streaming down her cheeks. He had never lied to her, because until that day she'd never had the courage to ask, afraid of what the answer would be.

She stood there in abject misery, watching him drive away. She hadn't intended to start a fight with him. She'd planned to be pleasant and encouraging, and through subtle means find out just how Gavin felt about seeing Alexandra. And, by extension, how he still felt about Barbara. But everything had gotten out of hand. Driven by a jealousy so deep she couldn't contain it, Erica had lost control.

She knew that this would only drive Gavin further from her, but she couldn't help herself. The more she needed him to reassure her that he loved her more than Barbara, the less he was able to do so, and the more desperate she was to hear it. It was a vicious cycle that had continued for over thirty years, ever since Gavin had married Erica—his second choice.

Second choice. The knowledge had haunted Erica for all her married life. She knew she would go to her grave without ever having that special confidence that she came first with Gavin.

She'd thought it would change when Barbara died. After all, Barbara was gone, and Erica was there, loving Gavin totally, without reservation. But somehow it had only gotten worse. She knew that Gavin never stopped thinking of Barbara. And in his memory she became an idealized fantasy that no other woman, especially Erica, could match.

Now Barbara's daughter was back, looking astoundingly

like her mother, and reminding Gavin of what he'd lost when Barbara had rejected him.

Erica felt a deep hatred for Alexandra well up within her. She almost hated her more than she'd hated Barbara. At least Barbara had died. But Alexandra was there, alive and well and living among them. A constant reminder to Erica that she would always be second choice.

II

DAVID BENEDICT PINCHED BACK the throbbing at the bridge of his nose. The pain shot up his forehead and dug in deep, pounding with each pulse of blood through his veins. As he reached for the ever-present bottle of prescription pain relievers, he glanced at the group of family photographs on the corner of his desk. In one photo, his son, Nicholas, sat astride his favorite polo pony at the Pebble Beach Equestrian Club. David frowned at the reminder that Nicholas squandered his life on expensive hobbies instead of applying himself to a career. At forty-five, Nicholas should have long since established himself in something, *anything,* as long as it was productive.

Next to Nicholas's photo was one of Valentina posed next to her race car. As always, she looked vibrant and reckless, and the tight-fitting racing suit revealed far more of her body than David felt was appropriate. Her helmet was off, and her long auburn hair hung wetly around her shoulders. She'd been doused in champagne as she held aloft the coveted first place trophy for winning the Formula One Grand Prix race at Long Beach two years earlier.

Her husband at that time, team driver Marco Charteris, stood in the background, frowning as she kissed team sponsor Enzo Fabi with slightly more than the natural winner's enthusiasm. Only a few months after the picture was taken, Val had divorced for the third time.

Her personal life was like her racing—high-speed, dangerous, constantly moving on to the next challenge, and leaving everything else behind. David had no idea who his daughter was seeing now, but he was sure there was someone. There always had been. From the moment that David had pulled her out of that expensive Swiss finishing school at fifteen when he learned she was having an affair with a ski instructor, she'd gone from one unsuitable man to another. David had long since given up trying to have any control over her, and simply prayed that she didn't embarrass the family too badly.

Beside the picture of Val was one of his wife, Charlotte Sloan Benedict. The picture had been taken at the annual Cascarones Ball, and Charlotte was dressed in a beautiful authentic Spanish gown and mantilla. An organizing member of the ball committee, she was pictured accepting the accolades of the other members. Charlotte was everything her daughter wasn't—demure, reserved, a lady in every respect.

David shook his head in frustration, wondering how on earth he and Charlotte had managed to produce two such unsatisfactory children as Nicholas and Valentina. He and Charlotte had each sown their share of wild oats when they were young, but by the time they married, in their late twenties, they'd settled down, exactly as people were supposed to do. Their two grown children looked as if they would never settle down.

Then his gaze fastened on another picture—a family portrait taken many years earlier, when David was still young enough and foolish enough to believe that all his hard work, sacrifice, and careful scheming had led to the perfect life he'd dreamed about as a poor, struggling law student from a lower-middle-class family. This picture had been taken at Christmas, when Valentina and Nicholas were adorable-looking children who hadn't yet disappointed their parents. His father-in-law—a commanding figure—stood at the edge of the family group that included Gavin and Erica, Charlotte and David, Alan and Barbara, and their baby, Alexandra. Rafe was absent from the picture. In those days he was the badly kept secret that everyone knew about but no one openly discussed.

Staring at Barbara, David was struck by the amazing resemblance to Alexandra. They had the same oval face, the same gray-blue eyes, the same fragile beauty. Seeing Alexandra again had been like traveling back through time. She had her mother's proud bearing and gentle voice. Val had been right, Alexandra could almost have been a ghost.

But she wasn't. She was very real, a poised, well-educated, successful young woman who, as a child, had survived a living nightmare. Now she had returned to confront it, to remember, and in doing so forced them all to remember, whether they wanted to or not.

Reluctantly, David remembered his own past. He had been a brilliant, fast-rising legal star with the law firm of Taylor and Hardison in San Francisco when he first met Charlotte Sloan in 1951. His position with the firm gave him an entree to the haut monde of San Francisco society, and Charlotte, who was living in San Francisco at the time, was very much part of that society.

Charlotte wasn't beautiful. When David first met her, she had mousy-brown hair which she kept too short to be really attractive or feminine. But she had long, slim legs, and dark, golden skin that made up for a lot, and the money to buy very expensive designer clothes that made up for even more. And she had great bone structure, inherited from the Marin side of the family, that defined her face with interesting angles and accentuated her only really pretty feature, startlingly deep blue eyes.

She was very bright, and had attended Vassar. She knew a great many of the people that David wanted to know. And, most important, she was wealthy. She drove a Chrysler convertible, partied with friends who lived in Nob Hill and Pacific Heights mansions, spent long ski weekends at her family's luxurious "cabin" in Lake Tahoe, and even longer vacations at their Oahu beachfront estate.

Through the grapevine he heard stories of wild parties and unsuitable men—an actor, a sidewalk musician, a charter fisherman. It was rumored that she bought him a boat as a parting gift when they broke off. It was also rumored that her father, Paul Sloan, had lost patience with his reckless daughter.

By contrast, David was very conservative and very ambitious. He was impressed by Charlotte's uninhibited sexuality, her wealth, and her name. It offered the connections he would need to go as far as he was determined to go.

Charlotte made no pretense at hiding the fact that she wanted him. The first time he asked her out, they ended up in bed together. By their third date he had moved into her spacious Post Street apartment. Soon he was spending time at her parents' home in Carmel, sleeping in the guest room, of course. Colleagues openly teased him about all the advantages of being married to a Sloan. He was more than aware of those advantages.

In November they went down to Carmel for Thanksgiving. The entire family was there, including Charlotte's older brother, Gavin, just back from college; Mac and his wife; Charlotte's widowed father, Paul; and various cousins. At one point he overheard a conversation about someone named Rafe, whom he assumed was another of the Sloan cousins. Later he discovered that Rafe was Charlotte's half brother, from Paul's affair with a Mexican-American woman.

After dinner Paul invited David into his study for an drink, a cigar, and a talk. Outside the house, in exclusive Del Monte Forest, mist rolled in off the ocean and shrouded gnarled and bent cypress trees, tall pines, and eucalyptus. Inside, a fire crackled at the hearth and the firelight sparkled in the cut facets of a crystal brandy decanter. The pungent aroma of burning logs and expensive hand-rolled cigars blended with the lingering aroma of roast turkey, tart cranberry, and spicy pumpkin soufflé pie.

"Charlotte tells me that you're ambitious," Paul said bluntly as they sat in deep leather chairs facing the fireplace.

David wasn't sure what the proper response was, so, cautious as always, he said nothing.

Paul went on. "I like that in a man." He rolled the big cigar between thumb and forefinger. Several more plumes of smoke jetted into the air. "I'm no fool," he went on in a contemplative voice. "I'm aware that what Charlotte lacks in beauty she more than makes up for on a financial statement. Someday she will inherit a significant stake in this company. That will make her a very rich woman."

He gave David a no-nonsense look. "The man who marries her will be very rich."

David didn't know what to say to this blunt assessment of Charlotte's attributes, as if she were a piece of valuable property. What Paul said next stunned him even more. "I want Charlotte to settle down with the right man. I think that's you, and I'm willing to make it worth your while."

Before David could frame a suitable response, Paul took another drag on the Cuban cigar, then continued. "She's had her little period of rebellion to get back at me for being unfaithful to her mother. It's time for her to get married and have children. She seems to want you, and I'm inclined to give her exactly what she wants. Besides, the company could use a good lawyer. If you marry Charlotte, I'll make you legal counsel for the Sloan Land Company."

David cleared his throat, then began nervously, "That's, uh, very generous of you, sir."

There was more. "In addition, on the day of the wedding I will sign over to you a five percent share in the company. Charlotte wouldn't need to know about it. The shares could be placed in a dummy corporation. You're a lawyer, I'm certain you can take care of the details. And if you're half as smart as I think you are, you've already done your homework on what that could be worth."

Paul didn't wait for a reply. "Mind you," he continued, "I don't expect fidelity." His expression sobered. "I'm not that big a hypocrite. I do, however, expect discretion, especially where a scandal might affect the reputation of this family and the company."

David was stunned. And intrigued. Paul had just made him a very lucrative offer to marry his daughter. But it would mean leaving Taylor and Hardison. He gave that careful consideration for a moment. He was the newest of several junior attorneys. All of them hoped to be offered a full partnership one day, but only one or two would make it. It would be years before he could hope for such an offer, if at all. Any lawyer at the firm, including the senior partners, Taylor and Hardison, would have given their firstborn child for the opportunity to represent the Sloan Land Company. It was being offered to him on a silver platter in exchange for something he'd already seriously considered anyway.

"I care very much for Charlotte," he began, only to be cut off by Paul.

"I don't for a minute believe that you're in love with my daughter. It's not a requirement for an agreement between us."

Paul stubbed out his cigar in the ashtray beside his chair. "You don't have to give me your answer today. Think it over, enjoy the weekend. I'll take you out to the ranch tomorrow. There's quite a legacy that goes with it—over one hundred thousand acres of prime California coastal property and the last original Spanish land grant in the state."

David knew that Paul had every intention of making certain he knew just how much he was being offered.

"The old family hacienda is out there. I love the place." He hesitated, then went on. "Charlotte doesn't care for it. Neither did her mother. If you marry Charlotte, you'll live in Pebble Beach, of course. The family owns a lot that's just the right size for a house for newlyweds."

They both stood then, and Paul walked with him back to the family dining room, where dessert was being served. Charlotte looked up from across the table and smiled at David. As they rejoined the family, Paul leaned over to whisper to him, "I'm not a patient man. Don't make me wait too long for your answer."

David and Charlotte became officially engaged that weekend. They were married three months later and honeymooned in Tahiti, compliments of David's new father-in-law. By the time they returned to Pebble Beach to oversee the building of their home, Charlotte was pregnant.

David wasn't in love with his wife, but he was satisfied with their marriage. They were compatible, and Charlotte quickly settled into her role of devoted wife and mother and society matron. Only after some time had passed did David begin to realize that he'd made a pact with the devil. The new house at Pebble Beach, the cars, the club memberships, *everything* belonged to the Sloan Corporation. Nothing was in his name except his paycheck, which wasn't much bigger than it had been at Taylor and Hardison. When he complained to Paul about his salary, Paul merely shrugged and reminded David that he didn't need a lot of cash. Everything about his life-style was taken care of for him.

The five percent share ownership in the Sloan Land Company looked important on paper, but the truth was that it wasn't enough to make a difference on a company vote. The assets were controlled by Paul.

The gilded cage David had so eagerly stepped into began to close in on him. He owned nothing, he controlled nothing. But he'd live very well—as long as he remained married to Charlotte.

His position of power within the family as the corporate attorney was an illusion. Eventually, David learned to use that illusion of power. It attracted people—like Andrea.

She was young and sexy. David was very discreet, convinced that Charlotte knew nothing of the affair. He always made certain he met Andrea when Charlotte was out of town on shopping trips to San Francisco, or visiting friends.

Then one weekend Charlotte returned early. He explained that he had a dinner meeting with a client. For once it was the truth.

"Cancel it," she said as she crossed the living room. There was a look in her eyes that he'd never seen before.

She seduced him then, just as she had seduced him the first time, with a blatant need that hadn't waited for the bedroom. As he lay beneath her, David wondered if she sensed—either by lingering taste or smell—the wildly erotic night and morning he'd spent with Andrea. If she did, it seemed only to sharpen her appetite.

He felt his body respond to Charlotte, and he loathed himself for it. Then he was inside her. She quickly climaxed. But instead of being satisfied, she sat astride him and began to move again. When he finally came, she climaxed for the third time, and David couldn't help but think that what he felt must be what a whore felt.

That night he began to hate Charlotte.

Eventually Andrea grew tired of waiting for David to divorce Charlotte, and left. Other affairs followed, but nothing ever came of them. He took from them what little pleasure he could, and remained married to Charlotte because he would have less than nothing if he left. His father-in-law had made certain of that.

But Paul had never envisioned the day might come when the Sloan ranch might be sold. It had always been unthinkable. Now it was a reality. And when it happened, the capital from that five percent interest his father-in-law had signed over to buy a husband for his daughter would be David's ticket out.

His secretary buzzed through on the intercom, reminding him about his meeting with Gavin. They were flying to San Francisco later that morning for a meeting with the Nakatome Group about negotiating the sale of the Sloan ranch in Big Sur.

They'd first met with Nakatome over three months earlier, right after the Sloan Land Company had been notified about the change in tax status on the ranch property at Big Sur. Because of the historical significance and the size of the ranch, the story had been printed in all the newspapers. Within days the Nakatome Group had contacted Gavin, making aggressive overtures to purchase the ranch. Gavin had immediately called a meeting of the board of directors, which consisted of the other family shareholders besides himself—Charlotte, Valentina, Nicholas, Mac, and Rafe.

David had provided the legal expertise for the sale. In turn, his brother-in-law laid out a convincing argument. The Sloan Land Company survived on a diversified portfolio of agriculture and several commercial developments Gavin had pursued on family-owned property within the urban areas of Carmel and Monterey. But the days of the old Californio ranchos was long over. Cattle ranching was no longer profitable.

Now the state had stepped in and passed new tax legislation in order to prop up a failing state economy. It had unilaterally changed the zoning of the ranch land, a move that escalated the tax base on over one hundred thousand acres of prime California real estate. That forced the family into a desperate situation.

Gavin had outlined their limited options. there was no choice but to sell off the ranch. Everyone was in agreement—except Mac and Rafe.

Mac had gone on and on about the preservation of the land that represented the Sloan family heritage—a heritage he stubbornly refused to admit they could no longer afford to keep. Rafe, the illegitimate half brother Gavin could barely tolerate, had listened until the argument died down, and then raised his own proposal to develop the land themselves instead of selling out to the Japanese.

The family immediately divided into two camps, those in favor of the sale on one side, Mac and Rafe on the other.

"I'm not worried," Gavin had assured David with his usual confidence. "Rafe and Mac are the only holdouts. Together their shares aren't enough to block a vote for the sale of the ranch. Valentina, Nick, and Charlotte will vote for the sale. With my shares, that gives us enough leverage to override Mac and Rafe."

And now Mac was dead, and his shares would be divided among the family.

His secretary buzzed him again. Charlotte had just arrived and was on her way to his office. He quickly gathered up the portfolio with the prospectus they'd put together for potential buyers of the ranch. He was just rounding the corner of his desk, on his way to Gavin's office, when Charlotte came in.

She was immaculately dressed, as always, her hair still short but expertly streaked with blond now, and not a strand out of place. She was still lithe and trim. Valentina had inherited her mother's sleek body. David couldn't help acknowledging that Charlotte had become much more attractive in the years they'd been married. But he didn't feel the least desire for her.

"Am I late? I was afraid I might have missed you," she began. "The guild meeting went overtime. I swear I'm not going to take this on again next year. Five years in a row is enough."

His response was automatic. "You say that every year."

"This year I mean it." She hesitated, then asked, "Are you feeling all right? You look a bit pale."

"I'm fine," he insisted.

"You've been working too hard on this Japanese deal. Or perhaps," she suggested with a watchful look, "it's our long-lost cousin, Alexandra."

David opened the file in his hand and pointedly focused on it. "I don't know what you're talking about."

"Liar," she said softly, still watching him. She wondered

how many other things he'd lied to her about over the past forty years.

Without looking up or acknowledging what she'd called him, David said, "My flight leaves in less than two hours for San Francisco. We'd better get into that meeting with Gavin. He wants this deal very badly."

"All right." She picked up her purse and followed him as he left his office and headed down the hall toward Gavin's. She knew that Gavin wasn't the only one who wanted this sale so desperately.

Two hours later the small commercial jet taxied down the runway at the Monterey airport. Charlotte sat behind the wheel of the Jaguar coupe in the adjacent parking lot and watched as the jet lifted from the tarmac and quickly gained altitude out over the Pacific Ocean.

Charlotte Sloan Benedict had no illusions about her looks or her options in life. From the time she was a little girl, it had been made very clear to her. She had no real money of her own, not the kind that would have given her freedom and independence. They money was controlled by the family and the company. The company paid her bills, bought the cars she drove, and the house she lived in. And she knew, too, that the company had bought her a husband. David had married her for that illusion of wealth. She had married him for love. She had loved him deeply, obsessively, and had done everything she could to be the kind of wife he wanted.

But he had never loved her. Perhaps, she thought bitterly, if she'd been beautiful, like Barbara, David would have loved her. She knew he'd been extremely attracted to Barbara, and why not? Barbara was beautiful. Charlotte had even dyed her hair the same color as Barbara's in an attempt to look like her.

When she thought of what she'd put up with from David—what she'd done for him to try to win his love—she felt sick inside. None of it had worked. And she'd been forced into the pretense of a solid, successful marriage.

Now they were forced to sell the ranch, and she was glad, because finally she would have money of her own. Her father had been raised at the ranch, and loved it. But Charlotte, like her mother, hated it. It was too remote, too rustic. The main house had been built in 1854. There had been additions and modern improvements over the years, but it was still a ranch house, and couldn't compare to her ultramodern redwood-and-glass Pebble Beach home.

Her father spent a lot of time at the ranch without his wife and children. Then one summer when her father was out of town on business and Gavin was away at camp, Charlotte and her mother made one of their rare visits to the ranch for the weekend. Charlotte was twelve, still enough of a little girl to love horses, and there were a lot of horses at the ranch. That was the only thing she liked about it.

They left early that morning, driving down Highway 1 in her mother's Lincoln, and arrived at the ranch shortly after nine o'clock. It had been months since Charlotte had been out there. Eager to change into her riding clothes, Charlotte leapt out of the car almost before it stopped and ran up the adobe steps to the front entrance. As she charged into the house, a young woman came out of the kitchen, and stood staring at her in dismay.

She was small and beautiful, with waist-length dark hair, olive skin, and large dark eyes. Charlotte's gaze fastened on the rounded fullness of the young woman's stomach beneath the loose summer dress she wore.

"Charlotte! For heaven's sake!" her mother called out as she came into the house. "You didn't even wait until I stopped the car. Don't ever do that again."

She came up behind her daughter. "Charlotte? Why are you standing there like that?" Then she saw the young woman.

There was a moment's stunned silence, then her mother ordered her sharply, "Go back to the car, Charlotte!"

"But we just got here."

"We're *not* staying."

Charlotte started to protest that she wanted to go riding before they left, but her mother grabbed her by the arm and said furiously, "Go to the car, now!"

As Charlotte retreated through the front door, she heard voices—the young woman calling for someone, and then a man's voice. "What is it, *querida*? What's happened?"

Charlotte whirled around. "Daddy?"

"Oh, Christ!"

What followed was ugly and was forever imprinted on her young mind, along with the endearment her father had called the young woman—*querida.* Charlotte was studying Spanish in school, and knew that it meant "lover."

Charlotte's mother led her to the car, then returned to the house, leaving Charlotte to sit there alone and confused. Eventually, her parents came out to the car, and they all drove home together in a strained silence. But her father hadn't stayed with them. He had driven back to the ranch that night.

In the days and weeks that followed, her mother refused to speak about what had happened. Her mother closed herself away in her elegant rooms and refused to see anyone. Charlotte gradually came to realize that the woman she had seen at the ranch had been staying there with her father. But she kept it a secret, refusing to talk about what she had seen.

She learned that the young woman's name was Amelia Estrada. She had been living at the ranch for several weeks. With that single murmured endearment as he came out of the bedroom at the hacienda, Charlotte also knew that Amelia Estrada was her father's mistress. And she was pregnant.

Charlotte was thirteen when her half brother, Rafael, was born. Her own mother died the following year. It was labeled an accidental overdose of prescription sleeping pills and alcohol, but Charlotte believed it was suicide. She never forgave her father for his mistress, his bastard son, or her mother's death.

For years she rebelled against her father, trying to hurt him as bad as he had hurt her. There were many boyfriends and lovers. Her father disapproved of all of them, and she enjoyed his disapproval.

Then she met David Benedict. He was everything her father wanted in a son-in-law. It stunned Charlotte that she wanted David, too, in a way that she'd never wanted anyone or anything in her life. She'd never had any illusions about the reason David married her. She was smart enough to guess at the truth. As the years went by she realized how much he hated being owned by the Sloan family.

She also know about all his affairs. But he always came back to her, and she always kept his secrets, just as she'd kept her father's.

Now the ranch was to be sold, and she was glad. Ever since that summer she had hated it. When it was gone she would finally be rid of all the old demons. It made it all the sweeter that Rafe so desperately wanted to keep the place. In the end he would lose everything, and the heritage her father tried so hard to pass on to his two sons—not his daughter—would be gone forever.

12

NICHOLAS SLOAN URGED THE surefooted purebred gelding to race faster down the choppy polo field of the Pebble Beach Equestrian Club, chasing the wooden ball. His was the number-two position, the hustler, who went after the ball to set it up for scoring play. Polo required a keen eye, an aggressive nature, and a fast horse. The gelding, Andio, born and bred and trained to the polo field in Argentina, was fast. Nicky had paid five hundred thousand dollars for him the year before, and the gelding had made the difference last season between the championship and a second-best finish in the national field trials.

After last season Nicky had improved his handicap from four to seven. This year, his goal was the coveted ten handicap. No one in the history of the modern game had ever jumped three places in their handicap in one season. But then, few had a horse like Andio. As every polo player who'd ever challenged the game knew, the horse was as much as seventy-five percent of the player's ability.

He'd bought Andio out from under the English trainer for the Duke of Castleberry by topping the trainer's final authorized bid. It had practically wiped him out, but the gelding was worth it. By the end of this season, the ten handicap would be his.

They were in the last period of play against the South American team. His number-three player swung across the field, took control of the wood ball, and fed it downfield to Nicky. He took the ball on a single strike of the mallet and then braced just before his Argentinian opponent slammed into him.

They raced headlong down the field, a tangle of swinging elbows and mallets, each horse and rider maneuvering to cut the other off as they fought to control the ball. The game was brutal, often a test of sheer strength as the players pushed and shoved at one another atop their horses.

Then Nicky took a powerful swing at the ball. He was thrown off balance and the side of the mallet glanced off the ball, but it was enough to break it out of the pack. He jerked Andio back around and swung again, this time sending the ball downfield right into the field of play of his number-one player. His teammate, Michael Parkman, angled in front of his opponent, who was protecting the goal, staggered him off position with his horse, then drove the ball into the goal for the winning score.

Nicky's team slowly regrouped, both men and horses exhausted, and cantered across the playing field to shake hands with the Argentinian team members.

He removed his helmet and tucked it under his left arm as he walked Andio back to the sidelines. His naturally wavy, dark hair lay in wet clumps against his head, and sweat molded the team shirt with number eight to his back and chest. There were smudges of dirt on his previously gleaming white riding pants, and a bad bruise along one forearm where he'd connected with an opponent's mallet. Perspiration streaked his face, yet he grinned broadly, his keen blue eyes glinting in stark contrast to his deeply tanned face.

Freddie, one of the team trainers, met him at the sidelines and took Andio's reins as he dismounted. "Good game, Mr. Sloan. You gave 'em a run for their money," he chuckled in an accent that was pure cockney. "It was close till the final chukker."

Nicky's grin deepened. "A little revenge for that drubbing we took last year." He laid his gloved hand on the gelding's sweaty neck. "But this fellow made the difference. Wouldn't you say, Freddie?"

"It's been a rare long time since I've seen a beast as fine as this one. 'E knows 'is game. Loves it as much as any man does, I'll wager. I could see it in the way 'e leads downfield. And 'e's not afraid of runnin' down another 'orse. Some of 'em shy away, y'know."

Nicky lovingly stroked the sable-colored neck, then ran his hands down long, powerful legs. "He was bred to win. He'll take us to the championship." Already the gelding had recovered from the strenuous afternoon game. He was no longer blowing heavily, and as a group of junior players came onto the field for a practice session, his ears perked up in anticipation.

"You've had your exercise for today," Nicky scolded the gelding as if he were capable of understanding. Then he turned to Freddie. "Walk him out slow and give him a good rubdown. He's earned it."

"Right yer are, Mr. Sloan." Freddie gathered up the reins and spoke soothingly to the horse as he turned him toward the long row of gleaming, immaculate stables where horses resided in privileged comfort. He called back over his shoulder, "By the way, Mr. Sloan, there's a gentleman wot was askin' for you up at the club'ouse. Said it was a business matter 'e wanted to discuss with you."

"Did he give a name?" Nicky asked quickly.

"No, sir, 'e didn't."

Nicky's teammates called out to him to join them at the outdoor pavilion, where an elaborate reception was already under way for both teams. Champagne, wine, and other drink flowed in abundance. White-damask-draped tables were covered with silver platters of fresh shrimp, crab, and oysters as well as other delicacies. An elaborate ice sculpture of a polo player astride a horse dominated the center table. Overhead, the red-and-white-striped canopy fluttered in the afternoon breeze blowing in off the ocean. In the distance, along a curve of beach, golfers dotted the landscape as they attempted the next hole of the fabled course.

Nicky flicked a worried glance at the clubhouse, then quickly made his decision. He turned and strode in the opposite direction, toward the pavilion. The crowd included both teams, other players who trained regularly at the Pebble Beach club, wives, families, and polo enthusiasts from all over California who had come to watch the international competition.

Among the guests was the daughter of a former member of the Argentinian team. She was an exotic beauty, with long black hair, captivating green eyes, and a delightful English accent developed in the most exclusive boarding school in England. Her name was Miranda, and she and Nicky spent the rest of the afternoon together. By the time they parted, after arranging to have dinner later at the Del Monte Lodge, Nicky had consumed a staggering amount of champagne, followed by his customary gin and tonics.

Miranda left in a bright red Ferrari, the top down, her long hair streaming in the wind. She waved and blew him a kiss as she circled the parking lot and sped out onto Seventeen-Mile Drive.

Despite his physical exhaustion and slightly befuddled state from all the liquor, his pace quickened as he headed for the stables to check on Andio before leaving. Miranda was an intriguing diversion, but she was just another woman. Andio meant far more to Nicky than all the Mirandas he'd ever known, and there had been many.

Except for the horses, the stables were almost completely deserted, since most of the other players and trainers had left. Across the exercise yard a teenage stable boy whistled as he led a blanket-draped horse inside an adjacent wing of the stables. Ocean air blended with the fragrance of pines, eucalyptus, fresh-cut grass on the playing field, and pungent stable odors. Inside the long stables, horses moved restlessly in their stalls, and made occasional snorting noises. As Nicky entered, the horses caught his scent and several heads were thrust over gates in anticipation of a gentle hand or an extra portion of grain.

He talked to them as he passed by, calling them by name. Most of the horses were boarded there on a regular basis. Two of them belonged to his teammates. Along the other side were several horses of the Argentinian team. Andio's stall was at the far end, near the rooms occupied by the stable boys.

As Andio heard the sound of Nicky's riding boots and caught his scent, he whinnied in greeting. Nicky looked for the finely sculpted sable head thrust over the end of the stall, but was surprised not to see it. He whistled softly and again there was an answering sound, but still no Andio. Nicky slowed as he approached the stall and opened the gate. In the shadows he could see the gelding standing at the back. The horse looked up at him expectantly, and at that same moment Nicky saw the dark shape of a man standing in the shadows, holding Andio's halter.

He was dressed in an expensive business suit, hands perfectly manicured, expensive shoes gleaming with fresh polish except for the soft dust of the stables across the toes. When he spoke, his voice was measured, articulate. "A very fine animal, Mr. Sloan."

Nicky stiffened. "What are you doing here?"

"I'm here to remind you about your agreement. And to check up on the collateral."

Nicky reached out and took hold of Andio's halter, pulling the gelding out of reach of the man. "I've paid back almost half the note. The other half will take just a little more time."

The man frowned. "With the Sloan name, repaying your gambling obligations should be no problem at all. My employer was patient in the beginning. But it's been four months. The note was for three."

"I told you, I need just a little more time," Nicky insisted, trying desperately to muster a tone of bravado.

"You bet on today's game."

It wasn't a question but a statement. An uneasy sensation slipped down Nicky's back. They knew every move he made.

The man went on in that same polite tone. "We'll take your winnings from today as a down payment on the balance. But my employer expects the debt to be *fully* paid within thirty days. He's already been more than generous. He's no longer in a generous mood."

Nicky's air of false bravado crumbled. He had a good idea what happened when men like the one he owed money to decided to get difficult. He said hurriedly, stumbling over his words, "I explained the situation to him. All I have is a monthly allowance from a trust, and that isn't nearly enough to repay the debt."

"And yet you can afford to board a fine animal like this at the club."

"It's all taken care of through the family, even the house I live in. Look, I don't have access to that kind of money right now, but I will have. The company is selling the Sloan ranch. As soon as the sale goes through I'll have my own money, a lot of it, more than enough to pay off my debt."

The man shook his head. "I told you, Mr. Sloan, my employer is out of patience."

"I can't force the sale to go through any sooner!" Nicky insisted, sounding more and more desperate. "It's being negotiated right now. My father flew up to San Francisco today to meet with the buyers."

The man's expression hardened. "For your sake, that sale had better go through. *Soon.*" He reached out, stroking Andio's glossy head. But instead of running his hand down the horse's muzzle, he used the cold, hard butt of a gun to do so. As the horse shied away from the object, the man went on. "You realize, of course, the collateral won't cover what you owe. I would still have to take other measures." He said sharply, "Understand?!"

Unable to speak, Nicky nodded.

The man smiled, as if glad that they understood each other, then brushed past Nicky and walked out of the stall. In a moment he was gone.

When he was alone, Nicky slowly let out the breath he had been holding. He knew the man meant every word he said. If Nicky didn't come up with the money soon, he would lose Andio. And that wasn't all.

His only hope was the sale of the ranch. When that happened, he would be a very rich man. He would have more than enough money to pay off his gambling debts, and he would finally be free from the control of the Sloan family.

Throughout his entire life he had been made to account for every penny he spent. As if that weren't bad enough, he was constantly reminded that he had a family reputation to live up to. For several generations Sloans had been movers and shakers in California society, as his mother never ceased to remind him. Well, screw the family. It meant nothing to him other than the financial freedom his inheritance would give him when he finally got hold of it.

Suddenly a disturbing thought struck him. Could the unexpected appearance of Alexandra somehow affect the sale? She was, after all, one of the heirs to the estate. Then something else occurred to him that he realized he should have thought of earlier. She had probably inherited a sizable piece of the estate from her father. After all, Alan had been the principal heir.

The panic that had been building within him ever since he found the stranger in the stall got worse. My God, what if Alexandra screwed everything up? His hand shook as he took a handkerchief from his pocket and wiped the sweat that had broken out on his brow. The sale *had* to go through. His freedom—even his life—depended on it.

13

In spite of the cool October air, heat shimmered off the asphalt surface of the meandering racecourse. The grass on the rolling hills was brown from the lingering dry season. It contrasted with the brightly colored metal bodies of the sleek race cars that streaked the course in red, bright yellow, silver, and white, the logos of team sponsors blurred by speed.

Laguna Seca was a brutal, challenging course with a series of tight corners, downward curves, unexpected hairpins and doglegs that lured the drivers in with the illusion of a straightaway that all but disappeared more than a dozen times. It demanded everything from man and machine, and had been rated one of the best racecourses in the world.

The cars sped by at alarming speed, the engines winding up to six and seven thousand rpm, then whining in a sudden downshift chorus as a half dozen cars bottlenecked through a turn meant for one. Then they hurtled out of the turn, accelerated to maximum speed, only to whine down again, accompanied by the ever-changing sounds of tires as weather conditions and traction changed.

Race fans filled the stands at the starting line and at intervals along the circuitous track. Campers, RVs, minivans, sports cars, and motorcycles filled several parking lots. Fans of car racing, along with ice chests and picnic baskets, spread out from the stands across the rolling landscape. They sat in lawn chairs, on blankets, the tailgate of pickup trucks. Camera crews from various sports programs as well as still photographers sat poised with their equipment, documenting the race, while sports announcers from ESPN and the networks commentated the race.

A deep metallic-blue Lola-powered MacLaren with silver and white logos banked high against the outside of turn number five behind the yellow and gold Miller racing team car, lulling the other driver into overconfidence as he shot down the middle of the course. At the last minute the blue MacLaren drew the fake, plunged low to the inside of the turn, and edged by the Miller car close enough so that the gold and yellow was forced to back out to avoid a collision. The blue and silver car edged ahead of the pack coming out of the turn, gaining precious time and the second-place position behind race leader Rick Mears.

They tore through three more turns, the front of the blue car never more than scant inches off the rear of Mears's car. The driver of the blue MacLaren continued to push, edging closer, refusing to back off, waiting for that single moment's hesitation at a corner that would give the edge.

Then, outside turn nine, black smoke began to pour out of the MacLaren. It gradually dropped back in the pack to positions it had overtaken earlier, then farther back until it safely dropped to the inside shoulder and limped off the course.

As the car rolled to a stop, emergency personnel rushed over, along with a mechanic from the driver's pit crew, and a tow truck. The canopy was removed and the driver wedged up out of the tight compartment. The chin strap was unfastened and the sleek racing helmet removed. Then the snug-fitting flame-retardent fabric hood and face mask were peeled off. Long auburn hair tumbled over the driver's shoulders.

One of the pit crew offered a water bottle to the driver. Valentina Sloan Rothman Charteris pushed it away as she scrambled out of the race car. "Where's Bill?" she demanded furiously.

The mechanic from the Sloan Racing team answered, "He's back at the pit."

She pushed past him, ignoring the paramedics who were always present anytime a race driver came out of a race unexpectedly. She ran over to one of the track attendants who were posted at regular intervals around the course in their small pickup trucks to give whatever assistance might be needed during a race. "Take me back to the pit area."

"The tow truck will be going back as soon as they get the car hooked up, Miss Sloan. You can ride back with them." Then, turning his back on her, he spun the truck about and drove back to his position at the next turn.

There was nothing for her to do but wait, or walk.

She waited. Less than half an hour later Val and the crippled MacLaren were delivered to the pit area. She slammed out of the tow truck. "Where's Bill?" she demanded of one of her mechanics.

He jerked a thumb over his shoulder in the direction of the repair truck that housed most replacement parts that a race car might need during the course of a race. Bill was inside, checking tools and equipment.

Val hurried over to the truck. "Dammit, Bill, that race was mine!"

He looked up slowly, apparently in no hurry to deal with her. He was used to drivers' furious outbursts, but Valentina Sloan was the worst. Over the past four years he'd gradually gotten used to her. It took a particular sort of woman to push her way into the male-dominated sport of auto racing. Several had tried, but only a few had succeeded. It took nerve, ruthlessness, and calculated calmness. Val had everything except the calmness.

"Seems to me that Mears had that race," he said simply.

She squared off at him. "Only after my engine blew! I could've had him, Bill!"

"*Could have* doesn't count in racing. You ran a good race. The engine just didn't have it. It had too many hours on it. They last only so long, and you were out there running against new engines."

"I know that!" Her voice rose in frustration. "That's what I've been telling you for weeks. I want that new Buick engine

If I'd had it today, we'd be headed for the winner's circle right now. Do you know the sort of sponsors that attracts?"

Bill shifted the massive power-boost starter to the far side of the van. The look he gave her was barely tolerant. "I've spent my whole life in racing," he reminded her as he came out of the van. "You don't have to tell me about sponsors. But I'm going to tell *you* something. You want that new Buick engine, you've got to come up with two hundred thousand to set it up. They aren't just sitting on a shelf in the local auto-parts store."

Before Val could form a scathing response, he went on. "This is a rich man's sport—or rich woman's," he amended reluctantly. "The bottom line is, I can't get the engine without the money. I've been scabbing parts to keep that car glued together for the past two races. You want to play in the big leagues, girl, you got to come up with the money. Ain't no free ride. That's why ninety-five percent of the teams on asphalt are corporate racing teams with big-time corporate sponsors."

"I've got a sponsor—" she began.

But he interrupted her. "Then go ask him for the money. When you've got it, we'll talk engines." With that, he threw down a greasy cloth and walked over to the car to supervise loading it onto the trailer.

Val watched with barely suppressed fury. There was nothing she could say. He was absolutely right. She turned and headed for the trailers that had been provided for drivers, but she didn't bother to shower. Instead, she quickly stripped out of her racing suit and pulled on expensive designer jeans, a thin white tank top that emphasized her full breasts, and boots.

When she left the trailer, a young man was waiting for her. Josh was twenty-two, a recent graduate of Cal Poly who was doing graduate studies at Cornell. He'd come home on quarter break to see her race and visit his family. He was the baby brother of the girl who'd been her best friend all through private school in Monterey before she went away to Switzerland. But he was no baby—not anymore. Val had seen to that.

As she stepped down from the trailer, Josh came up to her, slipping his arms around her in concern. "Are you all right?"

"Yes, of course!" she snapped.

He pulled her close, pressing his body against hers. "I was worried about you."

Suddenly she was very bored by this kid. She pulled back. "Look, Josh, I need to go home. It's been a long day."

"If you want to go home and sleep, that's all right. I just want to be with you," he said with a puppy-dog eagerness that she'd once found appealing. Though she'd grown tired of his pathetic adoration of her, she hadn't entirely forgotten how deliciously energetic he could be—and how nice his hands, his mouth, his body, could feel.

"Let's not go to my house. It's not convenient," she lied effortlessly. "Some of my family are coming over soon." She went on. "I know a place close by."

Within minutes they were speeding down the two-lane that connected Laguna Seca to the rest of the world. Josh drove to the nearby Holiday Inn. He checked them in using the company credit card Val gave him, then they drove around to the poolside entrance. Within minutes they were in a fourth-floor room with a view overlooking the ocean. It was identical to all the rooms they had used before.

Val was restless, impatient, still keyed up from the race. When Josh began to kiss her, she hastily pulled his shirt from his pants and peeled it back off his shoulders. She sunk her teeth into the hard, round flesh at his shoulder while her fingers unfastened his button-fly jeans.

Her mouth hungrily found his as she slipped her hands past the loose waist of the jeans, down over firm young buttocks. Josh groaned as his arms went around her. Then he shuddered as her fingers closed over his rigid erection. "Oh, God!" he murmured against her hair.

Val laughed, a deep, throaty sound as she pulled away from him. "I have to be home in an hour," she said teasingly as she went into the bathroom. She ran the tub full of hot water, and then emptied in the bottle of herbal-scented shampoo provided by the hotel. The water was warm and slick as they climbed into the tub together, then Josh was warm and slick inside her. Val marveled at the strength of his young body as the tension of the failed race poured from hers.

Perhaps, she thought, she hadn't entirely grown tired of him yet. . . .

It was just past six when Val slipped the key into the front door of the beach house at Big Sur. She had dropped Josh off an hour earlier, then driven down the coast to the enclave of million-dollar private residences that lined Yankee Point. Her hair lay in wet clumps down the length of her back, and her skin smelled of the herbal shampoo and sex. It was a delicious smell, reminding her of the hour they'd spent together. She shook her head and laughed when she thought of Josh and his sister, Anne. A tagalong, he'd been two years old when she and Anne became friends, four years old when she went away to school in Switzerland.

She'd seen him again through the years when her parents dragged her along to social engagements that his parents dragged him to. The last time had been five years earlier, when he was still in high school. Like most teenage boys, he was into cars, and was suitably impressed that Val competed in races. Then he left for Cal Poly, and Val didn't see him for a while. When he came home this summer, it happened to be at a time when Val was in between husbands.

They met at one of the parties given at the Pebble Beach golf classic. Val couldn't believe the changes that college had made. They danced, then went for a walk along the links. They hadn't waited for the hotel that night. He was eager and she was experienced. They made love in the darkened office of the club manager at Pebble Beach Country Club.

Val saw him when it suited her, usually in hotels or motels, once at a charming little bed and breakfast in Pacific Grove. Originally he had planned to change colleges and go to the East Coast in the fall. After becoming involved with Val, he said he'd decided to stay in California.

Val had been adamant. "No way! You've made your plans. You need to be at Cornell. You've planned it for a long time."

"But I want to be here with you."

Without hesitation she told him the hard truth. "Let's be honest with each other. What we've had this summer has been great sex. Period. Everything is changing now. We both need to move on."

He'd been stunned at her blunt, unromantic appraisal of their relationship. "But I love you!"

She shook her head. "No, Josh. It's over."

"You mean I can't see you again?" he asked in dismay.

She shrugged. "Call me when you're back in town. If it's convenient, we'll get together."

Josh had argued, but she was adamant. He was hurt and angry when he left. But, as she expected, he called the next time he was in town.

This past week it had been fun, but now Josh accepted it for what it was—mutual sexual attraction and gratification, and nothing more.

She moved through the house. As she peeled off the clothes that Josh had so hastily removed an hour earlier, her frustration and anger over the race returned. Despite what Bill had said, she *knew* she could have won that race. If only she had a decent engine.

She walked up the stairs to the master suite on the second level. The bedroom had huge floor-to-ceiling windows with a magnificent view of the sun slipping into the Pacific Ocean. On the nightstand beside the bed a red light flashed on the answering machine. Pressing the button to retrieve her messages, she listened with only halfhearted interest as she walked into the large closet.

There were three messages. The first was from Bill about the car. "Val, the engine is completely gone. It's got a blown turbo." There was a pause, then he added, "I put in a call to Jimmy Cassidy. We could have the new engine in time for the next race, but he needs half up front. It was the best I could do. Let me know in the next couple of days."

Damn! she thought. There was no way she could come up with that kind of money that fast.

The second message was from her mother. "Gavin and your father flew up to San Francisco this morning for the meeting with the Nakatome Group. He called afterward. It went very well. The Japanese have made an offer. Gavin is calling a meeting of the board first thing Monday morning for a vote on the sale. It's merely a formality, but you and Nicky should be there. Call me to confirm this."

Thank God. She breathed a sigh of relief. For once she would be happy to call her mother back.

Val's hand was about to take a red and black paisley robe off a hanger when the third message played back. She immediately recognized the deep voice with its thick Australian accent. "Finished up my business in L.A. earlier than anticipated. My flight should get in around six this evening. I've already phoned ahead for a car, no need to meet me. I'll see you at the house."

There was a brief pause. Then, suggestively, "There's only one thing I want for supper, luv."

Then the message clicked off.

The machine gave the date and time the message came in, then reset itself. Val glanced at the ormolu clock on the fireplace mantel across the room. It was already a quarter to seven. Given the time it took to drive from the Monterey airport, he should be arriving in a few minutes.

Instead of the paisley, she picked out a sheer floor-length nightgown that she'd bought a few months before on a trip to London with the Australian media mogul who'd been keeping her. It was moss-green satin with a black lace eyelet panel that swept low over the breasts, and another at the back that dipped below her waist. Thin black satin straps held the gown up.

After slipping it on, she went into the bathroom and began applying makeup. She thought of Bill's call. *Money*. It always came down to that. All her life it had been doled out to her with a stinginess that drove her crazy. Even now, in her late thirties, at an age when she should have been considered mature enough to handle her own finances, she received only a meager stipend through the company for shares she had inherited on her twenty-first birthday.

It wasn't enough. Not nearly enough.

She frowned as she clasped a Cartier diamond bracelet on her darkly tanned arm, then dabbed Paloma Picasso perfume at the bend of her elbow, the curve of each wrist, and around each breast. At least the sale of the ranch should finally take care of the money situation, she thought, brightening slightly. They couldn't keep from turning over her rightful share of the inheritance then. But it would take a while, at least a month, if not longer, to finalize the deal, and she was impatient. She wanted it *now* so she could compete in the next scheduled race.

She returned to the bedroom, her bare feet padding silently

across thick, pale blue carpet that complimented dark blue satin-covered walls. Once more she looked out through the expanse of tinted glass at a multi-million-dollar view. The house, perched on a cliff above a private stretch of beach, wasn't terribly big. There were two bedroom suites upstairs with their own bath, and downstairs a large, open living room, dining room, and kitchen.

But then, it didn't need to be big to suit its owner's purpose. Val was the only person who was ever there with him. They never entertained, because if they were too public, word might get back to his wife that he kept a mistress here in breathtaking isolation. He didn't want to upset his wife. On some level he loved her and didn't want to humiliate her.

Val bitterly resented being kept a secret, as if he were ashamed of her. She had to constantly remind herself that he was generous—the house, the Ferrari, jewelry, trips all over the world. More critical than all those things was the fact that he was the single sponsor for Sloan Racing. Once she had her own money, she thought, her full lips curving into a lethal smile, she wouldn't need to rely on her lover's generosity.

But tonight . . .

She met him at the doorway, her auburn hair shimmering to her waist, her breasts straining against the black lace. She began to undress him at the doorway, then continued as they climbed the stairs to the foot of the huge platform bed that lay under the wall of windows. She whispered seductive phrases as her hands and mouth moved over him. She forced herself not to compare his sixty-five-year-old body to that of the boy one-third his age whom she'd made love to only hours earlier.

As she pulled the enticing gown off and straddled him, she thought of her mother's message. In three days they would vote to sell the ranch. Soon she would have all the money she would ever need, and she would never again have to sell herself to a rich old man.

But as she expertly brought the man to orgasm, a frightening thought occurred to her—what if Alexandra's reappearance delayed the sale? The thought of having to please this boring old man for much longer made her sick. As he groaned, and his body shuddered with release, another thought made the feeling of nausea in the pit of her stomach grow worse. What if Alexandra somehow screwed up the deal completely?

Valentina turned her head away so her lover wouldn't see the grim expression on her face. There was no way she would let that shrinking violet, Alexandra, mess up her life.

14

ALLIE DROVE THROUGH THE open gate to Rancho Sureno and headed up the road toward the house. She wasn't sure why she'd come out here. She knew only that if she kept running away from the ghosts that haunted this place, she would never be free.

She had called earlier, and Miguel and his wife Cathy were waiting for her. They stood together in the open front door, welcoming her with warm smiles. As soon as she saw them, Allie knew she'd done the right thing. Instead of the fear she'd expected to feel, she experienced a reassuring sense of homecoming. The brief time she had spent with Mac was precious to her, and now she allowed herself the luxury of remembering that happy time, and taking comfort from the memory.

Cathy had prepared a wonderful lunch and Miguel served it out on the patio, where Allie had eaten with Mac. Afterward, Allie asked Miguel to saddle a horse for her. "One of the gentler ones," she specified, adding with a self-deprecating smile, "I'm not that good a rider."

On this beautiful, clear day she didn't want to sit around the ranch house. She wanted to see more of the ranch before Gavin sold it and it was lost forever.

Miguel explained to her which path to stay on so she wouldn't get lost, and she set off.

She had been riding for only a few minutes when she saw another rider approaching her. At first she assumed it was simply one of the vaqueros, but as the rider came closer, she recognized him.

Rafe.

He rode up to her, stopping a few feet from her. Today the helmet and leather jacket had been replaced by an old Stetson and blue chambray workshirt. But the well-worn hat, a bit battered about the edges and heavily stained, seemed as natural a part of Rafe as the Harley-Davidson had been.

She'd steeled herself for his response to her. Their only previous encounter, at the funeral, had been anything but congenial. He'd been angry, cold, and blunt—"Go back to wherever it is you came from. There's nothing for you here."

Now he was equally blunt. "What are you doing here?"

"Looking at my heritage one last time, before it's destroyed." She paused. "I might ask you the same question."

"I was working and decided to take a break." In the same breath he went on coldly, "I told you to go home. You shouldn't be here."

"Why, because I might remember the truth?" she shot back instinctively, without thinking.

He looked even angrier than he had the night of the funeral. She couldn't understand why she seemed to bring out such anger in him. She knew only that from the moment they'd first met, he had reacted to her as strongly as she'd reacted to him, with the kind of instantaneous combustion that happens when you toss a match into a pool of gasoline.

He glared at her. "The truth isn't always pleasant."

"I don't care," she retorted, sounding more like a petulant child then she cared to admit.

To her amazement, he smiled in spite of himself, and shook his head. "You were a stubborn little kid. Determined to do things your own way. Obviously, you haven't changed."

The slightly crooked smile exposed the soft crease of one dimple at his left cheek. That quicksilver smile held a lethal edge that made it all the more compelling. Allie was reminded of what she'd thought of him when she watched him from the balcony outside her room at Casa Sureno—a potent sexuality that had undoubtedly made female hearts turn over from the time he was a teenager.

The smile transformed his eyes from angry black to something equally dark, but unsettling in a different way—as if, like the deepest recesses of her memory, his eyes held secrets in their depths. His smile hinted at those secrets—and even more disturbing emotions than those that had previously been revealed.

She found herself being drawn to him in a way that thoroughly disconcerted her. To cover the confusion of her violently mixed response to Rafe, Allie said tightly, "I really don't care what you think of me."

His smile deepened. "You're not a very good liar, Allie. Which is a refreshing change from most of the people in this family, who are very practiced liars."

Allie had a sudden flash of insight—Rafe was as changeable as his moods. He could be remote, guarded, even angry one moment, then unexpectedly warm and open the next.

Before Allie could respond, he went on. "But being essentially honest can be dangerous."

"How could honesty possibly be dangerous?"

"Sometimes it forces people to confront things they don't want to confront."

"Such as the past?" she suggested pointedly.

His smile dissolved in an instant. "The past can be especially dangerous."

"Why is that?" she demanded.

"Because it can never be changed."

"Would you like to change the past?"

Something behind his eyes shifted, as if he were remembering something in the past that he desperately wanted to forget. "As I told you before, sometimes it's best to leave things in the past. Dwelling on it can't change anything."

"Sometimes it can," Allie said softly, recalling how profoundly the events of the past few weeks had changed the past as she knew it. "Sometimes the past is a lie. You have to know the truth before you can move on."

Rafe looked at Allie and asked sharply, "Is that why you're

here? Do you think that what everyone said happened here is a lie?''

She said carefully, ''I think that part of it is a lie. I want to find out the truth. I need to do that. And the only way to do so is by being here, where it all happened.''

''Well, take a quick look around, because it may all be gone very soon. If Gavin has his way, it'll be sold off to a group of Japanese developers who will pour concrete over every square inch.''

His expression was grim. ''Gavin's in San Francisco right now, trying to wrap up the deal with the Japanese. He'll call a board meeting Monday morning to announce the terms. That gives me less than two days to put my plan together and try to dissuade everyone else on the board.''

''Do you really think you can do that?'' she asked.

He shook his head. ''No. But I have to try.''

For a moment they sat there on their horses, silence enveloping them as they each thought about what was going to happen to this land that was their mutual heritage. Then, to her surprise, Rafe said, ''Come on, I'll show you around the ranch. You'll get lost by yourself.''

Allie wanted to reply tartly that she was perfectly capable of finding her way without getting lost, but somehow she didn't want to turn down the invitation. ''All right,'' she said, and they set off.

Rafe led Allie away from the path that Miguel had told her to stick to. At first the idea of a few hours on horseback didn't seem so bad as her muscles adjusted to the worn saddle and the easy gait of the cattle pony. It was, in fact, no pony at all, but a full-size horse at least fifteen and a half hands high. Still he was calm, surefooted, and patient.

At the end of an hour, though, after plodding over uneven terrain, she was forced to reassess the situation. She was beginning to feel the saddle in places she didn't recall having.

For the most part, they had ridden in silence, her horse trailing behind Rafe's, single file, as they traversed the rolling hillsides. He seemed content to ride in silence, except for the occasional landmarks he pointed out.

She recognized the names from Elena's journal, and as she rode in peaceful silence, she remembered the last passage she'd read.

Elena's Journal, August 7, 1852.

Today Papa met with Ben Sloan in Monterey. He bought more cattle for his rancho. This time they didn't talk the entire time about the ranch. I discovered that he doesn't have a wife. He is living in Salinas with his younger brother, who is visiting from this place called Virginia.

We talked about his family and about his plans for his small rancho. It is not nearly as big as El Sureno, but he hopes one day to breed very fine cattle.

There are times when I think that I like Ben very much, and other times when I am a little in awe of him. He is very ambitious. I listened to his ideas about ranching. Then he surprised me by asking about my ideas for El Sureno. None of the men my father knows would ever ask a woman's opinion about anything. But he asked me!

I don't know what to make of Ben Sloan. . . .

Suddenly Rafe interrupted her quiet reverie. ''Mac talked to you about the sale of the ranch, didn't he?''

She was a bit startled. It was the first thing he'd chosen to say to her in over half an hour. ''Yes,'' she admitted.

''He loved this place. He fought like hell to keep Gavin from selling it.''

He'd reined his horse to a halt. She stopped her own horse and they sat side by side. As she straightened up in the saddle, feeling a slight stiffness in her back, it seemed she would definitely pay for her impulsive decision to go for a ride.

His dark eyes seemed to have gone darker still as he contemplated her from beneath the brim of the hat, the personification of the rugged cowboy, comfortable in the saddle. She supposed a man had to be a bit of a rebel, or at the very least a free spirit at heart, to be a cowboy or to ride a motorcycle. Ben Sloan had been a bit of a rebel, she realized, leaving behind his roots in Virginia to make a new life in California. Elena had been a rebel, too, refusing to conform to the rigid restrictions placed on women in her time. Through her father, a trace of that same blood flowed through Allie. Perhaps, she realized, that was why she'd pursued a career in architecture, notoriously difficult for women. She was a rebel, too, in a way. The thought pleased her inordinately.

"And?" he asked.

"What is there for me to say?"

"For starters," he pointed out, "you're one of the heirs. You own a percentage of the Sloan Land Company, through your father."

She hadn't considered that. Mac hadn't mentioned anything about it, and she assumed he would have if it were of any importance.

"I didn't come back for any inheritance," she said tightly, convinced that he was afraid she'd try to take what he felt was his.

"If you didn't come back for what you could get, then you're not much of a Sloan. They all seem to be out for money."

"I wasn't even aware there was an inheritance."

"Like everything else that you weren't aware of for twenty-five years?" There was an edge to the question as if he didn't quite believe her.

She retorted, "That's right. And if I hadn't started having nightmares about the night my mother was bludgeoned to death, I wouldn't be here right now!"

She tried to contain the sudden, explosive anger that welled up within her, but it spilled out. "All in all, there are times I'd trade everything to be able to forget what happened that night! It's not a pleasant memory! But there are moments that make me feel that it's worth dealing with the pain!"

He didn't flinch or back down from her anger. But his voice softened, as if he realized that he had been too hard on her. Or, she thought, perhaps he, too, remembered that night and the horror of what followed. "What moments?"

She took a deep breath, then looked around at the breath-taking landscape. Nothing quite like this existed anywhere else on earth. She answered slowly, "Moments like this . . . a place like this . . . reading about Ben and Elena. And most important, getting to know Mac, even if just for a brief time."

She struggled to explain to Rafe a feeling she could hardly define for herself. She'd only recently discovered that she'd been searching for something her entire life, and the key to finding it was right here. "It's knowing I'm connected to something . . . a place . . . where I can have hopes, dreams . . something that defines who I am. Something I can leave my mark on."

He said with a grimace, "Now you sound like every other egotistical architect I've ever worked with."

She didn't take offense. She'd heard it too many times before. Julia herself had been one of the people to say it warning Allie that she'd be accused of trying to imprint her own identity onto her work, make it truly and distinctly her own out of sheer ego.

At the time Allie had been stunned to hear Julia echo tha criticism. "You've done that very thing," she pointed out "Everyone knows your work. It's as distinctive as Frank Lloyd Wright."

"Not everyone likes it, though, and they resent me for it," Julia had answered.

"Yes, but they recognize it as yours. That doesn't mean it's good or bad architecture. It means that it's *yours*." She went on passionately. "To me that would be the most wonderful thing in the world—to feel that connection, to have something that is uniquely mine, something that will last."

She realized now that she'd always been searching for the same connection in her personal life as she had in her work Now she knew why there were times she had felt that odd aching sense of emptiness. The emptiness had been the dark void within her memory—the lost years with her parents, the Sloan family, and the connection, however short the time o tenuous the bond, to this land.

"There are times," she went on to explain to Rafe, "that can *feel* the memories that are still blocked somewhere inside me. Right now, at this moment, I *know* this place. I'm certain I loved roaming over it."

"This *is* a special place,"he said in an uncharacteristically gentle voice. "This is where it all began."

At her questioning look, he gestured to a grassy knoll several hundred yards away. It overlooked the highway and the ocean below. Without a word he turned his horse, leading the way to the low hill.

The view was spectacular. Early morning mist had long since rolled far out to sea, and even the lingering haze, so often found along the coast, had dissipated in the brisk breeze. It was sunny, bright, and brilliantly clear along the entire coastline. Allie could see all the way north to the curve of the Monterey peninsula, and then south for several miles.

The wind fluttered the long sleeves of her white cotton blouse and whipped her hair about her neck and face. It was like standing at the prow of a ship, or climbing high above the ground in the trees on her grandparent's farm. She felt on top of the world.

Rafe dismounted. Holding the reins in one hand, he reached to hold hers while she dismounted. Together they led their horses to a large stone at the edge of the knoll. It was massive, like a black wedge that had been driven into the ground by the powerful contortions of the earth hundreds of thousands of years ago as the rocky coastline was being formed. In one spot there were scratch marks in the surface of the rock.

"It's magnificent," Allie breathed, meaning it. Her response to this spot seemed to come from deep inside her. As she had experienced when she first met Rafe, it was a sensory recognition, an awareness of being somehow bonded to this place—of having been here before.

"I know this place," she said with absolute certainty.

He looked at her intently. "This is known as Elena's Point. It's been called that for as long as anyone can remember."

It was uncanny. Here on this remote hillside, with the wind buffeting her and the sea spray jetting hundreds of feet into the air so that she could almost touch it, she felt as if she belonged.

She walked on ahead, then knelt before the huge stone and studied the scratchings. It was an inscription. And suddenly another memory slipped into place. . . .

"*This is a very special rock, Princess.*" She could almost hear her father's words as he told her about Elena and the history of the ranch. "*This is the southern boundary of the ranch—El Sureno. It's the first place Elena Marin's father saw when he came here from Spain.*"

"*He came in a boat, Daddy.*"

"*That's right. The governor of old California gave him this special land, and he stood on this very spot and called it El Sureno."*

"And he used to bring his little girl here."

"That's right, sweetheart. And when she grew to be a beautiful young lady, she came here often. It was her favorite spot."

"Ben Sloan and Elena Marin were married here," Allie said, repeating the other information her father had told her that day.

He nodded. "A priest performed the ceremony on this hillside—on this very spot. My father told me the story. And his father told him, and so on, back to Ben and Elena. That's part of what being a family is all about, Allie. Knowing where you came from, and honoring the people who came before you. . . ."

Now, Allie looked at the wedge of rock and exclaimed in surprise. "Here it is! The date—May 3, 1853, and their names."

"Elena wrote about it in her journal," Rafe said simply.

She looked at him with some surprise. "You know about the journal?"

"Everyone in the family does, though few have read it. It's not exactly easy deciphering the old Spanish."

"But you've read it."

He shrugged. "The summer I turned fifteen I got into a lot of trouble. Your father gave it to me to read as sort of educational punishment. He said it was time I learned about my family heritage."

Rafe went on. "The journal is a rich history of the Sloans, much like the old family Bible is in other families. All the Sloan births, marriages, and deaths are recorded in it. Elena started quite a legacy when she began writing her diary. The local historical society has been dying to get their hands on it for years. About five years ago Mac finally allowed them to hand-copy it. He read somewhere that photocopying can destroy old documents."

Rafe chuckled. "It took them a year to hand-copy all the pages."

"Did you read all of it?" she asked.

"Pretty much. Like I said, the old Spanish was hard to decipher, especially since my knowledge of the language was minimal."

"Then you didn't speak it when you were growing up?" It seemed a natural question, but as soon as she spoke, she realized she'd probably touched on a sensitive area. She expected Rafe to react angrily, but to her surprise he answered matter-of-factly.

"My mother spoke both English and Spanish, but she encountered a great deal of prejudice when she was growing up, and she felt it was important that I speak only English. She wanted me to be as Anglo as possible."

There was more than a hint of bitterness in that last statement. Feeling that it was best to steer away from it, Allie asked, "Then how did you learn any of the language?"

"My grandmothers and my uncles all spoke Spanish. Of course, it wasn't Castillian Spanish as Elena was taught by the Franciscan nuns in Monterey. It was the peasant Spanish."

Allie wondered if Rafe made self-deprecating comments like that as a sort of one-upmanship—putting himself down before someone else had a chance to do so.

She said tentatively, "It must have been hard on you, the situation between your parents."

"No harder than yours was," he responded in a tight, hard voice. He'd wanted to hurt her, and he'd succeeded. He immediately regretted the angry impulse when he saw the color drain from her face. "I'm sorry. I didn't mean to bring that up."

"Yes, you did. At least have the courage to be honest about it."

"All right," he admitted, "I had that coming."

She went on. "You're curious about me, just like everyone else in this family. They can't seem to accept that I remember very little of the first seven years of my life."

He pushed the hat back off his forehead and the sun fell across his face, illuminating the shadows behind his dark eyes. Staring at her intently, he said, "You really don't remember?"

She forced herself to meet his look squarely. She wasn't sure why it suddenly seemed so important to make him understand. Perhaps she felt that because of his own painful childhood he could empathize in a way that no one else could. "My memory of my childhood until I was seven is limited to the night my mother died. Even then, I have only bits and pieces of distorted images. And none of the pieces fit."

"My God," he whispered.

Suddenly she couldn't bear the intense scrutiny of his gaze. Turning away, she stared out at the expanse of the Pacific Ocean that rose up to meet the even larger expanse of infinite blue sky. She went on shakily, trying hard to control the slight tremor in her voice. "It's like a huge jigsaw puzzle. Somewhere in all the pieces I have to find the first two that fit together. Then the next one, and the next. Hopefully, one day I'll be able to see the entire picture—to remember what it is that as a child I chose to forget."

"Maybe you're better off now knowing."

His voice was almost harsh, and it startled her after the compassion he'd shown earlier. She answered defensively, "I can deal with the truth. It's the thought of not knowing . . . of never being able to be certain of anything that I can't live with."

For the first time she put into words what she had only sensed until that moment. "I have to find out who killed my mother. I know it wasn't my father."

"My God," Rafe said wearily. "First Mac, now you."

"What do you mean?" she demanded.

"He always believed that Alan was innocent—that he could never have killed Barbara."

"You lived here with my parents. Do you believe my father killed my mother?"

He didn't answer for a moment. He thought back to that night, over twenty-five years ago. As far as anyone knew, he had been miles away. But he would never forget exactly what happened that night. It was the reason he ran, and kept right on running for so many years.

"I didn't want to believe it," he said finally, carefully qualifying his answer.

"He *was* innocent," Allie said with absolute certainty. "I *know* that he didn't kill my mother."

Rafe looked at her, his eyes dark behind narrow slits. She hadn't said, "I refuse to believe my father killed my mother," or any number of responses that came from that basic human refusal to believe something bad about people we love. She had said it as if she knew for a fact that Alan Sloan hadn't killed his wife.

"Have you remembered something else from that night?" Rafe asked, feeling himself tense inside as he waited eagerly for her answer.

"No, not really," she lied.

She wasn't certain why she didn't tell Rafe the truth. She knew only that she couldn't tell anyone. Not yet. Not until the memory returned fully, and she knew exactly who it was she had seen that night. At the moment the memory was only a fragment, a flash of certainty in her heart, that she had fled in terror that night, not *away* from her father, but in search of him.

"We should be starting back," Rafe said with a glance toward the afternoon sky. "It's getting late, and we still have a two-hour ride ahead of us."

Allie went back to her horse and Rafe held the reins while she remounted. Then he mounted his own horse, swinging his tall, lean body up onto the animal with an easy grace. They rode north, cutting across rolling grazing land, through thick stands of oaks, until the roar of the ocean was muffled, and only occasionally carried on the changing wind.

For a long time they rode in silence. Finally, Allie gathered her courage and asked, "You lived here with my parents. Could you tell me about that time?"

He answered tersely, clearly reluctant to discuss this subject. "I was here for only a few years, off and on. I didn't know that much about anything that went on."

"But you must know *something*," Allie insisted.

"Look, the family couldn't quite decide what to do with me," he snapped. "I was the secret that everyone knew about but nobody wanted to acknowledge. I lived briefly with my father, but it didn't work out." His expression hardened. "I didn't get along with Gavin and Charlotte. They were furious at having to admit to all their friends that I was actually their half brother."

There was an old bitterness in his voice that he was clearly still struggling to deal with. "Then my father died. By that time Alan had married Barbara and was running the Sloan Land

Company. They brought me here to live with them. They . . . said they wanted me.''

In spite of himself, his voice softened, as did his expression. When he looked like that—boyish, vulnerable, unguarded, Allie thought he was the most compellingly attractive man she'd ever met.

He went on. ''I can tell you one thing about your father. He loved the ranch more than anything except, possibly, your mother. It surprised me that Barbara felt the same way. After all, it wasn't her heritage. She wasn't even from around here. It was foreign territory to her. But she took to it right away, and was happy to live in the ranch house that had been abandoned for a long time.''

''What else can you tell me?'' Allie asked, greedy for more details about her parents.

To her surprise, Rafe's mouth curved in the barest hint of a smile. ''I remember when I met you for the first time. It was at some sort of family gathering at Mac's house, shortly after I went to live with my father. You were only three, and I thought you were a pest.''

''Why?'' Allie asked indignantly.

''Because you were,'' he replied easily. ''You kept bugging me, wanting me to play with you, to pay attention to you. I was thirteen, and didn't want to bother with a toddler. Then, when I moved out to the ranch, it got worse. You were always following me around. Your parents called you my little shadow. I called you Brat.''

Allie colored in embarrassment at the thought that she'd made such a nuisance of herself with Rafe. ''But I was just a little kid,'' she insisted defensively.

''Yeah—a really irritating one.''

Before Allie could figure out what to say to that, Rafe went on. ''But when I came back a couple of years later, you weren't so bad. At least by then you didn't ask the same questions over and over again, and cry if you didn't get your way.''

''Where did you go during that time?''

''I was a guest of the California Youth Authority,'' he said dryly. ''I got into a bit of trouble over a stolen car. The law has a tendency to frown on that sort of thing, even if it was a harmless prank and the car belonged to my brother.''

"You stole Gavin's car?" She wasn't so much shocked as amused.

"It seemed like a good idea at the time. Unfortunately he didn't have much of a sense of humor about it. Your father tried to talk Gavin out of pressing charges, but Gavin was adamant."

"I don't suppose there was anything like revenge behind it," Allie suggested with a grin.

Rafe saw a hint of Barbara's kindly smile in that ingenuous grin, and something more that was Allie's alone—an ability to laugh at herself. He couldn't help but smile in response. "That might have had a little something to do with it."

"Just a little?"

"Well, maybe a lot. I was pretty wild in those days."

Allie said easily, "From what I've seen, you still are."

To her surprise, Rafe laughed. He had a nice laugh, deep and unselfconscious. And it made him even more appealing.

She said innocently, "You should laugh more often. It gets rid of that perpetually angry expression, and makes you look almost nice."

He stared at her thoughtfully for a moment, then said, "Come on, Brat. It's time I got you home."

It was almost five o'clock when they finally reached the ranch house. Rafe dismounted quickly, but Allie took a bit longer. He noticed her reluctance. "You're going to have to do it sooner or later."

"Just give me a minute," she said, trying to figure out some way of moving that didn't hurt her sore behind. "I want to try this gradually."

He came around her horse and looked up at her with a sly grin. "It's usually best to get it over with all at once." With that he gently grabbed her with a hand clasped over each hip and pulled her from the saddle.

She had the presence of mind to bring her right leg over the front of the saddle as she slid to the ground between Rafe and the horse. Her knees were a bit wobbly, and as her feet touched the ground, she felt her bottom throb. Rafe steadied her, his hands on her hips. She instinctively clasped his forearms to brace herself.

The moment their bodies came into contact, with her fingers

clasping his strong arms and his fingers digging softly into her hips, she felt it. Heat. A wild, raw energy connecting them.

Hot and fast. Those had been Valentina's words, spoken in her husky voice, when she greeted Rafe after the funeral. Allie instinctively understood what she had meant, and suddenly realized that Val had been wrong. There was more than one way to burn. It could be either hot and fast, or a slow simmer. The first was instantaneous combustion, gone almost before it happened. The other was a heat of the blood that built along every nerve ending and then exploded in tiny flash points just beneath the surface of her skin.

The chemistry between her and Rafe was so unexpected, so intense, her head came up and her gaze fastened on his in wonderment. His dark eyes were hidden in the shade of the wide-brimmed hat. It was impossible to guess the expression in them. But he couldn't hide the expression on his face. His lips opened slightly in surprise, and she heard his sudden indrawn breath. Then his fingers tightened over the curve of her hips. Allie went absolutely still.

"Are you all right?" he finally asked.

The question was loaded with all sorts of intriguing possibilities. She focused on the most obvious. "I'm fine. Just a little sore. Well, maybe a *lot* sore." Her voice sounded as uncertain and edgy as she felt.

She pushed one hand back through her windblown hair. Rafe's hands still rested on the curve of her hips. She could feel the pressure of each finger through her jeans—not painful, but something far more disconcerting than pain. The contact was vaguely possessive.

Then unexpectedly he reached out and she felt his fingers against her cheek. "Next time you should wear your hair tied back, or a hat," he suggested, trapping the sun-streaked strands between thumb and forefinger. "The wind left tangles in your hair."

Slowly, gently, he loosened a strand of hair, then brushed it back from her cheek.

The gesture was so tender that Allie didn't know how to react. Tenderness seemed an incongruous quality for a rebel like Rafe. Yet in the past few hours she'd discovered that he was an extremely complex man who tried to keep as much of himself hidden as possible. He was an enigma, a puzzle, like the fragmented pieces of her past.

Breaking the physical contact between them, he gathered the reins of both horses and turned toward the barn. She fell into step beside him. "There may not be a next time if the sale of the ranch goes through," Allie reminded him.

"I may be able to persuade the board against the sale if I can come up with backers to finance my own development."

"Condos, health clubs, and restaurants, with self-serve gas stations, convenience stores, and video parlors on every corner?" she speculated.

He frowned. "It's called *progress*. The ranch can't survive as a working cattle ranch any longer. Maybe someplace like Idaho or Montana, but not in California. It's impossible. The north and south coasts are filling up with people."

"Border-to-border concrete and skyscrapers? Quite a legacy for the future." Her tone was scathing. It wasn't the first time she'd encountered this sort of mentality. She and Julia had run head-on into it over the Edgewater project. "There *are* alternatives, you know."

"Not the sort that would attract enough of a tax base necessary to support a city."

She grabbed his arm, stopping him. "Is that what you're proposing for El Sureno? A planned city with all the support facilities that go along with it, and uncontrolled urban sprawl?"

"It's been very well thought out," he assured her.

Allie though of the natural beauty of El Sureno, virtually untouched since creation. She said angrily, "I don't even have to see detailed plans of your proposed development to know that what you want to do is exploitive. You're no better than Gavin trying to sell it off to the Japanese. It's just a different package, but the result is the same."

"Dammit, Allie, you don't know what you're talking about!" he said furiously.

"Why does it even matter to you? You have a percentage of ownership just like everyone else in the family. If Gavin puts the sale together with the Japanese, you'll be a very rich man."

His dark eyes pinned her. Then he pulled loose of her grasp. "I don't care about the money."

"What is it, then?" But even as she asked, she already knew

the answer. He'd given it to her himself as they stood out at Elena's Point. "It's revenge, isn't it?"

Ignoring the accusation, he started to walk away from her, but she walked right along beside him. "Isn't it?" she demanded.

He turned to face her, looking as if he were about to explode. She felt herself flinch, as if she were expecting him to hit her. For the first time that day, she felt a return of that fear she'd felt when she'd first seen his photo in the newspaper.

Seeing her sudden expression of fear, his anger dissolved and he said, "You don't back down, do you. You just keep at something."

"I discovered a long time ago, it's the only way to get what you want."

"What do you want, Allie?"

"The truth."

"What will you do to find it?"

"Whatever it takes."

His smile was grim. "We're not so different after all."

"Oh, yes, we are, Rafe. I wouldn't destroy this place just to get revenge. You should care about what happens to it. Like it or not, it's your heritage too!"

"Dammit, I do care! I've spent a lot of time, and my own money, trying to put this together my way, to save it from the Japanese."

"But only for the name of 'Rafe Sloan, Developer' on the plans. Right? That must give you a real sense of power, to think that you might be able to control what happens to all of this."

"It's not about power."

"Isn't it?" she accused him. "You just want to beat Gavin at his own game."

"That's right."

She didn't say anything, and he went on slowly. "You think I'm wrong about the development." It irritated him that it should matter at all what she thought. But it did.

"I haven't seen it yet."

He cut her another sideways look as they led the horses into the barn. "You've already said quite a lot about something you haven't seen."

"I've worked with a lot of developers and contractors. They can sometimes be shortsighted about a project."

"You don't mince words, do you?"

"I don't believe in bullshit."

"I don't either." Then he added, "I suppose you'd like to see the plans—professional curiosity, of course."

She shrugged, trying to appear casual. "It's strictly personal curiosity. After all, I have no say in any of this."

"That's right, you don't," he snapped.

Then, to her surprise, he smiled. "You haven't changed in twenty-five years. You're still a pest."

"Oh, I've changed all right. Now I'm big enough to really pester you, Rafe Sloan."

15

IN HER HOTEL ROOM that evening Allie turned back the bedcovers, then went to turn on the faucets to the large sunken bathtub. She intended a quick bath and then a couple of hours of reading in Elena's journal with the help of a Spanish-English dictionary that she'd bought. But the muscles that hadn't seen the back of a horse in more than twenty years convinced her a nice long soak was advisable.

When she stepped out of the bathtub an hour later, she felt tired and sleepy. She decided to just look at a page or two of the journal, and then go to sleep early. She crawled into the massive Mediterranean mahogany bed and opened the journal.

April 8, 1853.

Finally, the rains have stopped long enough for the roads to dry out. The vaqueros have started the spring roundup. The corn, beans, and squash that were planted early in the season now have long sprouts. Papa informed me today that Señor Sloan will be coming to the rancho for several days. There will be a fiesta. There is much to do.

Papa has become very friendly with Ben Sloan. They

have met several times in Monterey. Papa speaks of this Anglo with admiration. I think he likes him very much. For the fiesta Papa suggested that I wear the new gown he purchased for me in Monterey, and he asked Luz to fix my hair with Mama's combs.

In spite of her fatigue, Allie couldn't put down the journal. She continued reading.

April 11.

Ben Sloan arrived today. As a gift he brought a horse for Papa. It is a magnificent animal—very tall, with long legs, and specially trained. It is called a Tennessee walking horse because of its peculiar gait—a gentle, rocking motion that is supposed to be very comfortable. Papa was most pleased.

April 12.

The fiesta was a grand affair. Our neighbors for many miles around came to celebrate with us. It is exactly forty-five years ago that Papa first came here with his parents from Spain.

There were horse races and cock fights. Luz and the other women prepared the food. There were over forty tables set up for the guests. After the supper there was dancing. Papa hired musicians who came all the way from Monterey. He and Ben Sloan and some of the older men played cards and smoked the expensive cigars that Papa prefers.

Antonio came to the fiesta with his family. After the siesta, he asked me to walk with him, but Papa quickly intervened and reminded me that I had neglected my duty to our guest. I asked Ben Sloan if he would like to see more of El Sureno. We rode out to the southern point where El Sureno begins.

Allie realized that Elena was describing the place where she and Rafe had ridden to that day—the southern boundary of the ranch, where the wedding rock was.

She glanced at the clock on the nightstand. It was already past midnight, and she was exhausted, but she couldn't stop reading.

April 14, 1853.

The last of our guests left this morning, including Mr. Sloan.

He and Papa spent the entire morning together, riding out over the ranch, talking of future plans. I have not heard Papa speak of these things since before Francisco's death.

Then, as he was leaving, Ben Sloan thanked me for riding with him yesterday. He held my hand a very long time, but it wasn't at all unpleasant. He has very strong hands with long fingers. I don't find him offensive like so many of the other Anglos. He is very well mannered. And he has the bluest eyes I have ever seen.

There are times when it seems he is looking right through me. Sometimes his eyes can be very cold. Other times, they burn hot like the summer sky.

When Mr. Sloan left, I returned to the house and found Papa watching me curiously.

Later, before retiring, Papa insisted on speaking with me in private—a very important matter, he said. We went into his special room where only the men are allowed, and where he used to speak with my brother about matters of great importance.

He went on at great length about my responsibilities now that Francisco is gone. There is no one else who can do what must be done. He pleaded for me to be an obedient, loving, reasonable daughter. Many times he repeated how much he loved me, and explained that he had made a very grave decision which I must abide by.

At first I didn't understand what he was saying. Then he explained that everything had been arranged. Everything that my father has built in this land, the future of El Sureno and our family, depends on me.

I must marry the Anglo, Ben Sloan.

When Allie awoke the following morning, Saturday, she felt as if she had hardly slept at all. She had tossed and turned all night, once more haunted by dreams that were an uncomfortable blend of old nightmares and images from Elena's journal.

In spite of the long hot soak the night before, her muscles were as sore as she had feared they would be. Going on such a long ride when she hadn't ridden in years had been foolhardy. But she had badly wanted to see the ranch. And, she admitted reluctantly to herself, for some reason she hadn't wanted to back down from the implied challenge in Rafe's invitation.

She wasn't sure why it mattered so much to her to stand up to him. She knew only that she didn't want to give way to the subtle but constant fear she felt whenever she was around him. Try as she might, she couldn't figure out where that fear came from. Since he had lived with her family for a while, she thought that perhaps he had tormented her as a child. Yet that didn't seem to be the answer. Wherever the feeling came from, she knew it was much more than the normal awkwardness she had always felt around men and had never outgrown.

Now, as she got dressed, she felt at loose ends. Her plans were as unformed as they had been the day she arrived. She had no idea how long she was going to have to stay in order to remember everything she needed to remember to clear her father's name. With Mac gone, she felt that she had no one to help her in her quest, no one who would share her conviction that her father was innocent.

She knew she couldn't turn to her family. They were convinced she'd come back only for her inheritance. Mac had told her endless stories about her family, trying to help her get to know them. But they still felt like total strangers, people she couldn't relate to. Except for Elena.

Allie picked up the journal from her bedside table. She felt a bond between her and her great-great-grandmother. Elena was a kindred spirit. Like Allie, Elena had suffered the loss of family. And like Allie, she had been faced with momentous changes in her life. Allie was eager to read more of the journal, to find out how Elena handled those challenges.

Remembering Rafe's invitation to look over his plans for developing Rancho Sureno, she decided to call him. He had said he would be in the office, even though it was Saturday.

"Sloan Land Company." It was Rafe.

"This is Allie. I took a chance I might reach you." She hesitated, unsure if he had been serious the day before when he offered to let her see the development plans. She forced herself to continue. "I thought I'd take you up on your offer."

She heard what sounded like a low chuckle. "I was wondering how long you'd wait to call. I've never met an architect yet who can resist looking at plans that someone else drew up."

Without taking the bait, Allie merely said, "Then the offer is still good?"

"It's good. Where are you?"

"At my hotel. I can be there in ten minutes."

"Okay. The front door will be unlocked."

Allie found the office building easily. It was on Lighthouse Avenue, in the old cannery section of Monterey—the area immortalized by John Steinbeck. Cannery Row had been transformed into an eclectic mix of shops, restaurants, and the world-famous Monterey Bay Aquarium. The hillside angling up and away from the cannery was filled with old woodsided, one- and two-story summer homes that had been transformed into small apartments, bed and breakfast establishments, and business offices tucked away in Victorian-style turrets and charming clapboard niches. Several renovations were under way. Houses built in the cannery era were being scraped, sanded, painted, and reroofed, preserving the Old World charm of the area.

Ben Sloan had established the original office on a site overlooking the wharf when his ranching interests expanded into shipping from the small loading docks at Point Sur to the port of Monterey. In those days Monterey was a major commercial center for the central coast, midway between the ports of San Francisco and Los Angeles.

The shell of the original building remained—a low adobe-and-mortar bungalow of the hacienda style, much like the hacienda at the ranch. When Ben Sloan built it, horses were tied in front. Allie had seen old pictures in Mac's den at Casa Sureno. Now the sturdy posts with iron rings were gone, replaced by the requisite amenities of modern civilization—

curbing and pavement. An adjacent lot that once provided a holding pen for Sloan cattle awaiting shipment had been transformed into a tree-shaded parking area. Mac had mentioned to Allie that at least four of the trees were original oak seedlings from the rancho at El Sureno, planted by Elena Marin.

The parking area was empty and gated against tourists who crowded the streets with RVs and vans overflowing with children, all on their way to the aquarium. The curbside parking was full.

Allie pulled into the driveway entrance of the parking area as far as the gate would allow, then walked up a tiled walkway that led from the street under the shaded overhang of a second-story veranda. A heavy wood sign on the side of the building was etched with gold lettering—SLOAN LAND COMPANY. Underneath the name was written in Spanish, ESTABLECEDO EN EL AÑO 1858—ESTABLISHED IN THE YEAR 1858 .

As Rafe had said, the front door was unlocked. The moment she stepped inside, Allie experienced the same sensation she had at the ranch—an awareness of the passage of time and the importance of tradition that came from thick adobe walls that muted sound better than any modern insulation, the soft creak of original wood flooring underfoot, and the smell of ocean air mingled with the cool earthiness of old whitewashed walls and rich oils from darkly stained wood furnishings.

History surrounded her and enveloped her as it had at the rancho, but with none of the fear she had experienced there. Reaching out to touch the wall of the entry, roughened by the swirl of an ancient hand trowel as the plaster was spread, she felt a memory stir dimly in the recesses of her mind. She was a child, running excitedly into the building to meet her father, her white patent leather shoes gleaming immaculately. She had stopped here and laid her hand against the cool wall as she waited for her mother to catch up with her.

Standing there, Allie remembered looking back over her shoulder, waiting impatiently for her mother to catch up. Then the sudden burst of pleasure as her mother finally came through the door, all breathless and beautiful, the sun glinting off her rich blond hair.

With soft laughter Barbara had admonished her, *"Don't run, Allie. Daddy might be in a meeting."*

Pulling at her mother's hand, Allie had led her down the hallway to his office.

"I thought you might have decided not to come after all."

Allie whirled around, half expecting to see her father standing there, so vivid was the memory. But it wasn't her father, it was Rafe. She felt an unreasoning jolt of disappointment.

"Traffic was heavy down at the Embarcadero."

"It always is on Saturdays." Rafe looked at her speculatively. "Are you all right?"

"I was just discovering some old memories. They keep sneaking up on me unexpectedly."

He stood at the side of the hall, leaning a shoulder into the wall just outside his office. Casually dressed, he wore what she was beginning to realize was his preferred style—faded jeans that softly molded his lean hips and long legs, a hand-tooled leather belt at the waist, and an immaculate white shirt, with the long sleeves rolled back to the elbows, exposing the dark bronze skin at his arms. Instead of the boots she had seen him wearing on previous occasions, he wore Top-Siders as worn as the jeans. His expression was contemplative, his dark eyes watchful.

"Memories have a way of doing that," he remarked. "They don't let you forget."

"Sometimes they do," Allie replied.

"Maybe you're better off," he suggested.

Somehow their casual conversation had become anything but casual. "What would you like to forget?" she asked.

"Sometimes I'd like to forget that I'm a Sloan."

"And I'm trying to remember that I'm a Sloan."

"It looks as if we disagree on more than what should be done with the ranch." He smiled then, but it was impossible to know the mood behind that enigmatic smile.

"Speaking of the ranch, you promised to show me your plans."

"Maybe I thought you wouldn't take me up on it," he speculated.

"Maybe you were wrong."

"It wouldn't be the first time."

He made a sweeping gesture with his hand. "Step into my office, such as it is."

Hardly an office, it was more like a storeroom with a simple desk and a drafting table with all the familiar accoutrements of the trade. Rolls of site plans and preliminary elevations lay atop a huge old refectory table that sat against the far wall below a bank of paned windows. Allie's fingers itched to unroll those plans.

"Go ahead," Rafe said, reading her thoughts. "I have nothing to hide. Let's see what the lady architect thinks." There was no derision in his voice, only curiosity.

Allie removed the rubber bands from the heavy rolls of plans and spread them across the top of the table. For the next three hours she was entirely professional—turning back sheet after sheet of site plans for the development, firing off questions, then demanding more information than was outlined on the plans. She read engineering reports, core sample reports, topographical studies, mineral reports, environmental impact reports, and scanned maps that had been drawn more than one hundred fifty years ago. Mac was right. Rafe Sloan was thorough. He'd spent thousands of dollars in preliminary studies, preparing all the information necessary to satisfy prospective financial backers. This was an interesting and concise set of site plans drawn up by a reputable architect.

"What is the cost breakdown for the initial phase of the development?"

"Four hundred million dollars. That includes the airstrip and the first phase of the marina."

"You'll never get FAA approval for that airstrip," she commented casually.

"What makes you think that?" he asked, challenging her.

"In order to get approval for a commercial strip, you have to show that any adjacent airports are overmaxed on their capacity. The Monterey airport is currently in an expansion program. I noticed it when I flew in. Your location is too close for you to hope for any kind of approval within the next twenty years."

He studied her thoughtfully. She'd cut through to the heart of the biggest problem with the development, and the reason their ancestor, Ben Sloan, had established a port at Point Sur—poor accessibility, making it difficult to link the rancho with the Monterey peninsula.

"All right, Ms. Sloan. What is your solution?"

She had been bending over sheets of plans all morning, losing herself in what she loved best, digging through complex numbers, facts, and calculations. The problems in developing a project the size and location of El Sureno were monumental, but not impossible to overcome. It was the sort of challenge she loved. Now she looked up with a bemused expression.

"You won't like my ideas, and you won't like my fee."

He sat behind an old desk made of dark wood, the heavy, cumbersome design revealing that it came from another era. His feet were casually crossed at the ankles and propped at the corner. He asked, "What do you mean?"

"I don't work for free, not even for family."

"I haven't hired you, and we can hardly be considered family."

"We are both Sloans," she pointed out.

"I barely qualify. And besides, we have nothing in common."

"We have more in common than you think. Neither one of us wants to see the ranch sold off."

Leaning his head against the back of the chair, he closed his eyes and pinched the bridge of his nose as if trying to physically drive back the pain that had begun there. "It doesn't much matter what either of us wants."

"I take it that means you haven't had any luck getting financial backing for the development."

He opened his eyes, and she was startled to see a hopeless expression in them. "I spent last night and this morning talking to them again."

"On their own time? I'm impressed. Bankers usually won't meet with anyone after three o'clock in the afternoon on a *weekday.*"

"These are private investors. I've worked with them before on other projects in southern California. Commercial banks wouldn't even talk to me with the economy the way it is. They say this isn't the time for undertaking big developments."

"What excuse did your private investors give you?" she

asked, surmising correctly that they had also turned him down.

"They want to take a more conservative posture over the next twelve to thirty-six months, until there are more signs of economic recovery."

"*Time,*" Allie commented thoughtfully.

"Which I don't have," Rafe snapped. "Monday morning Gavin is going to present the offer from the Nakatome Group to buy El Sureno."

"How much of a vote would be necessary to block the sale?"

He read her thoughts. "More than either you or I have. And don't forget the rule of male inheritance stipulated by Elena Marin's father before he deeded El Sureno over to Ben Sloan."

At Allie's look of confusion, he explained. "Your shares are automatically excluded, even if you did support my plans for development."

He went on dryly. "A bit shortsighted on the part of our dear ancestor. At the time he was taking every precaution to make certain that the land remained in the Sloan-Marin family. The only way to do that was to restrict the line of inheritance. If it's broken, the property reverts to the State of California. It's an archaic stipulation. But believe me"—Rafe grinned sardonically—"there are whole teams of lawyers in Sacramento who would like nothing better than to enforce that rule."

"Or force the sale through escalated taxes," Allie concluded, recalling what Mac had told her.

"Either way, they get their hands on a prime piece of real estate." He threw down his pencil in disgust. "Hell, I'd rather let the state have it than see the Japanese get their hands on another piece of U.S. real estate."

He looked at her intently. "Have I offended your artistic sensibilities as an architect? Art for the sake of art and the rest be damned?"

"You might be surprised at my sensibilities," she shot back at him.

"Is that right?"

"Yes, that's right. I've never sacrificed a project for my own motives no matter what label you want to put on it."

"If that's true, Ms. Sloan, then you're an entirely new breed of architect. Most of them can't see past their own ego."

"I checked my ego at the door when I went to work for Julia Winslow. If you try to get past the door with it, she soon takes care of it for you. Your work may be brilliant, but if it doesn't embody the total concept of function and environment, it gets scrapped."

"And you love it," he said in some surprise. He understood enough about himself, the dreams and ambitions that had driven him, to recognize those things in someone else.

"Yes, I do."

He contemplated her for several moments in companionable silence, watching as she returned her attention to the plans spread before her. Her honey-blond hair streaked with lighter shades of gold fell forward in soft disarray. Her chin was propped on one fist, her eyes lowered as she studied the plans. Those blue-gray eyes that were so like her mother's . . .

"Sometimes you'd be better off not remembering." He had said those words to Allie, and meant them. How many times, he wondered, had he wished that he didn't remember the night Barbara had died?

"Let's get out of here," he said suddenly, swinging his feet off the edge of the desk and standing up in one fluid motion. "I try not to be depressed over this project for more than six or eight hours every day." He grabbed a leather jacket from the back of his chair and put it on.

Allie looked up. "Can I take these with me? I'd like to look them over in more detail."

"Sure."

He helped her roll up the plans and slip them into long tubes. Then they walked out together, and he locked the doors behind them.

"Thank you for showing me the plans," Allie said sincerely.

"They're not what you expected, are they?"

"Frankly, no. Not after what everyone—"

"Not after what everyone said about me? The outsider who doesn't belong."

In spite of her uneasiness around him, she found herself feeling sorry for him. Perhaps, she thought, because they were both outsiders. "You don't give a damn about them, do you?"

"No, I don't. Mac was the only decent one of the bunch. The rest can all go to hell as far as I'm concerned."

"And the devil take the Sloan name?"

He looked at her. "I already have."

"Are you a devil in disguise?" she shot back.

"No disguise, Allie." Then he leaned toward her, so close that she could feel his warm breath on her face. "But I will tell you a secret."

She forced herself not to pull back. "What secret is that?"

"I'm starved. How about lunch?"

"Well, I—"

"I refuse to believe that you already have a date."

"Is that what this is?"

"Not at all. Just a casual luncheon invitation. Besides, I won't accept no for an answer. I've got something I want to show you."

"What?" she demanded warily.

"You're interested in the ranch, aren't you?"

"Yes, of course."

"This has to do with the ranch. But you have to have lunch with me first."

"No choice in the matter, huh?"

"Absolutely none. I always extract a payment for everything that I do. Your payment is to have lunch with me."

She glanced at her watch. It was already past twelve. If she needed any further encouragement, her stomach grumbled loudly.

"That settles it." He grabbed the tubes of plans and threw them into the back compartment of a vintage 1961 red and white Corvette convertible. Then he held the door open for her.

After a moment's hesitation she slipped into the smooth red leather seat. He came around and sat behind the wheel on the other side.

"Somehow I was expecting the Harley," she remarked as she fastened the seat belt.

"I use it only for formal occasions," he said with a wry smile.

They pulled away from the curb and shot down to Lighthouse Avenue. Rafe drove fast, expertly cutting through the streets that he obviously knew well, leaving the Embarcadero behind. Then they were out on the highway and the wind made conversation impossible.

Glancing at him surreptitiously out of the corner of her eye, Allie thought what a complete contradiction Rafe Sloan was. He built multistory high-rise office complexes and hotels that were masses of high-tech design, all sharp angles, walls of glass, enclosed atriums, made of steel, concrete, and cold slabs of marble.

At the same time he perpetuated the image of the rebel, riding a restored Harley-Davidson, rattling around the ranch in an ancient four-wheel-drive jeep, and driving a classic Corvette convertible that probably should have been in some collector's private showroom. And he did it all with an irreverent abandon.

But the same man who clearly valued these things from the past had also drawn up plans for a gleaming concrete-and-glass multi-billion-dollar resort that would destroy an invaluable piece of history.

It made no sense to Allie.

They cut over to Highway 68, turned off just before the airport, then pulled into a parking area next to an old stone house. The yard was filled with animal sculptures and arbors with brilliant blooming bougainvillea. The rustic building had wood floors, whitewashed walls, arched doorways, and a glass case that displayed homemade pies and cobbler. A weathered sign out front said TARPEY'S ROADHOUSE.

Country and western music emanated from a dining room at the back, where tables were covered with checkered fabric tablecloths. Allie half expected a wine bottle with a candle stuck in it for atmosphere. Instead, there was an old-fashioned oil lamp at each table along with an impressive wine list.

The menu was of the hearty meat-and-potatoes variety, featuring chicken-fried steak, pork chops, roast venison and turkey, and southern fried chicken.

As they were seated by a plump, middle-aged waitress who called both of them "Hon," Allie found Rafe watching her with an amused expression. He took the menu from her. "I'll order lunch, you order the wine."

A few minutes later she found herself, for the first time in her life, sipping an expensive, crisp *Pouilly-Fumé* from a glass in one hand while munching a feather-light, crispy fried chicken leg in the other. She had to admit, it wasn't bad.

Neither said much as they ate. When they had finished, and Rafe had poured the last of the wine into her glass, she asked, "Now, are you going to tell me what it is you wanted to show me?"

"You have to come with me."

"Wait a minute. I agreed only to lunch."

"I can't *tell* you about it. It's one of those things you have to see for yourself."

Outside, they got back into the car. Rafe swung back out onto the road and headed for the airport. He placed a call from the car phone.

"Is everything ready?" He flicked a glance at his watch, and assured the person on the other end, "I'll be there in less than five minutes. I'm bringing someone along."

Allie wondered what on earth she'd gotten herself into.

16

ALLIE GLANCED UNCERTAINLY AT Rafe as they turned in at the airport entrance. He stared straight ahead, saying nothing. After cutting along the back service road past the commercial gates to the private flying service hangars, he pulled into a parking lot.

As he came around to her side of the car, he asked with a sly grin. "How do you feel about flying?"

"I think it's usually best done with wings," she said dryly.

"I agree." Opening the door, he took her hand and helped her out of the car. "Come on, you have to go up if you want to see it."

He led her toward a gleaming twin engine Cessna sitting on the tarmac about a hundred yards away. In the cockpit the pilot had turned on the turboprop engines, letting them warm up. To Allie's surprise, Rafe led her past the Cessna to another aircraft nearby. Long and low, it had an incredibly wide wingspan, and one wingtip rested gently on the ground. There was no propeller.

Allie stopped abruptly. "Wait a minute. I like my airplanes to have at least one engine, preferably two."

Rafe was busy pushing back the canopy, revealing a

double-seat compartment with two foot pedals, and what she might irreverently refer to as a joystick. There were no fuel gauges, or gauges to measure engine speed or oil pressure, only an altimeter and a compass.

"Do you like to fly, Allie?"

"Yes," she answered hesitantly.

He stood beside the cockpit. "There's nothing like flying in a glider for a rush of pure adrenaline. It's the closest thing there is to natural flight. No engine noise, only the sound of the wind lifting the wings."

He gave her that challenging look she was beginning to know well. "Afraid to take a chance, lady architect?"

It was a dare and she knew it. She also knew it was probably unwise. But she couldn't back down.

"Is there some sort of helmet you're supposed to wear when you go up in one of these things?" she asked, coming over to the cockpit.

He handed her a red helmet. A second one sat in the pilot's seat.

Glancing at the Cessna, whose engines were revving loudly now, Allie asked, "Is he towing us?"

"Yup."

As she struggled with the chin strap, she quipped, "What's the survival rate?"

Brushing aside her hands, Rafe expertly clamped the chin strap firmly into place. "I haven't lost anyone yet."

Then he helped her climb inside the tilted craft, carefully buckling her into the seat that molded around her.

Rounding the nose of the glider, Rafe climbed in beside her and pulled the canopy forward over their heads. It snapped into place. He secured it by turning two inside clamps, then buckled his own shoulder harness.

"Ready?" he asked.

Allie clamped her teeth tight together and nodded. She was more nervous than she was about to let him see. Rafe spoke into the headset inside the helmet. She heard the answering response and caught sight of the pilot's wave from the Cessna. Then she heard the pilot rev the engines to higher rpms and slowly roll away from the nose of the glider. The line between the two aircraft went taut. Instinctively, like that tautened line, Allie braced every muscle.

They started to roll forward, pulled by the Cessna as it taxied down the runway. Allie noticed small support wheels at the tip of each long wing on the glider. Gradually, as they gained speed, the wing on her side of the glider came up level with the other wing. Beside her, Rafe made a few small adjustments, working the pedals with his feet, keeping firm hold on the control stick. Beneath them, the runway rolled past, faster and faster.

The Cessna reached the end of the runway ahead of them and soared into the air. They were pulled along behind for several more feet, then the rumbling of the runway ceased completely, and Allie realized they, too, were airborne.

They were towed higher and higher in a slow-building ascent. Occasionaly, allie felt lift beneath the wings and the towline would momentarily grow slack. She watched the numbers on the altimeter—one thousand feet . . . two . . . three . . . four . . . five . . . Then she heard the pilot over Rafe's headset. He responded, nodding to her at the same time. Then he gestured to the Cessna.

The towline had gone completely slack. The glider was now carried aloft by the wind. There was a loud snap, and the towline dropped away from the nose of the glider and trailed loose behind the Cessna. Moving the stick at the same time he worked the foot pedals, Rafe steered the glider away from the path of the Cessna.

Rafe had described the sensation as the closest thing to natural flight, and he was right. It was breathtaking, Allie thought in amazement. Her nervousness was gone as she gave herself over to the sheer joy and freedom of flying. They soared and glided on the changing wind currents in ever-widening arcs that gradually took them over the California coastline.

The only sound was the wind rushing past the canopy. There were no engines droning incessantly, drowning out the sensation of flight. In the glider there was only the wind, the sun, and the man beside her.

Rafe handled the glider expertly, allowing it to sweep naturally across the sky. He adjusted the flaps and tail rudder only fractionally as they lost the pattern of the wind, then found another that lifted them several hundred feet higher in the breathtaking climb through the cloudless blue sky.

He pushed aside the mouthpiece of the headset. "It's all a matter of thermals." He explained the dynamics of their engineless flight. "The heat builds up over the land and rises. The cooler air comes in off the ocean and settles. When they meet, it creates air turbulence."

"Updrafts and downdrafts?"

He nodded, not at all surprised at her quick grasp of the scientific principles involved. He'd already learned she was a very smart young lady. He liked that in a woman.

He grinned. "The tricky part is being able to differentiate between them. A strong downdraft can slam a plane right into the ground."

The momentary fear she felt at the thought of that dissolved as she looked out over the nose of the glider through the canopy. She saw nothing but blue sky, with a few wispy streamers of clouds high above them. "So how do you tell the difference?" she asked.

"You learn to read the wind, and you need a good understanding of wind patterns. A downdraft is created by the action of an accompanying updraft."

She gave him a sideways glance. "So there should always be an updraft at the edge of a downdraft."

He grinned as he reassured her, "That's right. Theoretically speaking, of course."

Her eyes, framed with soft dark lashes, seemed a more intense blue with the reflection of the pristine blue sky that surrounded them.

He went on. "Of course, there are always unexpected situations." He felt the sudden shift of her shoulder, molded against his in the tight compartment, as she took a deep breath.

"Such as?"

"Weather patterns that change unexpectedly. It's not unusual to encounter some showers up here. Then, of course, there are the recent El Nĩno weather patterns we've been experiencing in California."

"Is that bad?"

"It makes it very interesting." To demonstrate, he changed

the angle of the stick drastically. The glider swooped in a downward plunge. Changing the angle of the stick once more, he angled the glider off its previous course. An updraft immediately lifted them.

"You have to watch the striations in the clouds." He pointed aloft at the faint wisps of clouds that hung like gossamer strands in the sky. "There's a downdraft several hundred yards off the starboard wing. We'll catch the edge of it and use it to maneuver into the pattern of another updraft."

"What if you miss?"

He laughed. "You'll just have to trust me. You used to. When you were little."

Trust him? she thought warily. The man she'd felt afraid of from the first moment she saw his photograph in a newspaper? Her uncertain gaze met his. "I don't remember . . ."

His hand folded over hers. "Maybe you will one day."

Suddenly, just as he predicted, she sensed the pressure on the wings as he angled the nose downward with his other hand. Then he maneuvered again and she felt the sudden upward lift. His fingers threaded with hers, reassuring her. To her surprise, she didn't pull away, but held on tightly.

For the next half hour they moved almost effortlessly through the sky, spiraling, swooping, gliding out over the coastline. Below them the rocky cliffs fell away to the churning, endless ocean. Above them the sky was a canopy that went on forever. Mist formed across the canopy, then was gone.

Like an enraptured child, Allie took it all in, her eyes wide with wonder as her fear gave way to pure enjoyment.

Rafe pointed beyond the canopy to something in the ocean below them.

Then she saw several somethings and exclaimed with delight, "Whales!"

"We caught them on a run. They're migrating south to warmer water for the winter. We see them frequently this time of year."

Allie tried to count them as they broke the surface and then plunged back into the water. There were at least two dozen, probably more. As Rafe pointed out, it was difficult to spot the smaller calves from this altitude.

Then he pointed toward the rocky coastline. "That's what I wanted you to see. That's Yankee Point—the northern boundary for the rancho." He gradually angled the glider down the coastline, weaving between the cooler ocean air and the warmer inland temperatures. Then, as the Santa Lucia Mountains rose to the east, he took the glider farther inland.

"We'll catch the updrafts off the western slopes of the mountains. Here we trade warmer inland temperatures for cooler temperatures over the water."

"Have you done this before?"

"Yup. We'll be able to see the entire ranch all the way to Elena's Point. It'll give you a better grasp of the enormity of the Sloan legacy."

They spent another half hour spiraling over the ever-changing landscape, picking out seasonal stream beds and year-round creeks. Rafe angled over Marin Bay, where his proposed marina and resort were to be built, then they swooped toward the mountains to pick up another updraft.

Gradually, the panorama of land unfolded below her—ravines, small hidden coves, and inlets, along a stretch of the most beautiful coastline in the world, just as it was laid out on the topo maps included with his site plans. It was all there.

"Look"—Allie pointed—"the hacienda."

The ranch spread out below them—pastures, outbuildings, and grazing land speckled with Ben Sloan's sturdy brown and white Virginia cattle. The one-lane dirt road threading across hills and gulleys, and through stands of trees, disappeared into nothing.

As they swept over the land at a low altitude, suddenly they came upon that distinctive outcropping of rock, like a giant wedge hammered into the ground—the wedding rock. They were so low that Allie could see the faint scratchings of the names and dates that were etched there, although it was impossible to read them from that distance. Then they were swooping out over the rocky cliffs below and immediately surged upward on a sudden updraft that took them high over all of El Sureno once more.

It was beautiful, nearly as serene as it must have been the day Don Marin first rode across it and claimed it for his own—as far as he could ride on that sturdy Andalusian stallion in seven days. This was the legacy he had entrusted to his daughter and the man he had arranged for her to marry.

Tears glistened in Allie's eyes as she turned to Rafe. "Thank you," she said softly. "There is no place I'd rather be than here. It's like climbing all the way up to heaven and holding a piece of it in your hand."

"I never quite thought about it that way, but I suppose you're right. If you're inclined to believe in that sort of thing."

"Seeing all this"—Allie gestured beneath the wide canopy—"is enough to make anyone believe. It's also a bit humbling."

"That's quite a statement for an architect. Are you trying to tell me that you aren't going to go out and design some lofty imitation of all this?"

"How could anyone possibly imitate any of it?" she asked, gazing at the coastline of El Sureno that passed below them. Then she asked herself quietly, "How could anyone destroy it?"

It took them more than an hour to work their way back up the coastline, moving in a reverse pattern of the way they had gone down it earlier. The return trip took longer, but it was by no means boring. Allie could have stayed up there forever. It was disappointing when they finally glided in over the trees that lined the airport, then dropped low and gently bumped down onto the runway.

The glider gradually slowed as Rafe firmly applied the foot brakes. They rolled to a stop, one wing dipping down to the tarmac like a huge, magnificent bird once more returned to land.

They rode back to Monterey in silence. At first Allie thought of the ranch and how magnificent it had looked from the air. But gradually her attention focused on Rafe, and the new side to him she had seen that day. There was a wildness about him, a need to push everything to the edge. He drove that way, and flew the glider the same way. And yet, even as she sensed him pushing that edge, she wasn't afraid for her safety, because somehow she felt confident that he knew exactly what he was doing and wouldn't take stupid chances.

She felt a vague stirring of memory. It had been triggered earlier when he said, "When you were little, you trusted me." But try as she might, she couldn't make the memory come clear. She knew only that it was something positive and reassuring, and distinctly at odds with the instinctive fear she felt toward him.

It was almost seven o'clock when they drove into Monterey.

"Are you hungry?" Rafe asked, shifting down at a traffic signal.

After the substantial lunch of fried chicken, mashed potatoes, and biscuits, Allie was surprised to discover that she *was* hungry. Still, she hesitated to accept Rafe's invitation.

Accurately interpreting her predicament, he flashed a wicked smile. "I can be trusted, at least until midnight."

"What happens after midnight?"

"We could make a really long evening of it and find out."

Allie was struggling to come up with a suitable response when Rafe turned sharply at the next corner, Alvarado Street, and pulled to the curb, cutting the engine in front of Cibo, Ristorante Italiano.

Inside the restaurant Allie was a bit self-conscious that they were the only people in jeans, casual shirts, and sneakers. Tables were set with heavy damask tablecloths, china, crystal, and silver. Rafe was clearly unconcerned that they weren't properly dressed.

"They may ask us to leave," she commented as the hostess approached them.

"No, they won't," he whispered confidently. "I know the owner."

The hostess smiled in recognition. She couldn't have been more than twenty-one, with thick dark hair that hung past her shoulders in a naturally wavy mane, and a voluptuous figure that threatened to spill out of the low-cut dress that looked as if it had been poured over her.

"Rafe!" she exclaimed with obvious pleasure. "It's been a while."

"Work keeps me out of trouble," he replied with a smile that flashed white against his bronze skin.

The young woman cast a sideways glance at Allie. "Work?" she asked.

"*Work*," he said firmly. "Can we get a table this evening?"

"I should make you wait, since you don't have a reservation. But if I know you, you'd just leave."

"Or speak with the boss," he said pointedly.

Her expression hardened, and suddenly she was studiously polite. "Follow me."

As they were seated, the young woman made a point of introducing herself to Allie. "My name is Stephanie. Rafe and I are . . . old friends."

"Allie Sloan," she responded. "Rafe and I are family."

She saw a look of mingled relief and disbelief cross Stephanie's lovely face.

"Please send the waiter over," Rafe asked.

Their waiter appeared and presented the menus. They ordered shrimp Milanese with angel hair pasta. The waiter left, then returned a moment later with a basket of warm bread and a small plate of olive oil and red wine vinegar sprinkled with fresh herbs.

As she dipped the fresh, warm bread in the mixture of wine vinegar and olive oil, Allie asked, "What was it like, living at the ranch?"

"Don't you remember anything about it?"

"Just bits and pieces, a flash here and there."

Rafe took a sip of red wine. "Living there with Alan and Barbara was probably the only really stable time in my life."

He leaned forward and slowly twirled his wineglass, staring down at the crimson liquid. He told her what she already knew. "I'd been in trouble. Alan and Mac wanted to straighten me out. Barbara just felt sorry for me. She had more compassion for people than anyone I've ever known since."

"What about Gavin?"

There was the smallest flicker of pain in his eyes, quickly masked by a wicked grin. "Let's just say that I wasn't his favorite person. After all, I *did* steal his car."

"Sibling rivalry?"

"It was more than that. Gavin hated me and made no attempt to hide it. I can't say that I blamed him. I pretty much hated myself. We had that much in common."

"Why did you feel that way?" Allie asked, genuinely interested in understanding this man.

"I was an outsider, and I was never allowed to forget it. I was the product of Paul Sloan's sleezy affair with a *Mexican,* an affair that could never be legitimized by marriage because he was already married in the eyes of the church. I was a Sloan, but the name I went by was Estrada, my mother's name. It was legally changed when my mother died and I went to live with my old man.''

''Did you see him when you were growing up?''

''Not until his wife died. Then once a month he would send his big car for me and I would spend the weekend with him. During that weekend I was a Sloan. I ate fancy food and wore fancy clothes and slept in my own room. On Monday, when I went back to school, I was an Estrada. I lived on the edge of Monterey in a farmworker's shack, and slept on the floor because my grandparents had the only bedroom and my mother slept on the sofa.

''That can be rather confusing for a kid,'' he finished tightly.

Her heart ached for him, torn between two worlds, one white and rich, the other brown and poor, knowing he didn't really fit in to either one. She could imagine the taunting he would have gotten from the other kids—words like bastard and half-breed would have been thrown at him, because kids can be cruel. How on earth had he survived all that? she wondered. How had he managed to not only avoid being destroyed, but actually succeed?

For the first time since she had learned the truth about her parents, Allie felt her anger at her grandparents' deception completely dissolve. They had given her a life filled with love and security, and had lied to her only because they were trying to protect her. Her life with them had been infinitely better than Rafe's.

She decided that the first thing she would do when she returned to Seattle would be to visit her grandmother and apologize for being so angry at her.

Looking at Rafe, Allie said matter-of-factly, ''So you rebelled.''

''I didn't want to be a Sloan *or* an Estrada.'' His expression was filled with genuine regret. ''I made life hard for my grandparents. After my mother died, I ran away a couple of times and lived on the streets. Finally, they called the old man. He had the authorities pick me up. And I went to live with him.''

''What happened?''

"Let's just say that I was no match for Gavin. He's almost fifteen years older than I am. It gave him a certain edge."

"But you were just a kid," Allie said.

"It didn't matter. I was his father's bastard son. He resented it and he made sure I knew it. He beat the hell out of me, and I ended up in the hospital for a couple of days."

"What?" Allie was flabbergasted. Gavin had seemed so polite and reserved.

Rafe said bluntly, "I swung at him."

At her startled expression, he went on to explain. "It was my first important lesson in street fighting—never swing on someone unless you're certain you can either knock the other guy out or outrun him. At thirteen, I didn't have enough of a punch to knock anyone out, and my legs were a great deal shorter than they are now."

"Why did you try to hit him?"

"He called my mother a whore."

Allie had no idea what to say to this. While Rafe tried to sound matter-of-fact about it all, she sensed that even now, years later, the memories were profoundly painful."

"Was that when you stole Gavin's car?"

"Yeah, when I got out of the hospital. I *borrowed* it for some joy-riding. But he didn't see it that way. He had me arrested. It was a big mess. The old man died right in the middle of the whole thing."

Allie noticed that he always referred to Paul Sloan as "the old man," never as his father.

Rafe continued. "Gavin was determined to press charges. Because of my age and the fact that I had no prior arrest record, I was sent to the California Youth Authority. I spent eighteen months there. When I was released, Alan and Barbara took me to live with them at the ranch. It seemed the best place for a kid with a lot of anger burning inside him—one hundred thousand acres of wide open land to roam around in."

"What did you do?" Allie asked curiously.

"I rode with the vaqueros, went to school with their kids at the small schoolhouse in Big Sur, and for the first time in my life felt as if I truly belonged. Alan was like a father and a big brother all in one. And then, of course, there was Mac. He was like a grandfather to me."

He looked at her intently. "You were just a little kid then."

"A pest," Allie said with a smile, reminding him of what he'd called her.

"Yeah. But a cute one."

The waiter brought their dinner and refilled their wine-glasses.

"I remember so little of that time," Allie said sadly. "It's as if everything has been swallowed into this dark void. I keep trying to remember, but I can't. My only clear memory is of that last night."

Rafe's expression, which had grown gentle, changed abruptly. He asked quickly, "What do you remember about the murder?"

She didn't want to talk about it, but somehow she felt that she must. "I remember hearing voices that night—angry voices."

"There were a lot of people in the house that night," Rafe pointed out.

She shook her head. "No, they had left by then. I heard my mother's voice downstairs. And I heard someone else. They were arguing. I came downstairs, then I saw their reflection in the mirror in the entry.

She hesitated, then went on slowly. "That mirror holds the key to retrieving my memory of what happened to my mother."

"What exactly did you see in the mirror that night?" he demanded.

"There was someone else in the den with my mother. And it wasn't my father."

He frowned impatiently, clearly not believing her. "Of course you want to believe that—"

"No," she insisted, "it's not wishful thinking. It's the truth. Someone else was there."

"Who?"

She shook her head in frustration. "That's just it, I can't remember. I keep trying to, but I can't."

"Allie, look, it's natural that you wouldn't want to believe your father could do such a thing."

"It *wasn't* him," she repeated adamantly. Remembering the

words he had spoken to her that last time in prison, she said, "He loved her."

Rafe said quietly, "Mac was always convinced that Alan was innocent. He refused to believe that he could have killed Barbara."

"What about you? What do you believe?"

He closed his eyes and said wearily, "I didn't want to believe it."

Suddenly a question occurred to Allie. "Where were you that night?"

Without quite meeting her look, he said, "I'd gone out."

"But—"

He cut her off curtly. "Look, there's no point in rehashing it all. It won't change anything."

Gesturing to the waiter, Rafe called him over and asked for the check. It was just after nine when they left the restaurant and Rafe drove her back to the Sloan offices where she had left her rental car. Allie said nothing during the brief drive, but she was disturbed by Rafe's refusal to talk to her about that night, to help her remember.

She retrieved the tubes of plans from the back compartment of the Corvette, then asked, "When do you need these back?"

He said briefly, his earlier friendliness gone, "I have copies. Keep them as long as you like."

"Will you be at the board meeting Monday morning?"

"I'll be there. I stopped running from the family a long time ago."

"Then you haven't given up."

His expression hardened. "I'm meeting with my investment group tomorrow."

She was surprised. "On Sunday?"

"I still have twenty-four hours to pull this off."

"And if you don't?"

"Then the sale to the Japanese will be approved, and soon you will be a very wealthy young woman."

"And you'll be a very wealthy man."

"There are some things that money can't buy."

He didn't elaborate, but she wondered if revenge fell into that category.

Feeling a little awkward, she held out her hand. "Thank you for lunch, a wonderful afternoon, and dinner."

He took her hand. The contact was brief, perfectly innocent, but the response it aroused within her was anything but innocent. It was the same disturbing response she'd felt the day before when she'd felt the pressure of his fingers at her hips.

"Get in your car," he ordered. "I'll follow you to the hotel."

"I'm perfectly all right," she insisted.

"Get in, Allie."

She didn't argue.

He followed her to Lighthouse Avenue. From there she cut over to Highway 68, then took the Carmel exit. As she pulled into the hotel parking lot, she glanced into her rearview mirror. For the first time in a long while there was no fear of what she would see reflected there. There were no frightening images, no monster hands reaching out from the darkness of old dreams. There were only the headlights of Rafe's Corvette as he pulled away.

17

ON MONDAY MORNING ALLIE accepted an invitation from Elizabeth DiMaggio to join her for breakfast at her shop. The Sobrante Gallery was tucked away off Dolores Street, at the back of a brick courtyard filled with a profusion of colorful flowers. It looked like an English country garden, and Allie found it enchanting. Elizabeth, watching for her from the door of the gallery, came down the brick walkway to greet her. "The flowers are almost all bloomed out," she remarked. "But I don't have the heart to take them out just yet."

"It's wonderful. I feel as if I've stepped into a fairy woodland." Gesturing to the surrounding shops that lined the courtyard, she went on. "It's so—"

"Quaint?" Elizabeth suggested. "That's what we usually hear."

"Uncommercial," Allie decided. "And completely refreshing. No fast-food restaurants, no video parlors, no MTV blasting from an electronics warehouse."

"It's that way deliberately. The city council sets very strict standards to ensure the quaintness and charm. It's part of the appeal."

"It certainly is. I could spend the entire day here."

"Well, you're certainly welcome to. I'd love to have you. Come on in." Hooking her arm through Allie's as if they were already fast friends, she said, "I hope you like croissants. I got them from a French bakery here that's marvelous."

She rolled her eyes and grinned good-naturedly. "Of course, they're terrible for my waistline," she groaned. "But at my age, I've decided not to be obsessive about things like that." She leaned closer as if divulging a secret. "Besides, as I've learned through a succession of husbands, it's not my waistline they're after." She winked. "It's my money."

"I love croissants," Allie replied. She went on. "I appreciate your invitation. I've felt a little at loose ends since Mac died."

Elizabeth's smile dissolved and the look she gave Allie was filled with sadness. "I know. He was such a dear man. I shall miss him terribly. But if there is a bright spot in this terrible loss, it's the fact that he got to see you before he died. That meant a great deal to him, you know."

"It meant a great deal to me as well," Allie said.

Elizabeth's expression brightened. "Good. Now then, come inside and see my gallery. We'll eat and we'll talk." She squeezed Allie's hand affectionately. "I imagine there's a great deal you want to know."

They sat out in the courtyard, talking quietly. Occasionally a customer ventured in, and Liz let them wander through the gallery, which displayed works by several of the most renowned local artists. If they had questions or showed interest in a particular painting, Liz excused herself, dealt with them quickly, then returned. The interruptions gave Allie a chance to collect her thoughts as they talked.

An hour later the pastry box sat on the table between them, empty. Liz had just brewed a second pot of fresh hazelnut coffee, and she refilled Allie's cup.

Allie asked, "When did you first meet my mother, Liz?"

"Just before she married your father. I had just returned to the area, after my divorce—my first divorce. I was twenty-three and my parents were determined I wouldn't make the same mistake twice. They insisted that I attend all the right social functions and meet a 'suitable' second husband instead of the unsuccessful artist I'd run off with the first time. I met

Barbara at some deadly dull charity fund-raiser. We were both bored to tears and looking for an escape route. Unfortunately, there wasn't one. We spent the entire evening in the corner, talking, and from that moment on we were good friends. I think it was a case of opposites attracting."

"How do you mean?"

"Barbara was gentle and sweet, and I'm anything but that. However, she had a wicked sense of humor that hardly anyone ever saw except, perhaps, Alan. It leavened her 'niceness,' and made her more interesting than some people gave her credit for being. They thought she was simply too nice."

"Why too nice?"

"It attracted people to her—that caring quality. Men, especially, felt they could talk to her and she would understand. And, of course, she was so beautiful that more often than not they fell in love with her."

Allie frowned. "That's why the rumors started."

Liz's voice turned hard. "Oh, yes, people were quick to talk, especially women who were jealous of Barbara's popularity. It was so hypocritical of them. Pebble Beach is practically Sodom and Gomorrah, you know. It's full of bored rich people who have nothing but time on their hands, and they frequently spend that time having affairs."

"But my mother wasn't like that," Allie said defensively.

Liz's hard expression softened. "No, Allie, she wasn't. But people judged her by their own low standards. Someone would see her talking privately to someone else's husband, and not realize that she was simply providing a shoulder to cry on. Or they would see that some man was obviously drawn to her, and assume that she encouraged him."

"Did she know that people talked about her that way?"

"Oh, yes. She wasn't stupid, you know, she had a really first-class mind, which ran counter to the popular image of beautiful blondes. But the gossip didn't really bother her. She shrugged it off. Until—"

Liz stopped, and suddenly looked uncomfortable.

Allie finished for her, "Until my father began to believe it."

"I'm afraid so. It devastated her that he could believe such a thing of her."

Allie said adamantly, "He didn't kill her."

Liz's discomfort grew. "I . . . I found it difficult to believe that he could do such a thing. I had known Alan for several years, and I knew how much he loved Barbara. He fell in love with her the moment he saw her."

Her lips curved in a wry smile. "But Alan was no saint. There had been plenty of girls through college, and afterward. For a while I was one of those women, and hoped I might be the one to catch him. But I got tired of waiting for him to settle down. That's when I married my first husband."

Allie was amazed. "You were in love with my father?"

Liz laughed. "Only briefly. We weren't right for each other. Too much alike, I suppose. It was ironic that your mother became my best friend. Watching her and Alan together, it was obvious they were made for each other."

Allie repeated obstinately, "He didn't kill her. I *know* it. I saw what happened that night."

Liz was stunned. "My God, Allie, you poor child! What did you see?"

Allie told Liz about hearing the angry voices, going downstairs, and seeing the images in the mirror. For the first time since she'd talked to the hypnotherapist, she articulated the horror of watching her mother be bludgeoned to death, and the childhood memory of those monster hands.

Liz said soberly, "No wonder you suppressed all memory of that time, especially that night. And to think that for all these years everyone believed that you were upstairs asleep and didn't witness anything."

"That's what my grandparents wantea everyone to believe, including me. They wanted me to forget all about it, put it behind me. I understand their reasons. But I had to come back. I had to find my family, and, hopefully, the truth."

"Everyone was so devastated by what happened," Liz said sadly. "Your mother's death and then Alan's execution the following year shattered the family. Mac was never the same afterward, not until you returned. I saw him briefly after that first day you were here, and there was a light in his eyes then that I hadn't seen in years. You did that for him, for all of us. Seeing you was like having Barbara back again, in a way."

Allie grimaced. "I'm not sure my other relatives were as happy as Mac was at my return."

Liz smiled wryly. "Did you see the look on everyone's faces at the church? I thought Gavin was going to have a coronary on the spot. He looked as if he'd seen a ghost."

Allie nodded. "Val made a comment about that."

"Yes, well, subtlety has never been one of her strong suits. And then she was probably just a little put out about the inheritance."

"But I don't have a big inheritance," Allie responded. "Just a few shares that were put in trust for me when my parents died." She went on uneasily. "Although, I suppose Mac must have left me something because his lawyer called me first thing this morning and asked me to be at the reading of the will today. But it can't be much."

"No matter how little you're getting, your relatives would resent it. They're a greedy bunch, especially Valentina and Nicholas. They both have very expensive habits, and are probably already counting every penny they're going to inherit."

"I can't believe they all resent me for that," Allie said in amazement. "They're so rich."

"Well, it's true that Erica doesn't need it. She has plenty from her own family. No, it goes much deeper with Erica. She hated Barbara. Seeing you must have been like rubbing salt in a very deep, very old wound."

"Why did Erica hate my mother?"

Liz gave her a sympathetic look. "I can see that Mac neglected to fill you in on some of your family history. The fact is, Gavin once hoped to marry your mother. But she met Alan, and it was all over for Gavin. Erica was nothing more than a consolation prize for him."

Allie shook her head in amazement. "I had no idea."

"It wasn't surprising. As I said, men were drawn to Barbara like moths to a flame, whether she wanted them or not. David Benedict was rather attracted to her himself. And, of course, Nicholas had to maintain his reputation as a budding young playboy by making a pass or two at her. Even Rafe had a sort of boyish crush on her."

"Rafe?"

Liz chuckled. "Oh, it was just a typical teenage boy's infatuation with a beautiful, slightly older woman."

As Elizabeth talked, Allie glanced at her watch. "Oh, dear," she said, "I'm afraid I have to go. I'm supposed to be at the lawyer's office in Monterey in half an hour, and I'm not sure how to find it."

As she rose, Elizabeth stood up beside her. "I can give you directions. What street is it on?"

Allie told her, and Elizabeth gave her the directions to find it. Seeing Allie's nervousness, Elizabeth reassured her, "Don't worry, Allie. It will be all right. You're a survivor, you know. Mac told me so, and he was a good judge of character."

Impulsively, Allie gave her a warm hug. "Thanks, Elizabeth. For everything."

A few minutes later she arrived at the attorney's office in an old building in downtown Monterey. It was one of the spectacular fall days on the peninsula, the air warm, almost balmy, and no fog out over the ocean. Allie didn't want to sit in the lawyer's office with her relatives, whom she was certain wouldn't want her there. She would have far preferred to go back to Casa Sureno and sit out on the patio where she had sat talking to Mac, and wrap his memory tight around her, like a warm shawl. But she had no choice. She had to respect Mac's last wish.

She ran into Rafe as she entered the building. Seeing her nervousness, he said, "It'll be over fairly quickly. Mac had his will drawn up years ago, and he told all of us what the provisions were. The majority of his estate will go to Gavin, since controlling interest has to go to a direct male heir, and the rest is divided up pretty equally among the rest of us."

Several chairs had been moved into the attorney's large office. Rafe and Allie were the last to arrive, and took the last two remaining seats at the back. As she had expected, her relatives were surprised, and dismayed, to see her there, but no one said anything, not even Valentina.

"Now that we're all here, let's begin," the elderly attorney announced. "Everything is pretty straightforward. Mac made several provisions for people outside the family who were special to him, including a bequest of a small house in Pacific Grove for his longtime housekeeper, Inez Garcia. There is also an additional bequest for the family of Miguel Escalante, caretaker of the Sloan ranch. There are several charitable bequests, which I believe you're all familiar with. I'll go into them later. Those provisions were all made several years ago."

He hesitated, then continued carefully. "Recently, Mac made several changes to his will regarding the remainder of his estate."

Gavin sat up in his chair, his full attention now on the attorney instead of on the portfolio before him, which undoubtedly contained information regarding the pending sale and the board meeting the following morning. "I wasn't informed of any changes. What are they?"

"If you'll please hold your questions until I'm through," the attorney said firmly. He continued. "Less than a week ago Mac contacted me about the changes. He knew the precarious nature of his health. He was especially concerned that the changes be made as soon as possible, and in a manner that could be questioned by no one."

"Dammit, what changes?" Gavin demanded.

"They are very straightforward. In the simplest terms, Mac made the following provisions: in keeping with the restrictions of the family land grant, fifty-one percent of his inherited interest in the Sloan Land Company has been willed to Rafael Sloan, son of his cousin Paul Sloan and Amelia Estrada."

Allie felt Rafe tense in surprise next to her. Clearly, he hadn't expected this.

Gavin started to erupt in fury, but the attorney drowned out his protests. "The remaining forty-nine percent of his inherited interest in the Sloan Land Company is hereby willed to Alexandra Wyatt Sloan, daughter of Alan Sloan and Barbara Wyatt Sloan."

The provisions regarding Rafe had caused surprise and consternation, but this announcement was utterly shocking. Everyone spoke at once, and the attorney had to shout to be heard above the uproar. "The ranch house is not part of the Sloan Land Company or any of its holdings, but owned separately by Mackenzie Sloan. It is willed free and clear to Alexandra Wyatt Sloan, as is his house on Seventeen-Mile Drive, and all of its furnishings and contents."

"This is ridiculous!" Gavin came out of his chair. "Mac made his will years ago! We all knew what his wishes were!"

"Nevertheless, he instructed me to make these changes," the attorney insisted.

Val was furious. Her face was almost the same color as her brilliant hair. "He can't just change his mind like that! It was supposed to be divided up among all of us." She turned to her father. "You're a lawyer. *Do* something!"

Next to her, Nicholas sat in grim silence, his face white.

The attorney rapped a paperweight against the top of his desk, like a judge calling for order. "I assure all of you, the changes are quite legal and binding!" he shouted above the confusion and loudly voiced objections.

In the midst of all the uproar, one thought was uppermost in Allie's mind—the contents of Casa Sureno included Elena's journal. Mac had said it was his most valued possession, and he had left it to her. She was touched beyond measure, and it was all she could do to control the tears that sprang to her eyes.

The paperweight slammed down again. "Please, sit down!" When everyone had finally calmed down enough to listen, he continued.

"I knew Mackenzie Sloan for over thirty-five years. He wasn't a foolish man, and he certainly wasn't senile or demented. He fully anticipated the reaction these changes would cause. He took several precautions that preclude anyone contesting the will. He made monetary bequests to every other member of the family, referring to them as a guarantee. By making these bequests, he knew there was no way anyone could contest the will by saying they had been left out. He left every member of the family, except Rafe Sloan and Alexandra Wyatt Sloan, the sum of ten thousand dollars."

"Ten thousand?" Nicky was incredulous. "That's nothing!"

The attorney gave him a sharp look. "As I said, he took steps to ensure that the will could not be contested." He looked out over the angry group sitting there, glaring at him in disappointment and outrage. Fixing his gaze on Allie, he explained. "Last Saturday Mac asked me to bring the new will with all the changes to his house for him to sign. That afternoon, in my presence, he had the validity of the will and his competence verified by three other individuals. You'll find their signatures on the last page, as witnesses."

His glance moved to Gavin. "I think you'll recognize the names of a federal court judge, the deputy mayor of Monterey, and his personal physician. In addition, he requested that a videotape be made of the entire matter so that there could be no doubt of his wishes or his ability to carry them out. I have that tape, should you care to see it. You may consult your own attorney if you so wish."

Looking at David Benedict, he went on. "But I assure you, these changes will stand."

He rose from behind his desk. "Copies of the will are available for everyone."

Everyone rose at once and began filing out of the office.

"Well, I suppose this isn't really any great surprise, is it?" Val snapped as she passed Allie. "If I thought all it took was a little kissing up, I would have done it a long time ago."

"C'mon," Rafe said, taking Allie's arm. "Let's get out of here. You look like you're about to collapse."

"Alexandra Wyatt Sloan?"

She glanced at the attorney standing just behind Rafe. "Yes?"

"This has obviously come as a bit of a surprise to you."

"I didn't know . . . I didn't expect anything."

"I know. Mac told me you were unaware of the provisions of his will. He also told me to give you this." He handed her a videocassette. "It's an additional tape he made just for you. He knew time was running out, and there were some things he wanted you to know. It's all here."

Allie shook her head in amazement. "Why . . . why would he do this? He hardly knew me."

The attorney's businesslike expression softened. "Mac seemed to think that you were a very remarkable young woman. His heart may have failed him in the end, but his judgment never did. Good luck."

"Thank you," Allie responded shakily.

Rafe followed her back to the hotel. Allie was stunned and could barely think, much less comprehend what Mac had done. To her disappointment, when Rafe had seen her safely there, he said he couldn't stay because he had things to attend to.

Before he could leave, she asked, "Why do you think Mac did this?"

"I have no idea why he made the bequest to me. It doesn't make sense. But I can understand why he left you such a large inheritance. He probably wanted to make certain that you were taken care of."

She shook her head. "No, it was more than that." She looked at the tape she still held in her hand. "He wanted to make certain that El Sureno was safe. It meant everything to him."

Rafe said, "I have to go. I'll see you in the morning." At Allie's look of confusion, he explained. "Gavin changed the board meeting to tomorrow. I think he was hoping that he'd get most of Mac's shares in the company, and could easily steamroll the sale through."

He smiled grimly. "Well, he must be feeling rather disappointed right now."

"Does this mean the sale could be stopped?" Allie asked quickly.

Rafe shook his head. "No. Neither of us has enough shares on our own to do that. Gavin will still win." He added, "If you'd like, I'll pick you up and take you to the meeting."

"Thanks. I appreciate that."

As she stood on the front steps, watching Rafe's Corvette head down the driveway and out the gate, she thought of going to the meeting tomorrow and watching helplessly while the land that Mac loved was sold off to the highest bidder. It made her angry and sad, but she knew there wasn't a damn thing she could do about it.

It was almost midnight and Allie sat in her room, staring at the tape. She had felt reluctant to watch it, afraid that it would be too overwhelming emotionally so soon after Mac's death. But she told herself she was behaving like a coward. Mac wanted her to see this, and he would be disappointed in her if she put off dealing with it.

She forced herself to put the tape in the video recorder and turn on the television. But as his image filled the screen, she felt as if her heart would break.

"Dearest Alexandra," he began, sitting in his chair in the study. "I'm making this tape because I want to tell you that I love you very much. I thank God that I was granted the time we had together these past few days. It was a rare and special gift. You have questions for which I have no answers. But I am confident you will find them. They lie within your memory, and the past. Both are part of El Sureno."

Allie fought the tears that tightened her throat.

"You know how much I love the ranch. It is the legacy of the Sloan and Marin families. You can't put a price on it, though Gavin will do everything in his power to do so. My hope was to prevent that, but time was not in my favor. I have given you part of your legacy, my dear, in the bequest that I have left to you. I gave the majority share to Rafe, because by the terms of the Sloan trust I had no choice but to bequeath it to a direct male descendent. If I could have given it all to you, I would have. Still, something tells me that the two of you together may be able to do something interesting. He has fierce determination and you have great heart. Who knows what you might be able to accomplish together."

He finished in a voice that had grown exhausted. "You are so like your mother. I know your feelings about the ranch are genuine, as hers were. Read Elena's journal. The future of El Sureno is in your hands."

Barefoot in spite of the chill night air, shirtless, and clad only in jeans, Rafe stood on the deck overlooking the plunging cliffs of Big Sur. When he first bought this house, it was nothing more than a two-room shack falling down over the edge of the cliff, its wood foundation rotted away by years of weather. He tore it all down and started over, like he'd started over so many times in his life.

First the foundation—solid concrete poured around steel stanchions that went deep into the cliff, anchoring almost five thousand square feet of floor space. Then glass, stone, and wood walls reaching up to thirty-foot ceilings that disappeared into the tops of pine trees. Built on three levels, it was a blend of rustic, modern, and traditional, like all the elements that had shaped his life.

In the daylight he could see the north and south coast for miles in either direction through twenty-foot glass panels. Six inches of heavily insulted walls protected against the coast winds. The carpets were soft and light, the walls rough and dark, in stark contrast, like the conflicting moods that drove him.

It was after midnight. The moon was obscured behind clouds and the night was black out over the ocean. He could hear the water below, moving restlessly over the rocks, in eddies and tidepools, then surging up in a frothy mist that all but disappeared before it reached the deck.

Frustration ate at him. He took another swallow of wine from the goblet balanced precariously on the ledge of the deck railing.

Everything that he'd worked for the past several months was about to slip through his fingers. He didn't like losing. He'd been a loser as a kid, a throwaway, caught between the world of his very rich, influential father and the lower class of his mother's laborer family.

He never thought of them as his parents. Parents came in pairs and usually formed some sort of nucleus for a family, even in the case of a divorced couple. His had never provided any sort of nucleus.

Both his mother and father had talked to him about what brought them together. His mother, Amelia, had gone to work at the Sloan ranch as a girl of eighteen. By the time she was twenty, she was Paul Sloan's mistress. Rafe's father insisted that he had loved her, and said she gave him the few truly happy moments in his life. They were stolen moments, because Paul was married and Catholic, and that created an impossible situation.

After Rafe was born, and his mother realized his father would never marry her, she ended the affair. Angry and bitter, she refused to have anything to do with Rafe's father again, or to let him help her financially.

He grew up the product not of a broken family, but of a family that never existed. For a brief time he found refuge with Alan and Barbara. It was the closest he ever came to actually feeling part of a happy, close family.

After Barbara's death and Alan's execution, Rafe had left and swore he'd never come back. Mac persuaded him to return by tapping into the things that drove Rafe, the need to prove that he belonged, just as much as any of the Sloans, but particularly Gavin.

El Sureno was his only hope to beat Gavin, and now Gavin was about to win, just as he'd been winning all their lives. At ten o'clock in the morning he'd present the offer from the Nakatome Group, and take the cursory vote, which he controlled through the majority shares he owned in the company.

The fifty-one percent that Rafe had inherited from Mac's estate changed nothing, for Mac had been a minority shareholder. Even added to the small number of shares Rafe had inherited from his father, it still wasn't enough to stop Gavin. And there was no other direct male descendant in a position to stop him. Mac had accomplished nothing with his last-minute manipulations.

Rafe stared down at the wine in the long-stemmed goblet. It glittered darkly in the half light from the dimly lit room at his back. There was movement behind the glass at his back. A woman appeared at the door, wrapped in a blanket, her long hair disheveled from sex.

"Are you coming back to bed?" she asked in a soft, sultry voice. "I have to leave in a little while."

Without turning around, he said, "Let's call it a night."

In the shadows at the door the woman tossed back her hair. "Will you call me?"

There was no immediate answer, and she knew he'd already dismissed her from his mind. She started to ask again, then thought better of it. From past experience with Rafe, she knew that demands would get her nowhere.

"I'll call you," she said, then retreated into the room and retrieved her clothes. A few minutes later the headlights of her sports car snaked down the driveway that connected his house to the road that led to the highway.

In less time than it had taken for her to turn away from the windows of his bedroom, she was forgotten.

All Rafe could think of was the bitter knowledge that once more Gavin had won. He'd beaten Rafe physically once, hurting him and humiliating him. Now he'd beaten him in an even more profound sense.

In fury and frustration Rafe hurled the wineglass into the dark sky. It glittered briefly in the light from the bedroom, then hurtled down onto the rocks. The crashing of waves obliterated any sound of shattering glass.

Standing at the edge of the deck, the knuckles of his fingers white as he grasped the railing and stared into the black night, Rafe recalled something he told Jim Collier that day at the ranch—"No one is going to stop me. I'll do whatever it takes."

Suddenly he realized the full significance of Mac's inheritance. And he knew what he had to do. . . .

Allie was jolted awake. For a moment she was disoriented, then gradually everything settled back into focus, and she realized she had fallen asleep. The television screen was snowy white. The only other light came from the bedside lamp. Then she heard a loud knocking at her door, and realized that must have been what woke her.

Going to the door, Allie hesitated, then called out, "Who is it?"

"Rafe. Let me in."

She wondered what on earth he was doing at her hotel room this late. Opening the door, she asked anxiously, "What is it? What's happened?"

"I have to talk to you."

She stepped aside as he strode into the room. He was dressed only in jeans, boots, and a white T-shirt, in spite of the fact that it was cold and damp outside. The misty night air had plastered his shirt across his shoulders and chest, emphasizing every muscle underneath and the dark bronze of his skin. His hair was damp also, clinging to his head in dark waves. There was a wildness about him that spelled danger, and she felt afraid.

Wrapping her satin robe more closely about her, she closed the door, then demanded angrily, "What's this all about? Do you know how late it is?"

He turned on her, and she saw an intense expression in his eyes that made her feel more afraid. "This can't wait. We barely have time to fly to Tahoe and be back before the board meeting at ten."

She looked at him with confusion. She was tired, and she had no idea what he was talking about. "Fly to Tahoe? Don't be ridiculous. Why would I want to do that?"

"To prevent Gavin selling off the ranch."

She pushed her hair back from her forehead. "We've been through all of this. There isn't any way to stop him."

His gaze never left hers. "There *is* a way."

A small warning tremor slipped across her skin. He was completely serious, and in spite of the wild look about him, there was something rational and calculated in his expression.

She asked in confusion, "How could we possibly do that?"

"An arrangement between you and me—strictly business, because that's the only way either of us would want it."

He added, "We have to get married."

18

"MARRIED?!" RAFE MUST HAVE lost his mind, Allie thought. Shaking her head, she added heatedly, "This is a really lousy joke!"

He looked at her evenly. "It's no joke. I've given it a lot of thought. Believe me, if there were another way, I would have come up with it. This is the *only* way to stop Gavin from selling El Sureno."

Allie stared at him as she pushed her hand back through her hair. It was late, and she was exhausted. She wasn't in the mood for this. "You're crazy."

"Maybe. At least listen to what I've got to say."

"Forget it, Rafe, there's no way I would even consider such a ridiculous idea! It's crazy—"

"It's the only way!" he insisted, interrupting her. "Do you want to hand over everything to Gavin, or do you want to fight him and win?"

She hesitated. This was stupid, she told herself. She couldn't possibly consider it. She should tell Rafe to go away. But somehow, seeing him standing there, so intense and determined, she couldn't. Instead, she closed the door behind him. Crossing to the small sofa on the far side of the room, she sat down, curling her legs under her.

"All right," she said in a tone that clearly meant *persuade me*. "What exactly do you have in mind?"

He crossed the room and stood over her. "Think about the rule of primogeniture—only a direct male descendent can inherit controlling interest in the ranch. Elena's father made that restriction for a specific reason."

She nodded wearily. "To keep the ranch in the Sloan-Marin family." Rubbing her temple with an index finger, she tried to massage away the dull ache she'd been fighting ever since they'd left the attorney's office. She went on. "But Gavin owns controlling interest. The fact that Mac chose to leave you and me his shares doesn't change anything."

Rafe took a piece of paper out of the hip pocket of his jeans, then sat beside her on the sofa, spreading the paper out between them. He was so close, their shoulders brushed. Allie saw that his dark skin was damp with a sheen of moisture, and she knew that he hadn't paused to put on a jacket in his rush to get over there to talk to her.

Suddenly she was reminded of the day at the ranch when he'd lifted her down from the horse and she'd grabbed his arms to steady herself. That day his skin had had a fine sheen of perspiration from riding all afternoon in the warm sunshine. Even now she could remember the heat of his skin—could almost feel it at her fingertips, along with the other wildly sensual feelings he'd evoked that afternoon with just the simplest touch. She clasped her hands together to hide the faint tremble at the memory.

"Take a look at this," he said.

As she did, he bent his head low beside hers, so that she could almost feel the damp coolness of his cheek, smell the wind in his hair. She yearned to touch him. Instead, she forced herself to concentrate on the paper he'd spread out. It was a page from a copy of Mac's will, outlining the distribution percentage of share ownership of the entire estate, including Rancho El Sureno.

She shrugged. "This merely shows that Gavin has majority ownership. You have the next highest percentage as the next direct male heir, and Nicky has the least."

"Your percentage share is more than Nicky's," he pointed out.

"That's irrelevant because I'm not a direct male descendent. I have no real power. There's nothing new in any of this." Her voice was edgy and she made no attempt to hide her frustration.

Unfazed, Rafe countered, "But look what happens when you add some of the numbers together." He added his percentage and hers together, then boldly circled the resulting number.

Allie stared at the figure. The individual shares they'd received from their parents, together with the shares they'd inherited from Mac, were surprisingly substantial when added together. In fact, they were just slightly more than Gavin's, and considerably more than anyone else's.

"But we can't vote those shares together," she reminded him, still staring down at the figures. "According to the original terms of the land grant, mine don't count. Or I could have simply voted with you and Mac against Gavin."

"They don't count unless they're all owned by a direct male descendent, through inheritance or . . ." He let his words trail off suggestively.

She looked up with a stunned expression as she finally understood what he was getting at. "Or through marriage," she whispered.

His dark gaze, usually so closed and remote, met hers directly. "The only way we can stop Gavin is to get married so that I control your shares as well as mine. I can outvote him then, and we would control El Sureno."

Stunned by the simple yet devastating logic of his argument, she got up and paced around the room, her arms wrapped about her tightly. He was absolutely right. This could work. But at what price? she wondered.

"Is it legal? Is it even possible? After all," she pointed out, "we *are* cousins."

"We're second cousins twice removed. It's perfectly legal for us to marry. Once we're married, I control majority interest in the Sloan Land Company and I can cancel the sale to the Japanese." Rafe spoke in a matter-of-fact tone, as if he were discussing a normal business venture.

But this wasn't business as usual, Allie told herself. It was a marriage. A *marriage*—just the thought of it made her head spin. For a moment she said nothing, letting it all sink in. The whole idea was preposterous, yet at the same time perfectly logical.

"Do you realize what you're suggesting?" she asked.

"Yes, I do. I'm making you a business proposition, Allie. I know that's the only way you'd agree to it. We both want the same thing here—to prevent Gavin selling Rancho El Sureno. You know as well as I do it's what Mac wanted too."

"Yes, but this way?" She shook her head. "It's . . ."

"Crazy?" he repeated with a self-deprecating smile.

"Yes!"

"You're right. It's also the only chance we have."

His eyes locked with hers for one intense moment. She broke contact first, looking over at the clock on the bedside stand. "It's after midnight. The board meeting's at ten o'clock. How could we possibly—" She stopped, unwilling to say the words, "*Get married.*"

"It would be cutting it close," he admitted, "but we could just do it. We could fly to Tahoe tonight, get married on the Nevada side, and fly back just in time for the meeting."

Rafe was talking as if this could actually happen. Allie felt confused, stunned, yet strangely excited. "We probably couldn't even get a flight out of Monterey this time of night," she protested.

"I could arrange a private flight from here to San Francisco, then we could catch a commercial flight from there to Tahoe."

His dark gaze pinned her. "I'm very serious, Allie. I wouldn't be here if I wasn't."

"We don't even agree on what should be done with the ranch, and we still face the problem of the taxes that will be due in a few months."

Rafe was unconcerned. "Let's deal with one problem at a time."

"Meaning?"

"Meaning that we stop Gavin first, then figure out what we'll do about the development."

Allie said worriedly, "But *you'll* control the property. I

wouldn't have any say about it. You could do whatever you wanted.''

''What I want isn't so bad, Allie. It's a helluva lot better than letting the Japanese have it, or the state. If I control it, it will remain in Sloan hands.''

''Subdivided and sold off,'' she snapped.

''We could still keep a portion of the ranch intact, including the main hacienda, of course. Dammit, Allie, you have to be realistic!''

''I'm trying to be. But I see a plan that meets *your* objectives, not *mine,* and is risky at best. You know as well as I do that Gavin won't take this lying down. He'll fight us every step of the way.''

Rafe's voice was tight with repressed anger. ''Let him. I'm not a helpless thirteen-year-old anymore. I can deal with him.''

''I won't let the land be parceled off and subdivided,'' Allie said flatly. ''That would almost be worse than selling it. At least we wouldn't be responsible for destroying Rancho El Sureno. Mac would have hated that.''

''Mac is dead,'' Rafe pointed out more harshly than he intended.

Allie responded with righteous indignation. ''Well, *I'm* not. I won't betray Mac's wishes by letting Rancho El Sureno be sacrificed to urban sprawl. There are other ways to solve the tax problem.''

Suddenly he realized the direction she was heading. ''You want to develop it *your* way?''

''Yes.'' She challenged him. ''What's wrong with that? It's possible to develop the land and still preserve its integrity.''

''We don't have the time or the money to do that,'' he said heatedly.

''If we control the land, we can get the money. You said so yourself.''

He couldn't argue with that. ''All right,'' he said grudgingly, ''what are you suggesting?''

Suddenly it seemed their positions had reversed. Now he was defensive and skeptical while she was convinced her plan could succeed. ''I'm suggesting a completely different sort of development from the one you originally proposed—one that would preserve the integrity of the land, adhering as closely as possible to the original vision of Rafael Marin."

"What vision? There's nothing in the journal about that."

"It isn't spelled out, but it must've been the reason he set up the line of inheritance the way he did. He wanted to make certain that El Sureno could never be broken up and sold in pieces the way the other ranchos were. He saw it happening all around him. That's why he arranged for Elena to marry Ben Sloan."

She stopped abruptly as she realized that was exactly what Rafe was suggesting—an arranged marriage for the purpose of protecting the land. History was repeating itself nearly one hundred fifty years later. The thought was so astounding, she couldn't deal with it for the moment. Taking a deep, steadying breath, she said in a quiet voice, "I'll agree to the arrangement because it's the only way to save something that I feel matters very much."

Rafe's expression of surprise betrayed the fact that he really hadn't expected her to go along with his dramatic plan. Before he could respond, she went on quickly. "But we'll sign an agreement before we're married that states the development will be changed according to my specifications. *I* will be the project architect."

She could tell that he was angry at being manipulated this way. But she wasn't about to let herself be intimidated by his anger. She had no intention of marrying him and turning over her shares to him simply to enable him to get revenge on Gavin.

When he spoke, his voice was rigid. "That one condition alone could end it for both of us. I'm convinced that your way won't work. And even if there was any chance it could, we'd kill it by not being able to agree on anything."

Allie met his cold look without flinching. "I'll take my chances. How about you?"

He looked at her for several moments. Just when she was certain he was about to tell her to go to hell, he asked, "Is that all?"

"Yes. But I want it in writing."

"All nice and legal," he said with the barest hint of an ironic smile.

"That's right. After all, this isn't personal. It's business."

She could have sworn there was a glint of humor in his dark eyes. "You've got yourself a deal."

Allie looked at him uncertainly, caught off guard by his capitulation. She'd agreed to this outrageous scheme because she understood there was no choice, but she'd bargained hard for what she wanted out of it. Nevertheless, she couldn't quite believe she'd won—if that was an accurate description of what had just taken place.

Unexpectedly, the words Mac had spoken to her in his video came to mind. "*You'll know what to do.*" He had read Elena's journal countless times. He knew what was in it—knew that Elena's marriage to Ben Sloan was arranged by her father in order to save El Sureno. Could he possibly have envisioned she and Rafe doing the same thing? He would have felt that it would be wrong to suggest such a thing to them, but if they thought of it on their own . . .

Allie looked at Rafe, and forced herself to ask the question that was now uppermost in her mind. "What about afterward?"

"Since it will be a business arrangement only, and the marriage won't be consummated, we can have it annulled eventually. I assume that's what you would want."

She nodded soberly. "Of course." She felt doubt beginning to seep in, but she pushed it back. They would make this work—they had to. Both had something they wanted very much from this arrangement.

"Now what?" she asked.

"I'll make some phone calls. You get dressed."

Fifteen minutes later, Allie stepped out of the bathroom fully dressed and her hair and makeup done. Rafe looked at her in surprise. For their "wedding" she'd decided to wear the same dove-gray suit she'd worn to Mac's funeral. It was understated, almost severe, and emphasized the fact that this was a business arrangement. For one crazy moment he found himself wondering how she would have looked in a white wedding gown with her golden hair swept back by a veil. Telling himself not to be a romantic fool, he immediately dismissed the thought.

"It's all set," he said, and watched an expression of doubt cross her lovely features.

But if she had second thoughts, she didn't give in to them. Looking at him directly, she said, "You were able to arrange a flight?"

"A friend of mine who's a pilot owes me a favor."

"That must be some favor to be willing to fly you to San Francisco in the middle of the night."

He grinned, trying to lessen the tension of the situation. "It is."

"What did you tell him?"

"That it was a business emergency and we had to be in San Francisco for a three-fifty flight to Tahoe."

"I'm amazed that people actually make commercial flights at this time of night."

"It's a gambler's special. We'll catch the return special back to San Francisco. Scott will lay over in San Francisco and fly us back here."

"Can we make it in time?"

"We'd better. If Gavin successfully presents and passes the vote on that proposal, he'll be calling the Japanese buyers immediately following the meeting. I want to stop him before it gets that far."

"And our written agreement?" she reminded him pointedly.

"I'll write it up on the flight to the city. We can both sign it and Scott can be a witness, if that's all right with you. Then we can formalize it when we get back to Monterey. I'm sure Mac's attorney will be glad to handle it for us."

"That will be fine." She tried to sound matter-of-fact, but her voice trembled slightly.

He looked at his watch. "Okay, then, we'd better get going. We have only half an hour to get to the airport. I'll see if Scott has something I can borrow to wear. He usually carries a change of clothing in his flight bag."

The Cessna waiting on the tarmac at the Monterey airport was the same plane that had towed them aloft in the glider only a few days earlier. "We're even now, buddy," Scott said to Rafe in greeting as they ran from Allie's rental car to the waiting plane. "I left Diane in bed, alone, and not very happy." Looking curiously at Allie, he said, "I hope you enjoyed your trip aloft the other day, Miss Wyatt."

Allie smiled. "The flight was extraordinary."

Rafe helped her into the plane, then climbed forward into the jump seat beside his friend. "Enough small talk. If you can get us to San Francisco in time to make that flight to Lake Tahoe, she'll be Mrs. Sloan in a couple of hours."

"*Mrs.* Sloan?" Scott's bright blue eyes widened in amazement. "No kidding? But I just saw you with—"

Rafe interrupted him. "Just get us to San Francisco."

The flight took slightly more than an hour and a half. They flew straight up the coastline, then came in over San Francisco International Airport a little before three o'clock in the morning. Scott had called ahead on a private linkup, requesting a car to take them over to the commercial terminal. They barely made their flight to Lake Tahoe.

As Allie and Rafe stood in line to board the plane, she watched other bleary-eyed passengers lining up at the gates for flights to various domestic and international destinations. She found herself trying to guess at the reasons they would be traveling so late at night—vacation schedules gone awry, commuters held up by last-minute business, servicemen trying to catch a standby connection that would take them home. Other travelers with missed or cancelled flights tried to sleep in waiting areas. Whatever the reasons that had brought these people here, it seemed unlikely to Allie that any of those reasons were as improbable as hers. She was frantically trying to make a flight to Nevada to marry a man she wasn't in love with and who wasn't in love with her.

She was filled with doubt about the rightness of her action. But she had no doubt about one thing—this whole crazy scheme was the only way to save El Sureno.

It's just business, she kept telling herself. It meant nothing to either one of them beyond what the marriage could achieve in legally combining their shares of ownership. The wedding ceremony itself would undoubtedly be tacky, cheap, and quick, in one of those ridiculous wedding chapels next to a casino, where couples could walk over on impulse between dinner shows or after a bout with the slot machines and tie the knot.

As they boarded the plane, Allie found herself wanting to call her grandmother, to get some comfort or reassurance from her, as she had in the past when faced with a dilemma. What would she say when she learned what Allie had done? In a way

Allie was doing the same thing her mother had done—going off and impulsively marrying a Sloan.

"Are you all right?" Rafe asked.

She looked from the bank of public phones back to Rafe, knowing there was no way she could call her grandmother and tell her what she was about to do. "Yes, I'm fine."

"Having second thoughts?"

"Would it make any difference?"

He nodded grimly. "Yes. We don't have to go through with it. Scott can take us back to Monterey, and we can forget the whole thing."

"And let Gavin sell off El Sureno."

"Yes." He paused, then asked bluntly, "Want to call it off?"

She looked at him. "Do you?"

"We both know why we're doing this. It's just business, Allie."

Her expression was determined. "All right then, let's get down to business."

He took her hand in his, his warm fingers wrapping about hers as they stepped onto the plane. Her hand was cold as ice. Even after they sat down he held on to her, his fingers laced through hers, his palm cradling hers against his jean-clad thigh. Somehow the contact was reassuring, though she couldn't have begun to explain why.

The flight was filled with older couples, all of whom were headed for the mountain gambling resort on a ninety-nine-dollar special that included twenty dollars in gambling tokens at Harrah's, and nonstop gambling until the bus returned them to the airport twelve hours later. Allie thought they were crazy, but she realized that what she and Rafe were doing was even crazier. She told herself the marriage would be annulled within a year, two at the most. Then she could put it behind her and get on with her life.

"You look like you're about ready to pass out," Rafe said after they were finally airborne. "Why don't you try to get some sleep? I'll wake you when we get there."

"I don't think I could sleep," she replied, glancing at their rambunctious traveling companions.

"Just close your eyes and rest, then. It's going to be a long night."

She did as he suggested, shutting her eyes and leaning back in the seat. Conflicting thoughts filled her mind . . . this was a rash, impulsive act she would undoubtedly live to regret . . . it was the only way . . . Mac would have wanted them to grab this opportunity to stop Gavin . . . she was marrying Rafe . . . marrying Rafe . . .

"Allie?"

She stirred, then slowly awakened. As she sat up, she felt disoriented, and it was a moment before she realized that Rafe was still holding her hand, and she had been sleeping with her head on his shoulder. She pulled her hand from his in some embarrassment. "Sorry. That must have been pretty uncomfortable for you."

He smiled. "I've learned not to wake sleeping people unless absolutely necessary. Depending on their nature, it can be dangerous."

She wondered what other people he meant—women? Then she shook it off. It didn't matter to her whom he slept with. It was none of her business.

"Are we in Lake Tahoe?" she asked, determined to change the subject.

His dark eyes narrowed as he caught the quicksilver change of her mood. He had liked watching her sleep—the curve of dark gold lashes, the way her lips parted slightly, the way her honey-gold hair lay against her cheek, the even rise and fall of her breasts beneath the impeccable business suit.

In that moment when she first awakened, he saw something in those soft gray-blue eyes that he'd seen only once before, in Julianne's expression—a naked, vulnerable sensuality that reached deep inside him like a fist. It was gone almost immediately, replaced by an aura of rigid control that he sensed was a defense, to protect her all-too-fragile feelings.

That perfect control had wavered, revealing her true emotions, only a handful of times. At Mac's funeral, when her grief had been transparent . . . the day they rode out over the ranch together, when her love for the land and its rich history was evident in her enthusiasm and animated expression . . . and when he took her up in the glider, and she looked as if she had slipped free of the nightmares and painful half memories that had brought her back to Pebble Beach. On that silent, magnificent flight he had glimpsed a spontaneous joy in her that had stunned him, making him realize that she was like Barbara in more ways than just appearance.

Now she was awake, and she had retreated once more behind the wall she kept safely around her emotions. Unexpectedly, he felt closed out, put at a distance. Even more unexpectedly, he discovered how much he hated it.

"We just landed," he said abruptly.

The other passengers quickly moved down the aisle, eager to get to the gambling tables. When the last one had passed them, Rafe motioned to Allie to walk ahead of him, and they quickly deplaned. Picking up a waiting rental car outside the main terminal, he turned onto the highway into South Lake Tahoe. They passed closed commercial centers, the outlet shopping areas, motels with No Vacancy signs flashing.

On their left was the rim of the lake, illuminated by small coves, piers, and docking areas for boats, and expensive hotels. On their right were more hotels, restaurants, turnoffs into camping areas, and residential areas, and countless ski chalets and resorts, including Heavenly Valley.

"Do you ski?" Rafe asked after a few minutes of silence.

"Some, but not since college. I went on a trip with friends to Colorado."

"I've skied all over. Heavenly is a great resort. They have some really challenging slopes and bowls, and you can't beat the view. The lake stays open in winter, doesn't ice over. It's an intense blue right in the middle of all this white, then with blue sky above. From just about anywhere you can see the entire Sierra Nevada mountain range."

"It sounds beautiful," Allie said, meaning it.

"You'd love it. It's almost as good as flying in a glider. We'll have to come back—" Then he stopped, remembering that business, not pleasure, had brought them here, and they were unlikely to come back.

He went on carefully. "Maybe you'll get a chance to come back when this is all over." They had reached the south shore gambling area with its high-rise hotel–gambling casinos. Even at this hour of the morning—almost five o'clock—people strolled on the sidewalks, the casinos were lit up, and there was a surprising amount of traffic on the street. Pulling into the parking lot of Harvey's Casino, Rafe stopped at the valet parking between the two main towers of the hotel.

"We won't be long," he told the attendant who handed him a receipt for the car.

Allie looked at him skeptically as he led the way into the hotel. "What are we doing here?"

"The manager, Mike Wainwright, is an old friend of mine. I called him from your hotel room while you were getting dressed. He should have everything ready for us."

"You mean—we're getting married here?" she asked, surprised.

"Yes. I thought it would be better than one of those awful wedding chapels."

She breathed a sigh of relief. She'd expected the worst—an all-night wedding chapel with pink satin wall covering, white shag carpeting, gold-painted hearts on the doors, tape-recorded music, an attendant who handed her some half-wilted bouquet that had undoubtedly been used for a dozen other weddings that night, a paid witness, and someone officiating at the short ceremony who had undoubtedly just finished a floor show in one of the lounges.

In the lobby they found a house phone, and Rafe called up to the business office. While he was talking, Allie glanced around, taking in the noise of bells going off, dealers calling for bets, the incessant grinding of the slot machines from the casino. She found the atmosphere somehow depressing and couldn't wait to get back to the beauty and serenity of Pebble Beach.

Hanging up the phone, Rafe turned back to her. "Mike will be right down. He's made all the arrangements."

She nodded, unable to speak. Suddenly she was very nervous.

A couple of minutes later she saw a clean-cut man in a business suit walking toward them. He was rather short, with warm brown eyes and an infectious grin, and slightly thinning blond hair. He and Rafe hugged each other unselfconsciously, each slapping the other on the back.

"You sly old devil," Mike said. "You finally decided to do

it. I never thought it would happen. You swore you would never—"

"Yeah, I know," Rafe cut him off. "This is different."

Mike grinned. "Right."

Turning to Allie, his expression went from surprise to confusion. The woman standing there wasn't at all what he had expected of Rafe Sloan. She was tall and slender, with dark gold hair that hung straight to her shoulders, soft blue-gray eyes, and a curve of mouth at once amused and vulnerable. Her heart-shaped face needed little makeup to look exquisitely lovely. There was nothing flashy about her as there had been with most of the women his friend chose. She was all class, from her quiet demeanor to the understated clothes she wore.

Mike was particularly caught by the expression in her eyes. Unlike the other ladies Rafe had occasionally brought here for a night or a weekend, there was a cool intelligence in this woman.

"You're not quite what I expected," Mike said, offering his hand.

"This isn't quite what I expected either," Allie responded with a small laugh.

He looked at her dubiously. "Are you certain you want to marry this guy?"

She looked past him to Rafe. "He made me an offer I couldn't refuse."

"Jeez, it sounds like a business arrangement," Mike joked, completely unaware how close he had come to the truth. Looking at Allie, he made a quick assumption; a man married a woman like this for only one reason—he wanted to make certain she would be his forever.

Mike went on. "I've made all the arrangements." He led them down a hallway. "It's too bad none of your family could make it."

Allie and Rafe exchanged a brief, uncomfortable glance as they followed him past a video arcade for teenagers, a French bakery, and an ice cream parlor. As they turned down another hallway, the sounds of the casino seemed to disappear. They passed several closed office doors, then stopped at one marked Private in gold lettering. Opening the door, Mike gestured for Allie and Rafe to precede him inside.

"I did just as you asked," he told Rafe.

Allie was stunned as she stepped into the private lounge. It was elegantly furnished with several dark blue brocade sofas arranged before a huge fireplace, smoky-glass-topped tables set with vases of red roses, and a panorama of windows that revealed a magnificent view of the mountains. The sky was pale gray, just beginning to turn to peach as dawn came. The ambience was warm and comfortable with an understated charm, and not a neon light in view.

"This is one of our hospitality suites," Mike explained, looking at Rafe. "You said you wanted the best, and this is it."

Allie turned to Rafe. "I never expected this."

He smiled. "I can imagine what you were expecting."

Deeply touched by his unexpected consideration, she murmured, "Thank you."

"You're welcome. It seemed the least I could do."

"You two sound as if you were being forced to do this," Mike teased. Then, realizing he might have put his foot in his mouth, his expression changed and he colored slightly.

Rafe said quickly, "Don't worry, it's not what you think." Before Mike could respond, he added, "Can we get on with this? We have to be back in Monterey by ten o'clock."

Mike nodded. "The justice of the peace should be here any minute. By the way, I had them open up the jewelry shop in the lobby. Why don't you go down and pick out a ring while we're waiting?"

Rafe turned to Allie. "We'd better make it quick."

For some reason Allie hadn't thought about a wedding ring. The idea of picking one out with Rafe was disconcerting. "Why don't you surprise me?" she suggested. "A plain gold band will do. Size five."

Rafe nodded and left.

When he was gone, Mike turned to Allie, curiosity etched on his face. "You sure you don't want to help him pick out the ring? You never can tell what he might come up with on his own."

"No, I . . . no," Allie answered, flustered.

Mike looked at her thoughtfully for a moment. "Did Rafe tell you how we became friends?" She shook her head, and he went on. "It was in 'Nam. We were in the same platoon. Both just nineteen, scared stiff, and doing everything we could think of to hide it."

"It must've been terrible," Allie said sympathetically.

"Yeah, well," Mike replied with a self-conscious shrug. "Anyway, the point is, you get to know someone pretty well in that kind of situation. I know Rafe's not perfect—who the hell is? But take it from me, you can trust him. With your life, if you have to. *I* know."

But I *can't* trust him, Allie thought. I hardly know him, and what little I do know of him frightens me. She glanced away, unable to meet Mike's look.

Just then Rafe returned, and almost immediately the justice of the peace arrived. He was a short, balding man with a kind expression, and he looked as tired as Allie felt. Clearly, he'd been dragged out of bed for this ceremony. Still, he smiled at them both. "You're the happy couple?"

"Yes," Rafe told him. Allie nodded.

"I usually don't perform ceremonies at this time of night. It's nice to meet a couple who are so eager to get married. Nowadays, most people seem more eager to get divorced." He smiled at them both, then focused on Allie. "Are you ready, my dear?"

She nodded stiffly, overcome with the knowledge of the seriousness of the situation. She was about to be *married*—to a man she barely knew and wasn't at all certain she could trust. And all for business reasons that suddenly seemed crass and self-serving. Was she doing it just for the power of controlling the development of an enormous tract of virgin land? It would be a thrilling, once-in-a-lifetime opportunity for any architect, especially one as young as Allie. She knew what the Edgewater project had done for Julia's reputation. The development of El Sureno could do it for her. Was she motivated by sheer ambition? she asked herself frankly.

Then she remembered Mac, and his desperate determination to save El Sureno. She remembered the way she'd felt when she'd ridden over the land, and again when she'd flown over it in the glider. Mac was right. It was worth saving for its own sake, not for the sake of her professional ego.

The justice of the peace said, "Please join me by the fireplace. Mike will act as our witness."

They took their places before the roaring hearth. It was warm and cozy in the room, but Allie felt suddenly cold inside.

Rafe took her hands in his. Caught off guard by the unexpected gesture, her gaze met his in blank surprise.

Then the ceremony began.

As the justice of the peace spoke the brief, unsentimental words, Allie thought of her fantasies of her wedding day. She had always envisioned a white wedding gown, bouquets of wildflowers because her grandfather had loved them so, and candles casting a soft glow over the ceremony. The traditional wedding would be held in the small white-framed Church of the Glen outside Lake Stevens, and Allie's grandmother and friends would be there with her.

This was as far removed from those dreams as it could possibly be. It wasn't what she'd planned, nor was the man standing beside her the one she'd dreamed of. She had believed in all the romantic ideals of love and commitment, building a life together, and sharing what came, both the good and the bad. And children . . . several children, because she wanted a big, loving, happy family.

But this marriage was designed to last only as long as it took to accomplish their goal. They would build something together, but it wouldn't be a life, only structures of concrete, wood, and plaster. Rafe didn't love her, and she didn't love him. As soon as they'd accomplished what they'd agreed to do together, their marriage would be ended as quickly and unemotionally as it had begun.

Standing beside Allie, Rafe felt her shiver, and he slipped an arm about her waist to steady her. When the justice of the peace asked her if she took this man in lawful matrimony, her lips trembled. She hesitated, and for an instant he thought she wouldn't be able to go through with it. Finally, she responded "Yes" in a voice that was barely a whisper.

Only once before in his life had he considered marriage—to Julianne. He would have married her if she'd left her husband and gone with him. But she hadn't had the inner strength to take such a risk, and in the end she'd let him leave, alone. Since then he'd had only casual affairs, none of which had ever come close to marriage.

For Rafe, the idea of marriage signified family, and he'd had his fill of the hypocrisy of everything that word supposedly stood for. His father had broken his marriage vows to his wife to have an affair with Rafe's mother. He'd promised her marriage, but in the end he wouldn't give her what she desperately wanted. It was all a lie, and Rafe wanted no part of it.

The justice of the peace turned to Rafe and asked if he would take Allie as his lawfully wedded wife. Without hesitation Rafe said tersely, "I do." He had no second thoughts. He and Allie had an agreement. After it was over and they'd accomplished what they both wanted, they would go their separate ways. It was just business, he reassured himself.

"Do you have the ring?"

As Rafe slipped it on her finger, her hand shook slightly. The ring was a gold band, as she had specified, but it wasn't plain. It was carved in ornate scrollwork with a pattern of interlocking hearts. She wondered uncomfortably why he had chosen something so . . . well, romantic.

The justice of the peace finished with a flourish. "By the power vested in me as a justice of the peace in and for the State of Nevada, I pronounce you man and wife."

"All right, it's official, you two are hitched!" Mike said with a huge grin. "Aren't you going to kiss the bride?"

Allie stared in dismay at Rafe. Surely he wouldn't . . .

"Of course," Rafe said as if it were the most natural thing in the world. Turning to face her, he brushed his mouth against hers. It was the lightest contact, almost chaste, yet it was hardly innocent in the feelings it evoked. His kiss was warm, rousing unexpected emotions.

Allie pulled back abruptly, as if she'd been stung.

He looked at her quizzically as she nervously raked her fingers through her hair. Light gleamed off the gold band on her finger. The sight of the ring more than the perfunctory words they'd spoken brought home to her the enormity of what they'd just done. They were actually married—even if in name only.

If Mike thought they weren't acting like normal newlyweds he didn't betray the fact. He said easily, "I wish I could talk you into staying for a few days. I could see to it that you had the best suite in the house."

"We appreciate that," Rafe said sincerely. "But Allie and I have to get back. There are a lot of things to deal with."

"I understand. But I want you to promise that you'll bring her back for a delayed honeymoon—a ski holiday, on the house."

Instead of responding to the invitation, Rafe simply said, "Thanks for everything. I really appreciate it."

"Hey, how often is it a guy gets to see his best buddy get married? I thought it would never happen."

Ignoring the good-natured barb, Rafe said, "We need to go if we're going to make that flight."

"Forget the rental car," Mike told him. "I'll have the hotel limo take you back."

Within an hour from the time they'd arrived, they were back at the Tahoe airport. Two hours later they'd landed in San Francisco, and Scott was making the last preflight check before takeoff. Neither Rafe nor Allie had said a word to each other from the moment they'd gotten into the hotel limo for the ride to the Tahoe airport.

Scott grinned as they climbed aboard. "Well? Is it *Mrs.* Sloan?"

Allie glanced at Rafe as if for confirmation. He nodded to his friend. It's Mrs. Sloan."

Scott offered congratulations and pointed to a bottle of champagne sitting in a plastic bucket filled with ice, and two plastic cups. "It was the best I could do in the middle of the night with only the airport gift shop open. I stole the bucket over at the hangar when I refueled." His grin deepened. "They'll never miss it."

Rafe looked at Allie. "Champagne?"

She shook her head. "Why don't you save it for when we pull off the development deal?"

Rafe left the bottle in the bucket. "Right."

Again they both lapsed into an awkward silence. Allie tried to sleep on the flight back to Monterey, but they had picked up the edge of a weather front and the flight was bumpy. She remembered the day she and Rafe had flown over El Sureno in the glider and he had explained about thermals, updrafts, and downdrafts. The weather had been milder then. It was anything but mild today.

It was almost ten o'clock when they finally landed at Monterey Municipal Airport, just ahead of a storm. Rafe tucked the bottle of unopened champagne under his arm, quickly thanked Scott, and then he and Allie raced for her rental car in the parking lot. Twenty minutes later, after battling downtown traffic, they pulled up in front of the Sloan Land Company offices.

Rafe glanced over at her. "Nervous?"

"A little," she admitted. Actually it was more than a little. The thought of facing her relatives with the shocking news that she and Rafe were married, that Rafe intended to take control of the company, was nerve-racking.

Taking her hand as he had at the hotel only a few hours earlier, he said, "Come on, *Mrs.* Sloan. Let's give them a little surprise."

As they walked into the building, Allie forced herself to assume a calm, controlled demeanor that was completely at odds with how she felt inside. Over the past few hours, since Rafe had first shown up at her room with the wild idea that they get married, she had tried to imagine what this moment would be like, tried to mentally prepare herself for it. Now she found herself thinking of Mac. *"You'll know what to do."* I hope to God you're right, she thought.

Rafe and Allie walked past the secretary in the reception area and headed toward the conference room at the back of the building. As they neared the conference room, Allie could hear Gavin's voice. Then Rafe was pushing open the door, and he and Allie entered just as Gavin was outlining the terms of the offer.

"Since I have controlling shares for the Sloan Land Company, which in turn controls the ranch," he was saying, "I've already verbally committed to the terms of the agreement." He stopped abruptly as Rafe and Allie entered. The other family members sitting around the conference table looked at them in surprise.

"I thought you might have decided not to join us," Gavin said to Rafe. "I know how you loathe family meetings."

"I was especially interested in this meeting," Rafe replied in a deceptively even voice. "I think everyone should know that the Sloan Land Company won't be accepting the offer from the Nakatome Group. El Sureno isn't for sale."

The expression in Gavin's eyes was ice cold. "I've accepted the offer. I'm meeting with the Nakatome representatives this afternoon. There's nothing you can do to stop it."

"I've already done it. You'll have to cancel that meeting, Gavin. You don't have the legal authority to accept the offer."

"I might have known you'd try to create problems," Charlotte said bitterly as she half rose out of her chair.

"Sit down, Charlotte," Rafe ordered. Turning back to Gavin, he went on. "Allie and I were married a few hours ago. Her shares in the company are now mine. As of this morning, you no longer own controlling interest in the Sloan Land Company. *I* do."

19

"YOU SON OF A bitch!" Nicky practically jumped out of his chair, glaring at Rafe. "You can't do this!" Looking around wildly, he focused on Gavin and repeated desperately, "He can't do this, can he?"

Gavin sat in stone-cold silence at the head of the table. Allie thought his silence was somehow more frightening than Nicky's outraged protests. Gavin's mouth narrowed in a hard line as he stared down the length of the conference table. In a voice as cold as his silence had been, he said evenly, "I might have known you'd try something like this."

Looking at Rafe, Allie could see that he was savoring this moment. It must be sweet revenge for the brutal beating that had landed him in the hospital when he was thirteen. He said easily, "I didn't want to disappoint you, big brother."

Gavin turned to David Benedict, who sat in stunned misery. "Is this marriage valid? Isn't there some sort of legal restriction on cousins marrying?"

Rafe spoke before David could. "There's no law against second or third cousins marrying. Consult your family genealogy, or, better yet, consult your attorney. The marriage is valid."

"What about it, David?" Gavin asked tersely.

In answer, David muttered under his breath, "Shit!" Then, fighting to control his anger, he went on. "Rafe is right. He and Allie are only distant relatives. The marriage is legal."

"Not exactly *distant,*" Rafe corrected with a grim smile. "We're husband and wife."

An odd feeling washed over Allie. *Husband and wife*. It sounded so unreal. Looking at Rafe, she thought, I don't know this man at all, yet I'm married to him.

Turning back to Gavin, Rafe said, "Don't be a fool and try to go forward with this sale, Gavin. I'll slap you with a lawsuit that will keep you and the Sloan Land Company tied up in court for years. And then I'll break you."

Gavin lost his tenuous hold on self-control, erupting in fury. "I'll fight this! You'll lose everything!"

Rafe faced him down. "You don't get it, do you? I never had anything to lose. You and Charlotte saw to that."

Gavin had ignored Allie so far. Now he turned on her, his face flushed with anger. "He's using you! You know that, don't you?"

She answered honestly, "We're using each other."

"What the hell is that supposed to mean?"

"It means that Mac loved the ranch and didn't want it sold. Together, Rafe and I can save it."

Gavin looked at her thoughtfully, as if seeing her for the first time. "What a coincidence that you turned up *now*." Gesturing toward Rafe, he said, "He'll turn on you. It's just a matter of time. You think you can trust him, but you can't believe a word he's said. Whatever he's promised you to get you to agree to this charade is a lie. He doesn't give a damn about the ranch."

"And you do?" Allie shot back. "*You* negotiated the sale to Nakatome."

Even as she spoke, Allie realized she'd just sided with Rafe against the rest of the family. It was the two of them against Gavin, Erica, David, Charlotte, Nicky, and Val. When they were getting married in Lake Tahoe, she hadn't thought about that, hadn't fully realized what it meant. Now, staring at the angry, hate-filled faces of her relatives, she realized for the first time the full meaning of her rash action. She'd just lost the family she'd only recently found. Even though she didn't begin to care about any of them in the way she'd cared for Mac, it still bothered her to think she'd completely alienated them.

Then another, even more sobering thought, struck her. Was this how her mother had felt when she'd married into this family over thirty years earlier? Then *she* was the unwelcome outsider who showed up unexpectedly, just as Allie had done. The thought that she was, in a way, repeating her mother's experience, was disconcerting.

Gavin went on in a cold voice that sent chills down Allie's spine. "I'll destroy both of you. When I'm through with you, you'll both wish you'd never crossed me."

Rafe didn't bother to respond. Turning to Allie, he said, "C'mon, we're through here."

They stopped at Rafe's office, and he quickly put some papers and a few small personal possessions in the briefcase he'd brought with him. "For the time being, I'd better work out of my house," he said. "Until they accept the fact that I'm in charge now."

Allie said unhappily, "I wish it didn't have to be this way."

He had moved to the drafting table and was rolling up plans. Meeting her worried look, he said, "There was no other way it could be. Gavin saw to that a long time ago. He was just waiting for Mac to die so he could take control, and the rest of them were more than happy to let him do it."

"He meant it when he said he'd try to stop us."

Rafe didn't look particularly concerned. "Without a doubt. Gavin is going to come after us with everything he's got."

"Meaning?" Allie asked.

"First he'll check out the legality of the marriage. He won't just take David's word, even though he realizes that David's right."

"And then?"

He gave her a level look. "We should be prepared for anything. I've never trusted Gavin."

She didn't bother to point out that Gavin had just said the same thing about him.

Seeing how unhappy she looked, he went on. "Look, Allie, I knew this wasn't going to be easy or clean. Mac knew it too. He left us his shares for a reason—because he realized that together we would have the strength to fight Gavin.

"You're glad you have a reason to fight him," Allie said pointedly.

Rafe shrugged. "Gavin just happens to be the one with the most shares. It wouldn't have mattered to me who owned them."

She didn't believe him for a moment. "Wouldn't it?"

In the hours since the wedding, her doubts about what they'd done had steadily increased. Now she was overwhelmed by second thoughts. Was Gavin right? she wondered. Had Rafe lied to her about his motives and intentions?

"Beating Gavin is more important to you than protecting the ranch," she said slowly.

"Dammit, Allie, you know the alternative! What would have happened if we'd done nothing?"

"I know exactly what would have happened, Rafe! But I don't know what's going to happen now that you've gotten what you wanted!"

He looked at her. "You'll just have to trust me."

She started to argue, then realized it was pointless. He was right—she would just have to trust him. She looked at him as if seeing him for the first time. His face looked slightly haggard and there was a dark shadow of beard, reminding her that he'd had no more sleep than she had in the past twenty-four hours. He hardly looked trustworthy, but she had no choice.

She asked simply, "So what do we do now?"

"First, we get some sleep. We could both use some. Then we start planning the project. I've got to get the revised plans to the investors as soon as possible so we can make sure money comes in before the taxes are due on the ranch. And I've got phone calls to make, now that I own controlling interest in the ranch."

"*We* own controlling interest," Allie corrected him. "California's a community property state."

He grinned. "I meant *we*."

"Did you?"

"Of course."

Though she didn't entirely believe him, she didn't argue. Instead, she said, "The scope of the project is going to change drastically. We need to discuss exactly what it's going to be now."

"All right." He didn't sound pleased, but clearly he realized he couldn't argue with her. After all, he'd known what the price was for her cooperation.

Allie said, "Before I get started on preliminary site plans, I want you to see a project that I just finished working on. It has some important concepts that I want to incorporate into the development of the ranch property."

"You don't waste any time, do you?"

"We don't have any time to waste."

He gave her a hard look. "Did you have this planned all along?"

"*You're* the one who suggested we get married. Now that I've gone along with it, I have every intention of holding you to that agreement you signed."

"Or else what? You'll throw in with Gavin?" His tone suggested he thought that unlikely.

"No, but I won't sit back and watch you ruin the land. We have an agreement, and I expect you to stick to it."

He looked at her with a crooked half smile. "In many ways, you're a lot like your father. He was stubborn too." Before she could respond, he went on. "I don't have time to go looking at some little project you designed. There are legalities to deal with here, and I've got to arrange a meeting with my investors as soon as possible."

The moment he said *some little project,* Allie's face had set in a stubborn expression that anyone who knew her well would have immediately recognized. "This *little* project embodies all the principles I intend to incorporate into the development of Rancho Sureno," she said firmly. "This is part of our agreement."

Rafe frowned impatiently. "Are you going to constantly remind me of that?"

"If need be."

For a moment he simply stood there, looking as if he would gladly throttle her. But she was right, and he knew it. He gave in grudgingly. "So tell me about the damn project."

Allie breathed an inner sigh of relief. This was their first real disagreement, and to her amazement she'd actually won. She knew she'd better savor the moment of victory, because there would be many more disagreements as they tackled this massive project, and, Rafe being Rafe, she wouldn't always win.

"It's called Edgewater," she explained. "It's in the San Juan Islands, between Bellingham, Washington, and Victoria, British Columbia. I think you'll like what you see." She finished with just a hint of nervousness in her voice. "I need to stop over in Seattle and see some people."

"Your mother's family?" he asked bluntly.

"There's only my grandmother." Allie added quickly. "You don't need to meet her."

"You don't want me to act the part of the doting husband?"

"I'll see my grandmother alone. There's no need to upset her any more than she is already."

For some reason it bothered Rafe that she wanted to keep him a guilty secret. But he couldn't argue with her. After all, it wasn't a *real* marriage, he reminded himself.

Allie went on in an awkward voice. "I, um, expect I'll be moving into Mac's house shortly. There's no reason to continue staying at the hotel."

"It's your home now," Rafe responded, wondering why she suddenly looked so uncomfortable.

"The thing is," she went on, not quite meeting his eyes, "I think it would be best if you continue living at your house." She continued in an embarrassed rush. "There's really no need for us to live under the same roof."

Now he understood what she was getting at. He couldn't quite suppress a smile. "Don't worry—cohabiting wasn't part of the deal."

He was amused to see the look of immense relief that washed over her.

Rafe took Allie back to her hotel. When he bid her good-bye at the door, on his way to his own house in Big Sur, she reminded him, "I'll check out the flights to Seattle, and call you. We should go right away."

He smiled wryly. "I'll be ready to leave when you are."

When he was gone, Allie called Inez to let her know she'd be moving in to Casa Sureño that night. The note of warmth and welcome in Inez's voice cheered her considerably. After packing the few clothes she'd brought with her, she checked out of the hotel and drove to Casa Sureno.

With a careful juggling of schedules, Allie quickly arranged for them to catch a four-thirty commuter flight that afternoon for San Francisco, where they could change planes for Seattle. They landed at Seattle-Tacoma International Airport just before nine P.M. They'd spent at least eight of the past twenty-four hours in airplanes, and Allie was beginning to feel serious jetlag.

She picked up her car, which she'd left in long-term parking at the airport, and they drove to her apartment in the city. Rafe had offered to stay in a hotel, but Allie told him that was ridiculous. There was a sofa bed in her living room, and there was no reason Rafe shouldn't use it. They were both desperate for sleep.

When she opened the door to her apartment, after being gone for over two weeks, she expected to feel reassured by a sense of the familiar. The sense of homecoming was oddly missing, and she hesitated inside the doorway.

"Is everything all right?" Rafe asked in concern.

She turned on the entryway light and laid her purse and keys on the delicate rosewood table in the tiny foyer.

She laughed off the impression. "For a moment it just seemed strange . . ."

Coming in behind her, Rafe set down the single duffel bag he'd brought. "What seemed strange?"

She struggled to articulate her feelings. "Being back here again . . . somehow it doesn't seem—"

"Doesn't seem what?"

She shook her head in frustration. "It's not important." But she had wanted to say that it no longer felt like home. How could everything have changed so much in so little time? She rubbed her fingers across her forehead, trying to block out the weariness that was beginning to seem overwhelming.

"I'll fix the sofa bed for you," she began.

He interrupted. "I can do it. You look dead on your feet. Go to bed."

"Okay . . . well, then, I guess I'll say good night."

"Good night, Allie."

As she started toward her bedroom, he added lightly, "Just make certain you keep to the bedroom."

"What is that supposed to mean?" she flared defensively.

He held up his hands in supplication. ''I was only teasing. Lighten up, Allie. We'll get through this if we can maintain some humor about it all.''

She sighed wearily as she pushed her hand back through her hair. ''You're right. I'm sorry. It's just that it's been a rough time lately.''

''It's been rough for everyone,'' he reminded her. Then he smiled in a self-satisfied way. ''Particularly for Gavin.''

''You're really enjoying this, aren't you? Hasn't anyone ever told you that revenge can be dangerous? It can come back to haunt you.''

The smile dissolved in an instant. ''It's not just revenge, Allie. I want to prove something.''

''That you're a Sloan, along with all that includes,'' she said bluntly.

''It's not even about being a Sloan,'' he admitted for the first time. ''It's about not running away from the past any longer.''

''I'd say you quit running away when you accepted Mac's invitation to return to Monterey.''

''It's more than physically going back. It has to do with what's in here,'' he said, pointing to his head. ''And what's in here.'' He laid his hand against his chest.

''Heart,'' Allie said softly. Then, ''Mac spoke of that. He was concerned that you had enough determination to succeed, but not enough heart. It was the reason he feared giving you complete control of El Sureno.''

To her relief, Rafe laughed instead of taking offense. ''Mac was a crafty old bastard. Right up until the end—and beyond—he was determined to control everything.''

''How do you mean?''

''Leaving us his shares was his way of controlling El Sureno, and what happens to it, after he was gone. I'll bet he's out there somewhere laughing his head off at the coup he's pulled off against Gavin.''

Allie said dryly, ''I wouldn't figure you to believe in the hereafter, spirits, and that sort of thing. You seem more the type who believes in what he can hold in his hands.''

''I believe in the power of family ancestors to screw everything up. Call it whatever you like.''

Before she could comment on his bitter remark, he asked, in

a different tone, ''Is there any food in your kitchen? Or are you one of these modern career women who live from freezer to microwave, with a little fast-food thrown in between?''

''I tossed out most of the fresh things before I left. But you're welcome to rummage around in the refrigerator and see what you can find.'' She smiled. ''Or are you one of those Neanderthal types who thinks a woman's place is in the kitchen and the bedroom, and not necessarily in that order?''

''I can find my way around a kitchen.'' He paused, then finished in a deceptively casual tone, ''And the bedroom.''

She stared at him, for some reason completely unnerved by his response to her teasing. His dark eyes were fastened on her, reminding her of the way he'd looked at her at the ranch, stripping away every defense, looking straight into her soul.

She struggled to pull herself together. ''Well . . . in that case, I'll let you forage in the kitchen while I take a shower.''

''If I need to do some shopping, is there a market close by?''

''Two blocks over. Turn right outside the entrance to this building, then take the first left. You can't miss it.''

''Okay.'' He reached out and brushed back a strand of hair from her cheek, tucking it behind her ear. ''Don't forget to wash behind your ears, Brat.''

It was said teasingly, and Allie slowly let out the breath she'd been holding from the moment his hand had reached toward her.

''I'll try to remember.''

Then a faint smile curved his mouth and he leaned toward her. For one split second she actually thought he was going to kiss her, and her entire body tensed. But he merely said, ''I need the keys to your car and the apartment.''

Stepping around him, she went to the hall table, took the keys from her purse, and handed them to him.

''Do you always give strange men the key to your apartment so easily?'' he quipped.

''You're hardly a stranger. You're my husband.'' She'd meant to say it lightly, but as soon as the words were out of her mouth, she regretted the implied intimacy in them.

His expression shifted to something unreadable. But instead of responding to her words, he merely said, ''I'll be back before you're out of the shower.''

She watched as he left, then she went into the bathroom.

He was as good as his words. Slipping on a white silk robe, she went into the kitchen and found him busy at the stove.

"Hi, honey, I'm home," he called out.

"So I see," she remarked with a smile.

Her hair hung in wet strands across her shoulders, and she had scrubbed her face clean. He looked at her for a moment, then turned his concentration back to what was cooking in a wok on the stove. Peeking over his shoulder, she said, "That smells wonderful. What is it?"

"Everything but the kitchen sink."

"I beg your pardon?"

"That's what it's called—Everything but the Kitchen Sink."

"It looks . . . interesting," she said carefully.

"Don't worry, it tastes great. Actually I picked this up in 'Nam. Out in the jungle, we had to improvise when it came to cooking. There was no time to get fancy. We were lucky if we could have a fire." He smiled as he looked over at her, the lines about his eyes softening. "Instead of a wok, we used our helmets."

She made a face. "That sounds awful."

"It was. It was all awful. But if you survived it, it changed your priorities in life. Life became the only priority."

She said gently, "You seem to have survived it."

"I was nineteen at the time. A kid. You can survive a lot of things when you're young."

That's true, she thought, thinking of what she had survived as a child. Making a rather obvious effort to change the subject, she asked, "How soon will that be ready? Do I have time to make some calls?"

"Just a couple, but make them short. You have to eat this when it's ready, to enjoy the full flavor and the crispness of the vegetables."

In the living room Allie called Julia, letting her know she was back in Seattle. "It's just a stopover really," she explained apologetically. "I won't be staying. Things in California are still . . . unsettled."

"Take your time," Julia said without a hint of impatience.

Inwardly, Allie blessed her for her understanding. She went on. "I want to get over to Edgewater. I brought someone with me who needs to see the project. You see . . ." She hesitated, then said, "There's a chance of doing something similar in Big Sur. I'd like to talk to you about it."

"Sounds interesting. Let's get together first thing in the morning. By the way, you sound better than the last time we talked," Julia remarked. "Things must be going well in Pebble Beach."

"Not entirely. That's part of the reason I want to see you."

"Anytime, my dear. You know that."

"How's work?" Allie asked guiltily.

"Don't worry, we're doing fine. Naturally, I'd like to have my key architect back."

"What I have in mind in Big Sur might keep everyone very busy—Edgewater, but on a much bigger scale. I need your input."

Julia laughed. "You know how eager I always am to tell people what I think. I'll see you in the morning."

After hanging up, Allie called her grandmother. She knew it was late, but she took a chance that Anna would still be up. She needed to see her, and wanted to make certain she would be home in the morning.

"Oh, Allie," she said when she answered, "it's so good to hear your voice. Where are you?"

Allie heard the hopeful note in her grandmother's voice, and responded, "I'm in Seattle."

She knew the response that would bring. Her grandmother said with relief, "Oh, thank God. I'm so glad you're back, safe and sound."

Guiltily, Allie explained, "I can stay for only a couple of days, but I want to drive out in the morning and see you. If . . . if that's okay."

There was no censure in her grandmother's voice, only a deep disappointment that she made no attempt to hide. "You don't have to ask permission to see me. You know that, darling." She asked, "Is everything all right?"

Allie turned at the desk so that Rafe, visible through the open doorway to the kitchen, couldn't see her face. She felt such overwhelming emotions over the events of the past few days—Mac's sudden death had left her feeling lost and bereft, the stunning revelations of his will, and . . . Rafe.

She said slowly, "Yes . . . things are okay."

Then her grandmother asked the question Allie knew she really wanted to ask, "Have you remembered . . . more?"

"I've remembered some things. But nothing really helpful."

She hesitated, wondering just how she was going to explain her marriage. Maybe, she thought, there was no need to explain it. After all, her grandmother didn't *have* to know about it. In a year or two it would be annulled, and it would be as if it had never happened. Allie decided to make that decision later, before she went out to Lake Stevens in the morning.

Her grandmother asked, "Why can you stay only such a short time?"

"It has to do with the Sloan family ranch. I'll explain when I come out in the morning."

She heard the soft catch in her grandmother's voice. "I'll see you when you get here. It's so good to have you home, sweetheart."

"Good night, Gram." Allie slowly hung up the phone. When she turned around, she was disconcerted to find Rafe watching her. He'd clearly overheard the conversation.

He said, "I take it that was Barbara's mother. I never actually met her, but I saw her when she and your grandfather came to get you. What are you going to tell her?"

"As little as possible, and only what won't hurt her."

There was a pause, then Rafe said simply, "You love her a great deal."

"For much of my life she was my only family. She raised me on her own after my grandfather died when I was twelve."

"You were lucky to have her," Rafe said in a thoughtful tone.

Allie nodded. "Yes, I was." Then, changing the subject, she asked, "Is that just about ready? It may look awful, but it smells wonderful."

"Five minutes more—just enough time to dry your hair."

Returning to her bathroom, she quickly blow-dried her hair, then went back to the kitchen. Rafe had set the small round oak table in the breakfast nook with silverware and napkins, and had already uncorked the wine and poured them each a glass. As Allie sat down, he put a steaming plate in front of her.

After taking a bite, she said in amazement, "This really is delicious."

He grinned. "Don't sound so surprised."

For a couple of minutes she concentrated on eating. Neither of them had touched the unappetizing-looking airline dinner, and she was hungry. After a moment she looked up and found Rafe watching her intently. She colored in embarrassment. "What's wrong—do I have something caught in my teeth?"

He shook his head. "No. I was just thinking how beautiful you look."

She tried to laugh off her self-consciousness. "Oh, right, with no makeup on and my hair hanging straight down."

"You really don't get it, do you?"

"Get what?"

"Just how beautiful you really are." He went on. "You have the most perfect heart-shaped face, skin that any number of women I know would kill for, and those blue eyes just like your mother's—" He stopped, then went on in a husky voice "And your mouth . . ."

She could no longer meet the look in those dark, unsettling eyes. Glancing down at her plate, she murmured, "My mother was very beautiful . . . much more beautiful than I am."

Rafe reached across the table and touched her cheek "You're every bit as beautiful as she was. If she were here she'd tell you so."

She couldn't respond to his words, or the feeling behind them. Her gaze was fixed on her half-empty plate.

Rafe went on, his voice lowered. "There's sadness there too," he said thoughtfully. "You shouldn't be sad, Allie You're too beautiful to be sad. Someone should make you happy."

She thought of Dennis, and the few men she'd dated sinc their breakup. None of them had seemed particularly intereste in making her happy. In fact, they'd all wanted something fron her, either sex without strings attached or emotional support fo their various problems.

She forced herself to meet Rafe's look. Her voice wa determinedly casual. "Well, maybe someday I'll find someon who will make me truly happy. My grandmother always tol me there's someone for everyone."

"Maybe she's right."

"I think it's hopeful wishing on her part. She's afraid I'm so devoted to my career, I won't ever get married." Realizing what she'd just said, she looked quickly at Rafe and found him watching her curiously.

"What are you going to tell her about us?"

"As little as possible, I think."

They'd both finished eating now. Getting up, she picked up their plates and took them over to the sink, grateful to have something to do, something to distract her from his piercing gaze and unsettling conversation.

"Dinner really was delicious," she complimented him, stifling a yawn. The wine, and the late hour, were beginning to get to her.

"Go on to bed," he said, gesturing to the dishes that still had to be rinsed and loaded into the dishwasher. "I'll finish up in here."

"You haven't had any more sleep than I have in the past twenty-four hours."

He grinned. "Yeah, but I owe you for letting me stay here."

"You prepared dinner," she pointed out.

"Go to bed," he said firmly. "I'll clean this up. Then I want to go over some work I brought along. Mind if I use the desk?"

"Help yourself. Well . . . good night, then."

"Good night."

She went into her bedroom, closing the door behind her. Within minutes of falling into bed, she was sound asleep.

Rafe awakened just after midnight. Looking up from the sofa bed, he saw the numbers glowing on the front panel of the microwave oven in the kitchen. He made the quick adjustment to unfamiliar surroundings as he remembered the flight from San Francisco. Swinging his long legs over the edge of the mattress, he went into the kitchen for a glass of water. He leaned against the breakfast counter while he emptied the glass and contemplated the past two days. What an amazing forty-eight hours it had been. What a remarkable woman Allie was . . .

Then he heard the faint childlike cries coming from her

bedroom. Quickly he slipped on his jeans, then hurried down the hallway to her room and pushed open the door.

She lay on her side, turned away from the door and curled in a tight ball.

"Allie?"

She moved, and for an instant he thought she'd heard him. But her movements were jerky, spasmodic, thrashing. "No! Don't hurt her! You have to stop!"

Rafe realized she was dreaming, and sobbing at the same time. When she spoke again, it was in the voice of a child. "Please!" she cried out. "You're hurting her. You're hurting my mommy!"

Then he knew.

She'd told him of the nightmares that had triggered the first memory of her parents in twenty-five years—the memory of seeing her mother brutally murdered that night at the ranch.

"Mommy!"

He couldn't stand the pain in her childlike voice. It mirrored too closely his own pain as a child. He had no idea if it was the right thing to do, but he went to her anyway. Sitting down at the edge of the bed, he gently took hold of her shaking body. He could feel her violent trembling through the thin silk of her nightgown.

"It's all right, Allie," he said in a soothing voice, as if she were still the small child who used to tag along after him all those years before. He pulled her into his arms to comfort her "It's only a bad dream. It's not real. Not anymore." She resisted, crying out again for her mother as the ghastly images of the nightmare lingered. As he pulled her tight against his chest and held her, he saw that her eyes were open, staring filled with terror.

"Allie?" There was something in her eyes—a flash of recognition that mingled with the terror.

"No! Go away! Don't hurt me!" She fought and clawed at him.

He held on tightly. "Allie! It's over. It was only a night mare. It's gone now."

"No! It won't go away . . ." She gasped and shuddered "The monster!"

He held her tight against him. "It's all right, Allie," he kept repeating over and over, not knowing what else to say. "You're here, you're safe. The nightmare can't hurt you anymore."

Her breathing was ragged, filled with tears and the last remnants of childhood fear. Gradually, he felt her begin to relax against him as her tears fell against his bare chest. She clung to him, her cheek wet against his dark skin.

As Allie came out of the nightmare and into consciousness, she felt she was holding on to a lifeline. Rafe was strong and solid and real. His warmth seemed to seep into her, filling all the cold, empty places haunted by shadows and old dreams.

She felt incredibly safe in his arms, and her one thought was that she didn't ever want to let him go.

"Shhhh," he said quietly, his lips moving against the softness of her hair. "It's all right."

"The nightmare . . ." she said, her voice once more that of an adult woman.

"I know. It's over now. You don't have to be afraid."

"I saw it. It was so real, just like it was happening all over again. I heard voices. I saw my mother. There was someone with her. . . ."

Suddenly she pulled away. Those eyes, so like her mother's, were wide and haunted, filled with dark shadows. She pushed back her disheveled hair in what he recognized as a nervous habit.

"What is it?"

She shook her head. "I'm all right now. It was nothing."

"Allie . . ."

"Please! It was nothing. There's no need for you to be concerned. I'm fine."

"You're still trembling. Please, let me help, Allie. I understand all about fear and pain."

But she adamantly shook her head. "I'll be fine. We both need to get some sleep."

It was a polite invitation to get the hell out. "All right. But if you need anything . . ."

She didn't reply.

She looked at him, for the first time fully aware of how little he wore—how little they both wore—and the intimacy between them only moments before.

"I'm all right," she insisted in a trembling voice that betrayed her inner turmoil. "You . . . you can go now."

He returned to the living room then, leaving the door to her room open so he could hear her. As soon as he was gone, Allie got up and closed it firmly.

It was a long time before she was able to get back to sleep.

20

ALLIE AWAKENED TO THE sound of her shower running. At a glance she realized that it was almost eight o'clock. She'd slept longer than she intended.

Then she smelled the rich aroma of fresh-ground coffee. Fully awake now, she realized it was Rafe in her bathroom. Slipping on her robe, she went into the kitchen. The coffee had just finished brewing. She took down two mugs and filled them, then hesitated. Though she was married to Rafe, she had no idea what he took in his coffee, so she left it black.

When she heard the shower turn off, she took his cup of coffee and headed back to the bathroom, knocking lightly on the door. Rafe opened it, wearing one of her peach-colored towels wrapped around his waist. Beads of water spread across the dark bronze skin of his shoulders and chest—a chest that was thickly covered with dark hair.

Suddenly she felt extremely self-conscious. Clearly recognizing this, he watched her in amusement. "I like the service here. I'll have to stay again when I'm in town," he joked.

She swallowed tightly. "I don't know how you like your coffee, so I left it black."

He took the mug from her. "I take my coffee black, thank you."

He sipped the coffee, enjoying the rich hot liquid, and at the same time savoring the heat that built between them.

Allie quickly stepped back from the door, obviously not at all comfortable sharing her small apartment with a man she didn't know well. Rafe found that rather endearing somehow. It meant that she wasn't the kind of woman who had strange men going in and out of her life on a casual basis.

"We leave in half an hour," she informed him, then added with an attempt at a smile, "You're on *my* bathroom time now. I'll give you five more minutes."

Just a little over an hour later, Allie swung out of the French bakery, La Boulangerie, which was on the way to her office. Neither she nor Rafe had mentioned what happened the night before . . . her nightmare, the way he had comforted her, and the unsettling sense of both physical and emotional intimacy that they had briefly shared.

They ate in her car on the way to the office. Rafe took a bite of croissant, then shook his head. "A French bakery owned by a Chinese baker." Skeptically eyeing the croissant, he said, "I wonder if I'll find my fortune inside."

Allie grinned. "I know it's a little odd. But he makes the best French pastry in town."

Rafe nodded agreement as he finished the croissant, then took another one from the box.

A few minutes later Allie turned into the familiar parking area of the Bon Marché building and parked next to Julia's Mercedes coupe. She knew that Julia had probably been there since before seven. She liked to come down and work before the phone started ringing during normal office hours, when everyone else got in.

How many times, Allie wondered, had she brought Quon Lee's pastry to early work sessions with Julia? They'd drunk coffee brewed to the consistency of mud, and worked long hours, particularly during the Edgewater project, and Allie had loved it.

Now Allie wanted Rafe to meet Julia, to know the creative genius behind the project. She wanted him to see the site plans, sheet upon sheet of schematics, and countless elevations. Then she wanted him to see Edgewater itself, because this type of project, blended with its own inherent legacy of design, was what she wanted for El Sureno.

Turning to him as they entered the building, she said, "About Julia . . ."

"You don't have to warn me. I assume she's pretty tough."

That was the usual assumption about a woman who'd been in the business for over fifty years and been very successful at it.

"She can definitely be tough when she needs to be," Allie admitted. "But I think you'll like her. She doesn't compromise on things that are important to her. She's a bit like you that way." They entered the elevator, and Allie punched the button for the top floor. Taking a deep, steadying breath, she went on. "We should agree on how I'm going to introduce you to everyone."

"We *are* married, Allie."

"For business purposes only," she reminded him. "There's no need for anyone outside Pebble Beach to know it."

Rafe was surprised that her attitude irritated him. No, it did more than irritate him, it made him furious. Why should he care? he asked himself. Then he realized why he instinctively reacted against what she was suggesting—she wanted to keep her relationship with him a secret, just as he'd been kept a secret when he was a child.

All the old shame and anger welled up inside him, and he said tightly, "I'm not going to start keeping secrets now. And neither are you."

They had arrived on the top floor, and Rafe opened the old-fashioned elevator gate. As they stepped out, Allie said quickly, "I just want to find the right time to tell everyone."

"*Now* is the right time."

"But this so-called marriage is only temporary anyway," she argued.

"Then you can announce to the world when we decide to end it. But I'm not going to be some dirty little secret that you're ashamed to tell your friends and family."

She blanched as she realized how she must have sounded. "I didn't mean it that way."

"*Good.*"

"*Fine.*"

It seemed more and more of their conversations ended in anger. At this rate, they wouldn't even be speaking to each other by the end of the day.

They had reached the reception area, and the young red-haired secretary, Maggie, squealed as she came out of her chair and embraced Allie. "Allie! Welcome back! When did you get back?"

"Last night. But I'm here for only a few days."

"Does Julia know?"

"I called her after we got in."

"It's been quiet around here without you. The old work-horse even took some time off."

"So I hear."

Glancing around Allie, Maggie's eyes widened appreciatively as she saw Rafe. "I'm Maggie Dawson, the secretary here. Allie and Julia think they run this place, but I'm the *real* power behind the throne. I keep everyone in line."

"I'll bet you do a great job too," Rafe said, taking her hand, and holding on to it for just a moment longer than necessary. Maggie was charmed clear to her toes. He went on. "I'm Rafe Sloan." Before Allie could say anything, he said, "I'm Allie's husband."

Allie braced herself as Maggie slowly turned to look at her "*Husband?* Are you serious?"

Not really, Allie wanted to say. Instead, she replied evenly, "Yes, it's true."

"Wait till Julia hears!" Then, "Oh, my God, Don Chamberlain called!" Glancing guiltily at Rafe, she explained in a rush, "I'm sorry, I shouldn't have said anything. But don't worry, Mr. Sloan, they went out only a few times."

"That's all right, Maggie," he said with a smile. "This caught all of us by surprise."

Allie said quickly, "I'll take Rafe into Julia's office now, if she's free."

"Go ahead, she isn't busy," Maggie replied, still looking embarrassed about her faux pas.

As they walked toward the last door off the wide hallway, Rafe said in a low voice, "So who's Don Chamberlain?"

"No one you need to be concerned about," Allie answered tersely.

Rafe liked Julia Winslow immediately. He was familiar with her work. He found it functional yet with a real style that had a sort of timelessness about it. It would seem modern fifty years from now.

Julia herself turned out to be definitely no-nonsense, almost fanatically pragmatic, a daughter of the old school of Frank Lloyd Wright. Meeting her now, Rafe could see that she was a woman who had gone her own way, thumbed her nose at her critics and contemporaries, and, judging by the shelves covered with plaques and trophies, collected countless awards in spite of all of them.

When Allie introduced them, he smiled, then said, "I'm familiar with your work. I like it."

Julie eyed him critically, then responded, "I have two cardinal rules as an architect—never forget the client, and don't build monuments to yourself."

"It would be tough for any monument to live up to your reputation."

Julia laughed heartily, a laugh that was surprisingly big for such a small woman. "You have far more charm than is good for you. I like that in a man. What do you do?"

"I build things."

"A contractor, eh?" She glanced at Allie. "How did you get tied up with this fellow?"

"Well, actually . . ." Allie stammered.

Rafe said without hesitation, "Actually, we're married."

Julia was stunned. "I would say you're kidding, but clearly you're serious. Well . . . congratulations."

"Thank you," Allie murmured self-consciously, unable to meet Julia's look. She went on. "I need to pick up the plans for the Edgewater project."

In a tone that brooked no disagreement, Julia said, "While you do that, Rafe and I will chat."

Allie was more than reluctant to leave Rafe alone with Julia, but she had no choice.

When she was gone, Rafe glanced over at some architectural renderings framed on the wall. "Your newer designs are softer than what you used to do. They really blend in with the environment."

"Noticed that, did you?" She studied him approvingly.

"You have a good eye. Not the usual blind spot of most contractors. We're generally lucky if they can even read a set of drawings."

"I taught myself to read drawings a long time ago. I didn't have so much ego about my own expertise that I'd completely discount someone else's."

"Someone who likes to learn," she said, nodding again. Gesturing toward the glass-enclosed office across the way, where Allie was pulling rolls of plans from the drawers, she went on. "She's a lot like that." Then she added with some amusement, "I'm glad you like the improvements in my designs over the past few years. If you'll look closely at those pictures, you'll see some interesting references at the bottom."

He looked at each of the drawings of the finished projects, all exceptional works of art, showing full landscapes in brilliant, precise watercolors. Listed at the bottom was: Alexandra Wyatt, Architect, Winslow and Associates.

"Her projects?"

"For the most part, with a little guidance from me. I believe in giving credit where credit is due. She's very talented. She has a rare gift for seeing through to the heart of a project while at the same time never losing sight of its function or design. And she has absolutely no ego about her work.

"Take it from someone who's worked with some of the biggest egos in the industry, that girl is remarkable. She also has something else that most of us never have, or if we do, we somehow manage to lose it along the way."

"What's that?" he asked quietly.

"She has heart. It's in everything she creates. If she doesn't believe in it all the way, or believe that she can somehow enhance it, she'll walk away from it. I've seen her do it."

"That is sometimes called shortsightedness."

"No, my dear, it's called conscience. And God knows, few of us hold on to ours for long."

Julia watched as he stared through the glass at the young woman in the adjacent office, and realized that his expression was one of surprise.

"You two don't know each other very well, do you?" Julia commented bluntly.

"It was a rather sudden decision," he admitted.

"She's been gone a little over two weeks," Julia began in blunt summation. "Before that I never heard diddly-squat about you. The first time I heard anything about the Sloans was when she decided to take her leave of absence. Her grandmother called me."

"I see."

"No, I don't think you do." She sat down in the leather Gunlocke chair behind her desk. "I don't know all the details, but I know that whatever that young woman is about, she doesn't play games. Don't you play games with her."

There was a definite warning in her tone.

Rafe replied bluntly, "I don't play games either, Ms. Winslow."

"Good, then we just might get along."

Allie returned to find them sitting across Julia's massive desk from each other. She glanced suspiciously from one to the other. "What have you two been talking about?"

Before Julia could form an appropriate response, Rafe said with some amusement, "Personal style. We were both admiring yours."

"I see." She really didn't see at all, except to understand that they weren't about to tell her. She crossed the room and laid the armful of plans out across Julia's drafting table.

"I wanted Rafe to see the plans of Edgewater so that he could grasp the sort of development I have in mind. I thought we might fly over this afternoon, if there's time."

Julia looked at him with renewed interest. There was a great deal more to this young man than just the wedding ring he'd put on Allie's Wyatt's finger. She wanted to find out just how much more. "Why don't you drive on out to Lake Stevens?" Julie suggested to her. "I'll show him the plans. He'll understand most of it if he's as good as you say he is."

That caught Rafe off guard. He didn't realize that Allie had said anything to Julia about what she had to do.

"I don't know how long I'll be. I need to talk to my grandmother. There's a great deal I have to explain," Allie said.

Julie looked slightly amused. "Yes, there is. Take your time."

Rafe turned to Allie. "I'd like to go out with you."

He said it so simply, as if it were the most natural thing in the world for a new husband to want to meet family he wasn't yet acquainted with. Except that this wasn't the usual marriage, and he wasn't the typical husband.

"That's not necessary," Allie told him. "It would be better if I went alone."

"Why would it be better? We're in this together," he reminded her.

He went on. "We'll have lunch, because neither of us has had much in the way of a meal the past two days, and I'll drive you out to Lake Stevens."

She glanced across the desk at Julia. Julia's expression was one she'd seen countless times before when evaluating a client—keen appraisal, only occasionally followed by approval. What she saw now was definitely approval, and it stunned her. Julia never made snap judgments about people, and she was never wrong. In this case, for some reason, she approved of Rafe Sloan.

"It doesn't look as if I have much choice in the matter," she said, reluctantly giving in.

"I'll put in a call to Dan Culhagen," Julia said, referring to Edgewater's owner. "He'll welcome you with open arms. Probably give you the bridal suite at the inn."

Allie was distinctly uncomfortable at that thought, but she could hardly ask Julia to request separate rooms for them. It was a problem that was going to keep coming up. It had to be dealt with. Either that, or one of them was going to have to get used to sleeping on couches.

Rafe joined them at the elevator.

"Keep in touch, kiddo," Julia said with an affectionate hug for Allie.

"I will," Allie assured her affectionately. "We'll need your expertise if we can put this together."

"I can come down to Monterey with a few days notice," Julia said.

"I'm counting on it."

Julia rode down in the elevator with Rafe and Allie. "I'll help in any way I can. You know that. But this is your project, my dear. It has enormous possibilities."

"It's a little daunting."

With a glance at Rafe, Julia said, "With a top-notch team, you can do it."

Allie hugged her as they stepped out of the elevator. "Thanks for all your support."

Julia held her hand out to Rafe. "That project has promise, but it won't be easy."

He glanced at Allie. "I've already discovered that."

Julia caught the look that passed between them. There was a lot more going on than either of them had volunteered. But she decided to say nothing about it. Instead, she told them both, "Call me and let me know what's happening on that project."

"She likes you," Allie said as they swung out onto the highway that led to Lake Stevens.

"You sound surprised," he responded with a wry smile.

"I guess I am, just a little. She usually doesn't make snap judgments about people."

"How often is she wrong?"

Allie admitted reluctantly, "I've never known her to be wrong."

"Then maybe you should trust her judgment," he suggested, giving her a direct look.

Disconcerted, she turned her attention back to the road. He studied the soft angles of her features, the way the wind from the open window teased tendrils of soft gold hair against her cheek, the way she brushed it back when it tangled with the lashes of those clear blue eyes, or caught at her lips.

He was learning about her—the subtle changes of emotion in her voice, the careful control that she kept rigidly in place, the nervous gesture of pushing back her hair, the shadows that moved behind those blue eyes and revealed the pain she tried to hide. He saw those shadows now—deep, troubled shadows that turned her eyes from that clear blue to almost slate.

"I won't be a dirty little secret, Allie."

That had been *his* pain. Guilt filled him as he realized he hadn't considered hers.

They turned off the highway and skirted the peaceful little lake shimmering with the reflected gold, amber, and crimson colors of the trees that lined the banks. A lone, single-sail boat skimmed across the water. Winter was on the way in the Northwest. It would be kept at bay only a few more weeks.

Then Allie turned into a driveway and stopped the car.

She sat there as she had only slightly more than two weeks earlier, wondering how she would confront her grandmother about her memories of the murder of her mother. Now she was about to confront her with something nearly as devastating. Her slender knuckles went white over the curve of steering wheel.

Rafe saw the torment in her features. He laid his hand over hers at the wheel, curving his warm fingers over hers. "I didn't realize this was going to be so hard."

"Losing my mother was very difficult for my grandparents. She was all they had." Her voice was choked, barely under control.

"Until they brought you to live with them."

She nodded. "In a way, they transferred all the love for my mother to me. I can't bear the thought of hurting her more than I already have." She looked at him then, trying to make him understand, at the same time feeling a sense of futility about it. How could he possibly understand?

"She holds the Sloans responsible for my mother's death."

"I see." He drew a deep breath, then looked away. "We'd better get this over with as soon as possible. You did want to make that five o'clock flight out of Seattle."

She realized that he had no intention of remaining in the car as she had hoped he might. Pulling her hand from under his, she jerked the wheel and drove down the tree-shaded driveway. Cutting the engine, she got out of the car, not waiting for Rafe.

Her knees were wobbly, her stomach tied up in knots. The nervousness inside her now was different from the nervousness she'd felt a few weeks earlier when she'd come out to confront her grandmother. Then she had begged for the truth *from* her grandmother. Now she had to tell her grandmother something she knew would cause devastating pain. As she started to walk up the steps, Rafe caught up with her. She ignored his curious glance.

Anna opened the front door and came down the steps to wrap her arms around her. "Oh, Allie!" she exclaimed through laughter and tears as she hugged her hard. "It's so good to see you, sweetheart." She held Allie at arm's length and looked at her carefully through tear-filled eyes. "You look . . . fine," she said with more than a little surprise as she laid a hand against Allie's cheek. "Maybe a little thin. You always were too thin."

Then Anna Wyatt hugged her again, as if Allie were really safe now that she was back in Lake Stevens again, and in her arms. "It's *so* good to have you home!"

Allie slowly withdrew from her grandmother's embrace, but still holding on to that strong, warm hand that had comforted her through so many childhood fears and illnesses. She knew she couldn't delay introductions any longer. Taking a deep breath to ease the knot in her stomach, she held her grandmother's hand very tightly.

"There is someone I would like you to meet, Gram," she finally managed to say, glancing over at Rafe. She'd seen the expression on his face dozens of times over the past two weeks—aloof, impassive, completely unemotional.

"This is—"

His expression shifted ever so slightly, and he held out his hand as he cut off Allie's introduction. "My name is Rafe Estrada," he lied, taking Anna Wyatt's hand in his. "I'm a business associate of Allie's."

"Business associate?" Anna asked.

Allie stared at him with a mixture of disbelief and uncertainty.

He went on. "We're going to be working together on a project." His gaze met Allie's briefly. For an instant she saw a flash of something enigmatic in his dark eyes. Whatever it was, she was silently grateful for the lie.

Anna looked over at Allie. "I didn't know you were starting a new project. When did all this happen?"

Allie looped her arm through her grandmother's as she walked with her into the house. "It happened over the past few weeks. It's in California, Gram. The Sloan ranch at Big Sur." She felt her grandmother stiffen beside her.

"I thought you were home to stay."

"No," Allie said gently. "I wanted to show Rafe the

Edgewater project. We have similar ideas in mind for the ranch, and I wanted to get Julia's input as well. Hopefully, she'll be working on the project with us."

"I see." Anna couldn't disguise the disappointment in her voice. "Then this was a business trip."

"Not just business, Mrs. Wyatt," Rafe assured her. "Allie's main concern was to see you. I just decided to come along for the ride."

Anna smiled softly, her face softened with pleasure. "I see. Welcome, Mr. Estrada."

Over her grandmother's head, Allie gave him a grateful look.

"Actually, I'm the one who made Allie late coming out here. I met with Julia this morning about the project at Big Sur, and our meeting went late."

Anna beamed. "You're forgiven, Mr. Estrada, now that I have Allie for a few hours." As they went into the house, she asked, "Can you stay over?"

"We can't, Gram," Allie explained. "Rafe wants to see the Edgewater project. I made arrangements to take him out there this evening, and then we have to get back to Monterey."

"Well, come in. I want you to tell me everything. I have some wine." She glanced warmly at Rafe. "I even have some beer. Allie's grandfather used to like it."

"Wine will be fine."

It turned out to be an unexpectedly pleasant afternoon. Rafe left them to talk while he explored the farm. Allie's gaze followed him out the back door into the yard.

"I like him," Anna said. "He's a fine young man."

"You and Julia," Allie said with a shake of her head. She saw her grandmother's eyebrows go up. Anna knew how few people Julia liked.

Suddenly Allie was overwhelmed by conscience. Rafe had lied for her. She had no idea why. But she didn't feel comfortable continuing the lie, even though she knew the pain the truth would cause her grandmother.

"There's something I have to tell you . . ."

"About the Sloan family."

"Yes . . ."

"I read in the Seattle paper about Mackenzie Sloan's death." Then she surprised Allie by saying, "I'm very sorry, my dear. In the brief time your grandfather and I knew him, he seemed a very fine man."

"He was," Allie agreed with feeling.

"I suppose you know now that he wanted you to live with him and his wife, after"—she couldn't bring herself to say it, and simply finished by saying—"afterward."

"Yes, he told me." Allie shook her head sadly. "We had so little time together. But in that time I became very fond of him."

Her grandmother followed Allie's gaze into the backyard. "In many ways Mr. Estrada reminds me of Mac Sloan. Do you think that strange?"

Allie stared at her grandmother. Was it possible that she guessed?

"No, I don't think that's so strange at all."

Anna went on in a tentative voice. "Have you remembered anything more about . . . about what happened that night?"

"Bits and pieces," she admitted. Suddenly restless, she stood and slowly paced the living room.

"I know my father didn't kill her, Gram."

"Oh, Allie . . ."

"I remembered." There was silence in the small living room.

Finally, her grandmother said in a quiet voice, "Tell me."

Allie walked out to the small pen where her grandmother still kept chickens and a couple of pygmy goats. She found Rafe leaning over the top rail of the fence. In spite of the expensive short coat and the polished brown loafers, he looked as if he belonged there, casually resting his arms on the fence, occasionally tossing grain to the chickens on the other side.

"Thank you."

"For what?"

"For not saying anything about . . . us."

Rafe looked away from Allie. He was silent for a moment, then he began slowly. "I never knew my grandmother Sloan . . .

she was dead by the time I entered the picture. Not that she would have been happy about having a bastard grandson. After all, she *was* a Sloan of Pebble Beach, and the family has always been deeply conscious of the image it feels it has to maintain. But I do remember my grandmother Estrada. She loved me unconditionally, no matter what I did to break her heart. And I did plenty when I was a teenager."

Finally, Rafe looked at Allie, guilt written all over his face. "I've always regretted that. In many ways your grandmother reminds me of her."

"She's had so much pain in her life. Losing her only child, then her husband. I'm all she has, and I don't want to do anything that would cause her more pain."

Rafe looked at her thoughtfully. "What about *your* pain?"

"What do you mean?" she asked.

"I mean, maybe it would be easier if you would put what happened with your parents behind you. It's in the distant past. It's over."

"The past is never over," Allie said firmly. "I can't put it behind me until I understand what really happened that night."

Rafe frowned. "Sometimes you're better off not knowing the truth."

"I don't agree with that at all. It's always better to know the truth, even when it's painful."

"What if you never remember?"

"I'll stay there until I do," she finished stubbornly.

"I wish you'd give it up, Allie."

"Why?" she demanded angrily. "Why do you keep discouraging me from trying to remember what happened that night?"

"I'm not trying to discourage you."

"Yes, you are! From the very first, you've been dead set against it!"

"It's for your own good," he insisted.

"Is it?" she asked. Then, looking at him directly, she asked the question that had hung in the air between them almost from the first moment they'd met. "Are you afraid of what I might remember, Rafe?"

His face clouded with anger, and she knew she'd gone too

far. But she had no choice. She had to know what part, if any, he'd played in the tragedy that had led to both her parents' deaths.

But instead of answering, he said in a hard, cold voice, "We'd better be going. We have a plane to catch."

21

"I'LL GET YOU THE damned money!" Nicky shouted into the phone. His fingers splayed across his forehead as if he could physically remove the pounding that had started with too many margaritas and escalated to a crescendo with the call he'd been dreading.

The voice at the other end of the phone was utterly cold and without emotion. "When?"

"I just need a *little* more time," he pleaded. "There's been a minor delay."

"That's not what my employer has heard, Mr. Benedict. The sale of the Sloan ranch is off."

"That's not true!" Nicky lied. "The sale *will* go through. These things just take time." Using a phrase he'd heard Gavin utter countless times, he went on. "It isn't like selling some stinking piss-hole farm in Salinas. There are a lot of details to be worked out. The buyer's hesitant . . . the economy isn't good right now . . ."

He was fumbling for excuses, and he knew the caller was all too aware of it.

"That's not what we heard, Mr. Benedict. According to our sources, your uncle no longer controls the ranch."

"Fuck your sources!" Nicky exploded, then immediately regretted his outburst. He went on desperately. "I mean, they don't know everything. I admit there's been a delay, but it's nothing we can't fix. It'll be a matter of only a few more days." He could feel the slight tickling sensation of sweat rolling down his cheek, even though it was chilly in his bedroom. His palm was so sweaty, it slipped against the receiver that he held tightly.

"You told us everything was taken care of."

"It was—it is! Look, you guys will have your money, plus a very nice profit in interest. I need a little more time."

"Time just ran out." The phone clicked and went dead in his hand.

"Nicky?"

The naked woman in bed beside him moved closer, stroking his flaccid flesh.

"Come here," she murmured soothingly. "I'll make it all better."

Jerking away from her, he stood abruptly. Taking a pack of cigarettes with him, he stood at the window with the pricy ocean view. Condos in exclusive Spanish Bay weren't cheap, but Nicky didn't have to worry about the cost. The company paid for everything. *Almost* everything. Unfortunately, it wouldn't pay his gambling debts.

He lit a cigarette as he stood naked before the glass, looking out at the moonlight shining on the ocean, and the twinkling lights of houses around the curve of the bay. The exotic Argentinian with the proper English accent followed him to the windows, rubbing her bare breasts against his back.

"Who was that, darling?"

Nicky hesitated, then said shortly, "A business associate."

"At this time of night? What did he want?"

Turning to face her, he enveloped the slender woman in his arms. "He was calling about some money we need for a project. I tried to explain that I don't have it right now."

An image swam through his thoughts—*money*. Lots of money. It was all that mattered. He'd learned that long ago, and now, finally, it was almost within his reach. He would have had it now if *she* hadn't shown up—Alexandra Wyatt Sloan.

Damn her! he wanted to scream. If she hadn't come back, if

she'd stayed forgotten, everything would have been all right, and he wouldn't have to deal with this now.

He felt the woman in his arms press her body against his.

"I have some money," she suggested with a soft catch in her throat as his mouth wandered across a particularly sensitive spot. "If it's only a matter of a few thousand . . . I could get it for you tomorrow."

Nicky laughed, a hard, brittle sound. "A few thousand? Christ!" Then he closed his eyes and concentrated on her long, dark hair swirling about her bare shoulders.

He'd talk to them again in the morning. He'd make them understand. Tonight he had other things to do. . . .

He was standing by the phone when the call came in just before noon. He'd been phoning everywhere, trying to reach his "business associate" and becoming more and more frantic with each passing hour. Then a call came in from the equestrian club.

"Mr. Benedict? You'd better get out here right away. There's been some trouble."

"What trouble? What are you talking about?"

"It's your horse, Mr. Benedict. Your trainer just found him." He repeated helplessly, "You better get out here—"

The call ended abruptly as Nicky hurled the telephone against the wall. There was no need to go out to the club, he knew what he would find.

"That bitch! She'll pay! I swear she'll pay!" he cried as he felt the glory of the coveted number-ten ranking and his position on the polo team slip through his fingers.

Then, through his fury, a terrifying thought struck him. They wouldn't stop with destroying his horse. They would come after him.

Valentina drove recklessly, upset about her conversation with her brother. He'd been practically hysterical when he called her, and it took forever to finally get him calmed down. He kept saying there had to be a way to stop Rafe and Alexandra. She agreed, of course. Rafe and Alexandra had ruined everything for everyone, especially for her.

Married! My God, every time she thought about it, she

wanted to kill the bitch. Gavin and her father had been in meetings with attorneys since that awful board meeting, and Gavin was confident that with time there would be a way to stop them. But time was a luxury Val couldn't afford. She'd ordered the new engine the same day Mac died, planning to pay for it with her share of his estate.

Now, thanks to Alexandra Wyatt—*Barbara's* daughter, Val thought scathingly—Val couldn't afford to pay for the engine. Without it she couldn't race. And without racing, life was hardly worth living. It was too utterly dull to bother with.

Rafe and Alexandra . . . Val almost laughed as she thought of that prim, proper little mouse of a woman with a man as sexy as Rafe. He was wasted on a woman like that. It would have been funny if Val hadn't been after him so long herself. Feeling cheated, she slammed the gearshift down into low as she took the turn a little too fast, coming off the highway onto the Laguna Seca raceway road. She ground the car to a halt in a spray of dust and gravel outside the garage pit area, where crews were preparing for the next race two days later. This would be her first race with the new engine, and she wanted to make certain that nothing went wrong. She intended to win this race.

But as Val drew near her own garage area, she saw the long flatbed trailer parked in front. Rounding it, she read the logo across the door, then broke into a run. She found Bill and her line mechanic arguing with someone.

Forcing herself to slow to a walk and approach them calmly, she called out, "What's going on?"

"They've come for the engine," Bill said bluntly. "They'll take it and the car along with it if we don't pull it."

She faced the man who'd been talking to Bill. He was dressed in immaculate coveralls with the same logo as the truck. "No one is taking my car, or my engine."

Unfazed, he asked, "You the owner?"

"That's right. I'm Valentina Sloan Charteris, and I own Sloan Racing."

"I don't care if you're Mario Andretti. It's not your engine until it's paid for. Half up front, half on delivery. It was delivered, but your check for the down payment bounced. I've got instructions to pick up the engine."

"The hell you do!" Val exploded, humiliated by the knowledge that everyone around them could hear their conversation about her financial situation. "Look, I'm good for that money."

"Not according to your bank." Sidestepping her, he called out to two other men dressed in identical coveralls. "Let's get on with this."

"You can't just walk in here and take my car! You need a court order."

"I don't need a damn thing, lady. Until you pay for it, this engine isn't yours."

Desperately, she tried to stall. "I can get you the money, I just need a little time. But *please* don't take the engine. I have to qualify today. I can't very well do that without a goddamn engine!"

"Sorry. No money, no engine. Take it outta the car, or we'll take the car too."

Val tried to rein in her famous temper. "Give me until noon. I'll be back here with a cashier's check for the full amount, I promise. Just *don't* take that engine!"

For one moment she thought he was going to say no. Finally, he replied, "Tell you what I'll do. I've got a few deliveries to make down the pit line to some of the other garages. You got until noon, lady. If you're not back here then with a cashier's check, the engine goes on the truck. Is that clear?"

"Perfectly clear," she said in a tight voice. She went on to Bill, "I'll be back. Don't let them touch that car."

Outside the garage she climbed into her car and punched in the overseas number she had been instructed never to use unless it was an emergency. Well, she thought desperately, this was an emergency.

Called to the phone by a servant in his house in Sydney, Marcus Field was furious. "Dammit, Valentina, I told you never to call me here!"

"You said if it was an emergency—"

"What's wrong?" he snapped with a distinct lack of concern in his voice.

She closed her eyes, willing herself to sound seductive rather than desperate. "Something has come up . . . I need some money."

The moment he realized this was about money, not a life-or-death situation, Marcus Field's anger rose. "I left several thousand in your account, Valentina! That should be enough to keep you going comfortably till I get back there next month."

Val's voice rose. "It's not enough! You don't understand! Look, Marcus, things are very expensive . . . maintaining the house . . . car repairs . . ."

"Has the Jag broken down?"

"No, the damn Jag hasn't broken down." Taking a deep breath, she lowered her voice to a sensual whisper, "Honey, I need to pay a few bills on the race car."

There was a dead silence. Then, in a voice no longer angry but cold, he said, "So *that's* the emergency."

"Marcus, they're going to take away the new engine! I need it! I can't race without it." She heard the begging tone in her voice and hated herself for it. Her fingers tightened over the phone until they went white. Making it all infinitely worse was her knowledge that she wouldn't have had to do this, if only the sale of the ranch had gone through.

"I'm tired of supporting your expensive hobby."

"But you know how much I enjoy it, sweetheart." She swallowed against the bile that rose in her throat. "Just think how exciting it is when you watch me race. Then afterward . . ." She left the rest unsaid.

"I'm sorry."

"Marcus, I *need* two hundred thousand dollars. I've never asked for much . . ."

There was a burst of sarcastic laughter at the other end. "Two hundred thousand dollars?" Then, "Sorry, darling. You're good, but you're not *that* good. Maybe if you were twenty—"

She felt as if she were going to be ill. "God, Marcus, don't make me beg."

"I don't want you to beg, Valentina. It's not your style. Why don't you ask that young man for the money—the one you keep around for entertainment while I'm away. I hear his family is well heeled. Or better yet, ask your cousin, Rafael Sloan. He's worth quite a lot now that he controls the Sloan ranch."

She felt sick inside. "Marcus . . ."

"Good-bye, luv. I think we've enjoyed about enough of each other's company. By the way, I'll send someone around to take care of the house. Thirty days ought to be enough time for you to get your things out. Oh, and Val, don't call here again. I mean it."

Val sat in the car—the car that Marcus Field owned, along with the beach house. All she owned were her clothes and the few pieces of jewelry he'd given her over the past three years. The Sloan Land Company would arrange a place for her to live, perhaps a condo like Nicky's. And they would get her a car, a nice one. But the house and the car wouldn't be hers any more than Marcus's beach house or Jaguar had been hers. And the company definitely wouldn't buy her a two-hundred-thousand-dollar engine.

She was about to lose the only thing that mattered to her, all because of Alexandra Sloan. God, she hated the bitch. She could happily wring her little neck. . . .

Gavin stood behind the desk in his office, too angry to sit down. Leaning across the desk, he slammed his hand down hard. "I don't want to hear any more talk about *possibilities*!" he shouted at David Benedict. "You're the legal counsel for this company, dammit! I want definite answers! How can we stop them?"

"I'm looking into it," David responded, keeping his voice low so as not to irritate the pain that raged behind his eyes. He'd had constant headaches ever since the fiasco of the board meeting. He went on helplessly. "It's all rather complicated."

"But is their marriage legal?"

"On the surface—yes. It *appears* to be legal, and their combined shares are definitely enough to outvote you."

Gavin snapped, "Well, stay on those probate officials and that attorney who specializes in inheritance."

"I will—" David began, but Gavin cut him off.

"There has to be some way we can prove the marriage is a fraud."

David shrugged miserably, trying to contain his own feelings of almost unbearable disappointment. *Freedom*—it had almost been within his grasp. He said with a heavy sigh, "Proving fraud wouldn't be easy. In these kind of circumstances—"

Again, Gavin cut him off. "Just do it! That's what I'm paying you for."

David winced at the blatant insult *"That's what I'm paying you for."* Just as his father-in-law had paid him years ago—*"I'll make it worth your while to marry my daughter."*

"The longer this takes," Gavin was saying, "the greater the risk that we'll lose the buyers, and that son of a bitch will be able to keep control. I'm going to stop them. I don't care what it takes. And you're going to help me do it."

How? David thought miserably as he left Gavin still fuming, and returned to his own office. Opening a bottle of antacid tablets, he took several. A moment later his secretary buzzed him to say that his wife was calling.

Reluctantly, he picked up the phone and asked bluntly, "What do you want, Charlotte?"

"What are you and Gavin going to do about this situation?"

He didn't have to ask which situation she was referring to. "Nothing yet. We don't have enough information on the legalities involved."

"Why not? My God, David, you're an attorney. You should know how to handle this."

He could have explained to her, as he had at length to Gavin, about the complexities involved—the probate of Mac's estate, the co-mingling of married persons' property, almost two hundred years of legal restrictions tied to the original land grant. But he didn't bother.

"Don't you have something to take your mind off this—charity work or shopping or something?" he suggested, dismissing her as he'd learned to do through the years in order to survive.

Charlotte heard the disdain in his voice and hated him for it. All the pain that had festered just below the surface throughout all the years of their marriage suddenly felt unbearable. "None of this would have happened if *she* hadn't come back," she said angrily. "The ranch would have been sold. I would have been rid of the damn place, with enough money to finally do whatever I wanted with my life."

David noticed that she said *I*, not *we*, but he didn't care. He said nothing.

"David!" she demanded. "Answer me."

"I have to go now, Charlotte. I have a great deal to do."

Erica curtly dismissed the maid, who had come in with a breakfast tray and had started to open the drapes in the bedroom. Leaving the breakfast tray untouched, she sat down in front of the mirror at her dressing table. The only light in the room came from a small Tiffany lamp on the table. Slowly lifting her gaze to her reflection, Erica tentatively touched the swollen, discolored skin across her right cheek, and winced at the pain. This wasn't the first time Gavin had hit her.

Tears welled in Erica's large, dark eyes, all the larger now in the pale shadow of her bruised face. With shaking hands she reached for the bottle of pain reliever. She took three pills, one more than the prescription called for, hoping it would numb the pain at her cheek. But there was no pill she could take for the deeper wound inside her—a wound she'd carried for over thirty years.

Miserably, she remembered the argument early that morning.

"It's Barbara, isn't it? It's always been Barbara! And now her daughter's here, ruining everything, just like Barbara ruined everything!"

She knew her anger would provoke Gavin, but she hadn't been able to stop herself. When he responded as he always did in these situations, there was no element of surprise, merely a repetition of the same old physical and emotional devastation that Erica had experienced throughout her marriage.

Before the board meeting Erica had believed that everything was finally going to be all right. The ranch would be sold, and they would be rid of all the old memories—all the old pain. But Alexandra had crushed Erica's desperate hopes. It was as if Barbara had risen from the dead—still young, still beautiful, still capable of making men fall in love with her, and thus ruining other people's lives.

Laying her head down on the glass-topped vanity table, Erica cried until she couldn't cry anymore. Slowly lifting her head, she stared at her reflection in the mirror. Instead of seeing her red, swollen eyes and bruised cheek, she saw Barbara—and knew that she'd never really died.

Erica got up and walked over to the bed. Sitting down on the edge, she opened the nightstand drawer. Her fingers brushed against the small revolver Gavin had bought her for protection after a series of burglaries had plagued the area the year before. The gun felt cool and smooth, and fit her hand perfectly. It was, of course, loaded.

It would be so easy to use, she thought. Then Barbara would finally be dead, and Erica wouldn't have to share Gavin with her anymore.

22

THE SKY OVER THE magnificent Seattle skyline was crystal-clear and vivid blue as Allie and Rafe drove out of the city toward Sea-Tac Airport. Two hours later they took off in a small commuter jet, flying over the alluring maze of deep green that is Puget Sound. An hour and a half after that, they circled the small airport on Orcas Island, and touched down in a smooth landing. The San Juans, a cluster of mostly uninhabited islands in the northern inlet of ocean, had been a favorite vacation spot for Allie and her grandparents when her grandfather was still alive. Because she knew the San Juans so well, she had been particularly excited about working on the Edgewater project there.

Remembering how cold it was at this time of year, particularly after the sun went down, Allie had packed warm clothes into a small duffel bag. She'd done this many times over the past eight years, when the job required her to stay over. Arriving at the site, she would change into jeans, hiking boots, and a thick sweater and jacket, and tuck the latest changes to the plans under her arm, as she surveyed the site, accompanied by engineers and inspection teams.

Now she tossed the bag into the backseat of the rental car,

and she and Rafe left the airport and turned onto the road that hugged the coastline. The wind had come up off the sound, where the Strait of San Juan de Fuca met the Strait of Georgia. The crisp salt-sea air was distinctly different from the air over the central California coast—chillier, heavy with the moisture that was so constant most of the year.

Allie glanced over at Rafe, who was driving the rented four-wheel-drive vehicle. He'd worn only the leather jacket that he'd brought from Monterey, yet he didn't seem to mind the cold.

Twilight descended around them as they wound their way along the narrow one-lane from the airport to the main road that encircled the island. The sky was turning gray, and behind them the enveloping darkness of the forest was broken only occasionally by tiny clusters of winking lights.

"We're staying at the Inn at Edgewater," she said. "It's at the entrance of the village. Dan Culhagen's offices are there, and you can see the mockup of the entire project."

Keeping his eyes on the unfamiliar, twisty road, he responded briefly, "Good."

Short as it was, it was the longest exchange they'd had since leaving her grandmother's house. Rafe's refusal to answer her accusation that he might have something to hide left her feeling frustrated and angry—and also just a bit guilty. What if she were being unfair to him? Perhaps his lack of support for her struggle to remember the events of that tragic night was simply what he said it was—a belief that it was best to put the past behind her. After all, her remembering what happened couldn't change it.

But she couldn't agree with that logic. She *had* to try to remember who had killed her mother, if for no other reason than to clear her father's name.

As they headed toward the Edgewater resort on the other side of the island, Allie gazed with pleasure on the deep opaque blue of the water, contrasting so strikingly with the red bark of the madrona trees and the dense evergreens covering the island. The trees grew right down to the water's edge on the rocky coastline, interspersed with huge gray boulders.

Clearly impressed, Rafe said, "It's really something, isn't it?"

Allie nodded. Even though she'd spent so much time here, it still took her breath away. "Every time I come back here, it takes me back to my days growing up, when my grandfather was alive. We came here a lot on vacations, and spent most of our time around boats and water. He taught me about kayaking."

Rafe gave her a surprise glance. "You know how to handle a kayak?"

She smiled modestly.

"I'm impressed. I tried it once off Catalina Island, and failed miserably," he admitted.

"It's hard to learn, but my grandfather was a great teacher." Remembering her grandfather's loving encouragement and infinite patience, Allie felt a sharp jolt of longing for him. After all these years she still missed him terribly. He had always told her she could do anything with her life, be anything she dreamed of. It was his encouragement that had motivated her to become an architect.

"I imagine it helps that the San Juans are in a protected inland waterway, so you don't get the rough waves of the open ocean," Rafe pointed out.

"You'd think so, but that's misleading. Each tide forces huge volumes of water through the narrow passages between the islands, making the currents powerful and treacherous. And the water's extremely cold. You can't survive for more than an hour in it."

Rafe frowned. "Sounds dangerous."

"It is," Allie agreed, "if you don't know what you're doing."

They lapsed into a silence that was surprisingly comfortable. The tension Allie had felt at her grandmother's house dissolved as they drove past lush green fields dotted with black-faced sheep grazing on tall grass shimmering with moisture. At times the trees lining the road formed a canopy of green overhead where the branches intertwined.

They drove through several tiny communities consisting of a small hotel or restaurant, and a store or two, before finally arriving at the main community of Eastsound, located at the northern edge of the large bay that divided the island. A couple of miles on the other side of it lay Edgewater. A resort and private residential community, it was the embodiment of a completely planned development that preserved the natural beauty of the heavily forested island. Yet it also maintained a delicate balance between carefully controlled growth within the boundaries of a fragile ecosystem.

As they came up over the crest of a low hill, then started to descend toward the development, Rafe let out a low whistle of admiration. "You were right—it's incredible."

Allie was more pleased by his compliment than she cared to admit. Trying to sound matter-of-fact, she explained, "It was the brain child of Daniel Culhagen, the billionaire."

"I heard he's crazy."

Allie grinned. "Crazy, eccentric, a genius—whichever word you choose depends on how you feel about him. I admired him because he did what a lot of people said couldn't be done. He developed a project of this size without sacrificing the natural beauty and integrity of the island."

"I'm surprised he didn't go bankrupt doing it," Rafe said bluntly.

"No way. Julia doesn't get involved in projects that will bankrupt her clients. It isn't good for business."

"How did he do it?"

"He'd heard of Julia's reputation, and decided she was the only one who could pull it off. She was wary of *his* reputation, but loved the challenge of the project."

"Julia didn't strike me as someone who can be ordered around. How did they work together?" Rafe asked curiously.

Allie smiled, remembering what it had been like when the two stubborn, strong-willed people came together. "He told her what he wanted, she told him what was possible and what wasn't. Since the island was privately owned, a great deal was possible. Somehow they made it through the first meetings without Daniel firing her or Julia walking off the project. After several more meetings they agreed on the concept for Edgewater. Realizing that it was the only way Julia would take the job, Daniel let her have complete design freedom."

Rafe gave Allie a sly grin. "Is that what you want with Rancho Sureno?"

She returned his grin. "Hey, I'm willing to work with you. If Daniel and Julia could work together, surely we can." She went on in a more serious tone. "When I worked on Edgewater with Julia, I thought it was the project of a lifetime. But it pales in comparison to what can be done with Rancho Sureno. We can make it something truly special, Rafe, something that other people can learn from. We don't have to rape the land to save it."

Her tone had grown fervent with the passion she brought to the project. Listening to her, Rafe felt himself responding to her unselfconscious use of the word *we*. He never spoke in terms of "we," only "I." It was disconcerting to hear Allie use the word so naturally—disconcerting but somehow touching.

Allie added hesitantly, "By the way . . . thank you for not saying anything to my grandmother this afternoon."

"There's nothing to thank me for," he said, fixing his gaze on the road ahead.

He was obviously still unhappy about the fact that Allie had wanted to keep his true identity a secret. She said defensively, "I *will* tell her. When the time is right . . ." Her voice trailed off guiltily.

Before he could frame a response, they turned onto a well-marked road with a large hand-carved wooden sign that said EDGEWATER. Julia had called Daniel Culhagen's office at Edgewater that morning, letting his staff know that Allie and a guest were flying out, and the security guard at the entrance gate waved them through.

Faith Talmadge, the manager, met them in the rustic but chic lobby of the inn. An attractive brunette who looked younger than her forty-odd years, she greeted Allie warmly. "It's so good to see you again."

"Thanks. It's good to get over for a visit."

Faith told them that Dan Culhagen, who lived at the outskirts of the village in the private residential section of Edgewater, had already gone for the day. He'd left word that he would see them in the morning, and he'd arranged for them to have the finest accommodations Edgewater offered, overlooking the cove and marina.

Faith and Allie had gotten to be friends over the course of her work on the project. The inn itself had been completed almost five years earlier, well before the residential section was finished. Dan immediately brought in Faith as manager, and she and Allie saw each other every time Allie came over.

Faith said, "Everyone in the Winslow office has a standing invitation for the grand opening, including reserved rooms. We've scheduled it for Thanksgiving weekend, and we're already booked solid."

Allie didn't want to explain to Faith that she probably wouldn't be able to get back here for some time. Instead, she smiled politely and said, "That's very generous of you and Dan."

Faith looked past Allie to Rafe with more than idle curiosity. Allie wasn't at all certain how much Julia had told Dan about Rafe. Playing it safe, she merely said, "Faith, this is Rafe Sloan. He's involved in a similar project in the Big Sur area of California. I wanted him to see what we did with Edgewater."

"Well, you definitely have the best architectural team for the job," Faith responded. Then, grinning at Allie, she added, "I understand congratulations are in order."

Allie tensed slightly, still more than a little uneasy with the arrangement between her and Rafe. She answered simply, "Yes, I suppose so."

"When did all this happen?"

"A couple of days ago," Rafe answered when Allie hesitated.

Faith's eyes widened. "And you're working? Not much of a honeymoon. Well, we'll do our best to help that situation along," she insisted playfully, leading them to the front desk. She asked the desk clerk for the keys to the Premier Suite. From the plans and countless meetings and discussion, Allie knew that she was giving them the bridal suite.

"Oh, we don't want any special treatment," Allie said quickly, mortified at the thought of staying in a room reserved for honeymooners.

Faith insisted. "Dan said you were to have the best."

Allie started to protest, then, noticing Rafe's amused expression, decided it was best to say nothing.

Taking the keys from the desk clerk, Faith escorted Rafe and Allie to the second floor. The inn was limited to just two stories, including the ground floor, so that the roofline didn't reach above the tallest tree line. This was in keeping with the rustic design of the overall resort that blended with the thick forest covering the island. All the heavy exterior beams and timbers came from the land cleared for the project. Huge rock had been brought in from the creeks and stream beds that fed into the ocean and used to make mammoth fireplaces big enough for a person to stand in.

But the exterior that blended so uniquely with the physical beauty of the island gave way to elegance inside. Gleaming pale wood floors were overlaid with thick wool carpets, especially hand-loomed in a design of flowers and the symbols of the ancient native island dwellers whose culture predated early American and Canadian explorers and settlers.

Figures of majestic black and white orca whales and dolphins bordered the carpet. The San Juans were their summer feeding grounds, and through the summer months orcas were frequently seen in the bay on their migration to the north.

The walls of the inn were hand-rubbed pine, and every grain and burl gleamed softly in the lamplight. Etched dual-pane cathedral windows formed the front walls of the inn, providing a breathtaking view of the curve of the bay, enveloping resort, the pristine blue waters occasionaly dotted with whales, and the strait that expanded to the northern waters of the Pacific Ocean beyond.

As Faith led them to their suite, Rafe said admiringly, "I have to admit, this is a lot more than I was expecting."

Allie said proudly, "The inn sets the tone for the entire development. We used natural stone and rustic wood everywhere. We built footbridges across the streams instead of damming them or diverting them. That way, there's little effect on the natural wildlife."

Faith added enthusiastically, "It's nothing to see raccoons and squirrels on the second-floor balconies, and deer and foxes in the meadows, or even an occasional bear lumbering around the edge of the resort. It's very much a wilderness, still, and people—not animals—are the guests."

They had arrived at the rustic wooden double doors of the Premier Suite. Faith said with a smile, "I don't have to show you around, Allie. After all, you helped design it."

Inside, she crossed the large sitting room, with its heavy, overstuffed furnishings, thick carpet, and clear-heart redwood walls, to the bank of cathedral windows that followed the steeply angled line of the roof. Drawing back the curtains, she revealed glass doors that opened out onto a large railed deck.

She touched a panel of lights, illuminating the enclosed garden atrium at one end of the deck that included a bubbling, steaming hot tub. At the touch of another switch, the glass walls of the spa opened to the deck.

"We get a lot of snow in the winter," Faith explained. "The movable glass walls allow year-round use of the spa. Some people leave them open in winter. They like the combination of hot bubbling water and cold night air."

Then, touching another button, she set a fire blazing cheerfully in the stone fireplace. "Each fireplace is fitted with the latest in catalytic emissions arresters," she informed Rafe. "We have virtually no air pollution on the island. We get the firewood from areas on Vancouver Island set aside for forestation maintenance."

Rafe shook his head in amazement. Turning to Allie, he asked, "Was all this your idea?"

"Mine and Julia's. I told you that we can do a great deal more than just pour concrete over dirt."

As Faith left, she told them, "Dan said he would join you in the Blue Spruce Room for breakfast in the morning. He's looking forward to showing you around."

When Faith had closed the door behind her, Rafe and Allie stood awkwardly in the middle of the room. He could tell by the rigid set of her shoulders, and the nervous way she gripped the strap of her duffel bag, that she felt intensely uncomfortable, much more so than she'd been in her own apartment.

"Look, Allie . . ." he began.

Before he could finish, she said in a matter-of-fact tone, "I'll take the smaller bedroom. The larger one has the spa and a full sitting area, including a desk." Handing him the tube of plans for Edgewater that she'd brought along, she said, "You may want to look over the plans before you see the actual development tomorrow."

She was being determinedly businesslike about this. And why not? he asked himself. After all, in spite of the fact that they were in the honeymoon suite, that's what this was all about—business.

She went into the smaller bedroom, closing the door behind her and leaving him to take the larger one on the opposite side.

A few minutes later he knocked on the door she had left slightly ajar. When she opened it wide, he could see her heavy jacket lying across the bed, and the duffel bag sitting in the bottom of the closet. Out of the corner of his eye he noticed her hairbrush and other personal items set out on the dressing table. She had removed the band that secured her hair in a severe ponytail, and now her hair hung loose about her shoulders. It transformed the fragility of her features into a beguiling sensuality that he suspected she wasn't aware of. He'd never known a woman so unaware of her beauty, and he couldn't understand why there hadn't been a long string of men in her life making her all too aware of it.

"Are you hungry?" he asked.

"Yeah—starving."

"I was thinking about the Wine Press Room."

"All right. Just give me a minute to do something with myself," she said, starting to turn back into the room.

His fingers closed around her wrist, stopping her. "You don't need to do a thing to yourself."

Her free hand raked through her hair in the distinctive gesture he was beginning to know well.

In a husky voice he said, "You're beautiful just the way you are. Do you know that, Allie? Do you realize how beautiful you are?"

His touch and his words made her intensely nervous. Abruptly pulling her wrist from his gentle grasp, she brushed past him and moved into the sitting room.

"We'd better be going," she said with a self-conscious smile. "I think you'll like the Wine Press Room."

They ate fresh salmon grilled on an open-pit hickory fire, and drank delicious Washington wine. Allie made a none-too-subtle effort to keep the conversation within the safe boundaries of work. Only after they'd finished dinner and walked outside did Rafe persuade her to talk about the time she'd spent there as a child.

They stood on the deck outside the main entrance, enjoying the spectacular view of the lights on the water. The wide wraparound deck descended from different levels to a central deck with a fire pit in the middle. It was surrounded by chairs and tables, and rimmed with wooden bench seats.

"My grandfather brought me here several times to go fishing and kayaking," Allie began. "A friend of his owned a summer place at the other end of the island. The only way to get here then was on the ferry from the mainland. To get to his friend's cabin, which was pretty far off the only road, you had to go on foot, by horseback, or motor skiff."

"Sounds pretty isolated."

"It was primitive," she admitted. "No running water, only cold water from the pump shack, and an outhouse at the back of the cabin."

"And you loved it," he decided from her tone of voice.

"Of course. I was a child, and it seemed like high adventure. Real Robinson Crusoe stuff. We came out here every summer . . . until my grandfather died."

"It must have been difficult losing him," Rafe said gently.

"I loved him very much," she replied in a voice that trembled with the effort to suppress the sadness and loss that welled up within her. Propping her arms on the top railing of the deck, and looking out at the water, she went on. "He and my grandmother were the only family I had then. I wish I'd known I had other family. I wouldn't have felt so lonely."

"You were better off without them," Rafe said harshly. "I know from experience. I spent years trying to get away from them, and I probably would've been better off if I'd stayed away."

"Why did you leave after my father's trial?" she asked impulsively. She'd never asked before, though she'd wanted to.

He leaned back against the railing on bent elbows. His face was partially obscured by the darkness, and half illuminated by the light from inside the inn that shone through the wall of windows overlooking the deck. Allie had the sudden conviction that he wanted to hide in the shadows, to not let her see his expression.

He said slowly, "I was seventeen years old. Most of my life I'd been shuffled back and forth between my mother's family and the Sloans—not a situation that builds a sense of belonging in a kid. After my old man died, your parents and Mac were the only ones who gave a damn whether I lived or died. When Alan took me out to the ranch to live with all of you, it was the first really stable time of my life. After . . . after your mother died, Mac wanted me to live with him, but I figured I was better off on my own.''

''So you ran away.''

''I was used to being pretty much on my own,'' he said with a shrug.

It was a profoundly unsatisfactory answer to her question. Allie sensed that he wasn't telling her the whole truth, but she didn't feel she could challenge him. She knew only that more had gone on than he was willing to admit.

Allie was wearing only a cotton turtleneck shirt with a brocade vest over it. She shivered, as much from empathy for the aching loneliness of that seventeen-year-old as from the cold. Pulling off the V-neck sweater he'd worn over a blue chambray shirt, Rafe wrapped it around her shoulders. He held on to the long sleeves and looked intently at her.

''Now you'll be cold,'' she protested. As she met his look, she saw something dark and unreadable in his eyes, something that made her wary all over again about the bargain she'd agreed to.

Then he crossed the arms of the sweater and loosely tied them across her breasts. ''We do have to keep up appearances, Allie,'' he reminded her. ''We're supposed to be married, and I'm merely behaving like a solicitous husband.''

At the casual brush of his fingertips against her breasts, her breath froze in her lungs.

''You look very tired and very cold,'' he said gently. ''Let's go back in. We have a big day ahead of us tomorrow.''

She was tired, but neither exhaustion nor the cold prompted her to hurry toward the door leading into the inn. She wanted, needed, to put some distance between herself and this man who evoked such disturbing responses within her. As she passed the wall of windows, she caught the vague outline of her reflection in the glass, and instinctively backed away.

''What is it? Allie?''

Rafe's voice seemed to come from very far away. Then Allie felt his hand at her arm. Jerking away as if his touch burned her, she turned back toward the glass. Now there was nothing there but the thick glass, and on the other side the lobby of the inn.

Wrapping her arms tightly around herself, Allie responded distractedly, "Nothing. I . . . I'm just tired."

By the time they reached their suite, whatever it was that she'd experienced was gone. But she still felt tense. Glimpsing the Jacuzzi out on the deck, she thought how inviting it looked. A few minutes in that hot, swirling water might relax her enough to enable her to sleep more comfortably than she'd done the night before.

Catching her expression, Rafe asked, "Want to try it?"

She hadn't expected him to join her, and instinctively reacted against the idea. The thought of being in the small Jacuzzi with him was distinctly unsettling. But she was determined not to let it show. She wasn't about to act like a silly little fool around him.

"Sure, why not?" she responded with a forced casualness.

Neither had brought a swimsuit, but the hotel gift shop sold them, and in a few minutes they'd changed into their new suits. Rafe was already sitting in the spa when Allie came out of her bedroom. She felt extremely self-conscious as he watched her cross the room toward him. The selection of swimsuits available in the gift shop had been extremely limited, and Allie had been forced to buy a white maillot that was cut much lower across her breasts, and much higher across her hips, than she normally would have worn.

She slipped into the water at the far side of the spa from Rafe, and the hot water covered her up to her breasts.

"Nice suit," he said easily.

Feeling herself blush to her very roots, Allie stammered a polite "Thanks."

He went on, with the barest hint of a smile. "Of course, if we were in L.A., we wouldn't have bothered wearing anything. Everyone pretty much goes au naturel down there."

"Well, we're not in L.A.," Allie pointed out, forcing herself to meet his look.

"Right." He added with a mock sigh, "Too bad."

In spite of herself, she laughed. "You enjoy making fun of me, don't you?"

"Oh, I'm not laughing at you—"

"I know," Allie interrupted dryly, "you're laughing *with* me."

"Actually, I'm not laughing at all. It's refreshing to be with a woman who can still blush."

"I'm not all that unsophisticated or inexperienced," she insisted, feeling somehow that she was coming across as a naive hick from the boondocks.

"Hey, I wouldn't think of accusing you of being inexperienced. I'm sure you've led a life filled with dissipation and unbridled lust."

"Now you really are laughing at me."

"No." His voice softened. "Just acknowledging the obvious—you're a nice girl who isn't used to getting into hot tubs with strange men."

She decided to let that go. The conversation had already taken a far more personal turn than she'd expected. And besides, Rafe was right—she wasn't used to getting into hot tubs with men she'd known for only a short time. Even if this one was her "husband." But she felt certain that Rafe had a great deal of experience with a staggering variety of women in hot tubs.

The mood between them, the setting, the moment, grew increasingly erotic. While a cold breeze rustled the branches of the nearby trees, and water lapped at the rocky shore only a few hundred yards away, Rafe and Allie were warmed by the hot water of the Jacuzzi—and by a growing desire for each other that she could no longer deny to herself.

Looking at him sitting only a few feet from her, she was intensely aware of his body . . . his broad chest, covered with a mat of softly curling dark hair . . . his muscled shoulders . . . and, visible through the clear water, narrow hips and sinewy thighs. His body was hard and fit.

Everything about him was so completely masculine, yet when he reached out to take her hand, his touch was exquisitely gentle. His fingers played with her wedding band as he said, "One of the first things I noticed about you were your hands. The fingers are so long and slender, like a pianist's or a surgeon's. I couldn't understand why you weren't wearing a wedding ring. It seemed unbelievable that some man hadn't talked you into marriage."

Jerking her hand away as if his touch burned her, she said shakily, "Someone did. But we didn't make it past the engagement."

"Why?"

She couldn't talk about Dennis. Especially to Rafe. She didn't want to reveal how vulnerable she'd felt when he'd hurt and humiliated her with his casual infidelities. Part of her still felt that there must have been something lacking in her to send him off in pursuit of other women. Surely, if she'd been lovable enough, attractive enough, he wouldn't have wanted anyone else.

Looking away, she said quietly, "It just didn't work out."

For a moment Rafe simply looked at her with a thoughtful expression. Then, to her chagrin, he reached out and lightly stroked her cheek. "You're a very special woman, Allie. He was a fool to let you go."

She shivered, as though from a chill. But she wasn't cold. She was suffused with a penetrating warmth that had nothing to do with the hot water, and everything to do with Rafe's touch.

"You're trembling," he whispered.

"The wind . . ." she began.

But he shook his head. "It's not the wind."

His hand moved up to her hair that shone burnished gold in the moonlight. He curled a strand around his fingertip, then let it slip through his fingers.

She didn't move. She couldn't. He had moved along the underwater bench, and was so close now, she could feel the warmth of his breath on her cheek, could see the glint of passion in those dark eyes. His eyes were luminous in the moonlight as they stared into her own, willing her to be still, to not pull away.

"No." She wasn't sure if she spoke the word or merely thought it. Either way, it didn't matter. What had been building between them practically from the first moment they'd met was too strong to be denied by a feeble protest.

His thumb ran across her lips, pulling gently at them so that they opened slightly.

"How could any man who's ever kissed these lips possibly let you go?" Rafe murmured.

She was barely breathing now, the rise and fall of her chest hardly perceptible. Her body was rigid as she fought with all her self-control to rein in her rebellious feelings.

His hands moved to her shoulders. She could feel the strength in those hard, callused hands. Rafe pulled her close. When she tried to hold back, to resist, he slipped one arm around her back, holding her against him, her breasts just brushing his chest.

"Allie," he whispered, and on his lips her name sounded like an endearment.

Her lips parted slightly to murmur a protest. But before she could speak, his mouth was on hers, tender yet persistent. Her lips parted even farther, and when his tongue touched hers, the sensation of warmth she'd felt turned into a raging fire.

Without thinking, her hands went to his chest. But instead of pushing him away, her fingers curled in the tight mat of chest hair.

Rafe sighed with inexpressible pleasure as his lips finally left hers and moved to brush lightly across her cheek, her jaw, down the slender line of her throat. Then they returned to her mouth with a groan of desire that sent shivers up her spine.

His lips possessed hers again. This time she didn't just sit passively. Her tongue met his, her lips pressed against his.

While one hand cupped her face, the other moved in slow circles under the water to caress her breast, barely covered by the tight swimsuit. Allie leaned back against the tile rim of the Jacuzzi and half closed her eyes as Rafe continued the warm, wet massage of her body.

His hand moved down to her stomach, continuing the erotic circular movement. His touch, along with the sensuous feeling of the hot, swirling water, filled her with a sweet languor. Her entire being felt open, unguarded, yielding. She wanted to give herself to him, to hold nothing back, to be filled with him.

"I want you so," he whispered, and began to push her shoulder strap aside.

His voice, and the realization that in a moment she would be exposed to him, brought her to her senses. She didn't know this man. She certainly didn't trust him. It would be far too risky to become intimate with him.

Pulling back abruptly, she said in a ragged voice, "No! I . . . I can't."

For an instant she was afraid he wouldn't stop. He was so much stronger than she was, and could easily overpower her. He stared in surprise at her sudden resistance. But there was no anger in his expression, merely intense disappointment.

To her profound relief, he said slowly, "All right . . . I understand. Strictly business, right?"

"Right," she agreed quickly.

Then, before he could say anything further, she got out of the Jacuzzi, and, pausing only to wrap a large white bath sheet around her, hurried into her room, closing the door firmly behind her.

For a moment Rafe sat there, staring at her bedroom door, wondering what the hell had happened to make her stop. She'd wanted him as badly as he'd wanted her. He was sure of that. Finally, shaking his head in frustration, he, too, got out of the Jacuzzi. In his room he showered, then put on a heavy velour robe. Taking the Edgewater plans, he returned to the living room. As he added more wood to the fire, he glanced over at Allie's closed door, fighting the urge to ask her if she wanted to join him. Clearly, she didn't want to have anything to do with him. The thought irritated him enormously.

Unrolling the plans across the massive glass-top coffee table before the fireplace, he studied them carefully. But he could hear her moving around behind that closed door. So, he thought curiously, she was too restless to sleep.

Forcing himself to focus his attention on the plans, he spent the next two hours going over every detail of the Edgewater project until he was thoroughly familiar with it. It would help enormously when he needed to ask questions about the actual facilities the following day.

It was just after two o'clock when he noticed the light finally go out under her door. He wanted to go to her, to tell her there was nothing to be afraid of, that as long as he was there the dreams that haunted her nights couldn't hurt her. But he couldn't do that. After all, their relationship was strictly business. . . .

Allie had brought Elena's journal with her, and she read it in bed until it was very late and she couldn't keep her eyes open any longer. She felt such an affinity with her ancestor, empathizing with the uncertainties the young Californio girl felt about the sudden changes in her life.

Elena's Journal, May 5, 1853.

The celebrations went on for two days after the ceremony. All of our friends came from the neighboring ranchos. But Antonio and his family were not among the guests. Papa refused to speak of it, but I think that Antonio was very angry.

There was much drinking the night of the wedding. The men kept pressing Ben to drink, though he didn't seem to want to, and he fell asleep on a bench in the courtyard. Old Catarina put a blanket over him. I slept in my old room, alone.

The second night, there was also much partying, but Ben did not drink. After supper, Catarina said I must go and make myself ready for my husband. I was very nervous when he finally came to my room. He was hesitant, as if he, too, were uncertain. He asked me to join him in the courtyard for a walk.

As we walked, he said that he knew the arrangement between him and my father was very difficult for me, since my wishes had not been taken into account. He assured me that he would not "force himself on me," as he put it. I had not expected such kindness from him, and I found myself looking at him in a different way than I had done before. He explained that he was riding back to his rancho that night to make arrangements with his brother to bring cattle to Rancho Sureno. Then he said something that surprised me—that he married me not for Rancho Sureno but because he cared very much for me, and hoped that in time I might come to care for him.

He kissed me then for the first time, for he had not kissed me even during the marriage ceremony performed by the priest. I have been kissed before, by Antonio when Papa was not looking, but it did not feel like this kiss. I felt very strange inside. Not bad, just different than I have ever felt before.

Then Ben left. I won't see him again for three weeks. We are married in the eyes of God, yet he has not made me his wife. I pray that he will return soon, so that I can tell him what I have come to realize—that I, too, care for him.

For a long while after she turned out the light, Allie lay in the darkened room of the suite she shared with the man who was her husband. She thought how odd it was that her life had come to mirror Elena's. Both of them had married men who were almost complete strangers, had gambled their lives on a dream, and faced an uncertain future. Like her ancestor, Allie found herself confronting feelings she hadn't counted on. Especially the realization that, like Elena, she was beginning to desire the stranger she had married.

23

DAN CULHAGEN MET THEM for breakfast the next morning on the deck outside the Blue Spruce Room. It jutted out over the water beside the marina where die-hard sailors launched sailboats into the water. The morning ferry—the main source of transportation from the mainland—was just arriving.

Allie's gaze fixed on one sailboat—a Hobie Cat—similar to the one she'd seen through the window of the hypnotherapist's office weeks earlier. As she had concentrated on that boat, she had retrieved the repressed memory of what happened the night her mother died. Even now, weeks afterward, it was emotionally devastating to remember the moment when the memory had finally returned, clear and horrifying in its tragedy.

She forced herself to focus on Dan Culhagen, but she wondered if she would ever be able to see sailboats and water again without thinking of that morning in Janice's office.

Not at all the typical billionaire, Dan was neither sophisticated nor socially ambitious. A self-made man, he'd built his fortune first with logging. Later it grew enormously with his investments in housing developments as people flocked to Seattle. He had no desire to distance himself from his roots, and had spent his entire life in the Northwest. A short, stocky man, he had a ruddy complexion, piercing ice-blue eyes that carefully scrutinized everyone, and thick reddish-gold hair, beginning to turn gray, that hinted at his Norse ancestors.

"What's your interest in Edgewater?" Dan asked Rafe the moment they'd all sat down together at a round pine table.

Rafe replied, "I control a sizable area of land near Big Sur, California. I want to develop it, and Allie wants me to use Edgewater as a model."

Dan patted Allie's hand. "Julia and this young lady convinced me this was the way to go."

A half hour later, when they finished breakfast, Dan said, "C'mon, Sloan. Allie and I will show you something you don't see every day."

It was one of those rare Indian summer days that sometimes occurs in the fall. The crisp morning air warmed beneath the clear blue sky and brilliant sun as it shone through the thick trees surrounding the inn.

They spent the rest of the morning with Dan, walking the pathways that surrounded the inn and connected it to the village, the main commercial center of the development.

Rafe made few comments. But Allie could tell that he was rapidly being persuaded by what he saw.

Dan said to Rafe, "Maybe you'd like to see the whole thing from the air. It'll give you a better idea of the overall layout."

"I'd like that."

As they had driven through the different residential phases that included single-family dwellings as well as multifamily units, Rafe had looked at Allie with growing respect. He'd known from the beginning that she was smart and creative. Now he realized just how talented she was, with a rare gift of imagination and sound design sense. Along the way he discovered something else about her—that she was a dreamer. He saw her vision in truly unique aspects of the development that coincided with suggestions she'd made about preserving Rancho Sureno.

Julia Winslow's influence was definitely apparent, in a style as recognizable as Wright's. But somehow Rafe knew that Allie herself was responsible for the symbiotic blend of man with nature in the contrast of smooth woods with the sharp angles of rock and stone that imitated nature in structures nestled unobtrusively among towering trees, and the waterfalls and tumbling creeks that provided natural barriers.

He'd expected curlicues and gingerbread cornices with feminine latticework and chintz in every room of the inn. But her influence on the design of Edgewater wasn't whimsical. It was as strong and brave as the determination that drove a young woman to confront a brutal murder, and to face a family she hadn't seen for over twenty-five years.

He found himself looking at her now in a different way than he had done before. The architect who'd helped design Edgewater was not only talented and had enormous integrity, she was also strong-willed and believed completely in what she set out to do. A woman like that could be a formidable partner.

After eating lunch at the marina, Dan repeated his invitation to Rafe to see Edgewater from the air.

Allie said, "You two go ahead on your own. I thought I'd take a kayak out and explore some of the inlets I used to fish with my grandfather. It may be a long time before I have an opportunity to get back here."

Rafe agreed quickly. He wanted the chance to ask Dan questions without Allie around—developer to developer. As they walked back to the car for the drive out to the airstrip, they agreed to meet back at the marina at four o'clock.

After Rafe and Dan had gone, Allie walked down the marina steps to the rental office and arranged for a kayak. Her grandfather had taught her how to handle the single-seat narrow craft. When he was confident she could handle one by herself, they had set out together, each navigating their own kayak.

Before she began working on the Edgewater project, she hadn't been kayaking in years. But when she started making trips back to the islands, she found herself drawn once more to the water. Some of the happiest times of her childhood had been on this island and on the water surrounding it. Out on the water she found the sort of peace and solitude that made problems manageable, even made them vanish.

As she carried the fiberglass boat down to the water, the afternoon sun felt surprisingly warm for this time of year. But she knew that warmth was misleading. The water itself was freezing cold, and if she capsized and remained in the water, there was a real danger of dying from hypothermia. Within minutes the cold would begin to have a deadly effect, starting with a loss of dexterity in the hands, then cramps in the legs and feet, and finally a terrifying loss of judgment and sense of disorientation. Unless she was very close to shore, swimming wasn't an option, because of the strong currents. The only hope in the event of a capsize was to get back in the boat as quickly as possible, and get back to shore and into dry clothes.

As Allie slipped into her neoprene spray skirt and life jacket, then carefully stepped into the boat, she reassured herself there was nothing to worry about. Her grandfather had taught her well, and she didn't take chances out on the water. Pushing out into the bay, the narrow boat rocked jerkily back and forth as Allie struggled to attach the skirt to the cockpit coaming. She reminded herself of the two essentials her grandfather had taught her—keeping her rudder in the water and maintaining a solid grip on the paddle. It was critical not to lose it.

For the first mile or so she stayed close to the shore of Orcas Island. Among the rocks jutting out of the water, she could see brightly colored starfish, and occasionally a fish jumped out of the water nearby. Allie was glad she'd decided to take this rare opportunity to relax. It was a glorious day and the scenery was magnificent. It felt good to be out by herself, surrounded by nothing but peace and quiet, feeling the gentle swell of the deep green water.

Turning the boat out toward the channel, about a half-mile from shore, Allie felt a brisk, cool breeze whipping her cheeks. The wind made tiny ripples on the surface of the water. Alone out there, with no distractions, she found herself thinking of Rafe. So much had happened over the last few weeks, especially over the last few days, she'd had little time to think about the man she'd agreed to marry with such uncharacteristic impulsiveness. Her feelings about him were as contradictory and unfathomable as his nature seemed to be. One minute she felt drawn to him in a way she'd never been drawn to any man before. And the next she was frightened of him, and it was all she could do to keep from running blindly from him.

As an adolescent she'd fantasized about marrying someone like her grandfather, a solid, unassuming man with basic down-to-earth values and an aura of protectiveness. As a mature young woman with a professional degree, she'd assumed she would marry someone like herself, about her age, with similar education and goals. Now she found herself married to a man ten years older than she, who hadn't even finished high school, let alone gone to college, and whose ambitions were in many ways diametrically opposed to hers.

It's not a real marriage, she reminded herself, trying to take solace in the thought. But it was real enough—in the eyes of the law, their friends, and their family. And her growing attraction to him was definitely real.

Allie had no idea if Rafe was attracted to her in the same way. He was clearly a man who'd known many women. He'd probably been irresistible to women from the moment he'd become a teenager. When he looked at her with undisguised desire, when he touched her, kissed her, she figured he was merely responding as he had to so many women over the years. Allie admitted she was relatively inexperienced and naive about the opposite sex, but she knew Rafe was used to dealing with women. If they made love, she imagined she would be just another conquest. For some reason, the thought made her suddenly very miserable.

Glancing at her watch, she was surprised to see how late it was, well past four o'clock. She'd planned to be back at the marina by now. Realizing that she'd better hurry, or she'd be caught by a change in the current that could carry her off course and into open water, she turned the kayak around and headed back toward the marina.

She'd been so lost in her thoughts about Rafe that she hadn't noticed that the breeze had begun to pick up and she'd drifted farther out than she intended. She had to paddle hard to keep the kayak heading toward shore. She kept her eyes on her destination, a barely perceptible dot in the distance, concentrating on going forward in a straight line.

The breeze strengthened, and Allie felt it whip the end of her paddle as she raised it out of the water on each stroke. The water had been smooth, but now small whitecaps were beginning to dot the surface.

Then a sound broke Allie's concentration. Turning to look over her shoulder, she saw a bright yellow and white speedboat coming up behind her, heading straight toward her at full speed. It quickly bore down on her kayak, on a dead collision course, and she knew it was only a matter of seconds before it would hit her.

Allie froze. What was the driver doing? Didn't he see her? In her bright orange life preserver and red boat, she must have been clearly visible. Raising her arms, she waved them frantically overhead, and shouted at the top of her lungs. But the person driving the boat seemed to neither see nor hear her. He continued heading straight toward her.

She picked up the paddle and started steering frantically, even though she knew it was hopeless. There was no way she could get out of his path in time.

She braced herself for the force of the collision, and was amazed when it didn't happen. Instead, the boat veered off at the last possible moment, barely missing her, and continued on at full speed. Giddy with relief that he'd seen her in time, Allie laughed out loud.

And then it happened. A huge wake from the speedboat hit the kayak broadside, turning it over easily and sending Allie underwater.

The shock of the ice-cold water was nearly unbearable. Dumbstruck, Allie hung upside down, still seated in the boat, gulping in water for what seemed like an eternity. *Don't panic!* Gathering her wits, she remembered what her grandfather had taught her to do in just a such a situation. She disengaged the elastic of the spray skirt and did a somersault underwater to push herself free from the kayak. Desperate for air, she barely reached the surface in time. Grabbing on to the overturned hull of the kayak, she realized the worst had happened—her paddle was gone.

Looking around anxiously, she expected to see the speedboat coming back to help her. She was dismayed to realize that it was nearly out of sight. Whoever the driver was, he must have seen what happened to her, but he had deliberately left her out there, alone and helpless. Allie had been so frightened, so desperately focused on trying to get out of the speedboat's way, she hadn't gotten a look at the driver.

Kept afloat by a sealed cargo compartment at the stern and a plastic flotation bag filled with air in the pointed bow, the kayak rose and fell with the swell of the waves. Holding on to it for dear life, Allie tried to think clearly. The first thing to do, she told herself, was to look around for the paddle. Glancing around her, she was relieved to see it floating several yards away. But as soon as she tried to swim toward it, keeping one hand firmly on the kayak, she realized this wasn't going to work. The paddle was quickly moving away from her, and she would lose it at this rate.

A line was attached to the bow of the kayak. Reaching underwater, Allie searched for it with fingers that were already beginning to grow numb. When she found the line, she unhooked it with cold, clumsy fingers, tied it around her waist, and began to swim toward the oar, towing the kayak behind her.

At first she was terrified that she wouldn't reach it. The wind was even brisker now, and the whitecaps worse. Allie was lifted up on the crests of the waves, then dropped abruptly into the troughs. At one point she lost sight of the paddle and nearly panicked. Then, suddenly, there it was, right in front of her, nearly within arm's reach. Ignoring the cramping already beginning to hamper her feet and legs, Allie swam toward it. When her numb fingers closed around it, she wanted to shout with joy.

But there wasn't a second to spare. Her feet and hands throbbed from the icy water, and she had started to shiver uncontrollably. She had to get out of the water, and fast. To do that, she had to get the kayak upright, and pull herself into it.

After untying the line from her waist, and tying the paddle to it to make certain she didn't lose it again, Allie swam to the bow. She pulled the kayak around until it was upright, but with the cockpit full of water, the boat rose only an inch or two above the water. Getting the water out seemed like an insurmountable problem, since she had nothing to bail with.

Once more she started to panic. She was out there alone, with no one in sight, and in a matter of minutes she would die of hypothermia. Fighting desperately not to surrender to the terror that threatened to engulf her, she tried to remember what she'd learned to do in this situation. But her mind was already starting to reel from the effects of hypothermia, and she couldn't think clearly.

Come on, Allie! What did Grandpa tell me to do if I was out alone and this happened? There was some method . . . something a person could do by herself . . .

And then it came to her. There was one chance—only one—but she hadn't done it in years, not since she'd practiced the maneuver with her grandfather. He had been right there to help her. Now she was alone, and quickly losing all ability to function. Her rational mind told her it was hopeless, but she refused to give up. She wasn't going to let herself die this way, alone and terrified, and all because of some idiot driving a speedboat in a dangerous way.

All the water in the kayak was in the bow and cockpit section because the stern had a sealed compartment. Turning the boat over again so that it was once more upside down, Allie swam to the stern. Carefully avoiding the steel rudder, which could easily cut her flesh to shreds, she pushed with what little remained of her strength on the stern. The bow shot up into the air and water began pouring out of the cockpit.

Allie's arms ached unbearably from the effort to keep the bow up until all the water was gone. When it was finally done, she faced something even more difficult. In a tricky maneuver made infinitely harder by her numb hands, she flipped the stern around so that the kayak landed right side up without filling with water again.

The kayak was now upright, with only an inch of water in the cockpit. Now, Allie told herself determinedly, all you have to do is get back in the damn boat without turning it over again.

Climbing directly into the cockpit was out—without someone else to steady it for her, she would just overturn it again. The rudder, with its deadly sharp blades, was a big danger at the stern. But the smooth bow had nothing to hold on to. Allie realized that she was so cold and exhausted at this point, she would have only enough strength and coordination left to make one attempt to get into the cockpit. Though it was extremely dangerous, she would have to try the stern.

First she made certain the steel blade was turned down. Then, pushing down on the stern until it was slightly underwater, she threw her leg over it and straddled it as if she were riding a horse. Grabbing the elastic shock cords that crisscrossed the rear deck of the boat, Allie inched forward, desperately trying to hold herself steady. It seemed as if it took hours to reach the cockpit, though she knew it could have been only minutes. When she finally lowered her body into the cockpit, she simply sat for a moment, utterly exhausted and shivering badly with the cold. She no longer fought the tears that stung her eyes, but let them flow freely.

But she knew she couldn't let herself sit there, crying and feeling sorry for herself. She still had to paddle back to the marina. There wasn't a moment to lose, for already the current was beginning to turn against her.

Pulling in the line tied around the oar, she began paddling with uneven, jerky movements that were pathetically uncoordinated and weak compared to the way she'd handled herself on the way out. At one point her muscles ached so badly she simply wanted to give up, let go. But she heard her grandfather's words. "*You can do it, Allie.*" Ignoring the pain, she kept paddling.

Just when she thought she must have gone in the wrong direction, the marina suddenly loomed before her, only a few hundred yards away. Now her exhausted tears turned to sobs of joy, and she paddled with renewed effort.

Mike, the young man who managed the marina, saw her coming. From his small office on the dock he came running toward her as her kayak bumped into the loading platform.

"Miss Wyatt! My God, what happened? Are you okay?"

Allie's teeth were chattering so badly, she couldn't speak. She simply sat while Mike quickly tied the kayak to the platform, then lifted her out of the cockpit. "Did you capsize?" he asked.

Allie nearly laughed at the absurd question. *Of course I capsized!* she wanted to shout frantically. But she still couldn't speak. And besides, she reminded herself, Mike meant well. She'd always thought him something of an amiable dunce. Now she was deeply grateful for his help and concern.

Leaning heavily on Mike, Allie stumbled up to the inn on shaky legs that threatened to buckle at any moment.

All the while, Mike kept up a steady stream of nervous chatter. "We've got to get you out of these wet clothes right away. You'll catch your death."

I very nearly did, Allie thought wryly, with a hint of her normal humor.

Mike went on. "I can't believe it, you've never capsized before. What happened?"

"I . . . can't talk," Allie stammered through teeth that refused to stop chattering. She felt absolutely frozen, as if she would never feel warm again.

"Sorry," Mike said quickly. "Hey, you know, someone called and asked about you while you were out."

Allie looked sharply at Mike. "Wh-what? Who?"

"They didn't give a name. Just asked where you'd gone. I told 'em which direction you headed out in."

Though her thinking was still far from clear, Allie had the presence of mind to ask, "M-man or w-woman?"

Mike shrugged. "Couldn't tell. They were talking in a whisper, and I could hardly hear 'em. But it's kinda funny, isn't it? I mean, they sounded like they might be worried about you, and I didn't think nothing about it, but there you were in trouble all the time, so I guess they had a premonition or somethin'."

They had reached the lobby of the inn. Faith had been standing at the front desk, talking to the clerk. Seeing Allie in her soaking wet, disheveled condition, Faith came running up to her. "Allie! Are you all right?"

"I w-will be. I j-just need a r-really h-hot bath."

"Of course. You poor thing, what happened? No, don't try to tell me now. Let's get you out of these clothes. Maybe we should get you to the hospital at Friday Harbor."

Allie shook her head stubbornly. She didn't need a doctor. She needed a hot bath.

Between them, Mike and Faith managed to get Allie up to her suite with surprising speed. Mike seemed to want to hang around to make sure Allie was definitely going to be all right. But Faith ordered him back to the marina, and told him to let the authorities know about the errant speedboat. Allie had finally managed to stop shivering long enough to tell them what had happened. Faith then started a hot bath in the sunken tub, and helped Allie out of her soaking wet clothes.

Allie had expected to find Rafe waiting for her in the suite, or elsewhere at the inn, since it was well past the time he and Dan were supposed to return. But Faith told her that Rafe had come and gone, that he'd said he wanted to walk around on his own for a while. Five minutes later, assured that she was no longer needed, Faith left Allie alone to have a long, quiet soak.

As Allie lay in the tub, feeling her body thaw out and her mind start to function again, she faced something that she hadn't dared think about while she was struggling for her life out on the water. What happened to her was no accident. The speedboat's course wasn't erratic, as it would have been if the driver had been drunk. It had headed straight toward her, and when it veered away at the last moment, it was in a manner carefully designed to send a massive wave right at her. The driver of the boat must have seen that Allie had capsized. But he hadn't come back to help her. He'd left her to drown.

Who could have done that? Who wanted her dead, and why?

Just then there was a furious knock at her bathroom door. "Allie, it's me, Rafe! Are you all right?"

She hesitated, then answered slowly, "Yes . . . I'm fine."

Through the closed door she heard what sounded like a faint sigh of relief—or disappointment? she wondered.

Rafe replied, "Good. I'll be waiting out here for you."

She took her time in the bathroom, reluctant to face him, though she couldn't have said why. She knew only that her old fear of him had returned the moment she heard his voice calling to her through that door.

But she couldn't hide in the bathroom forever. Finally, she walked out into the sitting room, wearing a thick white terry robe, her wet hair hanging down her back. Rafe was standing at the windows, looking out, his expression grim. At the sound of her entrance he whirled around to face her. She could have sworn it was worry stamped all over his face, but somehow she couldn't trust it to be genuine.

"Faith told me you nearly drowned today! What the hell happened?" he demanded angrily.

His anger, so unfair and so inappropriate, touched off her own. "Why are you mad at *me*! It wasn't my fault someone tried to kill me!"

She hadn't meant to reveal her suspicions, but it was too late now to deny what she feared.

The worry evident on Rafe's face turned to confusion, then to a dawning understanding that left him looking even more grim. Without saying a word he went to the bar, poured a generous amount of Napoleon brandy into a snifter, then handed it to Allie. "Here, drink this."

"I don't want it," she protested. "I hate brandy."

"I don't care, you need it," he insisted in a tone that brooked no argument.

Reluctantly, she accepted the glass from his hand and took a tiny sip of the amber liquid. She rarely drank hard liquor, and didn't really care for it. But to her surprise, this tasted good going down. Actually, it wasn't so much the taste as the warmth it generated deep within her. The hot bath hadn't thawed her out completely. The brandy finished the job nicely.

"Now," Rafe said, "tell me exactly what happened."

She told him, leaving out nothing. When she finished, Rafe was silent for a moment. Finally, he said in a tight voice, "It's a miracle you weren't drowned."

"Thanks to my grandfather, I knew what to do. But even so . . ." Her voice trailed off. She couldn't bring herself to say the obvious—she had come within a hairbreadth of dying. A less experienced person couldn't have survived such an ordeal.

Rafe gave her an enigmatic look. "I'm glad you're smart enough to realize this wasn't an accident."

Suddenly doubting her own suspicions, Allie responded nervously, "Why would someone want me dead?"

"You've made some people very angry. One—or more—of them may have let their anger get the best of them."

"None of the Sloans would try to kill me!" Allie insisted vehemently, trying to convince herself as well as Rafe. "No matter how disappointed they may be about the sale of the ranch being cancelled, they're my family, for God's sake!"

"You place a great deal more trust in the idea of family than I do," Rafe said bitterly.

Without stopping to think, Allie shot back impulsively, "And what about *you*? With me out of the way, you could do as you please with the ranch!"

The expression of utter fury on his face was so intimidating that Allie shrank back from him as if she expected him to attack her then and there.

"You think *I* tried to kill you just to avoid an argument over developing the ranch? You think I'm capable of that?"

Scared as she was, Allie didn't back down. "I don't know what you're capable of. I hardly know you."

For a moment there was a tense silence between them. Allie had absolutely no idea what he would say or do next. She was beginning to believe he was capable of anything. Nothing would have surprised her.

When he spoke, his voice was no longer angry. Instead, it almost sounded hurt. "You're right, Allie. Don't trust *anyone*. Don't believe in *anyone*. I learned that lesson a long time ago."

And turning his back on her, he strode out of the room, slamming the door behind him.

Allie stood for a moment, torn by conflicting feelings. Then she ran into her bedroom, making certain she locked the door behind her.

24

ALLIE SLEPT POORLY THAT night in spite of her physical exhaustion. Waking early from a fitful sleep, she was eager to get back to Pebble Beach, determined to find out who had tried to run her down in that boat. She wasn't exactly sure how to go about it. But she thought a good starting place would be to check out everyone's alibis for the day before. If one of the Sloans *had* tried to kill her, they must have been away from Pebble Beach for at least that entire day, if not longer.

Had Rafe been at the controls of the boat? Was he so desperate to have complete control of Rancho Sureño that he would resort to murder?

She forced herself to face the plain, cold truth—if she were dead, Rafe would own everything outright, and wouldn't have to deal with her interference. The family might contest that ownership; in fact, she was certain they were taking steps to do so at that very moment. But Rafe could probably deal with that. And Allie would be conveniently dead—just as her mother had died twenty-five years earlier.

As always, when she thought of her mother's death, one terrible question overshadowed all others: *who* had killed her?

A dreadful thought filled Allie's mind. Perhaps, she realized unhappily, she simply hadn't wanted to confront it. But it had been right there in front of her all along, and she'd chosen not to think of it, just as she had chosen not to remember the events of that night for so long.

It had been a *family* party that night at the ranch. If it wasn't her father who killed her mother, then it might very well have been a member of the family.

Snatches of various conversations came back to haunt Allie . . . "*I can see there's a great deal that Mac didn't tell you . . .*" "*Your mother attracted men, like bees to honey . . .*" "*Gavin once hoped to marry your mother . . .*" "*Even David was drawn to her . . .*" "*Nicky made a pass at her . . .*"

And finally, "*Rafe adored her, but it was probably nothing more than adolescent infatuation . . .*"

Was it possible, she wondered, that the attempt on her life had nothing to do with the thwarted sale of the ranch? Was it connected, instead, with a twenty-five-year-old murder to which she held the key? Was someone afraid she might remember too much?

Did that include Rafe? Was it possible that the person she had seen murder her mother that night in the den was now her husband? She shivered at the thought, and felt herself grow cold with fear. She tried to tell herself she was being melodramatic. What had happened to her the day before was simply an accident resulting from a criminally careless driver. It couldn't have actually been an attempt on her life. No one in her family—including Rafe—would do such a thing.

When Allie and Rafe flew out of the small Orcas Island airport a couple of hours later, Allie had no visible bruises from her near brush with death the day before. The scars, like those from the loss of her parents, were deep inside, in a renewed uncertainty and fear.

Allie and Rafe barely spoke during the flight back to Seattle, then on to San Francisco, and from there to Monterey. They arrived in the early afternoon.

Two days earlier they had driven out to the small Monterey airport in Rafe's car. Now Allie wanted nothing more than to leave him, and go back to Casa Sureno alone. But she had no logical reason for refusing his offer of a ride home, so she reluctantly went with him.

As they drove toward Pebble Beach, Rafe said thoughtfully, "I'll bet Gavin knows all about our little trip. He's probably got someone keeping tabs on us."

"What is that supposed to mean?" Allie asked anxiously.

"I mean that this is going to get down and dirty, and you'd better get used to it. There's a lot at stake."

"Are you suggesting that it could have been Gavin driving that speedboat yesterday?"

"Despite what you may think about my motives, it's a definite possibility."

"It would make everything a great deal easier if you could convince the authorities of that, wouldn't it?" she snapped.

"What are you saying?"

"You'd have everything then—control of the ranch, and revenge against Gavin. Well, I don't think it's that simple, Rafe."

His dark eyes went darker still. "Whatever you're trying to say, just *say* it."

She was reluctant to voice her thoughts, afraid to actually articulate them, and even more afraid of Rafe's response. She said slowly, unable to meet his look, "If someone did try to kill me, it may have had something to do with my mother's death. That person may be afraid I'll remember who it was I saw in the den with her that night."

"But your father—"

"It wasn't my father I saw that night."

A momentary silence hung heavily between them. Then Rafe said slowly, "Go on."

"I think it was a member of the family."

"Me," he said tightly.

"I had heard that you . . . loved her," Allie said in a small voice.

He nodded. "Yes, I loved Barbara."

The look Allie gave Rafe was profoundly wounded and filled with painful questions.

He went on slowly. "She was the only truly kind person I ever knew. She was gentle and beautiful, and she didn't give a damn that I was Paul Sloan's bastard kid. She made me feel as if I belonged in the family, as if I was more important than just the dirt the people in this family walked on."

Taking his eyes off the road for a moment, he looked straight at Allie. "I loved her. And I didn't kill her."

She wanted desperately to believe he was telling the truth. But she was terrified that if her full memory of that night ever returned, it was Rafe's face she would see.

He saw the uncertainty, and the fear, in her eyes. It cut him like a knife through his heart. She was afraid of *him*. She actually thought he might be capable of *murder*! For the remainder of the short drive he kept his eyes focused on the road and said nothing. Allie sat quietly beside him, utterly miserable.

As they drove down Seventeen-Mile Drive toward what Allie still thought of as Mac's house, she remembered how she'd felt when she first came there three weeks earlier. Only three weeks, yet it felt like months. Everything had seemed strange then, but now it was all familiar. She recognized many of the houses lining the drive, and the turns in the meandering road.

Was it her memory of only a few weeks? Or was it a memory from her childhood, finally returning? She had no way of knowing. She knew only that she hadn't remembered anything more about her mother's death than she had when she first returned here.

As Rafe pulled into the driveway, Allie thought of the day when she'd first come through those gates. She'd been filled with anticipation at the thought of meeting the man whose voice had enveloped her in a feeling of warmth and welcome with a single telephone call.

That warmth had been there when he came out to greet her. Coming back here now brought everything back in a rush of emotion. In that short time Allie and Mac had rediscovered each other, his love had been immediate and unconditional. She remembered dozens of brief moments they'd shared—sitting out in the courtyard, watching the seabirds soar and swoop over the breakers . . . Mac's quiet, gentle manner, so like her grandfather's as he spoke of Rancho Sureno and the family legacy . . . his heavily veined hand warm around hers . . . the impish smile behind his imperious demeanor.

As Rafe pulled to a stop in front of the entrance, Allie half expected Mac to open the door and step out onto the flagstone walkway, impatient for her to get out of the car. When the front door opened, she found herself holding her breath, then releasing it slowly with a small, sad smile as Inez stood waiting for her. Allie murmured good-bye to Rafe without looking at him, and got out of the car. He immediately drove off.

"Hello, Inez," she said as she reached the steps.

Inez wrapped her arms about Allie in such a completely open, caring gesture that all of Allie's uncertainties about coming to live here, even temporarily, were dispelled. "Welcome home, Miss Allie."

Inside, Allie looked around, feeling Mac's presence in every room. The feeling was somehow comfortable.

Inez said, "You look very tired, Miss Allie. Are you all right?"

She nodded. "Yes, I'm fine now."

"Will Mr. Rafe be returning later?" Inez asked, catching Allie off guard.

Naturally, Allie told herself, Inez was bound to hear of their marriage, if not the specific reasons behind it.

"He . . . he won't be moving in for a while," Allie said awkwardly.

If Inez found this strange behavior for newlyweds, she didn't say so. "Why don't you go out to the courtyard?" she suggested. "I'll bring you some tea."

"Thank you. Are there any messages for me?"

"I wrote them down on a tablet in the library. I'll bring them out when the tea is ready."

Out in the courtyard, Mac's reassuring presence was even stronger. Allie recalled the video he'd made for her just before his death.

"You will know what to do. . . ."

Mac had been so certain. He had trusted in her. She wished she were as certain as he'd been.

Inez brought fragrant steaming tea out into the courtyard and set it on the table. The list of telephone messages was on the tray beside the silver tea service.

There were several messages from Mac's attorney, asking her to contact his office immediately. She supposed it had something to do with Mac's estate. And there were three messages from her cousin Valentina.

She frowned, wondering why Val wanted to see her. Their last encounter at the family board meeting had been anything but congenial. Val, like the other members of the family, had first been stunned, then furious at the announcement of Allie's marriage to Rafe. Under the circumstances, Allie didn't think Val could possibly be calling with a social invitation.

Inez had poured the tea and waited for further orders. "Is there something wrong, Miss Allie?"

"No," she said, looking up. "Everything is fine." Then she added, "Thank you for making me feel so welcome in Mac's house. It means a lot to me."

"He cared very much for you, Miss Allie. You made his last days very happy. He wanted you to have this house."

"I hope that you'll stay on. I can't imagine this house without you."

"That is very kind of you, Miss Allie. At first I thought about retiring. Thanks to Mr. Mac's generosity, I now have a very fine little house in Pacific Grove."

"I will understand if you want to retire. But I hope you'll stay."

Inez smiled. "I'm not such an old woman. If I retired, what would I do with my time—sit around and crochet, or gossip with my friends?" She made a gesture through the air. "Such a waste of time. That's for old people."

"Besides," she went on, "my daughter and her children need a place to live for a while. She's going through some difficult times. I thought I might let her move into the house in Pacific Grove. It would be nice to have them close. And I could stay on here, just as I did with Mr. Mac. If that's all right with you."

"I think that's a perfect arrangement. I'm very glad you're going to be staying on."

Inez turned at the sound of the front-door bell. "That is probably your cousin, Miss Valentina. She's been here several times, besides calling at all hours. I explained that I didn't know when you would be returning, but she's been very persistent."

Allie set down her teacup and picked up the list of messages. "I'll see her inside. I need to return these calls anyway."

Before following Inez inside, Allie paused to look back over her shoulder at the view that Mac had so loved. "I'll do my best not to betray your trust in me, Uncle Mac," she whispered.

Then she turned and headed into the house.

Val was pacing across the formal living room as Allie came in, reminding Allie of her first impression of her cousin as a sleek, restless panther.

She wore a catsuit in a vivid shade of fuchsia, with stiletto heels, and her brilliant red hair tumbled about her shoulders. She wasn't alone. Nicky shot to his feet as Allie came in. She was surprised to see that his handsome face was drawn and haggard. He looked as if he hadn't slept in days.

"So you're finally back," Val said impatiently, glancing past Allie as if expecting someone else. "Your husband isn't home?" she asked bitingly.

Allie considered refusing to answer the question, but decided it wasn't worth the effort. It would be best to find out what these two wanted, then send them packing. "Rafe is busy elsewhere," she said curtly.

Val was obviously disappointed. "I see. That's too bad. I wanted to offer my congratulations. Things sort of got off to a bad start the other day. The two of you caught everyone by surprise with that little maneuver—"

"Let's get on with this," Nicky interrupted rudely.

"Can I get you anything to drink?" Allie offered with studied politeness.

"This isn't a social call," Val responded, abandoning all pretense of civility.

"I didn't think it was. Why are you here?"

Val squared off like a fighter ready to do battle. "We are here to make you an offer."

"An offer?"

Nicky stepped around his sister and confronted Allie. "We're willing to sell you our shares in the Sloan Land Company."

Allie was stunned. She looked from one cousin to the other.

"Those shares will be worth a great deal once we develop the ranch. Why would you want to sell them?"

"For the money!" Val blurted out. "Why the hell else?"

"You have a great deal of money," Allie pointed out.

Nicky laughed, a cold, hard sound. "The illusion of money, dear cousin." His tone was scathing. "Everything is owned by the family business, and we're given a pitiful allowance. We don't have any real money of our own."

"Look," Val said, "the truth is we were counting on the sale to the Japanese to provide us with some hard cash for a change. But now that the sale is off," she went on, looking sharply at Allie, "we decided that you might be interested in our shares. We can't sell them to outsiders, but they can be transferred within the family."

Allie looked at her cousins in amazement. It didn't matter to them who they sold out to—the Japanese or her. All they wanted was the money their shares in the ranch could bring them. Their loyalty to the Sloan family interests was that easily bought and sold.

Allie came straight to the point. "I don't have that kind of money."

"Of course you do," Nicky argued. "You have this house, the ranch house, and the shares Mac gave you."

"All of that is tied up in the estate. Everything is taken care of through the trust," Allie pointed out. "I couldn't liquidate any of the assets that quickly even if I wanted to, and I don't."

Valentina's gaze narrowed. "It's the least you can do. You owe us that much. Before you came here, everything was just fine. That damn ranch was going to be sold. Now that's all screwed up. I've been kept on a short leash my whole life, with an allowance doled out every month for living expenses. *An allowance,* for Christ's sake! I'm thirty-five years old and still living on an allowance."

"Val, I'm sorry, but it just can't be done. The money isn't there. Even if it were," she asked, "why should I buy your shares when Rafe and I already have controlling interest in the ranch?"

"That's a very good question."

They all turned around as Rafe came into the living room. He took off his jacket, draping it casually across the back of a chair, as if both he and the jacket belonged there. Smiling at Allie, he slipped his arm about her waist.

She simply stood there, staring at him in undisguised amazement. Considering how hurriedly he'd left her only a few minutes earlier, she hadn't expected to see him for a while.

"From what little I heard as I came in," he went on, "your generous offer doesn't make a lot of sense, *cousin*."

Val said hesitantly, "I just thought you and Allie might be interested in buying our shares, since you seem intent on collecting as many shares as possible."

Rafe's smile was utterly charming—and deceptive. "As Allie explained, there are no real liquid assets in the estate. And if you wanted to make an offer, you should've made it to me directly. I control the shares."

Val smiled seductively. "I've been making you offers for years, darling."

She started to walk toward him, but he stopped her cold. "I'm telling you the same thing Allie did—it doesn't make sense to buy more shares when we already own controlling interest in the ranch."

Val's expression went from warm sensuality to ugly fury. "Such a touching little display of togetherness between husband and wife," she spat out. "Do you really think anyone believes you married her for any other reason than to get your hands on the ranch?"

"Be careful, Val," Rafe warned.

"Gavin and my father will stop you!" she said furiously. "They'll find a way, and when they do, you'll both end up with nothing!"

Nicky had come around behind her. "Stop it!" he hissed. "This isn't doing anyone any good."

She turned on her brother. "This was your idea. You said he would listen. You're just like all the other incompetent men in this family." Turning back to Rafe, she added, "Except for you. But then, you were never really part of the family, were you?"

"Get out, Valentina." Rafe's voice was harsh. "And don't come back."

Allie followed Val and Nicky outside. They had come in separate cars, and Val ran to hers, getting in and slamming the door of the sports car hard. She roared down the driveway, going so fast that the car fishtailed.

Allie laid a hand on Nicky's arm. "Look, I'm sorry, Nicky. I honestly can't help you."

He looked at Allie, his expression dazed and helpless. "Val really needs the money." He laughed then, a frightened, agonized sound. "I need the money." Then he went on desperately. "It's not too late, you can get an annulment and the sale can go through. You'd make a lot of money too, just like the rest of us."

When Allie didn't respond, Nicky went on. "You don't know Rafe, he's just using you. He's dangerous, Allie."

"Nicky, please."

He made a monumental effort to regain control. "All right," he finally said in a resigned voice, "but think about what I said. It isn't too late—yet."

Rafe had remained in the living room. As Allie went back inside, she wondered why on earth he had come back.

As if reading her mind, he said, "We have to talk. That's why I came back. Have you talked to Mac's attorney?"

"No, not yet. I had several messages from him, but I haven't had a chance to call him back."

"I had those same messages on my service when I checked in. Gavin's been busy while we were gone."

"What is it? What's happened?"

"Gavin is trying to have the marriage set aside."

Whatever Allie had expected, it wasn't this. "But the marriage is legal. How could he do that?"

"By proving it's a fraud."

She sat down in Mac's favorite chair. She knew this wouldn't be easy, but she hadn't thought Gavin would move so quickly. She'd badly underestimated him. "What happens now?"

"He'll try to prove that we got married strictly for the purpose of stopping the sale and gaining control of the estate."

"Allie frowned. "That's exactly what we did." She looked at Rafe. "What do we do now?"

"We have to appear to live together as man and wife."

Allie stared at him in amazement. Surely, he didn't mean . . .

Before she could speak, he went on quickly. "We have to prove that we didn't marry just for the purpose of defrauding the estate over control of the ranch."

"That wasn't part of the bargain," Allie said furiously.

"I know. If you want out, we'll call it quits and cut our losses."

She looked at him in amazement. Their marriage was the key to everything he wanted. Yet he was willing to give it up if that was what she wanted. Could she trust what he was saying?

"*You* have to decide," he went on. "The choice is yours." Though this meant so much to him, there was no hint of pleading in his voice. He would never beg for anything. "What's it going to be, Allie? Are you going to let Gavin win, or are you going to fight him?"

She knew what she wanted to do—to preserve the Sloan family legacy that had meant so much to Mac, to create something as special with Rancho Sureno as she and Julia had done at Edgewater. But all her doubts of the day before came back, and she felt the familiar terror building inside her. She couldn't trust him. She *couldn't.*

Then Mac's words came back at her. "*You will know what to do.*" Mac had believed in Rafe—enough to bring him back into the family, enough to entrust him with the majority of his shares.

Meeting Rafe's gaze, Allie said slowly, "All right."

He nodded. "Good."

Then, as if they were discussing something relatively unimportant, he added, "I'll stay here. That makes more sense than you moving to my place. It isn't very big, and it's pretty remote out there." He added, "I should move in as soon as possible."

Allie simply looked at him. "Of course."

But inside she wondered what on earth she was doing.

25

When Rafe moved in that evening, Allie was surprised at how little he brought with him, just some clothes, a small box of books, and no personal possessions, photos, or mementos.

"You travel light," she commented as he put his things in the small bedroom that connected to her larger one. It had once been intended as a man's dressing room, and most of the space was taken up with closets and built-in dressers.

"I've never been interested in having a lot of possessions. They tie you down," he said quietly.

"I see. You're the kind of guy who wants to be able to fold up his tent and slip away in the middle of the night."

Rafe cocked his head to one side, and gave her a wry glance. "I'm not quite that bad."

"You know," Allie said awkwardly, "there's a much larger, more comfortable guest bedroom down the hall."

"I'm aware of that. But in case anyone questions Inez, this way she can say we appear to be sharing the same bedroom. I'll make up my bed every day, to cover my tracks, so to speak. And it would be a good idea for you to make your bed look as if two people are sleeping in it."

Allie knew he was right, though she was extremely uncomfortable at the thought of him sleeping so near. She hadn't thought of this when she'd agreed to let him move in. She also hadn't thought of how difficult it would be to lie to Inez. When she'd told her earlier about the marriage, Inez had been surprised but thrilled for her. Her warm congratulations had left Allie feeling extraordinarily guilty.

"Well, um, I'll leave you to your unpacking, then," Allie said nervously. "Dinner's at eight. I'll see you in the dining room."

She went into her bedroom, closing the door firmly behind her. Only then did she discover that there was no lock on this door . . .

Inez insisted on cooking an elaborate meal that she referred to as a "marriage feast." Rafe seemed to enjoy it, but Allie could hardly swallow the food. The realization that she would have to live under the same roof with this man, to share meals with him, to pretend to be his wife, in every way and to continue to live this lie for as long as two years, made her feel miserable. Being dishonest, pretending to be something she wasn't, was completely foreign to her nature. She felt that she was caught up in something that just kept going faster and faster, getting more and more out of control, and she had no idea where it would all end. She hadn't considered any of this when she'd impulsively agreed to marry Rafe, and now she was having serious second thoughts.

Dinner was a tense, silent meal, and as Inez served each course, she gave Rafe and Allie surreptitious glances of concern. Clearly, she felt the newlyweds were having difficulty adjusting to married life, and Allie thought grimly that she wasn't far wrong.

The moment dinner was over, Allie rose from the table. "I'm going to turn in early." She started for the door leading from the dining room to the hallway.

"Allie."

The sound of her name stopped her, but she didn't turn around.

"We have to talk."

Still not meeting his look, she said, "There's nothing to talk about," and was gone.

Rafe sat in mute frustration. He hadn't expected things to be this awkward and uncomfortable between them. Why did it have to matter to her? The fact that he was now living with her didn't *mean* anything. He certainly didn't feel awkward about it. But as he carried on this one-way dialogue with himself, his fingers drummed nervously on the table, and he found himself longing for her company. This was a big, silent, lonelv house when you were alone.

Determined not to sit around feeling bereft, Rafe grabbed his jacket and left the house, an uneasy anger riding him. He told himself he couldn't care less that she seemed determined to live as separately from him as possible. His only concern had to do with the success of their plan. He couldn't afford for her to change her mind about their arrangement now. There was too much at stake, and dozens of things he had to do if they were going to pull this off. But even as he swung a leg over the Harley and started it, he looked up at the second-floor veranda, where he had seen her looking down at him the day of Mac's funeral.

He half expected to find her there now, watching him with that cool blue gaze that carefully hid her emotions. When she'd run from him in the dining room, as if afraid of what he might have in mind for the remainder of the evening, those emotions had been stripped naked, exposing her vulnerability. At moments like that, she seemed as defenseless as a child.

He'd wanted to take her in his arms and comfort the frightened child within her as he had done in her apartment, but he knew she wouldn't give him the opportunity to do so again. He understood fear, pain, and loss. He'd experienced enough of it for ten lifetimes. Even as he was telling himself that she'd been entirely unreasonable, and all he wanted to do was help, he faced an inescapable truth. If she had let him get close enough to comfort her, he knew he would have wanted more.

"It'll be strictly business, because I know that's the way we both want it."

He'd meant those words when he said them. Now he knew he'd been lying to himself as well as to her. When he'd kissed her in the Jacuzzi at the Edgewater inn, it'd had nothing to do with business and everything to do with desire. He wanted her as he hadn't wanted any woman since Julianne. Even his passion for Julianne paled in comparison to his complicated, powerful feelings for Allie.

Angry and frustrated, he revved the Harley, spinning out on the cobble driveway as he turned it around and headed out onto the street. Once on Seventeen-Mile Drive, he quickly took it through the gears and beyond posted speed limits.

Out on the highway he pushed it to the edge, cutting through traffic until he was winding along the south coast toward Big Sur, and the sharp blast of the wind obliterated everything, except the need for speed.

Allie lay in bed, wide awake, unable to sleep. She kept listening for the sound of Rafe's return. She wasn't sure which was worse, not knowing where he was and what he was doing, or wondering when he would return. She told herself she didn't care where he was, that it didn't matter what he was doing—who he was doing it with. Still, she couldn't sleep.

When well past midnight she finally heard his footsteps on the tile floor, she nearly jumped out of her skin. Only then did she realize how intently she'd been listening for that sound. She lay there, her body tense, listening to his steps come down the hall. When they passed her door, she breathed a sigh of relief. She heard the faint sound of his door opening and closing, and more footsteps as he crossed his bedroom.

Then she remembered the unlocked door connecting their two rooms. She stared at the door handle, expecting to see it slowly turn. She told herself she was being utterly foolish. Rafe might be a lot of things, but he wasn't the kind of man to force himself on a woman. He was far too attractive to women for that ever to be a necessity.

Still, she didn't relax until there were no more sounds in his room, and she knew he must have gone to bed. She couldn't spend every night like this, she told herself. Something had to be done.

The next morning Allie looked in the Yellow Pages for the name of a private detective. Selecting one whose advertisement promised discreet but thorough investigations, she made an appointment to see him later that morning. Then she called Liz DiMaggio.

"I'm so glad you're back in town," Liz said warmly. "I've been trying to get hold of you. So, I guess congratulations are in order."

Allie was surprised. "You heard?"

"My dear, *everyone* has heard. You and Rafe have set this town on its ear. There hasn't been this much excitement since your father surprised everyone by marrying your mother. When it comes to gossip, the peninsula is like a very *small* town."

"Liz . . ." Allie closed her eyes, struggling for the words to explain what she was feeling. She knew she could trust Liz with the truth. The only problem was, she was no longer certain what the truth was.

Allie went on awkwardly. "There's something I need to tell you."

Something in her tone must have revealed the depth of her unhappiness. "How soon can you get here?" Liz asked.

"Ten minutes." But I don't want to impose if you're busy."

"It's no imposition. I'll be waiting."

Twenty minutes later Allie was pacing back and forth in Liz's gallery. Liz had put up the Closed sign the moment Allie arrived, so they had the place to themselves.

"Will you please sit down and have some tea?" Liz asked for the third time. "You're going to wear a hole in that carpet, and I'll have you know it's a very expensive import."

Allie stopped and looked down at the pale plush carpet on the floor of the gallery. It looked very expensive but hardly the antique variety. Looking up at Liz, she found her grinning at her.

"Well, at least it got you to stop that damned pacing. *Sit,*" she commanded as she poured her a fresh cup of hot tea. Allie's had grown cold in her cup.

Allie sat in one of the deeply cushioned wing chairs before the cozy hearth at one end of the gallery that gave it the warm, inviting atmosphere of an English country cottage.

"So you and Rafe got married to keep Gavin from selling off the ranch," Liz said bluntly, cutting through all the complicated explanations and self-justifications Allie had just given her.

"Well . . . yes," Allie admitted, feeling like a fraud.

To her amazement, Liz grinned like the proverbial Cheshire cat. "Good for you two! It's about time someone made that family realize they don't have a God-given right to run things as they see fit."

Allie said unhappily, "I thought I could handle it. It seemed like the only way to stop Gavin and preserve the ranch. It seemed so *logical* at the time."

"And now?"

"Now I don't know. I'm really having second thoughts about what we did. It's wrong."

Liz shrugged. "Only from a legal standpoint."

Allie had no idea how to respond to that. Instead, she said, "I believe the only worthwhile reason to get married is that you love someone and want to make a life together."

Liz eyed her thoughtfully. "Do you love Rafe?"

"What? Of course not!"

"There's no *of course* about it. Rafe's one hell of a sexy man, and you're an extremely attractive woman. You've been thrown together in an extremely intimate situation, and it's not inconceivable that sparks could fly."

"That isn't part of the deal!" Allie insisted, trying hard to sound as if she meant it. She hesitated, then went on less vehemently. "I don't even know him."

"As I recall from some of my past relationships, that's not always a prerequisite."

"Well, for me it is. And anyway, Rafe is the *last* man I would ever—"

Liz raised her hand, interrupting Allie. "Please, spare me the detailed rundown on Rafe's faults. I'm sure he's a selfish pig and a womanizing jerk, and everything else you can think of to say about him. You're a nice girl, and nice girls are taught to avoid men like Rafe. But while you're criticizing him, remember he's also intelligent, driven, and fascinating, and far more decent than he likes to reveal. Mac was extremely fond of him, to the point that he entrusted him with an enormous inheritance. And Mac was a shrewd judge of character."

"But—"

"But what?" Liz asked innocently.

How could she possibly explain it to Liz—the fear that came

from not knowing what part, if any, Rafe played in the events surrounding her mother's death.

Sensing there was more bothering Allie than she had admitted, Liz took Allie's hands in hers. "What is really going on?"

Allie hated revealing weakness in herself. For years she'd worked at overcoming childhood insecurities, creating a strong, self-assured façade, especially in her work. But this had nothing to do with her career. It had everything to do with a frightened little girl who'd repressed the memory of one terrible night.

"I honestly don't understand my feelings about Rafe!" she said in frustration. "I know only that I can't trust him."

"Why not?"

Allie explained about the instinctive fear of Rafe she'd felt when she'd first seen his photograph in the newspaper, and her near-fatal "accident" at Edgewater.

Liz's expression sharpened with concern. "Do you really think it might have been more than an accident, and Rafe might be responsible?"

"I just don't know," Allie said helplessly. "It's just a feeling, especially that inexplicable fear I felt the moment I saw his face in the newspaper." She heard the desperation and frustration in her own voice. Unable to sit still, she walked over to the window and stared out at the idyllic scene, with its beautiful flowers, quaint storefronts, and picture-perfect weather.

Liz said thoughtfully, "When all is said and done, we have only our instincts to go on. It can be a serious mistake to ignore our gut feelings."

Allie leaned her head against the window. "I don't know what to do about Rafe. I'm so torn between wanting to trust him, yet feeling somehow that I shouldn't."

Liz was silent for a moment. She refilled her own teacup, then picked up Allie's, put it in her hands, and said, "Drink." As Allie finally sipped her tea, Liz began gently, "Let me tell you something about the time when Rafe came to live with your parents out at the ranch. He was wild, rebellious, angry, and in a great deal of pain. His father had just died . . . not that he had any sort of relationship with him. He obviously couldn't live with Gavin or Charlotte, who hated him. When your parents offered to take him in, it was nothing short of his salvation."

Allie nodded. "Rafe told me about it. He said it was the only happy time in his life."

"Maybe, but there were a lot of rough times in the beginning. He and Alan didn't get along at first. Rafe saw him as just another Sloan, and felt he was merely being pawned off on another unwilling relative. Of course, he was crazy about Barbara from the beginning, but in his eyes she wasn't truly a Sloan."

Allie found herself filled with curiosity about the sad, difficult boy that Rafe had been then. "What happened to turn things around?"

"Alan spent a lot of time with him, at first over Rafe's sullen objections. He took him everywhere, riding with the vaqueros, treating him as an equal, letting him ride hard and play hard, and work out his anger. Little by little, Alan began to get through to Rafe."

Liz smiled softly at the touching memory. "My God, he was such a handsome boy, with those dark eyes and that dark skin and hair. I told Barbara he would break a lot of hearts when he grew up. She just smiled in that gentle way she had, and said that his own heart had already been broken, and someday she hoped he would find the right girl to mend it."

"I'm sure he's found a lot of girls," Allie said with a hint of jealousy that didn't escape Liz's notice.

Liz went on. "I particularly noticed the way he treated you—pretending you were a pest, yet enormously protective too. Alan told me once that he never worried about you when you were with Rafe. He knew Rafe would watch out for you. He was like both the brother and son Alan never had, all rolled into one. He was a handful, but Alan believed in him."

Allie's expression was sober. "But what if my father was wrong about Rafe?"

Liz didn't answer immediately. Finally, she sighed heavily, and said, "The only advice I can can give you is to trust your instincts." Then she added, "And be careful. There's a great deal more at stake than the future of the ranch."

Jerry Carter, the private investigator Allie had called, had a small but nicely decorated office in one of the old Spanish-style buildings in downtown Monterey. He was nothing like the chain-smoking gumshoe Allie had expected. In his early thirties, he was a short, slight, bespectacled man who looked more like an accountant than a detective.

"Whatever your problem is, I assure you I can handle it quickly and efficiently," he began. "Nowadays, we investigators do most of our work via computer. Almost anything you need to know can be found out through computerized records of one kind or another. I don't even own a gun. I don't need one. A state-of-the-art IBM is much more useful."

Allie smiled self-consciously. "I'm sorry. I guess I've read too many Raymond Chandler novels."

"It's all right. Most people who come in here expect something quite different from what they find." Leaning back in his leather chair, he went on. "Now then, what can I do for you?"

Allie took a list of names from her purse, handed it to him, and explained that she needed to know where these people had been during the preceding forty-eight hours. She particularly needed to know if any of them had left the area.

To her surprise, Carter said this would be an easy assignment, and he could probably have the information for her by the next day. Glancing at the list, he read it quickly, then looked at her curiously. "I recognize the names. The Sloans are pretty powerful. If you're taking them on, I hope you know what you're getting yourself into."

"I know," Allie said simply. "Just get me the information as soon as possible."

When Allie returned to Casa Sureno, it was cold and chilly. The fog was rolling in, along with higher clouds that predicted rain. She pulled around to the garage in the back, then went into the house through the courtyard.

As she walked up to the open doorway leading into the den, she heard Rafe's voice. Stopping at the doorway, she saw that Rafe was on the phone at the desk. Allie stared in dismay at the transformed office. Mac's antique mahogany desk had been pushed back as far as possible against the back wall. A leather sofa and two chairs that had previously dominated at least half the room were now tightly clustered around the fireplace. A larger conference table with rolls of site plans and elevations on top now dominated the center of the room. And against the opposite wall were a sturdy oak drafting table and a stool.

Rafe finished his conversation and hung up. He met Allie's critical look. "We've got a lot of work to do, and not much time. I thought we might as well get started."

She couldn't argue with that. Going over to the drafting table, she ran her fingers over the smooth, hard wood. It was smooth as glass, and aged to a pale gold color, like old school desks. "This is solid oak," she remarked in surprise.

"It's not fancy, but it's sturdy. If you don't like it, you can get something else."

"Oh, I like it," Allie said quickly. "Julia has one like this in her office. She found it years ago in an antique store. But no one makes them out of oak anymore. Where did you find it?"

"I picked it up at a flea market in L.A. years ago. I've been dragging it around ever since. I thought you could use it."

She smiled softly. "Thank you."

Somehow she sensed that the desk was more than just a piece of office equipment. It was symbolic of his acceptance of her work and his tacit agreement to let her guide the project as she saw fit. She was touched beyond measure, but had absolutely no idea how to express that feeling.

Finally, she said awkwardly, "Well . . . I guess we'd better get to work, then."

They worked into the early evening, going over the site plans, referring to old land grant maps of El Sureno, reviewing the original set of working drawings that Rafe had made and discussing changes to them.

Pencil in hand, Allie began to sketch on the blank piece of drafting paper, outlining the coastline that bordered the ranch property, loosely sketching in the golf course, clubhouse, adjacent resort facilities, then jumping the Malpaso Creek and linking them to a central village, commercial facilities, and then a chain of residential areas, all linked by a bridge.

"You've left the bulk of the ranch untouched," Rafe pointed out.

"That's the main idea—maximum usage with minimum intrusion."

To her surprise, he suddenly broke into an engaging grin.

"You're really something, Alexandra Wyatt Sloan. I don't think I've ever met a woman quite like you."

For a moment their eyes met. In his she saw admiration and something more—a genuine warmth. She was afraid to even think of what he must see in her own eyes. Uncertain and self-conscious, she looked away, forcing herself to focus once more on the papers spread out before them. She had retreated, just as she always did, behind the safe protective wall of her work.

She knew it, and he knew it. But he didn't press it.

"Rafe, this way we would develop only twenty or thirty thousand acres out of the total ranch property of one hundred thousand acres."

"Preserving the bulk of the ranch as it is," Rafe concluded.

Just then Inez appeared in the open doorway and announced that dinner was ready. This time they didn't eat in awkward silence. They continued to discuss the project, throwing out ideas, arguing about them, accepting or rejecting them. Long after dinner had ended they sat at the dining room table, talking enthusiastically.

When Allie glanced at her watch and saw that it was nearly midnight, she was amazed. She yawned tiredly.

"You're exhausted," Rafe said. "We can continue this tomorrow."

She smiled contentedly. "I'm used to sessions like this. It's very creative. I thrive on it."

"Even when we disagree?"

"That's where the creativity comes from. It would be boring if we agreed on everything."

Pushing back his chair, he got up and came around the table to stand beside her. He leaned his weight on one hip, casually propped against the edge of the table. The gesture was so like him, Allie thought. There was always a hint of restless energy about him, as if he intended to spring up at any moment. The only times she had seen him completely relaxed had been astride a horse at the ranch and in the cockpit of the glider.

Now he reached out to gently stroke her cheek. His touch was disquieting. Pulling back sharply, she stood and said, "It's very late. I should be going to bed. There's a lot to do tomorrow."

Looking directly at her, he asked, "Why are you afraid of me?"

"I'm not—"

"Liar," he interrupted in a deceptively quiet voice.

Undeterred by her earlier reaction, he reached out, slipping his fingers beneath the sweep of soft gold hair that curved against her cheek. He tenderly tucked it behind her ear, his fingers tracing the delicate curve. "Trust me, Allie," he whispered.

She was tempted to do just that. But can I trust myself? she wondered.

Rafe took her left hand in his. The light from the crystal chandelier poised over the center of the dining room table caught at the simple wedding band on her third finger. His thumb lightly traced the polished gold scrollwork.

Looking into his eyes, she knew that if she stayed there one more second, he would take her in his arms and kiss her, and she would be utterly unable to resist. Jerking her hand back, as if from a hot surface, she stepped back, putting a safe distance between them.

She said shakily, "I . . . I need to go to bed now. Good night."

And she fled from the dining room, leaving him watching after her with an enigmatic expression.

Allie took a hot shower and then dressed for bed. Her hands shook as she buttoned the tiny pearl buttons of her white silk nightgown. She crawled under the thick feather comforter and pulled it up to her chin. As she had done the night before, she lay awake, unable to sleep, listening for the sound of Rafe's footsteps. But there were only the creaking sounds of the old house and the crashing of waves against the rocky cliffs.

26

DESPITE HAVING GOTTEN TO sleep so late the night before, Allie was up early the next morning. As she came downstairs, just after seven, she smelled delicious aromas coming from the kitchen—fresh ground coffee and cinnamon rolls. She said a silent prayer of thanks that Inez had wanted to stay on instead of retiring after Mac's death. Planning to quickly look over the plans from the night before, to check any changes Rafe might have made, she stopped at the den on her way to the breakfast room. But she stopped abruptly just inside the doorway. Rafe sat at the desk, with paperwork, maps, and reports spread out around him. On one corner of the desk sat a fax machine that hadn't been there the night before.

"Glancing up at her, he said easily, "Good morning."

"Good morning," she responded, her tone betraying her surprise. She hadn't expected to find him up and working so early. Then she noticed a thick wool blanket folded at one end of the sofa, and realized why she hadn't heard him come into his room the night before. "You slept in here last night?"

"I worked late, and decided just to crash on the couch."

Inez came in, carrying a tray with a pot of coffee, two cups and plates, and a basket of cinnamon rolls. Quickly clearing off a corner of the desk to accommodate the tray, Rafe said with a grin, "I was wondering if you were going to let us eat those, or just torture us with the aroma."

Inez set the tray down on the desk and filled the coffee cups. "Before his heart condition, Mr. Sloan always used to ask for my rolls in the morning when he came in here to work." She added with a pleased smile, "It is wonderful to have people to cook for, and to hear the sound of conversation in this house again. Who knows," she finished with a wink, "maybe there will even be the happy sounds of children one day. As my late husband, Ismael, used to say, you never can tell."

Before either Rafe or Allie could summon a response, Inez turned to leave. On her way out she picked up the wool blanket and neatly folded it, then put it away in the storage closet beside the hearth.

When she was gone, Allie turned to Rafe. "Do you think she knows?"

"What? That we aren't sleeping together?"

Allie hadn't expected him to put it quite that way. She responded awkwardly, "Well, yes, I suppose that's what I meant."

His dark eyes met hers, filling her with that familiar uneasiness. "Probably. I'd say Inez misses very little that goes on around here. But I'm sure she thinks we're just having problems adjusting to married life, like any newlyweds. The important thing is that if she's asked to testify in court, she can honestly say we're living under the same roof and seem to be sharing the same bedroom."

"Do you really think Gavin would go so far as to take us to court?" Allie asked worriedly.

"Absolutely. He isn't about to give up yet. But he'll have a hard time finding proof that our marriage is a sham. We spent the night together in your apartment in Seattle, and in the suite at the Edgewater inn."

"But taking us to court would cost him a fortune."

Rafe frowned. "Gavin plays for keeps. But so do I."

Allie looked at him, realizing that he meant what he said. He had done whatever he had to to get this far. He would do whatever it took to make it all the way to the end. His single-minded determination and apparent lack of scruples were disturbing. But, she reminded herself, she was hardly in a position to pass judgment. After all, she'd willingly, if reluctantly, gone along with this charade.

Without further delay they got to work. There were hundreds of decisions to be made, meetings to be set with engineers, and eventually with potential investors. But first Allie and Rafe had to agree not only about the scope of the project but the overall design.

They argued about it for several days. Allie made frequent calls to Julia in Seattle to back up her arguments for an Edgewater type facility. Three days later they had agreed that the project, now formally called El Sureno, was to be a rustic but elegant design of the old Californio style, to blend as naturally with the surrounding environment of the Big Sur coastline as possible.

By the following Tuesday they had located office rental space big enough to accommodate the draftsmen. Rafe brought in two men he'd worked with previously, and Julia was willing to lend one from her office who had worked primarily on the Edgewater project.

By the end of the week the small architectural office—a joint venture of Sloan Construction and Winslow & Associates—was operational. They ran it from the office set up in Mac's den at Casa Sureno.

After his first night at the house, Rafe had either slept on the couch in the den, or he'd gone out and stayed away all night. Allie had no idea where he spent those nights out. She told herself it was really none of her business, and she didn't care anyway. But it bothered her more than she would admit.

Suddenly everything seemed to be happening at once. They were notified by their attorney that Gavin had filed suit against them for fraud, and they received their first social invitation as Mr. and Mrs. Rafael Sloan—to the annual Cascarones charity ball. The premier social event of the season on the peninsula, the masquerade ball dated back to the time of the dons, and all the proceeds went to a local charity.

Sitting at her drafting table in the den, Allie stared at the invitation. After a moment she looked up at Rafe. "What are we going to do about this?"

Rafe sat at the desk. For the first time that morning the

phone with the new business number was mercifully silent. "We accept, of course."

"But—"

"Look, everyone will be there. It'll be an opportunity to show the world what a happily married couple we are."

Allie grimaced. "I'm not sure I'm that good an actress."

Ignoring the barb, he went on. "It's precisely what Gavin won't expect us to do."

"Are you looking for a confrontation with him?"

"No. But I'm not going to run away from one either."

Allie said uneasily, "Rafe, this is flirting with trouble."

"The only way to deal with a problem is to face it head-on. We can't avoid Gavin, or the other members of the family."

"You don't want to avoid them," she said angrily. "You want to rub their noses in the fact that you beat them."

"If I do, they've certainly got it coming," he snapped.

Gathering up an armful of plans, Allie headed for the door. She needed a quiet place to work by herself for a while. She wasn't sure why it bothered her so much to think of putting on a show of marital togetherness for the family and Pebble Beach society. But it did.

As she slammed out of the office, she heard the phone ring. It also sounded on the extension in the living room across the entryway. That meant it was the personal line. She heard Rafe pick up the phone. After his terse hello, his tone changed. Lowering his voice, he spoke in a more intimate voice. Obviously, this was a personal conversation. Allie had overheard similar conversations at least twice since he'd moved into Casa Sureno.

She told herself she should have no illusions about Rafe. He had undoubtedly enjoyed an active social life before she came along, before their "marriage." He was an extremely handsome man with a dangerous edge that attracted women. It was unrealistic to expect that simply because of their arrangement, his personal life would change. She certainly couldn't see him being celibate for the duration of their marriage.

But no matter how objective she tried to be about the situation, no matter how much she told herself it was really none of her business and she didn't care anyway, she couldn't stop feeling angry and hurt. Now she slammed into her bedroom, scattering folders, portfolios, and rolls of plans across the small sofa in the sitting area. As she crossed the room, she heard the sound of the motorcycle in the driveway. Going to the French windows, she watched Rafe roar out onto Seventeen-Mile Drive. He didn't waste any time after receiving that phone call, she thought miserably.

For a while she tried to concentrate on the preliminary plans that she'd worked on, but she found herself staring at the phone. Finally she picked it up. Julia's voice at the other end was genuinely caring and immensely reassuring.

"What's up, kiddo?" Julia asked. "Got your hands full?"

The innocent question could have been answered in a way that would have surprised and disturbed Julia. Instead, Allie forced herself to stick to business. "I was wondering when you can cut Stan loose to come down here and get started."

"How about Friday? That will give him the weekend to look over the site and then you can get him started on Monday."

"Great," Allie responded, although her tone suggested everything was far from wonderful.

"Problems?" Julia asked immediately in her no-nonsense, direct way.

Cradling the phone against her shoulder, Allie said, "I was wondering if you'd like to take a few days off and come down to Monterey. I'd really like you to see the ranch. It's spectacular, and to tell you the truth, I feel kind of cut adrift."

"You've got what it takes to do this," Julia reassured her. "This is a simply a larger version of Edgewater."

"Thanks for the vote of confidence," Allie responded gratefully. "But I'd really like you to see it."

"Well . . . I don't have anything planned for this weekend. I could fly down with Stan and take a look at what you've gotten yourself into." It was said with Julia's own brand of ironic humor, but instead of smiling in response, Allie felt on the verge of tears.

She said quickly, forcing her voice into a semblance of control, "Let me know what flight you're on. You can stay here with me."

As soon as she spoke, Allie realized she'd made a serious slip—you can stay with *me,* not *us*. She was sure it hadn't been lost on Julia. But to her relief, Julia didn't question her.

Julia said, "I'll see you the end of the week. Want me to bring anything along?"

Allie wanted to say, yes, a shoulder to cry on and your sound advice. Instead, she answered, "Just Stan, and your expertise."

"I think I can manage that. See you Friday."

When Allie hung up, she felt immensely reassured. At least with Julia there, she wouldn't feel so alone.

A half hour later she slid behind the wheel of Rafe's Corvette to drive to the meeting with the investors. At his urging, she'd returned her car to the rental agency the previous week, and had been using the Corvette, while Rafe drove the Harley. She was right on time for the meeting in the new office they'd just opened up in a 1920 stucco house that had been converted to commercial property. It had bay windows that looked out onto Lighthouse Avenue and Monterey Bay. This was now the new location of the Sloan Development Company. Rafe was already there, having gone ahead of her to oversee the last-minute arrangements. This meeting was critical, and he wanted to be certain nothing went wrong.

While the half-dozen wealthy, middle-aged men listened intently, Rafe and Allie laid out the entire scope of the project, focusing on the changes she had introduced. They reassured the nervous investors they were definitely in control of the land. Rafe gave each of them a copy of a letter from Mac's attorney, informing the investors that Rafael Sloan and his wife, Alexandra Wyatt Sloan, now controlled the Sloan Land Company and Rancho El Sureno.

Rafe himself brought up the issue of the pending suit Gavin intended to file against them. She had expected him to avoid the issue, and perhaps even lie about it, but he didn't. In blunt terms he confronted their questions and their doubts.

Allie was more than a little surprised. She had fully expected him to completely avoid any mention of the action. It would have been the typical thing to do. She'd seen developers do it countless time, concerned only with the success of the project and the money it could make them. But he'd deliberately jeopardized the project in order to tell the truth.

Rafe said insistently, "With our marriage, my wife and I control the ranch. There is absolutely no question about that. And no matter what Gavin tries to do, he can't change it."

My wife. It was the first time he'd referred to her that way. Allie felt a funny little jolt in the pit of her stomach.

Rafe went on. "And now my wife will go over the plans in detail, so you can see just how unique and special this development will be."

Taking her cue, Allie slipped into the familiar professional territory that she loved. Two easels had been set up at one end of the room. The rough outline of new plans that she'd put together over the past week changing the layout of the first phase of the development were displayed. As she explained each new site plan, she folded back the sheets to reveal the next.

Rafe stood back and watched admiringly as Allie behaved with grace under pressure. She moved confidently from one board to the other. In this professional environment there were none of the distracted, uneasy gestures that betrayed personal uncertainty. There was also nothing flamboyant in the way she handled herself, unlike most architects, Rafe thought. For Allie, this wasn't about ego. It was about love—her love for the land and the historical integrity she was determined to preserve.

In that cool, soft-as-smoke voice, she fielded questions with the calm assurance of someone who believed absolutely in what she was doing. She was smart enough to present aspects of the project that she knew appealed to cost-conscious investors.

As Rafe watched these men, whom he knew well by now, respond to her, he knew that he'd been right to turn the meeting over to her. She was utterly convincing and persuasive. But more than that, he realized that he was proud of her. Like himself, she didn't back down from a challenge.

When both Allie and Rafe had finished speaking, and had answered the investors' numerous questions, the meeting was over. Before giving their final decision, the investors said they wanted to discuss the project privately among themselves.

Allie walked outside, preferring the small outdoor garden to the barren interior of the drafting room with its tables, stools, and newly installed countertops for laying out plans. She lit one of the cigarettes she'd been carrying around in her purse for weeks, then just as quickly extinguished it in a sand-filled clay pot that sat at the edge of the walkway.

Following her out of the small building, Rafe frowned as he watched her light up the cigarette, then quickly put it out. Her fingers trembled slightly, and he knew she was nervous and worried. He was too, but he refused to let it show. Allie stood at the top landing of the brick steps leading down the slight incline to the garden. The crisp morning breeze lifted her rich gold hair from her shoulder.

She looked tired, he thought worriedly. There were faint circles under her eyes. He wondered if she'd had the nightmare again. She hadn't said anything about it, but then he realized she probably wouldn't confide in him anymore. There had been just that one time at her apartment in Seattle—the first time he had seen her frightened and vulnerable, haunted by old memories. They had been close that night, closer than either of them had wanted to acknowledge. Then they had gone to Edgewater, and Allie had nearly drowned. After that, things had changed between them.

A barrier had gone up after the accident at Edgewater. He saw it in her eyes, felt it in the cool, careful, professional distance she maintained. He knew she had her doubts about the marriage. God knew he had his own. But they were in it now, for better or worse, as the justice of the peace had said. Watching her, seeing how shaky she was, he felt the need to reassure her.

Walking up to her, he saw the sudden tensing of her shoulders, saw the barrier drop into place as he came near.

"You were great in there. You really had them eating out of your hand."

She colored slightly, embarrassed. "Thanks."

"If this works out, it will mainly be due to your efforts, Allie. I . . . I'm very grateful."

Reaching out, he touched her arm, his fingers warm, demanding, sensually charged, against her cool skin. Heat moved between them like an electric current. Rafe remembered when he'd warned Valentina that she could get burned. Allie was nothing like Val, whose passionate nature was there for all the world to see. Allie was cool and remote—at least on the outside. But inside, he sensed, was a fire just waiting to be ignited.

His fingers tightened over her arm as he looked deeply into her eyes. They were like blue crystal, ice-clear with the same intensity he'd seen in Barbara's eyes. She was so like her mother, in more ways than she could ever possibly know.

Rafe felt anger churn inside him at Allie's cool response. He wanted to get underneath that perfect, remote façade, and find out just what it would take to make her melt.

"Allie . . ."

Before he could say the words that were only half formed in his mind, she pulled her arm free. "We'd better go in and find out the verdict."

And without looking at him she brushed past and went back into the office.

He stood for a moment, forcing his wildly mixed feelings back under rigid control. Then he followed her inside.

From the moment she walked into the tiny front office where they'd made their presentation, Allie knew they'd won. She could tell by the way the investors smiled at her, that they had voted to back the project. She was almost sick with relief.

When Rafe came in a moment later, one of the men said, "You've got the money, Sloan." Nodding toward Allie, he added, "And you've got your wife to thank for it."

Rafe glanced briefly at Allie. She couldn't read his look. Instead of the triumph she'd expected to see written all over his face, his expression was enigmatic, almost as if he were concerned about something besides the financing for the project. But she found that impossible to believe.

Rafe walked out with the men while Allie remained behind. She heard him set another meeting with them the following week to take care of the financial details with a local bank that would be issuing the funds to begin construction on the first phase.

Euphoria followed that first cold feeling of uncertainty. She'd felt it several times before on projects, but never with this level of satisfaction and accomplishment. None of those projects had ever meant this much.

When Rafe returned he leaned a shoulder into the doorway.

hands shoved into the pockets of his slacks. "Not bad," he said dryly.

The earlier tension between them was momentarily forgotten. Somehow that had been personal, while this was professional—and therefore familiar and safe.

"I'd say it was a little bit better than 'not bad,'" Allie said happily.

The fatigue he'd seen on her face earlier was gone now. She was relaxed, confident, and very pleased with herself.

"All right," he conceded as a slow grin transformed the lines and angles of his aquiline features. "It was a little more than 'not bad.'"

She was all softness and joy, completely euphoric with their victory. "Oh, for heaven's sake, admit it, we did it! We got the financing, and now we can make it all come true. We can make the dream real!"

He acted purely on instinct. Flushed with victory, he grabbed her arms, pulled her against him, and lowered his mouth to hers. Their lips met in a kiss that was brief yet intense. Like that night at Edgewater in the Jacuzzi, the contact was sudden and startling. Besides that night there had been only the briefest contacts—his hand gently covering hers in the glider, his fingers loosely intertwined with hers when they were married; virtually no physical contact. Until now.

She pulled back abruptly from the kiss, but still pressed against him, she realized again how lean and hard his body was. Her own body responded unconsciously. Heat spiraled through her every place their bodies touched—his arms at her waist, her thighs against his, his hips molded to hers, her breasts pressed against his chest. The contact was intimate, thoroughly rousing, and frightening.

She felt the pressure of his hands through the fabric of her plain white silk dress she'd chosen for the meeting. His fingers fanned low at the back of her waist, then bit into the curve of her bottom as he held her against him.

Her hand pressed against his chest, near his throat. She stared, fascinated at the contrast of skin—hers pale, almost translucent, his the soft bronze of his Latino heritage, deepened by countless hours in the sun, darker still where soft black hair swirled at the open collar of the shirt. It was impossible not to imagine what the stark contrast of their bodies would look like without the barrier of clothes.

Impossible—and easy, just as it was so easy to forget why they were there, why they had married in the first place—not for love, but a business arrangement, because each had something the other needed. Remember that, Allie told herself. Remember why you're here and who he is. You can't trust him, except in business, and perhaps not even in that.

She pulled away from him, shaken to the core. Desperate for something to distract her, she hastily started to gather plans, portfolios, and reports. Then she pulled the revised site plans from the easels, rolled them, and put them into tubes.

All the while Rafe stood in the doorway, watching her, his expression contemplative. There was no hint that he felt any response at all to what had passed between them. He said quietly, "You're right, it was a great deal better than 'not bad.' It was outstanding and it deserves a celebration. Let me take you out to dinner."

She relaxed slightly as she realized he was putting what had just happened behind them. Ignoring the sudden pang of disappointment she felt at the ease with which he dismissed it, she retreated behind a wall of easy banter. "Are you asking me out on a *date*?"

He grinned, obviously as amused as she was by the irony of a husband asking his wife for a date. "Under the circumstances, I don't know what to call it. But we definitely should celebrate."

"All right," she said, joining in the festive mood. "What time?"

He looked at his watch. "How about an hour from now?"

"Four o'clock? Isn't that a bit early for dinner?"

"The place I have in mind is down the coast a bit. And, by the way, dress casual. I've got a few things to wrap up here, then I'll pick you up."

It was almost three-thirty before she got back to Casa Sureno Allie barely had time to quickly shower and dress, keeping in mind that Rafe had said casual. Because it was one of those cold, damp afternoons, she decided on black velvet stirrup pants tucked into black suede boots, and a black off-the shoulder, long-sleeved stretch lace top. As she dressed, she thought how strange it felt to be getting ready for a date with Rafe—her husband, even if only in name.

The phone rang as she was racing to finish dressing. When she answered, she heard the voice of Jerry Carter, the private detective she'd hired. "Mrs. Sloan?"

"Yes," she said slowly. Suddenly her stomach felt tied up in knots, and she held herself rigid, waiting for the information he would give her. "Mr. Carter, do you . . . do you have some information for me?"

"Yeah, it was easy enough to check on the whereabouts of the people on your list. Unfortunately, it wasn't very conclusive."

"What do you mean?"

"I'll go down the list here." He paused, then continued matter-of-factly. "Erica Sloan was supposedly home alone all day. But no one can verify that. It was her housekeeper's day off, she didn't have any visitors, and if she made any calls, they were local and can't be traced."

"In other words, you can't be certain she was actually at home."

"Exactly. Her husband, Gavin Sloan, and David Benedict were both off somewhere together on business. At least that's what they told their secretaries. Neither of them was in the office all day. But I can't trace their movements. If they flew anywhere, or rented a car, they used assumed names."

Which is exactly what they would do, Allie thought, if they wanted to hide a trip to Seattle.

Carter went on. "Charlotte apparently went up to the city for the day to do some shopping. But she went alone. And if she bought anything, she must've used cash, because none of her credit cards had any charges for that day."

Somehow Allie found it difficult to imagine Charlotte shopping at Neiman's or Magnin's or any of her usual haunts without running up some impressive charges on her credit cards.

Carter continued. "And that leaves Valentina and her brother, Nicholas. Wherever they were, they were together. The security guard at Spanish Bay, where he has a condo, saw them drive off together in her Jaguar early that morning. He has no idea when Mr. Benedict came back, because the residents don't check in and out at the gate. He noticed when they left only because he likes Jags and Valentina's is a particularly nice one."

So that was that, Allie thought in frustration. None of them had a foolproof alibi for the day that someone had tried to kill her. She told herself it didn't necessarily mean anything. After all, innocent people didn't worry about providing alibis for themselves. Only someone planning to commit a crime would bother trying to cover his tracks. For all she knew, each one of them might have been doing something that had nothing to do with her.

"Mrs. Sloan?"

Allie realized she'd left Carter hanging on the other end of the line while she considered this less than satisfactory information. "I'm sorry, Mr. Carter. I was just . . . thinking."

"I understand. Look, I'm sorry I can't give you anything more definite."

"It's not your fault. Thank you for dealing with this so promptly."

"You're welcome, ma'am. If you need anything in the future, I hope you'll call me.'"

"I will. Good-bye."

As Allie hung up, a thought struck her. If none of her relatives had an alibi, it meant any one of them could have been driving the boat. Rafe was far from being the only suspect. In fact, the more she thought about it, the more she wanted to believe this let him off the hook. After all, the other members of the family had much stronger motives for wanting her out of the way.

Just then she heard the motorcycle in the driveway. Ignoring the doubts that still ate at her, she hurriedly swept her hair into a simple French twist at the back of her head and anchored it with a gold comb. As she sat at the large mirror at the antique dressing table, she thought again of the old, haunting refrain . . . *Mirror, mirror, on the wall, who's the fairest one of all?* Searching for other images in the glass, she saw only her own image, her expression uncertain. For now, at least, there would be no terrifying memories forcing their way to the surface of her consciousness.

A moment later Inez knocked at the sitting room door and announced that Rafe was waiting downstairs for her.

Allie hastily gathered up her purse and black wool coat from the bed. "How do I look?" she asked hesitantly.

Inez smiled warmly. "You look wonderful, Miss Allie." Her brown eyes twinkled as she said, "I won't wait up."

Allie started to correct her, to say she and Rafe wouldn't be late, but she stopped herself. After all, they were supposed to be married, and she needed to play the part of a new bride.

As she reached the stairs, she found Rafe waiting for her in the entryway. She looked down at him, he looked up at her. At that moment their eyes met, she saw surprise, quickly followed by admiration in his expression, and she knew this might not turn out to be an early night after all.

27

''YOU SAID CASUAL,'' ALLIE reminded him as she came down the stairs, a little uneasy with her choice of attire. ''I wasn't certain how to interpret that.''

He smiled unexpectedly, the look in his eyes the same one she'd seen earlier that afternoon at the office, when everything had gone from strictly professional to shockingly intimate. ''You look perfect.''

The words were studiously polite, but something in his look, and the tone of his voice, made her blush. Embarrassed, she hurried down the remaining stairs and brushed past him. ''Well, we'd better be going, then. You said it's a long drive.''

As they went out the door, he called back over his shoulder to Inez, ''Don't wait up for us.''

He'd put the hardtop on the Corvette. As they got in, Allie asked, ''You said we're going 'down the road a bit.' Just how far is that exactly?''

He gave her a sideways glance as they pulled out of the driveway. ''Just sit back and enjoy the view. It's pretty spectacular.''

He was right. The winding drive along Highway 1 between Pebble Beach and Big Sur boasted some of the most magnificent scenery in the world. They passed the Point Lobos headland, a wilderness reserve, then crossed world-famous Bixby Creek Bridge, which arched gracefully over a deep chasm. Rafe acted as tour guide, telling Allie the names of the places they passed, and sharing bits of local color.

"It's breathtaking," Allie said, entranced, looking out over Point Sur, a long, sandy arm of beach that jutted into the water and massed itself into a 440-foot-high fist of volcanic rock.

"There were a lot of wrecks here before the lighthouse was built." Rafe pointed to a fifty-foot white lighthouse looming above the roiling sea. "One of the vaqueros told me that his grandfather used to tell stories about seeing the wrecks of eighteenth- and nineteenth-century ships on Point Sur Beach. Now it's a different kind of graveyard—the shattered remains of cars that have gone over the edge."

Allie shivered. "What a horrible thought."

Rafe gave her a quick smile, then returned his gaze to the sharply twisting road. "Don't worry. I'm actually a careful driver, believe it or not. Especially when I'm responsible for someone else's welfare."

Allie glanced at him, surprised that he felt the need to reassure her. Most of the time, his attitude seemed to be that he didn't care what anyone else thought of him. Suddenly she remembered what his friend, Mike, had said at their whirlwind wedding ceremony in Lake Tahoe. *You can trust him. With your life, if you have to.*

Can I? She wondered. She prayed she would never have to find out.

They'd been driving for about an hour when the road veered away from the deeply scissored coast, and they passed through the Big Sur River valley. The scenery—woodland, towering redwoods, and the estuary of the Big Sur River—was glorious. The highway passed alternately from shade to sunlit meadows. Allie felt there weren't enough words to describe the various shades of green—the emerald green of the maidenhair fern, the gray-green of the tall eucalyptus trees, and the mallard green of the feathery redwoods. Golden eagles and redtailed hawks soared above the rare Santa Lucia bristlecone firs.

Seeing the scattered shops and restaurants along the Big Sur River, Allie assumed they had reached their destination. But

Rafe kept driving, and soon the road had wound its way back to the coast again. Allie stared in wonder as the sea blasted through blowholes, curled roughly around the sea stacks that were once part of the rocky cliffs, and crashed with undiminished energy on the sandy beach. It was an exhilarating, windy, lonely place, and it epitomized the essentially wild character of Big Sur.

Now streamers of gray mist blended ocean and sky, and wisps of fog obscured the fiery ball of the sun as it sank below the horizon. From the highway above the high, rocky cliffs overlooking the ocean, Allie watched the day slowly fade.

Just when she thought they would be on this road forever, they turned off Highway 1 onto an even smaller road that wound through a ravine. They made the dramatic change from beach to forest in only a few heartbeats. Allie caught glimpses of phantom white orchids.

"There are wild boar, and even mountain lions, in there," Rafe said, gesturing toward the dark forest.

Allie grimaced. "Sounds dangerous."

"Only if you decide to go for a walk at night alone," Rafe said with a wry smile. "I wouldn't recommend it. There are better ways to spend your time here."

It was almost dusk, and the darkening sky was made darker still by the heavy canopy of trees as they plunged into the thick forest. Leaves scattered across the road and churned in their wake. The air through the open window was crisp, pungent with the heady scent of pine, oak, and plants Allie couldn't begin to name.

This area was remote and isolated, and there were no other cars on the road. Allie glanced uneasily at Rafe. His features were illuminated by the glow of light from the instrument panel, creating shadows in the angles and planes of his face. She shivered and pulled the folds of the wool coat more tightly about her.

"How much farther is it?" As she spoke, she heard the edge in her voice. As his gaze met hers, she smiled to disguise it.

"Not far," he answered, his eyes looking even darker than usual in the muted light.

She felt his gaze linger, then shift back to the road.

"We're almost there. It's just around the next curve."

They swept around the next bend in the road and shot into a large clearing rimmed with trees. Several cabins were clustered at the edge of the clearing. But most important, there was the reassuring comfort of lights. Rafe pulled the Corvette to a stop before the largest building.

Architecturally, it could be described only as in the rough-hewn log-cabin style. Rocking chairs were scattered along the length of the wide wraparound porch, and there were river-rock pillars on either side of the wooden steps leading up to the porch and the dramatic hand-carved double wooden doors. It looked as if it had stood a hundred years and would easily stand a hundred more.

Inside, the lodge was all glass, rough-hewn cedar-lined walls, and vaulted cathedral ceilings. A massive stone fireplace filled one wall. Several sofas and deep chairs formed a conversation area before the hearth. Guests sat quietly and talked, or read the evening paper, while sipping glasses of wine. Incongruous with the rustic atmosphere, Vivaldi played softly amid the hiss of the fire and the muted conversations.

Rafe checked on their dinner reservations, then slipped his hand around hers. "There's something I want you to see." Leading her to the opposite end of the lodge where more sofas and chairs were clustered, he stopped in front of a huge expanse of window that filled the entire wall.

The view beyond was breathtaking—the deep woods and the mountains behind them in one direction, the distant ocean through towering spires of pine trees in the other. The low coastal fog had not yet reached the forest, and the sun had slipped beneath the horizon, leaving a fiery crimson band over the surface of gray water. It looked like molten silver.

Rafe stood behind Allie, leaning very close so that one hand braced on each side of the deep window ledge before her, his cheek very near hers. "La Ventana." He said the name of the inn. "In Spanish it means 'window.' This is a window onto the backcountry of the Santa Lucia Mountains."

She felt the warmth of his breath against her cheek, the heat of his body, and experienced all over again that sudden ache of desire that she'd felt that afternoon.

Outside, it grew dark rapidly. Light behind them, from inside the lodge, reflected off the window. She saw his reflection on the glass and fought back a momentary flash of panic—that sudden inexplicable need to run, to get away.

Abruptly, she turned away from the window and stepped out of the circle of his arms. Even though it was warm and cozy inside the lodge, and she was still wearing the wool coat, she suddenly shivered.

Reaching for her hand, he said, "You're cold as ice. Allie? What is it?"

Her gaze cut away from his. She felt caught, trapped, afraid of what she had—and hadn't—seen in the glass. Before she could answer, the hostess found them and said their table would be ready shortly. "Would you like to wait out on the deck?" she asked.

Allie said quickly, "Yes! That would be nice."

"Very well. This way, please."

Allie felt Rafe watching her as they followed the hostess out of the lodge onto the wide deck at the back.

"Have you been to Ventana before?" the hostess asked congenially.

He nodded. "A few times."

"Then you're familiar with the location of the restaurant. Your table will be ready in about ten minutes, if you'd like to go in then."

"Thank you," Rafe said briefly, still staring at Allie.

It was dark now, the air was pure and crisp, permeated with the scent of wood burning in the main lodge. In the glow of light from the lodge Allie could just make out several divergent pathways leading to the cabins at the edge of the forest.

All the pathways were lit at intervals. One was hemmed by footlights that twinkled in the gathering darkness ahead like low-hung stars suspended just above the earth.

Rafe's hand closed around hers. She saw the questions in his eyes, but he didn't push her. His skin was warm against hers as he gently stroked the backs of her fingers with his thumb and spread the heat, driving away the coldness of fear.

"It's too cold just to sit here," he said. "How about if we go for a nice, invigorating walk before dinner."

"Are you sure you know where you're going?"

"All the pathways connect," he assured her. "The worst

that could happen is that we would find ourselves on some guest's doorstep."

He felt her hesitation and sensed that it was something more than reluctance to go for a stroll in a strange place after dark. But whatever she struggled with, she overcame it. Her rigid fingers relaxed as she held on to his hand.

"You can trust me," he said in a surprisingly tender voice.

She smiled nervously as they started down the path. "Were you a boy scout?" she asked, trying to make light of the uneasiness she felt at the surrounding darkness, unbroken save for the intermittent winking footlights along the path.

"No," he admitted, keeping a gentle but firm hold of her hand. "But I know how to survive." He added, "I won't lose you, Allie."

As the forest closed around them, Allie found herself holding on to him even more tightly. The pathway was nothing but a dirt trail. It wound through the trees until the lodge disappeared completely behind them. But the walk was easy enough. They crossed a wooden ravine and a dry streambed, following those twinkling lights. Somewhere in the stillness they heard the faint murmur of voices, possibly from other guests on their way to the restaurant or from a nearby cabin. Another path intersected the one they were on.

They walked down a gentle incline into another clearing and found the restaurant, which resembled the main lodge. Inside they discovered the same vaulted ceilings, a roaring fire at the hearth, and rough cedar walls that disappeared into intimate niches and alcoves where soft lights twinkled at the center of tables covered with embroidered tablecloths. Soft music came from a piano near the hearth. A hostess showed them to their table.

Allie thought how different this was from the first time Rafe had taken her out to eat, at Tarpey's Roadhouse. The restaurant at the inn offered rustic elegance, exquisite food, fine wines, and an intimate ambiance that seemed more appropriate for long-time lovers.

They ordered dinner, then Rafe ordered wine and hors d'oeuvres of shrimp and crab in a buttery-lemon sauce sprinkled over with fresh basil.

"Better?" he asked as she finished a glass of wine, and he poured her another.

"Yes, I was just a little tired," she answered, not wanting to explain, not even certain that she could.

"More bits and pieces of old memories?"

"They come back unexpectedly. I can't seem to get used to it."

He looked at her intently. "Have you remembered anything else?"

She shook her head. "That's the frustrating part. The brief glimpses seem to have stopped. I was told that I might not remember anything more than I already have. I'm beginning to be afraid that may be the case."

"But you might also remember more," he pressed.

"Maybe. There's just no way of knowing."

Tipping his glass lightly against hers, he toasted, "To new memories."

Their dinner arrived then, medallions of beef for Rafe and pork tenderloin with nutmeg and plum sauce for Allie. As they ate the delicious food, they talked about the meeting that afternoon and the tight time frame they had to produce the detailed plans needed for construction on the first phase. Rafe ordered a second bottle of wine—one with just a whisper of smoke in its smooth bouquet. The conversation turned to the construction company he'd started, and Allie felt herself begin to relax as he talked about the projects he'd worked on.

When their dinner plates were cleared away and Rafe had poured the last of the wine, Allie asked impulsively, "Why the Harley? Why not some state-of-the-art Japanese import?"

Rafe leaned back in the upholstered chair, his forearms resting on the padded arms, his wineglass cradled in long fingers. "Before I went into the service I worked part-time for a mechanic. He had the Harley in a box in the back of his shop, in pieces. The largest was a fender and it was badly dented and rusted. Some of the parts were missing altogether. He'd been trying to rebuild it for years, but he never got around to it."

He paused to take a sip of wine, then went on. "I thought it might be a quick investment—restore it, then sell it for a profit. I offered him a hundred bucks to take that box of pieces off his hands. He took it."

"And you rebuilt it," she concluded.

"It took the next ten years," he admitted with a self-deprecating grin. "But I finally finished it. I couldn't even find some of the parts I needed. I had to have them specially milled. Every time I moved, I packed up the pieces and took them with me. They became a permanent fixture in the living room of whichever apartment I was living in at the time."

"Wouldn't it have been easier to sell the lot, or pay someone to do the restoration?"

"Yeah, it would have been easier," he admitted, staring down into the wineglass cradled in his fingers. "Most of my life, up to that point, I'd done the easy thing, which usually meant running away from problems. I never *finished* anything. I suppose I thought that if I could just put all those damn pieces back together and have the thing work, it would be something I could point to and say, 'I finished that.' It became something I had to do."

He looked across at her then, a boyish smile curving his mouth. "That probably doesn't make much sense."

It made perfect sense to her. What he was really trying to do was put back together the pieces of a young boy's shattered life. She tried to imagine the aching loneliness that could come only from being batted back and forth between parents who could never provide a real family.

"Did it run when you were finished? she asked.

He shook his head and laughed. His expression was filled with irony. "I spent ten years working on the damn thing. It symbolized this important goal in my life. And it wouldn't start. I discovered it was a little more complicated than just putting everything back together. But I kept at it. Eventually, I got it running." He shrugged. "By then I couldn't stand to sell it. I'd put too much of myself into it."

"What about the Corvette? Was it in pieces too?"

"That was different. It just needed a lot of work."

Allie sensed it wasn't different at all. Both the Harley and the Corvette were battered classics that had somehow survived and endured—not unlike the man who had restored them.

"It gave me something to do after I had the Harley put back together," he explained. "Besides, I discovered there are some impractical aspects to riding a motorcycle."

"Such as?"

"Rain. And the fact that not everyone likes to ride one."

By that she assumed he meant some of the women he'd dated. Impulsively, she wanted to ask him if that included the woman who had called several times since they got back from Edgewater.

Allie had been so consumed with curiosity, she'd actually picked up the phone a couple of times and listened briefly before hanging up guiltily. It was always the same woman, her voice soft and sultry. After each call Rafe went out and didn't return until the following morning.

Thinking of this now, Allie told herself for the hundredth time it didn't matter where he spent those nights that he wasn't asleep on the sofa in the den at Casa Sureno. But as always, it didn't make her feel better.

"What about you?" he asked. "Why architecture as a profession? It can't be easy for a woman." The remark wasn't the least deprecating or condescending, merely an honest evaluation, and he was in a position to know.

"It's not," she admitted. "But Julia made it easier. She was one of the few women pioneers in the field. What she went through, the recognition that she achieved, made it easier for me to be taken seriously. But it was still up to me to prove myself."

"Edgewater," he said quietly.

"It was the first really big project I worked on. Julia gave me a chance and I took it. I've worked on other projects through the years, but it was the first one where the owners pretty much turned over creative control."

"Building a monument to yourself?" he asked pointedly, voicing his usual assessment of architects.

Her clear blue gaze, so much like her mother's, met his. "I wanted to be part of something that would last—something solid and real that endures and doesn't disappear."

He knew she was telling the truth. It had nothing to do with the usual reasons most architects chose the field—enormous egos and the need to build monuments to themselves. He suspected that for her, the reasons might be found in the memories of a terrified child trying desperately to hold on to something solid, safe, and enduring in a world that had become unsafe in one awful night.

"Well, now you're part of something very real," he concluded.

She knew he referred to their plans in El Sureno.

"Will that be enough for you?" he asked, and suddenly it seemed there was a great deal more that was left unasked.

"Yes, of course," she answered quickly. "What more could I want?"

Silence expanded between them, broken only by the soft sound of the piano. Instead of responding to her rhetorical question, Rafe abruptly drained his wineglass, then pushed back his chair, stood, and held out his hand. "Do you want to dance?"

Allie heard the familiar melody of "As Time Goes By." It was an old classic, like vintage motorcycles and cars, and one of her favorites.

"Are you a good dancer?" she asked teasingly.

"I'm no Gene Kelly, but I'll manage to stay off your toes." Reaching across the table, he took her hand. "Are you?"

She groaned. "After two weeks of ballet, I quit—though not at the teacher's suggestion. I'm afraid I felt I was hopeless."

"What about school dances?" he asked as they crossed the restaurant to the small open space before the hearth, where a few other couples had stepped out onto the floor.

"I was never asked," she confessed reluctantly.

Her voice had lowered to an embarrassed whisper, with what he knew must be remembered humiliation. He'd gone to only a few school dances, telling himself he had no use for them. But he knew that if he'd been at one of hers, he would have asked her to dance.

"Well, I'm asking now," he said as he turned around, still holding her hand. "May I have this dance?"

They received several amused glances from other couples on the floor. Most of them were older and moved easily to the dance steps. When she hesitated, he stepped closer and slipped his arm about her waist, pulling her close.

He murmured in her ear, "This is nice. Maybe I should have gone to more dances."

"Why didn't you? You're a wonderful dancer."

He smiled with inordinate pleasure at the compliment. "Let's see, why didn't I go to very many dances? Maybe because it seemed that the girl I desperately wanted to dance with always danced with someone else."

"What was her name?"

He screwed up his face in a thoughtful expression. "You know, I can't even remember now. And at the time it seemed like the end of the world."

"Did you ask her to dance?"

He nodded. "Oh, yeah. I spent two hours working up my courage and finally asked her."

"What happened?" Allie asked gently.

"She said in a very polite voice, 'No, thank you,' and danced with the other guy."

Allie remembered the newspaper photograph of Rafe at seventeen—achingly handsome, sullen, and wild. She decided the girl must have been either crazy or blind. "What did you do?"

"I went out behind the school auditorium with a bunch of other guys. We smoked and drank, the usual sort of stuff teenagers do to get in trouble."

"Stealing cars?" she asked. He had pulled her closer still, their bodies pressed together in intimate places, his cheek against hers. She heard him laugh softly, felt the warmth of his breath against her cheek, then the faint movement of his lips as he spoke.

He confessed, "That was the night I stole Gavin's car. If that girl had just danced with me . . ."

"You still would have stolen it."

"Yeah, I still would have."

The wine, the glow of the fire, and the man whose body was pressed intimately against her made her forget everything else. Allie closed her eyes and let herself drift with the music.

In the shadows at the edge of the dance floor, lit only by the fire at the hearth, they danced slowly.

She felt his hand press gently against her back, pulling her against him, much as he had done earlier that day at the office.

He felt the uncertainty in her, the hesitation as he urged her closer, the restlessness that shivered through her. His cheek against hers, he asked, "What are you afraid of, Allie?"

"I'm not afraid."

Ignoring her denial, he said, "There's nothing to be afraid of."

Only monsters, she told herself, but the unhappy thought left as quickly as it had come, dissolving in a happy mist of warmth and music and closeness.

They had stopped dancing as the music played around them. His cheek scraped gently against hers as he bent his head lower. Then she felt his lips at the corner of her mouth. She closed her eyes as the ache spread through her.

She *was* afraid. Afraid of him, afraid of the feelings he aroused in her . . . afraid of herself.

Abruptly, she pulled away from him. "The music's ended, and it's late. We should be getting back."

For an instant he looked almost as she imagined he must have looked when that girl had refused to dance with him. Then, without saying a word, he paid the bill, and they left the restaurant to walk back to the main lodge, where the car was parked. The footlights that marked the pathway now had halos of mist around them as fog filled the forest. As he had on the earlier walk from the lodge, Rafe insistently took her hand, giving her no room to object.

He said nothing as they walked back to the car. It had been a wonderful evening, filled with intimate moments and laughter. Now she sensed his hurt and anger and knew that she was to blame. Twice, in just the space of hours, physical desire had heated between them. Twice she had backed away, struggling to deal with the reality of the bargain they'd made . . . and her own fears.

Absorbed in her own thoughts, she stumbled on the pathway. Rafe's hand tightened over hers to prevent her from falling, and his other arm went around her. Without warning his lips captured hers in a hard kiss.

His mouth was demanding, giving her no time to protest, much less pull away. The tenderness he had shown earlier was gone. The kiss was filled with anger, impatience, and need. The anger and impatience were his. The need was her own.

Finally, breathlessly, they moved apart. He pulled the front of her coat more tightly about her, his dark eyes searching hers.

"I've wanted to do that from the first moment I laid eyes on you."

Then, before she could figure out what on earth to say, he added, "We'd better hurry, or we'll be fogged in here."

As they drove away from Ventana, the fog that had followed them on the highway swallowed the forest around them, making the return trip dangerous. Remembering what Rafe had said earlier about the wrecks of cars that had gone over the steep cliffs, Allie felt her fear increase.

He seemed to read her thoughts. "Don't worry, I know the road. And we might get lucky, this stuff might lift. It usually doesn't set in this heavy until early in the morning."

She glanced over at him. "I guess I'll just have to trust you."

Their eyes met briefly. She could still taste him on her lips, feel his hands on her body, and, God help her, she wanted more.

She turned back to the window on her side, trying to bring her emotions back under control as she fixed her gaze on the gray curtain that seemed to drape everything around them. They could see only a few yards ahead. The twin beams of the headlights reflected uselessly off the wall of fog.

Rafe drove with uncharacteristic caution. They encountered no other cars until they reached the highway. The fog was no better there, but at least there was reflective markers on both the centerline and the side of the road. By watching those markers, spaced only a few feet apart, they were able to maintain a fairly moderate pace.

Allie couldn't stop thinking about that kiss. She reminded herself they'd made a deal—marriage in name only. She was determined to make certain it stayed that way. She couldn't risk falling in love with him.

At that moment she almost laughed out loud. It was ridiculous—falling in love with her husband. She was certain he was in no danger of falling in love with her. Rafe had always done exactly as he pleased. He'd lived his entire life that way, leaving when he chose to, never looking back. Even when he returned to Monterey it was on his terms. She had to remember that—their relationship was business only. . . .

Allie was jolted out of her unhappy reverie by the glare of headlights coming at them out of the fog. There was no warning, they were just there, heading straight toward them.

Rafe braked fast and cut the steering wheel hard to the right. The Corvette went off onto the shoulder, lost even traction with one set of wheels on the pavement and the other in gravel, then turned sideways in the roadway. But even as Allie instinctively braced for the impact, the other car had passed them and disappeared in the heavy fog.

The Corvette came to a stop, straddling both lanes of the highway. It had all happened in less than a heartbeat, yet Rafe had managed to keep the car on the road, away from the embankment plunging down to a ravine on the east side, and the cliffs dropping away to the ocean on the west. Quickly jerking the wheel around, Rafe shifted hard and put them back in the northbound lane. He didn't stop—it would have been dangerous to do so.

After they had driven on for a moment, he reached across to lightly stroke Allie's cheek. "Are you all right?"

She nodded shakily. "That was close."

He agreed. "Too close. I don't intend to do that again."

Cutting a glance over at the side of the road, he obviously was looking for something. "We've been on the road about twenty minutes. At this rate of speed, it should be along here any time."

"What should be along here?"

"The road marker."

They drove on for another hundred yards, then he said, "There it is, Marin Bay."

After another two hundred feet he made a sharp left turn. Allie thought they would drop right over the cliff into the ocean. But the tires rolled over smooth pavement.

"Is this a shortcut?" she asked in confusion.

"In a manner of speaking," he answered evasively as they followed the road around several curves, then through a gated entrance anchored by pilings of railroad ties on either side. Rafe slowed as they drove through the entrance, and lights automatically came on, illuminating a long, curving driveway.

"Do you know who lives here?" she asked.

"I do."

The driveway seemed to go on forever. Allie began to doubt they would ever reach the house that must lie at the end of the driveway. The fog drifted in waves of low-lying clouds that seemed to eddy and swirl like an ocean current.

Finally, as the car approached it, lights automatically came on at the front entrance, illuminating rough rock steps leading to the large house. Perched on the very edge of a cliff, it seemed utterly isolated.

Allie could hear the pounding waves hitting the rocks below and the roar of the ocean. She could actually feel the heavy wetness of it.

"Does anyone else live out here?" she asked as they got out of the car.

"I like my privacy. I own this entire bluff," he said as he came around the car. "Watch your step. The first riser is a bit steep."

She followed him up the stairs, noticing as they reached the front door that the house was made of redwood, weathered to a silvery color by wind and ocean. She recalled something he had said when they returned from Edgewater and realized they would have to live together as man and wife, at least temporarily. He had said his house was too remote. Well, she thought, it was remote, all right. And isolated.

"Why are we stopping here?"

He entered the code for the security system and then unlocked the door. Lights immediately flooded the interior entry, revealing expanses of white walls, polished natural-wood floors, elaborate stonework, and walls of softly hued clear-heart redwood framing windows that soared to several different levels. He walked in ahead of her, and other lights came on.

"I thought it might be wiser for us to stay here tonight. We can drive into Monterey in the morning, after the fog has lifted."

She hesitantly stepped inside. Architecturally, the house was a blend of old and new, traditional and ultramodern, high-tech, state-of-the-art equipment and the raw forces of nature. There was contradiction in every element of texture, color, and light, very much like the man who lived there.

Houses, she knew, often provided the most revealing glimpse into a person's nature, an intimate canvas where all the aspects of one's life were spread out for anyone to see. Rafe's house was such a canvas, revealing, exposing, displaying all the diverse contradictions of his nature. But somehow they all melded into a vivid, complex picture that embodied a rebel.

Allie's quick interest in Rafe's home was soon supplanted by her concern at its isolated location. She couldn't disguise her uneasiness at being so far from the main road and any other neighbors. She knew it was unreasonable, but she couldn't help how she felt. Her gaze fastened on the clear windows. The reflective panes threw her own image back at her, and she hurriedly looked away.

"This is a hell of a lot safer than that foggy road tonight," he called out as he walked ahead of her into the house. "That was a narrow escape. I don't want to chance another accident."

Rafe had disappeared into one of the rooms opening off the large living room. From somewhere in the distance Allie heard the distinct beep of a telephone answering machine, and the equally distinct voice of a woman. There were several more messages, then silence.

Returning to the living room, Rafe frowned as he saw Allie still standing in the entry. She hadn't come more than a few feet inside, and the door was still open behind her.

"What is it?" He crossed the entry and reached out to her. "Is something wrong?"

She stepped back, looking at him in distrust. He had seen that look in her eyes before, at Edgewater following the "accident," and then briefly that evening when they were looking out the windows at Ventana.

"No, nothing's wrong," she said hastily. "It's just that I would rather go back to Monterey tonight." She stood, rigid, just inside the doorway, as if she might turn and run at any moment.

"You saw how bad the fog is. It would be better to stay here," he said patiently.

"I don't want to stay here."

He heard the thinly disguised fear in her voice. "Look, if it's the sleeping arrangements that are bothering you, there are two bedrooms."

She shook her head. "It's not that." Her voice quivered. "I have to get back tonight."

"What is so important that it can't wait until the morning?"

Her gaze met his briefly, and he was stunned to realize that she was very near tears.

"Please, take me back tonight. Or I swear I'll walk back."

"All right," he said gently. "If it's that important to you, we'll drive back tonight. But I wish you would tell me what you're afraid of."

Tell him? How could she possibly explain her deepest fears—the nameless fear she couldn't explain because it came in half-formed images on glass and in mirrors—but somehow Rafe was part of it. The fear that what had happened at Edgewater was no accident and that he might somehow be responsible.

Turning, she quickly retraced her steps to the car, got in, and waited for him.

The drive back to Pebble Beach was agonizingly slow, and it was after midnight when they finally returned to Casa Sureno. Allie hurried into the house, moving as if she were running from something. Following her, Rafe caught her at the top of the stairs, just outside the bedroom she occupied alone.

"Dammit, Allie, we have to talk!"

"I . . . I'm sorry, Rafe. Thank you for dinner. It was lovely." Then she nearly ran into her bedroom, closing the door behind her.

He heard the faint click of the lock.

Angry and frustrated, Rafe stormed downstairs.

Allie leaned her forehead against the door frame, fighting back the tears that stung her eyes. She knew it was stupid to lock the door, since the communicating door between her bedroom and Rafe's didn't have a lock. But the gesture had been automatic, a symptom of the unreasoning fear that had gripped her.

Feeling utterly exhausted, she changed into a nightgown, washed her face and brushed her teeth, then slipped into bed. But despite her tiredness and the late hour, she couldn't sleep. To soothe her troubled mind, she reached for the journal from the bedside table.

Elena's Journal, June 2, 1853.

Over three weeks, and still there is no sign of the vaqueros returning from the Salinas Valley with the cattle—and no sign of Ben Sloan. He is my husband, and yet I think of him as Señor Sloan.

Yesterday, Papa left for Monterey. I rode with him to the boat landing. Except for old Luis and his wife, I am alone.

Today, I rode out to the cliffs overlooking Sureno Bay. It is peaceful there and I can see the coastline for miles in both directions. I looked out at the rocks, the white sand beaches, the tall cliffs, and the brilliant blue ocean. I think there must be no more beautiful place on earth.

If only Francisco were alive. All of this was to have been his. Now it is mine. I vow that I will do everything to protect the sacred trust my father has placed in my hands.

Tomorrow I will have been married exactly one month, and yet my husband and I have shared less than a day together. I do not know this man I have married. He is a stranger to me.

Yawning, Allie put down the journal and turned out the light. But as she drifted into a restless sleep, she thought how oddly her own marriage mirrored Elena's. She, too, was married to a stranger. . . .

28

JULIA ARRIVED ON FRIDAY, and Allie was grateful for her presence. It wasn't so much a need for her professional expertise as it was her drive, energy, and focus. Those qualities helped Allie put aside her troubled thoughts and move past her uncertain relationship with Rafe.

As it always had before, work grounded her, defined who she was, what she was about. It was a safe haven where she could retreat from the confusion of her personal life, even though the two were now inextricably intertwined.

Since the evening at Ventana, when deep, dangerous emotions had erupted between them, both Rafe and Allie had purposely kept their contact with each other detached and impersonal. They communicated only when necessary to arrange the ground breaking of the first phase of the development at El Sureno.

Allie told herself it was better this way. This was what they'd originally agreed upon, and it was definitely safer and less complicated. But was it really what she wanted?

Later, after a long day working with Julia, Allie straightened in her chair, easing the strain in her lower back. She and Julia had been leaning over a drafting table for most of the day red-lining the necessary changes.

"I think it's about quitting time," Julia said with a tired sigh. "Everyone else, including Rafe has gone."

Rafe had come in before anyone else that morning. When Julia arrived, he greeted her warmly, and they had quickly reestablished the friendly and challenging banter that had come so easily in Seattle.

But he remained cool and distant with Allie, exchanging words only when necessary. He left as soon as he'd finished what he was working on, telling Allie where he could be reached if needed.

Allie knew he was taking care of the mountain of paperwork necessary to launch a project of this magnitude—endless forms to local and state agencies and to the zoning commission; clearances, permits, and necessary changes to reports already on file with the State Contractors Board, the Department of Transportation, Coastal Commission, F.A.A., and port authorities about the facilities being planned for El Sureno.

Allie knew that while Rafe had legitimate reasons for being out of the office, he also was spending as little time there as possible when she was around. He spent even less time at Casa Sureno. He joined her on the nights she dined with Julia and Stan, but on other nights, when she ate alone, he wasn't there. Allie tried not to let it affect her. Since Julia was staying at Casa Sureno, she was rarely alone. But late at night, when everyone had gone to bed, she found herself unable to sleep. Wandering downstairs to the den, she looked in vain for Rafe. It had been days since he had slept at the house.

Where was he sleeping? she wondered miserably. At the house at Marin Bay? And with whom? The woman of the sultry voice, whose calls to Casa Sureno had stopped abruptly?

Allie threw down her pencil on the drafting table. Turning to Julia, she said, "You're right, let's get out of here. How about a drive out to the ranch? You haven't seen it yet."

Julia watched her with a thoughtful expression. "All right," she agreed. "It might do you some good to get away from things."

It was a clear, cool, beautiful autumn day on the peninsula. Allie put the top down on the Corvette. Every time she drove it, she couldn't help thinking of the evening at Ventana. She decided she needed to get something else to drive while she was here.

They sped down the coastline toward Big Sur. The road was dry, the conditions perfect, and Allie let frustration and that uneasy restlessness of the past several days edge the speed upward.

When they were approximately halfway to the ranch, she found herself watching the signs at the far side of the road. The memory of that night jolted through her at the sight of the private-road sign for the turnoff at Marin Bay.

She quickly glanced down the road, to the cliffs, and the imposing house beyond that looked as much a part of the elements as the rough and craggy coastline. Was he there now? she wondered. And if so, was he alone?

Fifteen minutes later they turned onto the ranch road and drove back from the highway to the gate, which stood open. Rafe's job captain had already been moving in heavy equipment to cut in the new road for the development, and this was the only access. Once the road was cut, the private road to the hacienda would once again be a private road for use only by the owners.

"Want to talk about it?" Julia asked, staring hard at Allie.

"It's complicated," Allie responded hesitantly.

"It usually is where men and women are concerned."

As briefly and matter-of-factly as possible, Allie explained about the "accident" at Edgewater, and her mistrust of everyone—including Rafe—since she couldn't determine who was behind it.

"What makes you think it wasn't an accident? That sort of thing does happen. There are a lot of boats in those waterways and islands."

Allie shook her head adamantly. "It wasn't an accident. Whoever was driving that boat saw me and deliberately turned into the cove. It was as if he were looking for me. Afterward, he was gone."

"You said 'whoever' was driving the boat," Julia reminded her. "You didn't see the person, so you can't know if it was one of your relatives, or Rafe."

"No," Allie admitted, "there wasn't time. I heard the boat

first, then by the time I realized it was coming at me, there was no time to look to see who it was. Besides, I didn't really believe it was deliberate until afterward."

Julia said carefully, "I understand your concern. By taking over the ranch, you've made some pretty bold moves."

"I had to do it. There was no other choice. If we hadn't, Gavin would have sold it and it would have been lost forever." There was an angry desperation in her voice.

They had stopped at Elena's Point, overlooking the cliffs and the ocean beyond.

"My God!" Julia said. "This is magnificent!" She turned to Allie. "You were right to try to save it. Whatever you've had to do is worth it."

For a moment Allie wondered if Julia saw through her sham marriage to Rafe. In the next moment she knew she had.

Julia spoke bluntly. "Even if Rafe married you only to get control of this place, I don't think he's the kind of man to hurt anyone. Someone could have come over from the mainland on the daily ferry, or by private plane. And from what you tell me, there are several people with a great deal to lose because of what you've done."

She gave Allie the direct look she'd seen countless times across the conference table or a drafting board. It was challenging, demanding, and brutally honest. "What would Rafe have to gain if something happened to you?"

Allie stared out at the churning sea below Elena's Point. "Complete control of El Sureno, without any interference from me—complete freedom to build the project exactly as he chooses. He could make a lot more money doing it his way instead of mine."

Julia shook her head. "I think you're wrong. My gut feeling tells me he's not the sort who would go about it like that. He's too direct. When he's angry, I suspect everyone knows it right out front."

Like the anger that had been all too obvious almost the entire past two weeks? Allie thought unhappily. And what about the uneasiness she'd experienced from the moment she saw his picture in those old newspaper articles? How could she explain to Julia something she didn't fully understand, and couldn't remember?

She decided not to try. Tabling the matter, she drove on to the ranch house. There they changed from the Corvette to the battered old pickup. Then Allie showed Julia over the ranch, driving across rolling grassland, through wooded forest, across dry streambeds and shallow creeks, and winding through ravines that Elena Marin had ridden on horseback one hundred fifty years earlier, down to the pounding surf, quiet inlets, and coves below.

Only when it was dark did they finally return to the hacienda, where Miguel's wife had prepared dinner for them. It was colder now. Instead of the courtyard, where Allie had once spent an enjoyable afternoon with Mac, they ate in the formal dining room with its adobe walls and deep burgundy rug over muted-brown Spanish tiles.

After dinner they sipped a last glass of wine before returning to Carmel. They sat before a blazing fire at the adobe brick hearth in the great room, with its original hand-woven carpet over the wood floor and smooth, aged leather chairs made in Monterey.

This was the same room where Don Marin had once smoked fine cigars with his compadres—the first Californio dons—and arranged the marriage of his daughter to the Anglo from Virginia, Ben Sloan. And it was where Elena Marin and the husband she barely knew had eventually raised their sons and entertained their guests.

A hundred fifty years and six generations separated them, but Allie realized that she and Elena Marin were not so very different. Both found themselves forced into arranged marriages in order to save El Sureno, and both women had their own fears about that marriage.

How had Elena reconciled those fears? What had changed her feelings about the husband who was a virtual stranger when they married? Or had she merely endured the marriage, as so many women did, trapped in a loveless relationship of duty and responsibility, without options or choices? For Elena, a Catholic, divorce had been unthinkable.

As she sat in this room now with Julia, Allie felt a welcoming warmth wrap itself about her. She didn't fear the house, only one room in it, reflected in the mirror and seen through the eyes of a terrified seven-year-old child. Someday, she hoped, she would be able to sit here without thinking about that. Someday, if she was lucky, she would finally be able to put the past behind her.

When they returned to Casa Sureno, they found they had the house to themselves. Inez had gone to the little house in Pacific Grove to spend the night with her daughter and grandchildren.

Allie and Julia sat up late that night, talking. She told Julia the whole truth about her marriage. And then she went even further, and talked about her emerging memories of her mother's death. Julia listened in sympathetic silence, providing immense reassurance simply by her presence and unabashed caring. Allie hadn't expected Julia to offer any answers, but it helped to finally be able to voice all her fears and uncertainties, and to hear Julia's expressions of love and concern. Wrapped in thick robes, they sipped fresh coffee and watched morning finally lighten over the ocean from Mac's courtyard.

Allie realized that, unlike El Sureno, where she felt a connection to the land that in some way defined who she was, she would always think of this house as Mac's. He had made her feel welcome there, and his love still filled the beautiful rooms. But this place wasn't part of her blood. El Sureno was, in spite of the lost memories trapped there.

"I hate to have to say this, especially after all you've told me, Allie, but I've got to get back home," Julia said as the sun finally appeared at their backs, warming them.

Allie sighed heavily. "I know."

"I don't mean to abandon you, but I have projects that I have to keep track of and clients to keep happy."

Looking at Allie, she saw circles of fatigue beneath her troubled blue eyes that had nothing to do with staying up all night. She went on. "You know I'm there for you if you need me. All you have to do is call."

Allie reached out to squeeze her hand affectionately. "I know. Thank you, Julia. For everything."

Julia said tersely, "As far as that so-called husband of yours is concerned, for my money, I'd bet on him. I'll take one rebel over a dozen of anything else. You may not like what they stand for, but you always know where they stand."

For the first time in days Allie smiled. "Spoken like a true rebel."

"I've been called that," Julia agreed. "And worse." Then she added, "Give him a chance, Allie. He might just surprise you."

A chance? Professionally? She'd already done that.

Personally? Since she'd refused to stay in his house, and presumably share his bed, he'd made it clear he wanted nothing beyond the strictly professional, strictly business relationship that gave him precisely what he'd wanted from the very first, control of El Sureno.

And, Allie insisted to herself stubbornly, that was all she wanted too.

Two hours later she bade Julia good-bye at the Monterey airport.

"I'll send those changes up by the overnight as soon as I'm finished with them," she told Julia. "I want you to take a look at them."

"Think you can afford me?" Julia quipped. "I don't work cheap."

"No, but you can be had," Allie retorted with a grin. "And I want the best."

"*You're* the best for this project," Julia assured her. "You just need to believe in yourself. And maybe in that husband of yours as well." Then she was walking out to the commuter jet that connected to the flight out of San Francisco.

"Remember, trust your gut instinct," Julia shouted back at her before boarding the plane. Allie knew it was a reminder that, like Julia, she had once trusted in her gut instinct, about work, and about people.

Could she rely on that same gut instinct now? What about her feelings toward Rafe? Was her mistrust of him instinctual, or something else? Shaking her head in frustration, she realized she just didn't know.

29

NICKY PULLED THE INCONSPICUOUS Ford Taurus to a stop before the gated entry of the lavish Del Monte estate on Crescent Drive. He dare not drive the easily recognizable Porsche Carrera with its personalized plates that had seemed so clever and necessary, and were now a deadly label wherever he went.

He loathed the Taurus. The suspension was sloppy, it was nonresponsive, the sort of car that belonged to some bureaucratic government employee with a dumpy wife, 2.2 children, and a mortgage on some cul-de-sac split-level in Salinas, whose biggest concern was which health insurance plan would be provided by his pension plan when he retired in twenty years. It hardly fit Nicky's image, but at the moment his image wasn't important. His life was. Anyone looking for him would be looking for the Porsche, not a nondescript Ford.

For the first time in his life Nicky wanted anonymity. He wanted to blend in, or slip silently, unobtrusively, away. But even anonymity required money.

An hour later he paced the study in his parents' house like an animal that's been driven to ground, and, once cornered, becomes the most dangerous animal of all.

"Are you aware they're ready to break ground?" His voice rose, revealing the desperation of a man who was fast running out of choices. "What the hell is being done to stop them?"

David Benedict crossed the room and snapped the heavy double doors shut. "Keep your voice down!" he snapped. "Your mother is holding her final organizational meeting for the Cascarones Ball. Every well-connected matron in the area is in the living room. Do you want them to hear about your gambling debts?"

"What the hell difference does it make? I'm more concerned with my life than what other people think, for God's sake!"

"It could make a great deal of difference if we hope to get back control of the ranch."

"The ranch?" Nicky sank into the deeply cushioned sofa. "I don't give a damn about the stupid ranch. I need money *now.* You don't understand how serious this is." Sitting forward, elbows propped on bent knees, he drove his fingers back through his hair. "You don't know what they'll do to me."

"You should've thought of this before you got involved with these kind of people."

"I had no choice. There was no other way to get the money I needed."

"Needed?" his father lashed back at him incredulously. "A half million dollars for a goddamned horse? International tournaments, entry fees, staying in the finest resorts, enjoying the services of the world's most expensive whores? Is that your definition of *need*?"

Nicky lifted his face to stare at his father. His contempt for his father was almost as great as his father's contempt for him. "Just like you needed the Sloan family name and connections. Just like you need your freedom now. But you don't have enough money, or guts, to go for it, do you?"

"Damn you," David swore at his son.

"I'd say we're both pretty much damned, unless you and Uncle Gavin come up with something. What the hell are you doing about it?" he repeated, standing now, his body rigid, his fists clenched.

"Don't you think I'm doing everything that I possibly can? We're taking steps."

"Legal steps?" Nicky snorted with disdain. "They'll take forever and they probably won't work!"

"Keep your voices down!" Charlotte Sloan Benedict had slipped into the study, closing the doors behind her. "I could hear you in the living room. Do you want everyone on the entire Monterey peninsula to know about our problems?"

"I'd say they already do," Nicky shot back at her. "It's all over town about that bastard marrying my dear cousin and taking over the company." His hands were shaking, from the aftereffects of a great deal of alcohol and cocaine—and fear.

He turned to his mother, as he had done since an early age when he discovered that she carried the most authority, and had all the real power in their family—the power of the Sloan name and money.

He loathed his father for his impotence, but he hated his mother for her pretentious airs, her charity events, and precious social status that had to be preserved at all cost.

"All legal means are being pursued," she assured him tightly.

"Forget legal means! What's being done to get us all some money?"

"We've hired an investigator. We'll prove the marriage was a fraud, intended simply to gain control of the company."

"That will take time!" he exploded. "I need the money *now*. I have bills I have to pay."

"Oh, I know all about your bills," Charlotte told her son. "Your expensive toys. And your debts." Her voice dripped with venom. "You're just like Valentina. She's been here today too. You're both spoiled children who always expect someone else to bail you out financially."

There had been the usual explosive tirade from her wild daughter.

"Everyone in this family is too damned worried about the family name! I don't give a damn about the Sloan name! What has it ever gotten me? I know how to get results, I'll prove their marriage is a fraud!"

Of her two children, Valentina was the most passionate, volatile, and unpredictable. She was very much like her grandfather that way, and her uncle Gavin.

Valentina had left in one of her usual unpredictable rages

that always made Charlotte uneasy—there was no telling what Valentina would do.

But Nicky was different. His emotional outbursts were never serious and never lasted long, at least no longer than it took to write out a check. She went to the desk and took out the leather-bound portfolio. Quickly signing a check, she handed it to him, ignoring her husband's look of disgust.

"This should keep your creditors at bay for a little while. At least until we get some of the legal technicalities out of the way."

Grabbing the check, Nicky stared at the figure in disgust. "Fifty thousand? Do you really think this will fix it, Mother?" He waved the check in front of her. "This wouldn't buy the shit that I'm up to my neck in!"

"Nicholas!" she exclaimed, horrified at his crass language.

But Nicky was hardly foolish, and never as reckless as his sister. Instead of tearing up the inadequate check, he jammed in into his pocket.

"I need *five hundred thousand,* and I need it now, not six months from now, or a year from now, or whenever your legal wrangling will be resolved. If the sale of the ranch to the Japanese had gone through, everything would have been fine. But you let that bastard brother of yours screw everything up!"

Turning to the double doors of the study, he threw them open, not caring who heard what he had to say next. "If you don't find a way to stop Rafe and Alexandra, I will!"

Charlotte stared at her son for a moment. Then she said in a voice that was utterly cold. "I'll stop them. You can count on it."

30

Elena's Journal, June 25, 1853.

Today was my eighteenth birthday. Papa planned a big celebration, and our friends arrived all through the day. At sunset there was a grand fiesta and I opened my gifts. Then there was music and dancing.

Just after sunset one of the vaqueros rode in to say that many riders were coming. My husband has returned with the cattle from Salinas. He was very tired and dirty from the long ride. But he took time to greet each of our guests. Then he gave me a birthday gift, a black lace mantilla with pearls set at the edge. I had admired it many months ago on the trip to Monterey when we first met.

It surprised me that he remembered. Such things were never of any importance to Antonio. I have been warned that Ben Sloan is ruthless and ambitious. But I know that he is also kind and gentle. It is a contradiction that is difficult to understand. I do not know what to think of my Anglo husband.

Allie reluctantly closed the diary and laid it aside. She had put off dressing for the ball as long as she could. The

Cascarones Ball was always attended by the founding families on the Monterey peninsula, most of which were descended from the original Californio dons. Everyone dressed in traditional Spanish costume, which left Allie with a problem.

She'd brought a simple cocktail dress with her on the recent return trip from Seattle. It wasn't appropriate for a costume ball, but it was all she had. She'd had no desire to go shopping for something more extravagant, since she didn't want to go to the ball in the first place.

But like it or not, this was business. She was expected to make an appearance. Rafe's note had been explicit—*I'll pick you up at eight*—like the reminder of a business appointment.

She was exhausted, on edge. Despite the long, hard hours she spent working, when she finally crawled into bed at night she couldn't sleep. On top of that, she'd had the nightmare again the night before, waking in a cold sweat, haunted by the monster in the mirror.

She definitely wasn't in the mood to socialize with the other members of the Sloan family, all of whom loathed her. Her attendance at the ball with Rafe was nothing more than a phony public display of marital togetherness. And yet the future of the ranch depended on such displays. Otherwise Gavin might very well be able to prove their marriage a fraud.

At that moment Inez knocked on her bedroom door, then entered. "I've come to help you dress, Miss Allie."

"Thanks, Inez. Could you run a bath for me?"

Nodding, Inez went into the adjacent bathroom and filled the huge sunken tub.

Allie slipped out of jeans and sweatshirt—her favorite outfit for work when she didn't have to meet with clients—and stepped into the steaming bath. She lay back against the sloping end of the tub and closed her eyes. The heat eased taut muscles and the aching stiffness at the back of her neck. Fatigue was replaced with a sort of languid lethargy.

It will be all right, she told herself. I'll stay as short a time as possible. And I won't have to do anything like this again for a long time.

A half hour later she reluctantly stepped out of the tub and dried off. Wrapping a towel around her wet hair, she slipped on the thick terry robe. Just then Inez knocked on the bathroom door. "Miss Allie? I have something to show you."

Opening the door, Allie found Inez smiling at her excitement. "Come, you must see this."

Inez led Allie down the hallway, stopping before a door to a room that Allie had never entered. "This is a storage room," Inez explained. "Mr. Sloan had your parents' personal possessions placed in here. He was saving them for you."

"Why didn't he tell me about this?" Allie asked in amazement.

"He would have if he'd lived," Inez answered simply. Then she went on. "I've been waiting for the right time to show you these things. But you've been gone so much, and when you're here, you're so busy, I didn't want to disturb you. But now I think is the right time. I know you don't have a costume for tonight. Perhaps you will find something in here."

Inez opened the door, and she and Allie went in. The large room was empty of furniture, but it was filled with boxes and trunks. In a corner the door to a large oak wardrobe hung open, revealing numerous formal evening gowns, carefully enclosed in plastic garment bags.

"Most of these dresses belonged to your mother, but there are also some fine old things here," Inez said proudly. "Some of them are very valuable. The historical society asked many times for Mr. Sloan to donate them, but he always refused."

Walking up to the wardrobe, Allie gazed at the very dresses her mother had worn. There were gowns of silk and satin and velvet, in lovely shades of turquoise and sea green and lavender. The soft colors would have looked lovely on someone as fair as Barbara.

Unzipping one of the garment bags, Allie tentatively touched a sea-green satin ball gown. My mother wore this, she thought, entranced. She almost thought she could detect the faint scent of her mother's perfume on the dress.

Someday, Allie thought, when she had time, she would come in here alone and go through every single thing that had belonged to her parents. In a sense, this was like their legacy to her, a legacy she hadn't known existed. Overwhelmed by emotion, she had to brush a tear from her eye.

Inez said nothing, merely stood beside her in mute support.

Then, pulling out a drawer at the bottom of an old-fashioned wardrobe that had once stood in the house at El Sureno, Inez took out a long cedar box shaped very much like a small trunk.

"This belonged to Elena Marin," she explained as she set the box on the floor. "Mr. Sloan's wife, Joanna, once showed me what was inside."

Even before she lifted the hinged lid of the cedar box, Allie knew what she would find inside. There were packets of bound letters and several pieces of antique jewelry, none of great value—except for a thin wedding band. It was the wedding band Ben Sloan had given Elena Marin.

There were dried flowers wrapped in lace and bound with ribbon, faded tintypes of Elena Marin on her wedding day, her expression wistful and uncertain, yet her magnificent dark eyes shining with hope. Her hair shone thick and glossy even in the faded old photograph.

There were other photographs—of Ben Sloan, Elena, and their firstborn son; then other photographs, with two sons, then three. One of them Allie recognized as her great-grandfather. Another son, she knew, must be Rafe's great-grandfather.

Finally, there was a photograph of Elena Marin at the end of her long life. She was still beautiful and slender, dressed in an exquisite gown of the period, and wearing the mantilla Ben had given her for her birthday. Allie could only speculate that she might have been dressed for the Cascarones Ball.

The journal had told the story of Elena Marin's life, but these private, personal things were the mementos of a lifetime. They were Elena's memories.

Underneath the photographs, packets of bound letters, and sprigs of dried flowers, Allie found Ben's birthday gift to his wife. Carefully, she unfolded the mantilla. The workmanship was exquisite, the tiny pearls at the edge glistening pure white against black lace.

Unlike the lace doilies and tablecloths Allie's grandmother had in her house, and had starched with a vengeance to keep their shape, Elena's mantilla was made of the softest, silkiest lace, intended to hang from the crown of a woman's hair down the back in the traditional manner.

"There is something else," Inez went on, her voice nearly bursting with excitement and pride. From the faintly musty cedar-lined wardrobe she took out a plastic-encased gown—the very one that Elena had worn with the mantilla in the photograph.

When Inez unzipped the bag and took out the gown, Allie saw that it wasn't made in the traditional Spanish style. The signature sewn on the inside of the bodice revealed that it was a design of Frederick Worth, an exclusive couturier of the time. Allie realized that she held a priceless heirloom in her hands.

She also realized that Elena Marin had been a bit of a rebel in her own way. She had been caught between two cultures—the culture of her Spanish heritage, and the Anglo culture of her marriage—during a time of great change in California. With her marriage she had gone against tradition, willing to do whatever was necessary to save the land she loved. And in doing so, she had created a family dynasty.

The gown and the mantilla were representative of the dichotomy of Elena's changing life—her determination to move into the future while preserving the past.

Looking at Inez, Allie asked with a smile, "How are you at lacing corsets?"

By the time Elena had been photographed wearing the gown, she had already borne three sons. Allie found it difficult to comprehend how her ancestor had stayed so slim. The gown was so small at the waist, Allie feared Inez would never be able to close the countless buttons at the back. But if Elena Marin had owned a corset to help maintain her slender waist, it wasn't to be found in the wardrobe. They did, however, find a buttonhook.

While Inez closed the buttons down the back of the gown, Allie struggled with the ones at her wrists and silently praised whoever had invented zippers and Velcro. Glancing anxiously at the clock on the nightstand, she hoped Rafe would be late.

She wore her hair pulled back in the same style she'd worn it the night they went to Ventana. She told herself she didn't want to recall any memories of that night, this was simply the quickest way to style her hair in the little time they had left.

Once the dress was buttoned, Allie stood in the middle of the room, hardly daring to breathe as Inez secured the mantilla high at the crown with gold combs, so that it flowed down her back, over the skirt of the dress.

"How do I look?" Allie asked.

"See for yourself," Inez responded with a grin as she turned Allie around to face the full-length mirror.

"Oh, my," she slowly breathed.

She was taller than Elena by several inches. The hem of the gown, which trailed along the floor in the photograph, barely brushed the toes of her black velvet flat-soled shoes. The waist was incredibly small, pushing her breasts upward at the low-cut bodice.

"Dancing is definitely out," she murmured. "It's all I can do to breathe in this."

She jumped at the sound of a motorcycle in the driveway below.

Inez said eagerly, "I'll tell Mr. Sloan you'll be right down. Oh, Miss Allie, he will be so impressed!"

Allie checked her appearance one last time in the mirror. "Mirror, mirror, on the wall . . ." she whispered, wishing her mother was there, needing her strength, love, and wisdom now as never before. But she wasn't there. There were only the secrets in the mirror. Allie whirled around abruptly and hurried downstairs.

He was waiting for her in the entryway, his back to the stairs, pacing impatiently. She had expected him to refuse to wear a costume, and she was surprised to see he'd conformed for the evening, though on his terms. Instead of the elaborately decorated, brilliantly colored costumes worn by the affluent Spanish dons of old California, he had worn the costume of the vaqueros. Butter-soft leather pants hugged his hips and thighs, and flared over leather boots. The belt at his waist was also leather, but devoid of all but the simplest detailing. His shirt was rough-spun cotton, with long, full sleeves, and open at the throat, exposing dark skin and dark, curling hair. He wore a leather vest over it, tied with leather laces across the front.

Allie had seen Miguel wear very much the same type of clothing at the ranch. It was inherently a part of who Rafe was and fit him as naturally as jeans, leather jacket, or the Harley.

Turning, he watched her come down the stairs. He felt his breath leave his lungs as if he'd been hit low and hard. She was dressed all in black lace, the heavy skirt of the gown rustling about her as she moved, the bodice low over her high breasts, the black lace mantilla flowing over her soft gold hair and down her back.

A vague memory stirred of having seen the gown before, and he realized that she must have found it among the family heirlooms Mac insisted on keeping. Watching her descend the stairs, Rafe was amazed at how the modern, liberated, professional woman disappeared behind the sensual illusion of lace and pearls from another time. At that moment he wanted to forget all about their damned business arrangement, and discover the woman beneath the lace.

"I got your message," she said as she reached the bottom landing. "Eight o'clock."

He nodded, his mouth a hard, fixed line in his handsome, sculpted features, and said, "We don't want to be late."

It was said as easily as if they were discussing a business appointment. If she could have, Allie would have taken a deep breath to temper her slow rise of anger at his cool attitude. As it was, the only thing she could do was nod curtly. She would show him that she could be just as cool and detached as he.

They drove to the Hyatt Regency in silence. Rafe pulled in front of the hotel behind other costumed guests and waited for the valet to take the car.

Allie struggled with the heavy skirts as she got out of the low Corvette. Unexpectedly, he was beside her, his arm going around her waist. The contact was intimate and jarring, and her clear blue gaze met his in startled surprise.

His fingers spread across the silk bodice at her back. Instinctively, they curved inward at her waist, and he had to suppress the desire to pull her closer.

Dozens of hotel guests stared at them, impressed by their costumes. It occurred to Rafe that if he really wanted a public display of marital togetherness, he should kiss Allie, right there in public, for all the world to see. Everyone who saw them would believe they were genuinely husband and wife. It would accomplish exactly what they'd come there to do—prove to the rest of the Sloan family their marriage wasn't a fraud. But if he kissed her, Rafe knew that he would want and *need* more.

"He held her against him a moment longer, then released her. "Try to smile," he suggested. "There's a lot at stake."

She saw his expression, which had turned intense for a moment, shift back to a cool detachment. She reminded herself this was all a performance. "Be sure to cue me on my lines," she bit off angrily.

"I think you know them well enough by now."

Allie felt as rigid and cold as stone as they walked into the lobby of the hotel. There, a costumed attendant directed them to the ballroom, where the Cascarones Ball was already under way.

The huge ballroom was gaily decorated in a Spanish motif, and it was packed to capacity with the brilliantly costumed social elite of the peninsula. As Allie and Rafe entered, the other guests stared at them in undisguised curiosity. Their whirlwind marriage, and subsequent takeover of the Sloan Land Company had been the subject of rampant gossip and speculation.

"Allie?"

She turned at the familiar voice as Liz DiMaggio swept toward her in an elegant and colorful re-creation of a traditional Spanish gown.

"My God, you look exquisite. The very image of your mother." She hugged Allie affectionately. "Charlotte is going to go positively catatonic when she sees you in that gown. If I'm not mistaken, it's the same one she tried to get Mac to turn loose of for years. It belonged to your ancestor, didn't it?"

"Yes, it was Elena Marin Sloan's."

Turning to Rafe, Liz said, "You cut rather a dashing figure yourself."

His lips curved almost imperceptively in the barest hint of a smile. "Thank you."

"You two are impressing the hell out of everyone here tonight. They can't take their eyes off you. But you've really got your work cut out for you. That sale to the Japanese was just about the biggest thing to happen around here in a long time. It would have been even bigger than the sale of Spanish Bay to the Japanese two years ago."

Rafe's smile dissolved in an instant. "It isn't going to

happen. Allie and I control the company, and *we're* developing the ranch.''

Liz looked at them speculatively. ''Most people wouldn't choose to go up against Gavin. You two are *the* topic of just about every conversation here this evening.''

Rafe said firmly, ''It's about time someone stood up to Gavin.''

Then, turning to Allie, he went on. ''Since everybody's watching, we'd better give a good performance.''

Taking their leave of Liz, Rafe escorted Allie across the room, where the president of the Monterey Civic Club—Charlotte Sloan Benedict—was greeting all newly arrived guests.

As they walked toward Charlotte, Rafe laid his hand over Allie's, where it lay on his arm. Her fingers were cold as ice and dug softly into his sleeve. He knew she was nervous but determined not to show it. On this night she was doing more than confronting the family she'd only recently met and almost immediately antagonized. She was confronting the past and the monsters out of a child's nightmare. That painful past was inextricably intertwined with the Sloan family. Out of his own painful past he sensed the struggle that went on inside her, and knew exactly the courage it took to confront them.

His fingers laced with hers, he bent low to whisper, ''It'll be all right.''

The warmth of his breath and the brush of his lips against her cheek recalled Ventana. She glanced up at him, wishing she could read the look behind his eyes. Before she could say anything, she found herself face-to-face with Charlotte.

Her patrician features were fixed in a taut expression that wavered only slightly as her gaze swept the gown that Allie wore. Then she coolly dismissed both of them.

The guest of honor for the evening, the governor of California, stood next to Charlotte. It was Charlotte's official duty as president to introduce all guests to the governor, but she clearly intended to snub Rafe and Allie by refusing to make the introductions.

The look Rafe gave her was filled with contempt, and rage at all the years the Sloan family, with the exception of Alan, Barbara, and Mac, had so ruthlessly rejected him.

Now he had what mattered most to them—control of their company. If revenge was sweet, this moment was pure honey.

"Good evening, Governor," Rafe said with a smile. "My *sister* seems to have forgotten her official duties as hostess as well as her manners. I'm Rafael Sloan, and this is my wife, Alexandra."

He made the formal introduction himself, pausing ever so slightly at the word *sister*. His words were a slap in the face for Charlotte, who always prided herself on rigidly adhering to the social proprieties.

Allie smiled at the governor and exchanged brief pleasantries. Glancing at Charlotte, she thought, if looks could kill, Rafe and I would both be struck dead at this moment.

It was David Benedict, standing on the other side of Charlotte, who eased everyone past the awkward moment. Taking Allie's hand in his, he said, "You look as lovely as your late mother."

Allie was taken aback by his civility, which hinted at genuine admiration. But after all, she reminded herself, he wasn't a Sloan, and this wasn't really his fight. Still, she couldn't help wondering at the emotion evident in his voice when he mentioned her mother.

"It's good to see you again, David," Allie responded politely.

Nearby, Allie saw Gavin and Erica standing together. Erica stared at Allie as if she'd seen a ghost, and looked as if she might collapse at any moment. Allie noticed Gavin's fingers digging into his wife's arm, the skin across his knuckles showing white as if he were either warning her against saying anything that might embarrass anyone, or perhaps holding her up.

Turning to face Gavin and Erica, Rafe said easily, "Hello, Erica. You look beautiful tonight."

She raised deeply shadowed eyes to meet his look, and her hesitant expression suggested she was afraid he was being sarcastic. But somehow Allie knew he was sincere in the compliment. It surprised her that he would take the trouble to be kind to Erica.

"Thank you," Erica responded in a carefully controlled voice that almost managed to disguise a quiver of uncertainty.

Knowing that Gavin had once been in love with her mother, Allie realized that Erica had lived with that bitter truth her entire married life. When Erica finally looked at her, Allie felt the full force of her soul-destroying jealousy. It was there in the pain in her eyes as she confronted the living image of her archrival.

Looking directly at Rafe, Gavin said in an even voice. "Enjoy yourself, but be careful." He smiled artificially. "Don't drink and then drive. We do want everyone to get home safely tonight."

It was smoothly said, so that anyone who overheard it would have taken it as a considerate reminder from host to guests, or brother to brother.

"I intend to get both Allie and myself home safely," Rafe assured Gavin.

As Rafe and Allie moved off, he said under his breath, "I just love family get-togethers."

Rafe held Allie's arm and smiled down at her. They gave every outward appearance of being the happy, blissful couple they needed everyone to believe they were.

Liz rejoined them, and while Rafe chatted with an acquaintance, she took Allie around to meet her friends. Allie realized that she had indeed become the object of a great deal of curiosity across the Monterey peninsula. The Sloan name was an institution, one of the veritable pillars of Monterey-Carmel society.

Allie couldn't help thinking about her mother's entrance into this same society. Twenty-five years earlier her mother had entered the kingdom, so to speak, and died tragically. Her father had been tried and executed for the crime. When it came to scandal and sensationalism, memories were long. Most of the people at the ball were old enough to remember her parents.

Being Barbara Sloan's daughter made her a sensation. The fact that she'd married the illegitimate son of her father's distant cousin, and together they'd laid claim to the family empire, made her even more of a sensation. As Liz led her through the throng, pausing to introduce her here and there, Allie knew she was setting Monterey-Carmel society on its Cartier-diamond-studded ear.

The air of the Hyatt Regency ballroom was electrically

charged with so much speculation, rumor, and gossip that it was a wonder circuit breakers didn't go off, she thought with wry humor.

"I understand that you're an interior decorator," one woman remarked to Allie.

Liz almost choked on the olive in her very dry martini.

Allie smiled patiently. "Actually, I'm an architect."

"An architect? Good God, why would a beautiful young woman want to do something like that?"

Biting back a far worse retort, Allie said, "I like to build things." Smiling sweetly, she added, "Or take a wrecking ball to them."

As Allie and Liz headed toward the ladies' room, Liz said with a grin, "You're holding up marvelously."

"This is bullshit," Allie swore with uncharacteristic ill humor. "I have absolutely nothing in common with these people, Liz, I have to get out of here."

"Patience, my dear, you can make a discreet exit soon."

Liz greeted an acquaintance who was leaving the ladies' room as they entered it, kissing the air and whispering under her breath, "Those diamonds are fakes, absolute paste, and she wears them as if they're the real thing. Tried to commission a copy off of one of the artist's originals. Thought the idea was flattering to the artist. Cheap, just plain cheap."

Liz patted Allie on the shoulder. "And you're absolutely right, it *is* bullshit, but very lucrative bullshit. They'll earn a bundle for a good charity just by rolling the old dowagers out and fawning over them."

She went on. "Let me reconnoiter the stalls. I don't want you running into Val. She can be wicked when she's been drinking. Of course, she can be wicked when she's not drinking too. The woman has talons. Even her closest friends wear armor."

"In a way, I feel sorry for her," Allie said. "Her life seems very empty."

"Oh, she fills it up regularly." Liz rolled her violet eyes meaningfully. "With men, usually rich. In between rich, she goes for young." Then Liz looked at her oddly. "I hate to bring this up at this point, but exactly how do you go about it with those skirts?"

Allie laughed for the first time that night. Liz had enough money to buy and sell most of the matrons there, and yet she was the most unpretentious person Allie had ever met. She was a badly needed breath of fresh air in a very stuffy room.

Allie said ruefully, "I don't think I can do anything, there are so many layers."

"Oh, my God," Liz exclaimed as they sat before the long vanity and repaired their hair and makeup. "That's it."

"What's it?"

"That's the reason the women in those old photographs are all pinch-faced old prunes. They had to go to the bathroom. Thank God for elastic."

They were still laughing as they came out of the ladies' room. Liz went to look for Rafe, leaving Allie among the trailing Spanish-style arbors draped with real, blooming bougainvillea that decorated the ballroom. Allie preferred to stay discreetly at the edge, where she could watch everyone rather than be watched.

Authentic Spanish music was being played, a blend of guitar and violin. This was quite a festive affair, and under different circumstances, Allie thought she might have been able to enjoy herself.

"Well, if it isn't dear Cousin Alexandra."

Allie recognized that sultry, smooth-as-warm-honey voice even before she turned around. "Hello, Val."

Valentina Sloan Charteris looked sensational. Whereas Allie's gown was understated elegance in black lace, Val's costume was flamboyant, colorful silk, more in the style of Spanish Gypsies.

Her skirt clung to her slender hips and legs with the sort of transparent sensuality that revealed she wore little or nothing underneath, and the blouse of a bold red color rode low at her shoulders and across her breasts, revealing the nakedness there as well.

She was barefoot and tanned, her toes painted crimson to match her long nails. Her hair hung loose to her waist in a shimmering cascade of vibrant flame, and her dark eyes smoldered with another kind of fire—hatred. "How is married life, Cousin?"

"It's fine, Val. But perhaps you'd better ask Rafe."

"I intend to. Because I'm willing to bet that it's not so fine—perhaps not even consummated."

Allie responded coolly, "I don't have to discuss this with you," and she turned to leave.

"No, but you'll have to discuss it in court. You have to prove that your marriage is real."

"It's as real as any marriage," Allie insisted.

"Define real."

"What do you want, Val?" she demanded. "Bloodstained sheets from the wedding night? Isn't that a bit medieval?"

Val shrugged. "It would help if you had someone else to testify about your marriage."

This was ridiculous. Val was bluffing. There was no one to testify about the nights she and Rafe either did or did not spend together. Then she thought of Inez. Would Inez tell the truth in court—that Rafe often slept on the sofa in the den, and just as often went out late at night and didn't return until the morning?

Val went on. "I know Rafe doesn't spend his nights with you. Maybe someone would be more than willing to tell the court where he *does* spend them."

For just a heartbeat Allie suspected it might be Val whom Rafe was involved with.

Val grabbed her arm. "Come along, Cousin. There is someone I'm just dying for you to meet."

Allie jerked out of her grasp. Whatever sordid little scheme Val was up to, she wanted none of it. "I'm not going anywhere with you."

"Oh." Val pulled back in surprise, her sensual mouth curved in an appraising smile. "And physically strong too. Perhaps if your mother had been as strong, or had been faithful to her husband, she wouldn't gave gotten herself killed."

31

RAFE AND LIZ FINALLY found them. Rafe was furious. "What the hell are you up to, Val?"

"There's someone I thought Allie might like to meet," Val went on recklessly. They were starting to draw attention, but for someone who fed on being in the winner's circle, it was merely an aphrodisiac. She called out a name, drawing even more attention.

A beautiful, slender, dark-haired young woman slowly approached them.

Val said triumphantly, "Perhaps you would like to make the introductions, Rafe darling. After all, you and Melissa have been sleeping together for the past two years—before *and* after your so-called marriage. But then, who can blame you? After all, you're not sleeping with your wife."

"Damn you!" Grabbing Val's arm, Rafe saw the victorious gleam in her eye. He would have gladly broken that arm, or her neck, to wipe that smug, self-satisfied expression off her coldly beautiful face.

She wrenched away from him and turned back to Allie. "You're being used, just like your mother was used by her lover," Val spat out venomously. "Then you'll be discarded, just like she was. If you're not careful, you'll end up dead too."

Allie was deathly pale, the expression in her eyes profoundly wounded and filled with pain. Val's words had slashed at an already open wound. Allie had no strength to fight back, and so she simply turned and began quickly walking away, refusing to look at anyone. Her back was straight, and she held herself with pride, but she died a little more with each step she took.

The people in their immediate vicinity had stopped talking and turned to stare at the angry little circle. Allie felt their eyes on her as she made her way through the packed throng.

Someone gave instructions and the orchestra began to play to cover the embarrassing silence. The soft music of guitars blended with the traditional chords of violins.

Shoving Val out of the way, and coldly ignoring Melissa, Rafe went after Allie. He stopped her, his fingers closing around a slender wrist that seemed unbearably fragile. Everything about her seemed fragile, as if she were about to break.

"Don't let Val chase you out of here. Show them you don't care. Dance with me."

She shook her head, refusing to look at him, the lace mantilla shimmering over her soft, golden hair. She whispered, "Don't touch me."

She tried to pull away from him, but he held on more tightly, and then forcibly pulled her into his arms. His lips were against her cheek, which was cold as ice.

"Dance with me, dammit! Don't give them the satisfaction of seeing you cry. You're stronger than that. In some ways, you're the strongest person I know. Stronger than I am."

She didn't speak, and he stared at her perfect profile, the classically beautiful features, eyes now more gray than blue, yet crystal-clear and glassy with unshed tears.

"They're not worth it, Allie. Not one of them. Dance with me, just once, to prove to them they can't beat you down. And then I'll take you anywhere you want to go."

She danced, if it could be called that. Her movements were more like those of an automaton, jerky, stilted, more from sheer force of will. And gradually the dance floor of the ballroom began to fill around them. He held her tight against him, afraid that if he let go she would crumble, or, worse, run away from him. He couldn't bear the thought of that. It had been a mistake to come there. He knew that now. He'd allowed her to walk right into an ambush. And all to prove their marriage was no fraud.

Now it stunned him to realize he didn't give a damn about any of it. The only thing he cared about was Allie.

Then the dance ended.

Without looking at him she pulled out of his arms and hurried away from him. Others on the danced floor moved between them, momentarily preventing him from following her. He reached the lobby of the hotel just as she was passing through a gauntlet of photographers. Then she climbed into a taxi and sped away.

Rafe's car was hopelessly blocked in valet parking, and he had the attendant hail another cab.

It was just a little after ten o'clock when Allie arrived back at Casa Sureno. She had no money with her, and had to ask the driver to wait while she went into the house to get some.

Inez stood in the doorway, a bewildered expression on her face as Allie came back after paying the driver. ''Please help me undress, Inez,'' Allie asked. Then, in a voice that was barely a whisper, ''I don't think I can manage the buttons.''

''Mr. Sloan is not with you?'' Inez asked, but there was no answer.

Upstairs, she carefully removed the mantilla, then began unbuttoning the back of the gown. When the last buttons were unfastened, Allie was able to draw a deep breath for the first time that night. The breath sounded very much like a sob. Then she stepped out of voluminous petticoats and grabbed the first thing her numbed fingers could find—the jeans and sweatshirt she'd worn earlier that day and had left lying on her bed. She put them on, along with soft, rolled-cuff boots.

She heard the front door open, then slam shut.

Allie said to Inez, ''I don't want to see anyone.''

As Inez left the room, Rafe pushed past her. Glaring at Allie, he said, ''We have to talk.''

She replied in a trembling voice, ''There's nothing to talk about. It's none of my business what you do, or whom you do it with. But I could have done without the public humiliation."

"Dammit, Allie, there's a great deal to talk about, and you're going to listen," he insisted.

She shook her head. "I can't do this. I won't do it anymore. I won't go through that pain."

She tried to turn away, but he wasn't about to let her off that easily. "There's *nothing* between Melissa and me. That was just Val's way of trying to get at you."

She shook her head, as if it hardly mattered. "I know we had an agreement—strictly business—but I've been here before." Her voice was weary. "I won't ever go through that humiliation again. Not for anyone. You said I'm strong, but I'm not strong enough to endure that."

"Look, I admit I was involved with Melissa, but that was before we were married. I haven't slept with her since the night we flew to Tahoe. I ended it the next day."

His strong fingers bit into the delicate curve of each shoulder, as if he could physically force her to believe him.

She looked at him then. Her clear blue eyes—so like her mother's—were like reflecting glass for the emotions inside her. Clearly, she didn't believe him. "Why would you do that?"

When he reached up and gently stroked her cheek, she didn't pull away this time. She simply stood there as a tear slipped down her cheek. He brought his other hand up and gently cradled her face.

She was in pain, wounded, as if something inside her were broken, unable even to seek the comfort she so desperately needed. He ached as he touched her, wanting to offer comfort, wanting to touch her, yet terrified that she was so fragile at that moment, she would shatter in his hands.

His lips touched the cool skin at her forehead in a tender kiss as he whispered, "Because I don't want her. I want you."

Then he bent his head and laid his cheek against hers. He whispered again, "I'm sorry. I never meant for you to get hurt."

He'd rarely apologized in his life. But now he needed to say the words—"I'm sorry"—to her.

Allie felt cold inside. What Val had said about her didn't

matter. But what Val had said about her mother went deep, because there was still so much Allie couldn't yet remember. The pain was so intense, she was certain she would never again feel anything else. She wanted to hold herself tight against it.

But she was wrong about never feeling anything but pain. As Rafe held her, she felt heat—gentle, stirring heat—everywhere their bodies touched. It had been there between them from the very beginning. She felt it now in the warmth of his cheek, the tender roughness of his hand as he laid it against hers in such a stirring, sweet supplication, the hard strength of his body pressed against hers.

He was the last person she should need or want to turn to for comfort. But this had nothing to do with logic. It was primal and instinctive, and came from some dark, hidden place inside her. The pain melted, she closed her eyes, and turned to the heat of his mouth.

Because she thought she knew everything there was to know about the sort of man he was, she expected that same barely controlled violence of the kiss at Ventana. He stunned her with an unexpected tenderness as his mouth lightly brushed hers with such utter sweetness that the last traces of fear crumbled inside her.

He murmured, "What do *you* want, Allie?"

She felt his breath against her neck as his head came down low beside hers, felt the feathery brush of those incredibly thick dark lashes against her cheek, and without looking, knew that he had closed his eyes, waiting for her to answer.

He was offering her a way out. Once before, he'd given her that same choice. She had only to take it and she knew that he would accept her decision without argument.

If she chose to call it quits and walk out of his life, it would all end. He would lose everything. But what would she be losing? It came down to that one simple question—what did she want? She went on instinct, finding her answer in his. "I want you," she whispered, the words caught somewhere between a sigh and a sob.

For a moment they simply stood, Rafe holding her with one arm loosely encircling her waist, while his hand cradled her face against his, fingers buried in her hair. His only response was the faint flexing of those fingers as they dug in gently.

"Not here," he said in a low voice as he stepped away from her. "We need to be completely alone, just the two of us."

Crossing the room, he seized her heavy denim jacket from the back of a chair. He threw the jacket around her shoulders, then took her hand firmly in his and pulled her down the stairs with him. Encountering Inez at the bottom landing, he said, "We're going out." Then, picking up his leather jacket from the hall table where he'd casually thrown it earlier, he led Allie outside.

The heels of his boots scraped over the flagstones of the driveway. He didn't let go of her hand until they reached the Harley, when he swung one leg over the low-slung black steel-and-chrome motorcycle and straddled the cushioned leather seat. By letting go of her hand then, he was offering one last unspoken way out. He looked over at her, his eyes dark and intense in the glow of the driveway light. Reaching out to her, he said simply, "Trust me."

She hesitated only fractionally. Then she laid her hand in his, stepped to the Harley, and slipped her leg over the back. Even before she had settled on the seat behind him, the Harley roared to life with a deep-throated rumble that obliterated the distant sound of the ocean.

Wordlessly, Rafe reached back, sliding his hand along her jean-clad thigh to the curve of her hip. He pulled her forward until she was tightly pressed against his back. Then he handed her the helmet, ordered her to put it on, and wheeled the Harley out of the driveway.

"Hold on tight!" he shouted above the roar of the motorcycle. They turned onto Seventeen-Mile Drive and headed for the coast highway.

The night was clear and black around them, the buffeting wind sending icy shafts through every layer of clothing. Allie wrapped her arms about his waist, flattening her hands against his chest beneath the jacket, and buried her face at his back to keep warm. They sped south, the single beam of the Harley spiraling down the ribbon of empty highway.

The wind tore at her hair where it hung below the helmet, and made tears stream from her eyes. She felt at the edge of control, precarious, more vulnerable than she had felt in the glider with nothing below her but sky.

Rafe felt strong, warm, and solid. Under her, the Harley oared like a wild, untamed beast. It was like riding in the eye f a great storm. In its own way, this, too, was like flying.

The steady stroke of the motor hummed along every nerve nding and throbbed into the center of her, creating a wild, estless energy that coalesced into a hard knot of desire as her highs molded to his and the cleft of her body straddled his low t the hips.

It was a ride of the senses as the cold night air pounded at hem from the outside and the heat built inside their tightly nolded bodies to the rhythmic pulse of the motorcycle.

She had no idea how long they rode through the night, only hat she was aware the sound and feel of the motorcycle had hanged. They were slowing down, then turning. Then the peed was different as they jolted to a complete stop and he cut he engine.

He swung off the back of the Harley first, and she felt the olt of separation after the closeness they'd shared. He stood ilhouetted in the soft glow of light in the driveway at his ouse. She watched as he drove his fingers back through the vild mane of his hair, then held out his hand to her.

Sliding off the Harley, she slipped her hand into his. He ound his fingers through hers and led the way up the winding tone steps to the house.

She hesitated at the doorway, remembering her earlier uneasness, but that was all it was, a dim memory, no more. Now she vondered what else she might find besides that brief flash of nemory—reminders of his relationship with Melissa?

"It's only you and me," he said in a low voice. "There's no ne else here. No ghosts."

She stepped inside then, leaving her last doubts at the door, nd shivered faintly in the still-dark house. He moved ahead of er into the living room, moving with easy familiarity in the eep shadows. Then, unexpectedly, there was a spark and a ash of flame, and fire sprang to life at the Spanish tile hearth. he moved toward it and him.

They came together as suddenly as that spark at the hearth, and gnited like that flash of flame. Then they burned, wild and enzied, their movements driven by the pulse of the motorcycle hat still throbbed inside both of them.

His impatient hands peeled her jacket back from her slender shoulders. Hers unfastened the buttons of the rough-spun vaquero shirt. As her jacket fell to the carpet at their feet, her hands found the naked skin at his chest. His fingers sank into her disheveled hair as hers spread through the silken mat of darkness that spiraled down his belly to the waist of the leather pants.

And then he kissed her.

There was no tenderness in him now. The question had been asked and answered. He was all wildness and hunger, intense, barely controlled, his skin hot beneath hers, his mouth demanding and equally hot.

She wanted to taste the heat, she wanted to taste all of him. Allie cried out softly as need became a sharp ache deep inside, and she welcomed the penetration of his tongue between her lips. Then his mouth was moving over her in an urgent, whispered need of his own.

The skin at her neck was cool in dark shadows beneath her hair where it lay at her shoulders. He pushed it back with one hand as his other moved at her back and pulled her closer. Then he tasted her, running his tongue down the curve of her neck to that place at her collarbone where the sweatshirt stopped him. He wanted to tear it off her. Instead, he gently closed his teeth over the silken ridge of flesh.

Allie shuddered at the exquisite sensation, then her hands were impatiently tugging the shirt from the waist of his pants and pushing it back off his shoulders. Firelight danced across the bronze planes of his chest. Her hands and fingers were pale, almost white against his skin, the contrast startling and wildly arousing. She lowered her head and pressed her mouth against his shoulder. But she didn't stop here. She closed her eyes and let the taste of him fill her senses as she traced her tongue across his collarbone, then down through the dark swirls of hair.

Rafe had been certain he couldn't want her more than he had wanted her at Casa Sureno. Now he knew he was wrong. Then he'd felt a need to comfort her, and take away the pain he saw in her eyes. Her pain had touched something deep inside him, something out of his own childhood that he'd kept closed away.

But this was different. A raw, aching need filled him, and throbbed beneath his belt. It had been there from the moment he first felt her woman's softness molded against him on the back of the Harley. He had felt it move between them, like the powerful thrust of the engine, and there was damn little control left now as he stared down at the wild torrent of her golden hair brushing his shoulder, saw the pale pink of her tongue stroking his chest, then felt the wet velvet of it at his nipple.

She heard the soft groan of her name, then felt his hands at her waist, pushing the shirt up over her breasts, then jerking it off. She wore nothing underneath, and she was accutely aware of her nakedness as she crossed her arms over her breasts. He reached out and seized her arms, slowly drawing them away.

First she experienced those warm fingers circling the mounded flesh of her breast, then his mouth closing over a taut nipple. The heat of his mouth was wild, and burned with wet fire as he slowly circled her nipple, then drew the erect bud between his teeth and gently nibbled. Allie cried out as her fingers plunged back through his dark hair, pulling him to her other breast.

Her flesh ached and hummed with an urgency that spread downward from the gentle tugging at her breast to the awakening pulse at her womb. Then his mouth left her, and she gasped with the sudden ache of loss, only to draw her breath in sharply at the sensation of his hot mouth at her belly, then lower at the waist of her jeans, where they buttoned.

She felt the insistent tug of his fingers at the button, then heard the rasp of the zipper, followed by the exquisite torture of his mouth moving lower still. His hands stroked over her hips, slipping beneath the loosened waist of the jeans as he skimmed them off. Then he went down on his knees and nuzzled her through the thin silk of her underwear.

Allie trembled at the first touch of his tongue, the tender stroking, the feather-soft flicks, the insistent nibbles, until she thought she would shatter into a million pieces. She wanted to push him away for the exquisite torture he gave, but at the same time she pressed him against her.

She whispered indecipherable words in desperate appeal as she felt his hands urgent and demanding on her body. Then he was peeling away her silk underwear and pulling her down with him before the blazing fire.

Heat radiated around and through them in the cool air of the room. His bare flesh glistened like molten bronze. In the tanned-leather pants from a bygone era, naked from the waist up, with dark skin and handsome patrician features, he looked as if he had stepped out of the past.

Her fingers were pale and cool against his skin at the waist of the leather pants as she unlaced them. Then her fingers tangled with his as he stripped them off, and she discovered that he wore nothing underneath. He was dark and golden all over, including the thick, erect flesh that stood up against his hard, flat belly.

She was softness and light, her rich golden hair fanning out over the dark blue carpet beneath them, the color reflected back in the clear blue of her eyes. His were dark and intense as he watched her. In the glow of firelight that washed over them, her luminous skin was like pale satin, while he was all hard muscle and sinew beneath the sheen of dark flesh. Allie's slender fingers cupped, stroked, then closed around his sex as she drew him to her.

He fanned long fingers low over her belly, grazing his thumb over the hardened nub of flesh between her soft folds. Then he was parting those layers of skin and guiding himself into her. His other hand moved low at her back as he lifted her hips. She watched in stunned fascination as he pushed inside her.

Darkness and light, night and day, fire and ice. They came together in a wild torrent of need and desire.

Every woman he'd ever been with, except one, had been for the moment. But not this one. This one was forever.

Allie was slender and strong beneath him, her curves and softness yielding, drawing him in, even as those clear blue eyes drew in his soul. There was no need for words. He didn't think he could explain what he was feeling—that she touched something deep inside him that he'd tried to keep safe and untouched, that she challenged him, made him feel when no one had made him feel anything in a very long time. He wanted the kind of strength that seemed to come so naturally to her; at the same time he felt the need to protect her.

Need. It sharpened and focused on that one tiny word as he felt himself inside her and then watched as she arched her hips and took him deeper still. Then they moved together and their separate needs became one.

When he sensed the first faint spasms beginning deep inside her, he knew all he had wanted was to give her pleasure. He could have easily followed her, that first penetration was all he needed. Instead, he laced his fingers through hers and drew their clasped hands over her head, marveling at the strength in her slender hands as she arched against him, waiting for her body to cool, and passion to subside in those crystal blue eyes.

Then he slowly began again, fascinated with the transformation from cool ice to molten fire, wanting only to fulfill her needs, and in doing so fulfill his own.

This time he lifted her to him as he went back on his knees. Her slender arms circled his neck as he held her and guided her legs about his waist. Then he clasped her hips and rocked her against him. Her arms went around his neck, her breasts flattened at his chest.

He heard her startled gasp as it began, saw the stunned pleasure in the clear blue gaze that stared back at him.

"Rafe? I can't."

"Yes, you can, sweetheart. Let it happen."

She shook her head. "No, not without you. Please."

"No, not without me," he assured her. "But I want to feel it happening inside you first. I *need* to feel it, then I swear I'll be there with you."

"Rafe!" Tears glistened in her eyes.

"I know, *querida,*" he whispered in Spanish against her throat, unaware that he did so.

He watched the expression in her eyes at the sensation that lay somewhere between pain and pleasure, felt the powerful spasms that pulsed once more through her body, then filled her with his own need. . . .

They stayed by the fire. Neither of them had any desire to move. When they finally felt the cold against skin not warmed by the fire or each other, Rafe retrieved a comforter from the upstairs bedroom. He wrapped her in it, then wordlessly pulled her against him, and simply held her through what remained of the night.

Just before dawn he carried her naked through the house to the open glass shower on the second level. There they explored further the sensations to be found with water that they'd begun to explore in the Jacuzzi at Edgewater. He slowly cooled the water, and the fire that seemed to build so quickly between them. Then he pulled her from the shower and dried her off. She stuck out her tongue and pouted playfully as she tried to reach for intimate parts of him and he dodged her hands.

"Stop that," he warned her. "Or I'll have to punish you."

"Just how do you intend to do that?" she asked with the beginning of a smile that reminded him of just how seductive her mouth could be. He tenderly grazed the back of a knuckle against the slight protrusion of her lower lip.

"No sex."

She gave him a mock look of horror as she spun away from him, leaving the towel hanging limply from his fingers. She moved across the bedroom wearing nothing but her shoulder-length honey-blond hair that hung over her shoulders in damp disarray.

"No sex?" she asked impishly, already seeing evidence that he was a very bad liar.

"Allie," he warned, crooking a finger at her.

She shook her head. "Not a chance. I want to see you suffer." He lunged at her then. She tried halfheartedly to escape, but his hand closed around her wrist. He spun her around and jerked her against his hard body and even harder erection, refusing to let her go.

"I don't know which is harder to take, seeing your naked body or feeling it."

"Define harder," she said with a laugh.

He hadn't dried off yet. Water from the shower still lay beaded across his dark skin and glistened in the swirls of even darker hair at his chest. Smiling up at him, Allie pressed her open mouth against the curve of chest muscle and drank the water from his skin.

"Sweet Jesus!" he groaned as he set her away from him.

"You started this," she said.

He looked at her—his wife—and realized she was right. He went to her then, and kissed her fully, completely, with a blatant hunger and need that mirrored what they had discovered in each other over the past hours. When he felt her quiver against him, he gently released her.

"You're right," he admitted. "And I fully intend to finish it, but not right now." Then with a grin he walked past her and went downstairs. Since her clothes were scattered all over the living room floor, she had no choice but to follow. She deliberately took her time locating them, not putting anything on until she had found everything.

"Are you through?"

She looked up, saw the ridge of hardened flesh beneath the blue jeans that he'd pulled on, along with a white T-shirt, boots, and black leather jacket, and smiled innocently. "Just about."

He said dryly, "I thought you were shy."

"I was. Until I met you."

Ten minutes later they were astride the Harley and heading out the driveway. Her wet hair was pulled back into a ponytail, she didn't have a stitch of makeup on since she had none with her, and she was dressed in the jeans and sweatshirt she'd worn the night before. As she sat behind Rafe, with the sky just becoming light over the Pacific, she thought how right this felt.

Whatever else there was between them—the family, El Sureno, their difference of ideas over the development—*this* was right. She slipped her arms around his waist as they turned south once more, and she realized they were heading toward the ranch.

They ate breakfast in a small roadside café that catered to early-bird tourists in campers and RVs.

"Certain appetites have to be satisfied first," Rafe informed her as they got off the Harley, drawing a few stares as they did. He grinned as he pulled off reflective sunglasses, for the sun had just come up over the mountains behind them. "And there's no food in my house."

"You live way out here, and you don't have supplies for at least a year?" she quipped. "How do you ever expect to survive the winter?"

He slipped an arm around her waist, hugging her against his side. "You need other things to survive besides food."

"Name one," she replied, feeling her own stomach begin to grumble at the aroma of bacon, eggs, and muffins. At his silence she glanced across the table at him as they were seated. He grinned at her wickedly, and she quickly said, "Not here. We'll discuss it later."

After breakfast Rafe put gas in the Harley, then they got back on the road, still headed south. But instead of turning down the ranch road, he continued on. Allie settled comfortably against the solid strength of his back, enjoying the warmth of the sun through her jacket, and the gentle sway of the Harley around the curves in the road.

Finally they turned off Highway 1 and followed the paved connecting road as far as they could. When it disappeared, Rafe stopped, and they got off. He rolled the bike out of sight behind heavy tree cover, and took out the key.

"Where are we?"

"This is the ranch. We're not far from the south section." He gestured upward. "Just over that rise. And that"—he gestured toward the ocean—"is the old landing."

She immediately recognized it from their previous ride. She shaded her eyes as she scanned the hill behind them. "You mean cliff."

He shrugged. "Cliff, rise, it's all pretty much the same."

"Until we try to climb it," she speculated.

"I thought you were the adventurous type."

"I am, but I think we might need ropes, and rappeling equipment."

He shook his head. "Nah!" Then he took her hand and they walked back from the road, through clumps of brush, and discovered stone steps. "These lead to the top," he explained.

"How long have they been here?"

"Since the landing was in use." He pointed around the hill. "There's an old wagon path over that way, but I don't think the Harley would make it."

"So we climb."

"We climb."

It didn't take that long. The climb was easy enough with the wide, stone steps. Occasionally one had crumbled, but most of them were intact. They stopped from time to time during the ascent to look back over their shoulders at the Pacific, and what remained of the boat landing at the small cove—the future site of the marina at El Sureno.

Once they'd reached the summit they turned to look at the entire curve of the small bay, including the inlet where old pilings protruded from the water, and talked about the layout of the marina.

"It'll happen, Allie," he told her. "We'll make it happen, because it's ours. And no one is going to stop us."

Standing behind her, he put his arms around her and pulled her back against him.

"Not even Gavin?" she asked, remembering the hatred in his voice the night before.

He slowly turned her so that they were facing each other. "Especially not Gavin. He can't stop us now."

"A marriage consummated?" she asked, suddenly wondering if that had been the plan all along.

Reading her thoughts, he said firmly, "Last night wasn't about that."

She prayed he was telling the truth. But now, after the incredible intimacy of the past few hours, she found herself distrusting him again. Her emotions were wildly unsettled. It was as if everything had been turned upside down because of what had happened between them. Although, she thought, if she were honest with herself, she had to admit that what had happened between them had been coming from the very beginning.

Last night, during what was probably one of the lowest moments of her life, Rafe had been there, refusing to let the Sloan family win their little battle of wills and emotions. She had stepped aside from who she always thought Allie Wyatt was, and gone purely on emotion, because at the time that was all she had left. Rafe had touched that emotion deep inside her.

Their relationship was on an entirely different plane now, or perhaps on the one it had been headed toward from the start. She had no idea where that left them now. The only thing she was certain about was that she needed him in ways she'd never allowed herself to need a man.

And he was her husband.

Husband. She told herself if he'd needed proof that they'd slept together, it would have been easier to stay at Casa Sureno with Inez as a witness. Instead, he'd taken her off somewhere where they could be alone.

"Last night was about *this,*" he said, cupping her face between his hands as he bent to kiss her.

And just as it had the night before, Allie felt desire begin low inside her at the touch of his mouth against hers, intensified this time by the memory of everything that had happened the night before.

He slowly made love to her with his mouth, kissing, stroking, then penetrating her lips with his tongue as his body had the night before. And he didn't stop. His hands insistently pushed at her sweatshirt. She felt the cool rush of air against her breasts followed by the intense wetness of his mouth close over her nipple. She gasped as she clung to him—the only thing solid and secure in a world that suddenly shifted.

"What are you doing?"

"Object lessons."

"What . . . are you talking . . . about?" she finally managed to say as he insistently pushed her down onto the soft, rustling grass of the hillside and his mouth moved insistently over her.

"Proving what could be worse—being forced to only look at you, or only touch you. The question is—who is it worse for. You or me." He made an example as he pulled away from her, his eyes dark with that familiar intensity that spoke of other ways he'd like to touch her.

"Oh, God." The words shivered out of her as her fingers dug into the buttery-soft leather of his jacket and she pulled him down for her kiss.

"Don't . . . stop," she murmured against the curve of his lips.

"Don't?" he asked as his voice grew husky against her mouth, her throat, and then her breast.

She answered shakily, "Stop . . ."

"Stop?" His mouth moved low over her quivery stomach, until his teeth teased at the band of silk on her underwear.

She laughed, and gasped, and shivered all at once at the ridiculous word game and then the more serious game he was playing with her body.

Enunciating every word as perfectly as she possibly could so there would be no doubt, she said, "*Don't stop!*"

32

THEY SPENT THE REST of the weekend at Rafe's beach house at Big Sur. When Monday arrived, they reluctantly ended their idyll that had in fact been little more than twenty-four hours long.

Back at Casa Sureno, Inez glanced from one to the other with a polite, speculative expression. "I was worried about you, Miss Allie." Inez glanced over at Rafe. "I was concerned that something might have happened."

"As you can see, I'm fine," Allie reassured her. "We spent the weekend in Big Sur."

"Oh," Inez said. Then her eyes widened, and she added, "Oh, I understand."

Allie felt her cheeks go warm. "Is there any chance of breakfast before we go over to the office? We didn't eat anything before we came in this morning. Some people don't believe in keeping food in the house."

"I will make something special," Inez said with a smile.

"Food of any kind would be special," Allie retorted as she headed for the stairs. "I'm starving."

"Oh, by the way, Miss Allie," Inez reminded her, "I won't be here tonight. I'm going to visit my daughter." She looked from Allie to Rafe. "I hope that won't interfere with any plans."

Rafe assured her, "I think we can take care of ourselves." His gaze went to Allie on the stairs. "We've had a little practice."

In the bedroom Allie quickly applied makeup and loosely curled the ends of her hair, then changed her clothes. Actually, she liked the idea that Inez was going to be gone. On a day-to-day basis she didn't know what she'd do without her, since Inez took care of most of the details of running the house. But she liked the thought of being able to spend more time with Rafe, alone and undisturbed.

Inez was setting breakfast out in the dining room as Allie came downstairs. Rafe came out of the den, where he'd been making some phone calls. He grabbed her around the waist. "God," he said, breathing in the cool fragrance of her perfume, "you smell good enough to eat."

She brushed her lips against his, just lightly enough to taste him and experience another sort of hunger—that now-familiar ache to feel him inside her.

Her voice was slightly husky and filled with regret. "It'll have to wait until tonight. We still have a project to get off the ground," she reminded him.

Shaking his head, he said, "I'm afraid it'll have to wait until Wednesday night." At her look of surprise, he explained. "I've got to go to Sacramento."

"When?"

"Today. I just talked to Jim. There's been a snag with some of the documents submitted to the state. They're holding up approval on the development. I've got to get it straightened out."

"Can't someone else go?" There was no disguising the disappointment in her voice. Everything was so new between them—she wasn't even certain what label to put on it yet. Sex? Yes, certainly that, and, she hoped, a great deal more. They needed time together to sort it all out.

They'd been back less than an hour, and already they were being pulled apart. There was also the preliminary hearing on Wednesday on the lawsuit Gavin had filed against them. Allie didn't want to face that alone. "Can't Jim take care of it?"

"He's the project engineer, not the owner. I'm the only one who can answer their questions." Sensing the change in her, he slipped his arms around her waist and pulled her close. "It'll take only a day or two at the most. I'll be back for the preliminary hearing Wednesday morning."

Impulsively, he suggested, "Come with me."

"You know I can't. I've only just gotten started on the new preliminary site plans for the main resort."

"Don't worry about the changes."

She felt a faint ripple of irritation that he could dismiss this so easily. "I have to worry about them. Those preliminary plans have to be right before we can get the necessary approvals from the Department of Transportation for our access."

"I already have the go-ahead on my plans. It would save time if we went for the original site," he suggested.

"We talked about this. You agreed to go with the changes I suggested."

"I know. I also know that we're short on time for ground breaking on the first phase. I have investors to keep happy."

She pulled out of his arms, feeling more than slight irritation now. It was as if he were trying to go back on their agreement. "I told you I'll have the changes ready on time, and I will. I've never let a client down or been late on a project."

He looked at her intently. "That isn't what I meant."

"Then what did you mean? This was supposed to be all settled."

He circumvented the issue by taking her hand in his. "I'm hungry. We'll talk on the way to the airport."

Allie shook her head. "I have to get to the office. I'm already late as it is."

"I see. Work comes first," he said, and by the tone of his voice, she could tell he wasn't at all happy about it.

Allie tried to salvage something of the mood they'd shared earlier as she touched his hand. "In this case, I think it has to. For both of us."

His hand dropped away from hers. "You're absolutely right." Then he added, "I need to get out to the airport. I can probably just make the morning commuter flight."

"You're leaving now? What about breakfast?"

He was already headed for the den. "You said it yourself—work comes first." He slipped on his jacket. "I'll see you in a couple of days." Moments later the slamming of the front door was followed by the sound of the Harley leaving the driveway.

"Will Mr. Sloan be returning shortly?" Inez asked from the doorway of the dining room.

"No, he won't," Allie replied, trying to bring her emotions back under control. The morning had started so wonderfully. They'd made love, losing themselves in physical and emotional desire and need, closing out the rest of the world for a few more precious hours before they had to return and deal with the problems they shared. As long as they put aside the issues of the Sloan family and the future of El Sureno, they'd been able to connect. It had been almost perfect.

Now all the shared moments had evaporated, making Allie wonder if she had been foolish to think their fragile relationship might work. She poured coffee and grabbed a piece of toast, deciding to drive Mac's Mercedes into work since Rafe's Corvette was still at the hotel.

"It looks like it's just you and me for dinner," Allie told Inez.

"I'm going to Pacific Grove this afternoon," Inez reminded her, then suggested, "I could change my plans and go later in the week. It's just that the baby has been sick and my daughter doesn't have anyone to take care of him."

Allie had forgotten all about it. She shook her head adamantly. "No, go ahead with your plans. That's more important. Besides, I'll probably be working late. There's a lot to do."

"I'll make a fresh seafood salad before I leave today," Inez offered. "Then all you have to do is put on the dressing."

Allie smiled. "Thank you. I'll be fine. I hope your grandson is feeling better soon."

"It's the flu. The older ones had it and he caught it. The day care center won't take him when he's sick."

She squeezed Inez's hand on her way out the door. "It's not a problem. I'll see you when you get back."

There were still a great many issues to be solved. Glancing at the local newspaper over lunch, she saw that the scene at the Cascarones Ball had indeed been covered. She had no doubt that Gavin would use it as evidence in his lawsuit against them for fraud. But she had more to worry about at the moment than Gavin and his legal maneuverings.

She spent the entire day on the phone with the Department of Transportation going over the new site location for the road access. They were verbally in agreement, as long as she could get them a set of amended plans, so she got Stan started on the drafting. Then she called the Coastal Commission about the site for the marina, which should be no problem since it was now farther away from a known feeding habitat for seals and sea otters at Marin Bay.

In between, she made several calls to Julia in Seattle about different aspects of the project, red-lined more changes, and interviewed still another draftsman she wanted to hire. It was almost eight o'clock when she finally left the office.

Before leaving the office, Allie called home and checked the messages on her machine. There was a brief one from Inez, reminding her to set the security system after she got in that evening; a call from Liz about getting together for lunch later in the week; another from Mac's attorneys, and that was all. There was no message from Rafe.

It was probably foolish to hope that he would call her. They hadn't parted under the best of circumstances. Still, it was just a minor disagreement, and there were bound to be many. They were both strong-willed, opinionated people who were intensely involved with the ranch, and, now, each other. But it would have been wonderful just to hear his voice, to feel the connection that seemed to spring physically between them even when they were arguing.

The beautiful clear weather that she and Rafe had enjoyed in Big Sur was gone. It was foggy as she drove back to the Del Monte forest, mist beading across the windshield so thick that she turned on the wipers. She almost missed the entrance to the forest. The guard waved her through at the sight of the sticker on the front window of the Mercedes.

"Drive carefully, Miss Sloan. We've already had one accident this evening inside the forest. A driver hit a power pole. Couldn't see the curve in the road, twenty feet ahead."

"I'll be careful. Thank you."

She was glad when she finally reached the gate at Casa

Sureno. Punching in the security numbers, she watched as the gate opened and lights came on down the length of the driveway to the house.

Instead of parking in the carport at the side of the house, she parked in the circular drive close to the front door. She coded the security system and let herself in, then reactivated it.

Lights automatically came on when she unlocked the front door. She had always thought the house warm and inviting. Tonight it was simply lonely, with Inez gone to her daughter's and Rafe in Sacramento. Thinking of him, she went first to the den and the answering machine.

She replayed the three messages she had listened to earlier. The attorneys undoubtedly wanted to discuss the hearing scheduled for Wednesday. They could wait until morning. She suspected Liz was curious about Saturday night. She glanced at the desk clock. Even for good friends, it was too late to call.

There was a fourth call that came in after she had retrieved the messages earlier in the evening, but there was no message, the machine simply clicked off. She wondered if it'd been Rafe. Finding that she wasn't home yet, maybe he had chosen to try again later. She thought of calling him, then realized she had no idea where he was staying.

"Right along with hundreds of other things I don't know about my husband," she murmured unhappily. She'd kicked off her heels as she came in. Now she picked them up and went upstairs to change into something more comfortable.

When she came back downstairs, she took the sets of plans into the living room and spread them out on the massive coffee table.

Since Inez hadn't been there to light a fire, the house was chilly. Allie turned on the gas jet beneath newly laid logs and lit the fire, then set the glass doors back in place. Seizing a roll of plans, she went to the couch, curling her jean-clad legs beneath her.

The house was quiet. There was only the muted hiss of the fire behind the glass doors, and the sound of her drafting pencil on the tablet of paper at her knees as she made occasional notes.

Being alone had never bothered her. She had often worked alone in the office on various projects for Julia, and she had lived alone, cherishing her privacy and solitude. It gave her the opportunity to recharge in a career that often required long hours spent over the drafting table or with demanding clients.

She hoarded her private time, telling herself it was necessary. She liked moments alone, but never considered herself lonely. But tonight the quiet and solitude bothered her.

Instead of wrapping around her like a soothing blanket, allowing her to concentrate completely on the work she'd brought home, the silence made her restless. She was distracted, constantly forced to refocus her attention. She paused frequently, looking around expectantly.

When she glanced at the telephone on the Spanish-style secretary in the far corner of the large room for the third time in a half hour, she realized that she had been listening for it to ring.

"Like a foolish teenager waiting for him to call," she chided herself out loud. "God, don't we ever grow up?"

She was convinced it must have been Rafe who called, then hung up without leaving a message. One part of her wished she had been there when he called. Another part of her was glad she hadn't been. Her feelings for him were still so new, she hadn't had time to sort them out.

They were married and yet they were strangers. They didn't really know much about each other. She had jokingly teased him about wanting to date her the night he had taken her to Ventana, but in a very real way they needed to start at the beginning. And so far, it was a pretty shaky beginning.

She knew there had been a strong attraction between them from the moment they met. But there had also been that first uneasiness when she saw his picture. She assumed it was simply because none of the other faces in the newspaper articles were familiar.

Why his face and not the others? She had no idea. But the attraction was undeniable. It had been there from the beginning, pulling them together even as they were fighting each other over the plans for El Sureno.

Business partner? Husband? Lover? Rafe was all three, and yet she still didn't know what it added up to beyond their business arrangement and a powerful sexual attraction. They had yet to discover what more they could share.

Her previous relationship with her fiancée had been well-ordered, predictable. She'd never waited for a phone call, because he always informed her when they would see each other the next time. Now she was involved with the most unpredictable man she had ever known. And for the first time in a long time she desperately wanted that phone to ring even as she told herself it was ridiculous. Because she tried hard to convince herself she was being foolish, she jumped when it rang a few minutes later.

She reached the phone on the third ring, and quickly picked it up before the answering machine got it.

"Hello?" There was no answer. Again she said, "Hello?"

She thought she might have gotten there too late and waited for the recorded outgoing message to play through the receiver. But there was only silence.

Again she responded, "Hello?" And then, "Who is this?" The call clicked off on the other end. Allie slowly replaced the receiver, then went into the den. The answering machine seemed to be working properly. With a frown she returned to the living room and the plans she had been reviewing.

She worked for another hour, glancing at the mantel clock from time to time, wondering if it was Rafe who had tried to call. Then she heard the sound. It came from outside at the back of the house, a faint scraping sound.

She stopped working and listened for it to come again. But there was only the hiss of the logs behind the glass at the hearth, and the faint ticking of the clock.

"Old houses," she whispered to herself as she got up to put more wood on the fire. As she pulled the glass doors back across the front of the hearth, the room behind her went dark.

The fans at the hearth that forced heat out into the room went silent. Except for the fire at the hearth, there was no other light in the entire house.

Allie froze where she was standing. Then, remembering she had seen a flashlight in one of the desk drawers, she headed for the den. The light from the hearth extended only as far as the doors of the formal living room. The hallway beyond and all the connecting rooms were dark. As she bumped into the corner of the elegant long hall table, Allie mentally cursed all power companies.

The entry hall was completely dark as well. Allie hesitated, frowning to herself as she glanced in the direction of the front doors. She was certain that Inez had said the security system was on a separate power source, and yet there was no red light glowing back at her from the small security panel just inside the entry. Were the problems with the power because of the accident the security guard had told her about earlier? It shouldn't affect the security system. A faint uneasiness settled in the pit of her stomach as she quickened her steps to the den.

She bruised her hip badly as she moved to the desk, having forgotten about the drafting table in front of it. She rounded the desk and was about to pull open the first drawer, when she heard another sound—the shattering of glass.

Allie whirled around, the flashlight momentarily forgotten. Her uneasiness erupted into full-fledged fear.

It was late at night, and she was alone in the house. There were no lights and the security system was apparently out, which included the panic buttons here in the den at the desk, and in her bedroom upstairs. Then she heard more glass breaking.

Allie grabbed for the phone at the edge of the desk. The light was out on the answering machine, but she expected that because it ran off the house power. She hadn't expected the flat silence.

She depressed the receiver button several times, but there was no dial tone. The phone was dead. Groping along the desktop, she felt for the other phone, with the newly installed second line. Fear left a cold, metallic taste at the back of her throat as she practically knocked the phone off the desk. She steadied it, grabbed the receiver, then felt herself die a little more inside. It, too, was silent. Both phone lines were dead.

The house was silent now, except for the rapid pounding of her heart and her frantic breathing. She fought to bring both under control, along with the panic that threatened to engulf her. She had to remain calm. She had to think.

Someone was in the house. She was certain of it. Someone who had made certain there were no lights, no security system, no means of calling out. She was alone in the dark with no one to help her. She thought fleetingly of the phone call, and the ne she'd picked up earlier on the machine. It had probably een the same caller, checking to see if she was there.

The first call had been picked up by the machine. Clearly she vasn't yet home. When she picked up the later call, whoever vas on the other end knew that now she was. In the back of her rain she knew that if robbery was the motive, it would have een carried out when no one was home. The caller had wanted o make certain she was home.

The new fear could have easily overwhelmed her if she adn't lived with something very near it from her dreams ne past few months. A tiny shaft of reason illuminated itself. he was in the dark—but so was the person who had shattered ne window. That disadvantage might also be an advantage. he couldn't see, but then, neither could the intruder. And she as familiar with the house.

Then another terrifying thought surfaced. What if the in- uder was equally familiar with the house?

She had to get out. *Now.*

The front door was the closest, but she had to go back rough the living room to get there. There were two other ntrances, the one off the kitchen, and the one off the ourtyard, but they were both toward the back of the house, here the glass had been broken. She decided to go for the ont door.

It faced out onto the driveway that led to the street and other ouses on Seventeen-Mile Drive. Unfortunately, none of those ouses was close by. She quickly made her way across the den, etracing her steps in the darkened room. This time she easily oved around the drafting table, being careful not to bump into nything. At the moment, whoever was in the house didn't now where she was. This might be her only chance to escape.

The living room was dimly lit by the fire. That meager light uided her, but it also illuminated her to the intruder. She uickened her pace, circling behind the huge occasional chairs nd game table rather than taking the shortest distance between vo points. Reaching the open double doors, she repressed the rge to run down the length of hall to the front doors.

She held back in the dark shadows, straining to see any ovement. Then she heard the distinct squeak of floorboards. he knew the entire layout of the house. The entry hall was tiled, as was the living room. But the floor in the dining room was wood. The dining room was directly across the hall.

If she didn't move now, she might easily be cut off from the front doors, forced to flee into some other part of the house. But how close was he to the dining room doors that opened out onto that same hallway?

She felt trapped by her own fear, yet she knew the longer she hesitated, the less chance she had to make it to the door. Taking a deep breath, and casting one last glance back toward the dining room entrance, Allie bolted for the front door.

She slammed against it, groping for the heavy bolt. Behind her she heard the crash of a chair from the dining room. Her fingers seemed to have gone numb. She fumbled with the handle on the bolt, her cold, damp fingers sliding off the metal grip, then grabbed at it again, her terror building with every passing second.

Then she heard the rapid slap of soft-soled shoes on the tile behind her.

It was the same as it had been that night when she was seven years old—terrified of the dark, more terrified of the person she had seen—that horrible nightmarish monster who haunted her dreams seemed now to have come to life. The monster was chasing her.

Allie screamed, a low, desperate sound that came from frustration and terror as the sticky bolt held tight. Then suddenly it gave. Shoving it back all the way, she threw open the doors and ran into the night.

The intruder, whom she now thought of as the monster, was right behind her. She could hear it crashing through the house coming after her. She had to get away. Running to the car, she jerked open the door, then realized with mounting terror that she had no keys. Abandoning the car, she raced toward the gat at the end of the drive.

She was barefoot, and the edges of the driveway stone bruised her feet, but she barely noticed. When she reached th gate, she realized she was still trapped. All the security control were locked. With the power off, the only way to open the gat was to physically roll it back. She didn't have time for tha even if she had the strength.

Hurrying over to the stone wall, she leapt at the top of it. Sh grabbed the edges of several stones high up and began to climb. She didn't look back to see if the monster was coming after her, she just kept climbing until she was able to swing her leg over the top.

She dropped easily to the ground on the other side and began to run down the street. She headed toward the nearest light, which came from the house across the road, then pounded on the door.

"Hello? Please open up!" she called out frantically. "You've got to help me!"

But there was no answer. She tried again, but there was still no answer, and for the first time she noticed there were no lights on inside to indicate anyone was at home.

Turning away, she quickly ran to the house next door. There was no light on, but still she pounded at the door. "Help me! Please!"

She continued pounding and yelling as loud as she could, all the while refusing to look and see if the monster had followed her. It was back there, she knew it. She didn't have to see it, she could feel it.

"Open the door!"

Suddenly a light went on inside. Please God, Allie prayed, let them open the door.

33

ALLIE SAT IN A squad car in the driveway at Casa Sureno, a blanket draped around her shoulders, sipping a cup of hot, bracing coffee that someone had thrust into her hands. Calls came in over the radio in a never-ending stream of codes. A car belonging to the Del Monte Forest security patrol was parked nearby, along with a plainclothes policeman's car.

The house and grounds were flooded with light as uniformed police and security officers moved in and out of the house and explored the grounds. Lights from the patrol car cast blue and red beams onto the driveway, giving everything a surreal look.

It was well past midnight, and Allie was exhausted to the point of numbness. The coffee helped, the heat and caffeine working to calm her at the same time they energized her. The first numb shock at the realization that someone was trying to kill her was beginning to wear off, replaced by almost uncontrollable shaking.

The plainclothes officer came up to the open car door and knelt beside it. "How're you doing, Mrs. Sloan?"

Allie forced a polite smile. "Better now. Thanks."

Detective Martin had arrived right after the uniformed patrolmen, and had talked to her at her neighbor's house down the street. She had never met the elderly couple, but knew she would be eternally grateful to them for opening their door in the middle of the night to a young woman on the verge of hysteria.

Detective Martin was fortyish, with gentle, slightly droopy brown eyes, sandy blond hair that was fast receding on top, and the reassuring presence of a St. Bernard with a keg full of whiskey around its neck, seeking out avalanche victims. At the moment that was exactly how Allie felt, as if an entire mountain had come down on her.

"How's the ankle?" He asked.

She had hurt it in her headlong dash from the house, and Detective Martin had urged her to go to the hospital. But Allie had refused, insisting it wasn't that bad. And besides, she wanted to be here, to know as soon as possible what the police were able to find out.

Martin had recognized the Sloan name as soon as the call came in. Alexandra Wyatt Sloan herself was remembered by the older officers on the police force, who recalled her mother's notorious murder case. One of the officers had mentioned to Martin that he had been at the scene of the crime that night, and had seen the child. "She looked shell-shocked," the older man had said, shaking his head sadly. "Just like guys in 'Nam. It was terrible seeing a little girl like that."

Detective Martin knew Carmel-Monterey society as well as anyone. He often dealt with cases in those staid, expensive areas known as the Highlands, and Seventeen-Mile Drive. He knew the sort of people who lived in the elaborate, expensive estates, behind gated entrances.

On first meeting Allie, Martin had thought she seemed like the kind of woman police detectives rarely encountered except to locate their stolen jewelry or Mercedes. But this wasn't a case of stolen jewels or cars. The intruder hadn't stolen anything as far as they could tell. In fact, he'd left several items of substantial value untouched. He'd been after something else.

The overturned furniture indicated the path the intruder had taken as he had chased Allie through the house. Fortunately she was quick-witted and hadn't panicked. Even now she answered all Martin's questions clearly and succinctly, recalling as much as she could with a calmness that he knew must hide tremendous inner fear.

Taking out the power and the security system usually meant robbery. Burglaries happened here in spite of the zealous private security force and elaborate alarm systems. But disabling the phone system smacked of something else, and Martin knew that Allie realized this.

There were dark circles under her blue eyes—eyes that were watchful and filled with uneasy shadows.

"Can you remember anything else?" he asked as gently as possible. "Something that you might have seen or heard?"

She shook her head. "It was dark except for the light from the fireplace." She went on shakily. "I never did find the damned flashlight."

"You were probably better off without it. He couldn't see you in the dark."

Allie looked at him, that hard knot of fear in the pit of her stomach tightening.

Just then a uniformed officer appeared at Martin's side. "They're all through inside, sir. They're packing everything up now."

Martin nodded as he turned to Allie. "You might be more comfortable inside now, ma'am." He saw her expression as her glance cut past him to the house. "Whoever it was is long gone, Mrs. Sloan. We've fixed the alarm system, and one of the local security guys is going to remain on guard for the rest of the night. The intruder won't be back tonight."

But what about tomorrow night? Allie thought fearfully. And the next night, and the next . . .

Martin escorted her into the house. She hesitated at the front door, reexperiencing the desperation she'd felt earlier to get out those doors ahead of her pursuer.

Fear tightened her throat. She took several deep breaths forcing herself past it as she went inside the house.

They had just entered the living room when one of the uniformed officers interrupted them. "Sir, there's a guy out here who says he's her husband."

Without waiting for permission, Rafe pushed passed the officer, then stopped as he took in the scene in the living room. A lamp had fallen to the tiled floor, the shade skewed at a craz angle, the bulb shattered. In front of the hearth, architectural plans lay scattered all over the floor surrounding the large low coffee table, and the heavy wrought-iron fireplace set lay where it had fallen across the tile in front of the hearth. Several very old Spanish tiles, specially designed for the house, had broken under the crashing weight of the heavy pieces.

Rafe's gaze went to the police, then to Allie. "My God. What's happened?"

She stood and stared at him in bewilderment. "What are you doing here?"

Detective Martin glanced from one to the other, a little surprised at her response. Clearly she hadn't expected him home tonight.

"I thought you were in Sacramento," she went on.

"I was," he said as he came through the room, stepping over the toppled lamp. "I decided to drive back tonight."

When he reached her, he gently took hold of her shoulders. "Are you all right, Allie?"

She nodded.

Rafe knew she was anything but fine. She looked as if she was about ready to fall apart. Pulling her into his arms, he felt her shiver with a residual fear that he immediately recognized from the aftermath of her nightmares.

His breath was warm and reassuring against the side of her neck. She didn't seem to have the strength to put her arms around him, so she simply let him hold her, feeling his strength surround her.

Rafe looked over at the detective, and in a low voice demanded, "What the hell happened here tonight?"

Martin studied his reaction, noting the underlying edge of anger in the question. Anger was a basic emotion. It usually came from some inner hostility, sometimes out of fear, occasionally out of frustration. He wondered which was the source of Rafe Sloan's anger.

"There was an intruder," Martin explained. "As far as we can determine, nothing was taken," he reassured him.

Rafe persuaded Allie to sit down, then sat beside her, his arm around her shoulders, holding her close. He listened while Detective Martin filled him in on what had happened.

Martin finished by saying, "I take it you weren't expected back tonight."

Rafe looked at him with a level gaze. As a young man he'd had enough encounters with the authorities to know exactly what was behind the question. He kept his voice even, not wanting to upset Allie by getting into an argument with the police.

"I missed the commuter flight to Sacramento this morning, so I drove over. I had several business meetings set up for this afternoon that I would have missed if I'd waited for a later flight. After taking care of the meetings, I decided to drive back tonight."

"You didn't call to tell your wife that your plans had changed?"

"I tried," Rafe said. "But she'd already left the office. I called here later, but the phone wasn't working."

Allie listened, her head cradled against his shoulder. "Both phone lines were dead," she said in a low monotone.

Rafe glanced at Martin. The detective nodded, then indicated that he wanted to speak with Rafe privately. Rafe assured Allie that he would be right back, then followed Martin out into the entryway.

"The phone lines were cut," Martin said bluntly.

"You're certain?"

"The wires were tampered with, as well as the wires for power to the house and the separate power source for the security system." Martin watched for a reaction, then he went on. "Whoever the intruder was, he was after more than the usual video equipment, money, or jewelry."

"How were the wires cut?"

Allie had joined them. As they turned to look at her, she said as calmly as possible, "I think I have the right to hear this too."

Rafe knew the monumental amount of strength it took for her to say that, much less confront the truth.

Martin explained, "The power to the house and the separate source for the security system were cut at the electrical panel at the back of the house. It was a clean cut, probably with a pair of wire cutters, the kind you can buy at any hardware store."

Allie frowned slightly. "I heard the sound of metal scraping against metal."

"That was probably the electrical panel when it was forced open. The phone lines were undoubtedly cut before that." Focusing on Rafe, Martin added, "Whoever did this knew his way around here. He knew how to disarm the alarm system, and he knew there were two phone lines that needed to be cut."

Allie had known from the first moment the police arrived that this wasn't a simple case of burglary. Still, suspecting the truth was one thing; hearing it confirmed was an entirely different matter. She felt as if the room had suddenly tilted under her. She sat down heavily in a chair next to a narrow table in the entryway, feeling as if her legs would no longer support her.

Someone had been after her tonight. Just as someone had been after her at Edgewater.

"You've recently inherited a substantial interest in the Sloan family holdings, haven't you?" Martin asked her gently.

Her gaze met Rafe's. "Yes," she answered hesitantly.

Martin nodded, still thoughtful. "I imagine there were several people who were upset about that."

"What are you suggesting?" Rafe asked.

"I'm not suggesting anything. But money—a great deal of money—can make someone a target."

"You don't think this was a stranger," Allie concluded.

"We have to consider every possibility, Mrs. Sloan." Martin paused. "I've got to be going now. My people made temporary repairs to the wiring, but you'll need to get someone out here to make more permanent repairs. And you might want to consider a whole new system. One that can't be so easily disarmed."

"I'll take care of it," Rafe said curtly.

A uniformed officer came in. "We found this near the front wall." He handed over a wrought-iron fireplace poker wrapped in a clear plastic bag. It seemed to match the other pieces at the hearth.

Martin compared it to the deep gash in the wood at the front door. Clearly, the intruder had slashed the door when Allie slammed it shut behind her as she fled from the house. The intruder had picked up the poker to use against Allie, then dropped it at the wall after following her from the house.

Allie shuddered, remembering all too vividly the sounds that had followed her through the house—the scrape of metal as the electrical panel was opened, shattering glass, then the movement of someone stalking her.

"We dusted it for prints," the young officer said. "We didn't pick up anything."

"The surface is too rough to pick up a print," Martin observed. "But we'll run it through forensics, see if we can pick up anything else—possibly hair or cloth fragments, something identifiable."

Martin looked at Allie. "I need you to come in later this morning and sign a report. We're treating this as an assault case."

Unable to speak, Allie merely nodded.

When the police had finally gone, Rafe took Allie into the den and pulled her into his arms. "Are you sure you're all right?" he asked.

"I am now," she said, holding on to him tightly, too tired and shaken to be surprised at the need that came so easily. Her head lay against his chest. She closed her eyes, trying to shut out the events of the past few hours, concentrating on the steady, strong beat of his heart. But the images and Detective Martin's words wouldn't go away.

"This is the second time someone has tried to kill me," she finally said in a shaky voice.

He stroked her hair. "Don't think about it now. You've been through too much already."

She pulled back slightly. "I have to think about it, Rafe. Someone tried to kill me. *Twice*."

"It's all right, Allie, I'm here now," Rafe assured her. "I won't leave you again until this is resolved."

"What if it's never resolved?" Her fearful gaze held his. "What if it *was* someone in the family? Everyone has a great deal to lose since we took control of the ranch."

His eyes were dark and intense. "Only temporarily. Everyone in the family still has their shares. Once the development goes through, they'll get a big return on those shares."

She shook her head. "You know how they feel. They want their money *now*. And they would've gotten a lot more from the Japanese than they'll get from our development of El Sureno. Rafe, you know that Gavin swore he would stop us."

"Allie," he said gently, cutting her off, "stop it. You're exhausted. You've been through a lot tonight. It won't solve anything to go through this now. Why don't you let me take you upstairs? You could use some sleep."

He was right. She was exhausted and sounded hysterical even to herself. But she couldn't stand the thought of going upstairs just then.

"I'd rather stay down here for a while," she said, struggling to hold on to her composure.

"All right. I'll put more wood on the fire." Before he got up, he bent his head and tenderly brushed his mouth against hers. The kiss was warm, tender, and all too brief. Her hand went to the back of his neck, holding him, needing more. He paused for a moment, then broke away.

"Hold that thought. I'll be right back."

She shivered faintly as he crossed to the fireplace and opened the glass doors. Within minutes he had the fire going again, flames dancing around several large logs, heat and comforting light pouring into the large room. Then he rejoined her on the sofa.

"I was a jerk this morning," he said simply.

She managed a smile. "I won't argue with that."

"Allie . . . there's no excuse for my stupid behavior. It's just that somehow I guess I expected you to suddenly turn submissive. When we went back to the same old disagreements, I blew up. I'm sorry."

"Apology accepted," she said, then kissed him lightly.

"Anyway, what matters is your safety. I'm not letting you out of my sight until we find out what's going on."

As she curled up against him, Allie told herself his words were immensely reassuring. Yet deep inside her was a nagging doubt. Was it just coincidence that she'd been attacked the one night Rafe was away? It had to be.

When she awoke she was alone, covered with the blanket Rafe used when he slept in the den. It was daylight, the sun poking feebly through the fog that surrounded the house. A fire still burned at the fireplace.

For a moment Allie felt reassured by the safety and comfort of the cozy room. Then the memory of the night before came flooding back, and she sat up abruptly, looking around for Rafe. He was nowhere around. Then she discovered what had awakened her—the distinct sound of pounding at the back of the house.

With only a few hours sleep, fatigue fogged her thoughts, and she felt a moment of familiar panic at that sound, reminiscent of the night before. Then she gradually got hold of herself. Pushing back the blanket, she went in search of the sound, and her husband. She found both at the back of the house, at the service entrance. Barefoot, her ankle still a little sore, she stepped out onto the open courtyard.

Rafe was there, along with two workmen. He wore faded jeans, a pair of loafers, and a white V-neck sweater. His longish, dark hair lifted slightly with the wind blowing in over the seawall at the back of the estate. He stood holding a diagram in one hand, alternately looking at it, then back to the house.

In spite of the fact that it was cold, the sleeves of the sweater were pushed to his elbows, exposing the length of bronze forearms lightly dusted with fine black hair. Her gaze went to the V of the sweater, where more of that dark hair was exposed, and she felt that unexpected physical quickening low inside that she experienced whenever she saw him.

He was her husband, and now her lover as well. No matter why they had gotten involved, now it felt right. With a tiny jolt of surprise she realized she'd needed him, needed to connect with someone in this way, for a very long time.

"Good morning," she called out.

He looked up, a slight frown on his handsome face. Then the frown shifted to something more intimate, and the physical desire Allie felt took on the sharper edge of hunger.

"I think 'good afternoon' is probably more accurate," he said with a spreading smile as he came over to her. "I thought you might sleep the day away."

"I might have, except you were making too much noise out

here. What is all this?" She gestured to the two workmen in coveralls, their tools spread across the back walkway.

"This is Ben and Paul," Rafe explained, making introductions. "We're moving everything inside."

"Inside?"

He showed her the diagram. "I'm having everything rewired to a panel inside the service area. It will be more secure that way. It should have been done a long time ago."

It seemed a bit much to Allie. "Couldn't you have just put a lock on the panel?"

He shook his head. "I'm not taking any chances." When she started to ask another question, he stopped her with a kiss. Then he asked gently, "How are you?"

It took her a moment to recover. His mouth was wonderful—warm and tender, and so giving. "I'm better."

"Hungry?"

She nodded. "A little."

"There's some bacon and sausage in the oven, along with some muffins."

"Is Inez here?"

"No, I called her and told her not to come in until tomorrow. I thought we could use a quiet day today."

"Then who made breakfast?"

He winked at her. "I can handle frying up some bacon and putting Inez's muffins in the microwave."

She smiled. "What a talented husband I seem to have."

He laughed. "There's coffee too," he added as he put his arm around her waist and walked with her back through to the kitchen. "I make *great* coffee."

"That takes real skill," she remarked. "A few ground beans, filter, and automatic coffeemaker."

He pulled her into his arms, his hands both rough and tender as they skimmed down her back.

"I don't need any smart-ass comments from you," he said with equal tenderness.

"What do you need?" she asked as his hands moved down over the curve of her bottom and pulled her against him. She felt erect flesh between them below the thick closure of his button-fly jeans.

"I need you."

It was unexpected and said so simply that it caught her completely unprepared. She knew so little about him, but enough to realize those kinds of words didn't come easily. Because of his own painful childhood, she suspected that he'd learned not to expose his emotions, to keep everything carefully closed away behind the façade of a devil-may-care rebel, so that he couldn't be hurt again.

Because she hadn't expected it, or the intensity behind it, she didn't know what to say. It mirrored her own feelings, and all her own uncertainties. She felt need pulse between them—both physical and emotional. Financial need had brought them together in the first place, but that had nothing to do with the need they felt for each other now. If she were honest, she would admit there was an edge of danger to that need, just like the danger that gave an erotic edge to their lovemaking—the desperate need to lose oneself in the other, the empty aching awareness of being less than complete, needing the other to be fulfilled.

Allie felt a little breathless, and a little scared. Rafe had that effect on her. Glimpses of the person deep inside him were brief, intense, and unsettling. Loving him would never be easy.

That sudden realization—that she was in love with him—left her even more shaken. She pushed out of his embrace. "I think I need a shower to wake up," she said with a shaky laugh.

A half hour later she still stood under the warm spray of the shower, letting it sluice through her hair and down her body. Turning at the sound of the shower-door latch, she wiped streams of water from her eyes. Rafe stood there, a cup of coffee in his hand. His dark eyes moved over her entire body, then came back up to her clear bluc gaze.

"How are you?" he asked again, his voice low, his gaze intense and watchful.

Very slowly, her voice gone as low and husky as his, she said, "Still hungry."

Setting the cup aside, he reached inside the shower for her. He pulled her against him, one hand resting at her naked waist, the other pushing back through wet hair to the back of her head. Then he kissed her deeply, thoroughly, tasting beaded water at her mouth, feeling it at his fingers as his hand curved low over her.

Allie grabbed the front of his sweater to steady herself. She felt the nubby yarn of the sweater at her fingertips and breasts, then bare skin beneath her nails, the coarse scrape of denim against her thighs, the heat of the man underneath. Need focused in the sensations at her thighs, intimately joined with his, yet separated by the cloth barrier.

In a voice she hardly recognized, he whispered against her mouth, "What do you need?"

Allie cried out softly, "*You.*"

Then she was pushing the sweater back off his shoulders, their mouths parting only long enough to pull it over his head. She pulled him into the shower with her. His jeans and briefs fell to the bottom of the shower, and they were completely naked, their bodies sliding together under the rhythm of the water that beat against them.

"Allie . . ." He whispered over the hiss of water and the curling clouds of steam, his hands gliding over the gentle curves and sleek planes of her body, discovering her all over again. She wrapped her arms around his neck as she lost herself to sensations—the wet heat of his body sliding against hers, the dark hair plastered across his chest, the taste of him in her mouth.

The desire that she'd felt so strongly earlier hadn't lessened. If anything, it was sharper, more intense, because she had run from it. She was trapped by the sensual sting of the water, by the naked heat of his body. Now, there was no running away.

"You're so beautiful," he whispered hoarsely against her mouth. "Please let me love you."

He lifted her, his hands moving down over her hips, his long fingers circling and kneading her sensitized skin until she thought she couldn't stand it any longer. Then he lowered her, guiding her legs around his waist in a loving embrace as he pushed inside her.

This was the completeness she so desperately needed, that pure physical sensation that made her feel as if she had ceased to exist alone, and now existed as a part of him. It was a joining that went beyond the physical to the spiritual, until body and soul became one. They became one, intimately joined, their separate heartbeats felt as a single beat that began deep inside him and ended deep inside her.

His words washed through her as the water washed over them—*Please let me love you*—as if he were asking permission, this man who had never asked but simply taken, and always on his own terms.

She let him love her, and she loved him in return as she had never loved any man in her life. . . .

Wearing a thick terry robe, Allie sat before the lighted mirror at the long, tiled counter in the dressing area, trying to comb the tangles from her hair. With a towel wrapped about his hips, Rafe retrieved his jeans and briefs from the bottom of the shower and wrung them out.

He came up behind her, gently taking a handful of her wet hair and tugging her head back for his kiss. "You taste clean," he whispered against her throat.

"You taste . . . wonderful," she said, feeling the delicious warm ache deep inside from their lovemaking. She flattened her palm against his, then slowly entwined their fingers. She looked at his hands clasped in hers. A faint grin appeared at the corners of her mouth. "You're all pruny."

"You should see the rest of me," he said, pulling her close and nibbling the edges of that grin. The sudden ring of the telephone in the bedroom jarred them apart.

Rafe let go of her hair. "I don't believe the phone company got the phones rewired so quickly."

He went into the bedroom to answer it, then returned a moment later, frowning.

"What is it?"

He sat down beside her on the upholstered bench seat, lacing their fingers together as he cradled her hand in his. He stared down intently at their joined hands, rubbing his thumb across the cool gold of the wedding band he had given her.

"The illustrious press wants a statement about last night."

She slowly withdrew her hand from his as she stood and began restlessly to pace the dressing room. She pushed her hand back through her wet hair in a gesture so natural, he had come to expect it, it was so innately a part of her.

"Why can't they forget about what happened twenty-five years ago? Are they so desperate for news around here that they have to check out every little burglary attempt?"

Her brush with the press Saturday night after Val's confrontation had been bad enough. They were looking for sensationalism, and Val had given it to them. A statement now would only whet their appetites for more.

"It's not just the local press," Rafe said in a quiet voice. "That was the *Chronicle*."

"San Francisco?" She couldn't believe it. What were they going to do? "How are we going to go down to the police station this afternoon? They're probably camped out at the gate."

"The local security people will be able to take care of most of it. I could put a call in to Detective Martin and tell him it's out of the question."

She shook her head. "I have to go down there. If there were just some way we could avoid them. Damn!" she exclaimed. "I'm beginning to feel like my every move is being watched."

Her gestures were exaggerated, fueled by frustration and an underlying uneasiness. He went to her, pulling her against him.

"Let me take care of it."

"But how—" He silenced her by kissing her. When she started to protest, he kissed her again.

"Let me take care of it," he insisted. "I've dodged some unfriendly types in my time.

"The police?" she asked with the beginning of a smile.

"And 'Nam. Just leave it to me." He kissed her one last time. "Dress casual and be downstairs in a half hour."

She met him downstairs at the appointed time, dressed in a corduroy skirt, turtleneck sweater, and high boots. The skirt was slim, long, and pewter gray, accentuating her slender figure. The sweater was cobalt blue. It contrasted with the soft gold of her hair, left loose at her shoulders, and accentuated the clear blue of her eyes.

"That looks like an outfit I would enjoy taking off you," he said with an appreciative smile as he came out of the den wearing black jeans, white T-shirt, and leather jacket.

"Ditto," she said, then asked, "Are we riding the Harley?"

"The car will do just fine," he assured her. "As I said, I've had some practice."

The Corvette was in the carport. They went out through the courtyard at the back of the house. As they slowly drove around to the front of the house, the two workmen he'd hired swung around in front of them in Mac's Mercedes.

"What's going on?" Allie asked in confusion.

"They'll bring the car back tonight and pick up their truck. They can be trusted. They've worked for me a long time."

The electronic gate opened, activated from inside the Mercedes, and Ben and Paul swung out of the driveway at a fairly good pace. They were immediately followed by two cars that had been parked on a side street, out of sight of the security guards. As they disappeared down Seventeen-Mile Drive, Allie and Rafe drove out the gate and sped off in the opposite direction.

"Very good," she complimented him. "But I think you missed one."

Rafe glanced in his rearview mirror. "I think I can shake him. I know another road out of here."

That was news to Allie. As far as she knew, there were only two gates, one at each end of Seventeen-Mile Drive, the main road through the Del Monte forest.

Rafe made several quick turns down adjacent streets, cut back briefly to Seventeen-Mile Drive, then veered down a single-lane road that Allie hadn't even seen because the tree cover was so dense.

"It's a fire road, used only in case of emergency. Not too many people know about it."

She looked behind them and grinned. "Evidently not."

Within minutes they were out on a connecting road, leaving the Del Monte forest behind, and then cutting over to the highway into Monterey.

At the police station they went in through the back entrance, where prisoners were usually transferred to the city jail. Detective Martin was waiting for them, looking as if he'd worked straight through the night, his St. Bernard eyes drooping even more than usual.

He smiled at her. Showing them into his office, he said, "Mrs. Sloan, we'll try to make this as brief as possible."

She read through the official statement he'd had typed up from his report the night before. "This seems pretty accurate."

"You're certain there's nothing else you want to add—

something you might have remembered since last night that would help us identify your attacker?"

She shook her head.

He nodded. "Okay, just sign at the bottom of the statement." Then he explained that if she did remember anything else, she was to contact him immediately.

Allie asked straightforwardly, "Do you think it was someone in my family?"

Detective Martin's gaze flicked briefly over Rafe, then returned to Allie. "That's a distinct possibility. I would caution you not to take any chances." He added, "Be careful who you trust, Mrs. Sloan."

"I'll make certain she's careful," Rafe assured him. Then, as they were leaving, he asked, "Did you find anything on the fireplace poker?"

"Not yet. It takes a while to go over something like that. The people in forensics like to be thorough. Very often a case hinges on a single piece of evidence that they find. I'll let you know how it turns out, Mr. Sloan."

When Rafe and Allie left the police station, the sun had finally poked feebly through the fog. Within an hour it would close in again, Allie knew.

"I suppose we should go into the office and try to get some work done. We've lost almost a half day, and tomorrow we have the hearing," Allie added tiredly.

Rafe slid into the car beside her. "The boss is giving you the day off."

She looked over at him. "Is that right? And just who is this boss?"

"When it comes to your welfare, *I'm* the boss," he said. "You're taking the day off, to relax and have some fun. You need it."

"What sort of fun?" she asked suspiciously.

"It's called hide-and-seek—the best possible way to beat the press at their own game."

"How does it work?"

"By hiding in plain sight. We're going to play tourist."

The Monterey Bay Aquarium was packed with tourists. Allie and Rafe moved easily among them, blending in, hiding in plain sight if anyone had bothered to follow them.

They sat in the theater and watched the movie "The Living Sea," listened to a lecture for students at the tidal basin with all its live sea creatures crawling about, stood before forty-foot glass panels that opened onto waving tendrils of plant life in the kelp beds, and watched the antics of playful sea otters.

They spent the entire afternoon there, saying little, simply enjoying each other's company, each pulling on the other's hand when one of them found something unusual.

Afterward they walked through John Steinbeck's fabled Cannery Row, teeming now with restaurants, arcades, and shops. They ate fresh clam chowder and drank two bottles of Johannesburg Riesling from a Monterey vintner. By the time they returned home, Allie was more than a little relaxed.

It was barely nine-thirty when Rafe drove into the driveway and quickly closed the gate, shutting out the reporters who hung about outside. He parked in front of the house, then walked around to the passenger side of the car.

Allie had fallen asleep on the drive back. Now she stirred awake at the sudden rush of cold, damp air as the car door was opened. She leaned against Rafe as they walked up the steps and paused while he entered in the numbers for the security code. Through the fog of two bottles of wine and bone-numbing fatigue, she wondered when she had given him the code. She didn't remember doing so. But she must have, she told herself.

She put the thought out of her mind as he closed the door behind them and they went up to bed.

34

'HE FOLLOWING MORNING THEY went to the attorney's office) be briefed on the preliminary hearing scheduled for later that ıorning.

"The entire basis for the suit will be Gavin's claim that you ıarried for fraudulent purposes," their attorney explained. "It 'ill be put to his attorneys to prove that claim."

"How will they go about it?" Allie asked, eager to know xactly what to expect.

"They'll call in witnesses to support their claim, as we will) support ours." He hesitated then and looked down at the ·gal brief, as if the next matter was perhaps delicate.

"They may try to require a physical examination," he dded, bringing his gaze back up to theirs.

Allie let out a slow breath. "In order to prove that the ıarriage has been consummated," she concluded. She'd been xpecting something like this.

"That is correct. At this time it hasn't been stipulated. But may be in the future. I wanted to prepare you for it."

Allie nodded.

"This is bullshit!" Rafe came out of the chair beside her and egan to pace the room. "For your information, the marriage

has been consummated. If necessary, we'll testify to that i
court. But an examination? For Christ's sake, what is tha
going to prove? That my wife is no longer a virgin? We're no
living in the Dark Ages here, and we're certainly not a coupl
of innocent teenagers. We're adults, we've both had pas
relationships. How in hell will an examination prove anything
except to sensationalize this situation?''

Their attorney remained remarkably unaffected. ''I wa
merely trying to prepare you for what might happen. There i
every chance it may not go that far. And off the record, I agre
with you. But what *I* think doesn't matter.''

''I'm telling you right now, there won't be any examina
tion,'' Rafe insisted furiously. ''That's insulting to my wife.'

''Your refusal may be looked upon as an admission c
fraud,'' the attorney pointed out.

''Then it's up to you to prove beforehand that this marriag
is real.''

''That's exactly what we'll try to do, Mr. Sloan. Now,
think we should get over to the courthouse. We don't want t
be late for the preliminary hearing.''

As they left the office and made the short drive to th
courthouse in the attorney's car, Allie said to Rafe, ''I'll subm
to the examination if it's required. We can't afford to refuse.'

''No,'' he said flatly.

''You know how important this is,'' she started to argue.

''No. It's ridiculous. It's not going to happen.''

''It's *my* choice to make.''

''It's *our* choice. This is a marriage in all ways now.''

Allie was surprised—and deeply touched—by his attitude
He took her hand as they got out of the car and walke
briskly to the entrance of the courthouse, where the attorne
pointed to a group of waiting reporters. He said, ''Let's get th
over with quickly, without any comments.''

Allie held back slightly, reluctant to face the press. B
Rafe's hand tightened over hers as he pulled her on ahea
They were almost through the doors before they were reco
nized. The morning air erupted in a barrage of questions th
followed them to the courtroom where the hearing was to begi
in just a few minutes.

Their attorney and his assistant quickly escorted them in

the courtroom. Once inside, the press was bound by the rules of the court. They were allowed to remain but could ask no questions. They had to wait until the hearing adjourned.

Inside the courtroom Allie and Rafe took seats beside their attorney. This morning, both sides would enter their positions and assertions. Then a formal hearing date would be set for later.

It was necessary only for the parties directly involved and their attorneys to be present. However, all the members of the Sloan family were there, in what Allie wryly thought of as a show of familial unity. But she knew they were unified only so long as family loyalty translated into money—a great deal of it.

Gavin sat behind his attorney with an air of confidence, ignoring Rafe and Allie. He leaned forward several times to exchange words with the lawyer. Only when the judge finally came in and the hearing got under way did he finally glance over at them. For an instant, brother stared at brother, and all the hatred of the past seemed to leap between them, focused in that millisecond of eye contact. Gavin was the first to break the contact as his gaze shifted briefly to Allie.

Suddenly she felt cold inside. He had sworn to stop them, and as Rafe had said, she was sure he would do whatever was necessary.

Beside him, Erica sat perfectly still, as if desperately trying to hold herself together. She was beautiful, but all the beauty, perfect makeup, and designer clothes couldn't disguise her pain. She looked up briefly, her gaze locking with Allie's, and it seemed that all her years of suffering were focused in that one glance at a young woman who reminded her that she had always been second choice.

Charlotte was all coolness and perfect composure, her elegant patrician Sloan features fixed in the perfect mask she always presented to everyone. Not a hair out of place, and she wore a string of perfectly matched pearls—a gift from her father. In her pale blue Armani suit, she epitomized the wealth, power, and position of the Sloan family in Monterey-Carmel society.

David Benedict sat beside her. His head was bent forward as he discussed the case with the attorney. When Allie and Rafe had come in, his gaze had met hers briefly. His expression was haggard, his face deeply lined. He looked, Allie thought, like deeply worried and unhappy man.

What was he thinking? she wondered. Was he recalling th fact that both he and Allie were outsiders, somehow caught u in the tangled machinations of the Sloan family?

He had once been attracted to her mother. Like Erica, was h reacting to her uncanny resemblance to Barbara? Or was something else? Of all of them, David had been the only on ever to express any real kindness to Allie.

Then she glanced over at her cousin Nicky. When she'd fir seen the newspaper photographs of him, she'd thought him a extraordinary attractive young man with a lean athleticism an air of faint boredom. Now she thought how little he'd change But her perception of him had changed. He was merely a ma fast approaching middle age, still playing at little-boy game His expression was that of a spoiled, petulant child whos favorite toy had been taken away from him, leaving him angr and sullen. Nicky had never grown up. Allie doubted he ev would.

There was no need for her to seek out Valentina. H cousin's striking flame-haired beauty made her stand out in an crowd. This morning she was especially captivating to th members of the press as she talked freely with them. When th court was brought to order, Val gave Allie a cold, calculatin look, then went to sit beside her brother.

As she looked at the members of her family, Allie recalle what Detective Martin had said the previous afternoon—th whoever had broken into Casa Sureno knew their way arour in the dark.

"Someone who had been there a great many times."

"Someone in the family?"

"Be careful who you trust."

Was it possible? She didn't want to believe it. Just as sh didn't want to believe the truth about the night her mother die She had denied the truth about that night, locking it away in th subconscious of a terrified seven-year-old child. But there w no denying the horrible truth that confronted her now- someone in her family had probably been in the house at Ca Sureno two nights ago. That same person was in the courtroo at that very moment.

Which one was that desperate to stop her? Which one hated her enough to try to kill her?

Beside her she felt Rafe's reassuring warmth as he took her hand in his.

Be careful who you trust.

Remembering Detective Martin's words, Allie found herself giving Rafe a thoughtful look. No, it was impossible. She had to trust Rafe.

The preliminary hearing went quickly. The case was entered, both sides presented their claims, and a formal hearing date was set for three weeks from then. In a matter of minutes it was over.

"Now we really go to work," their attorney told them afterward. "I'll need a list of witnesses who can support your claim that you have a valid marriage."

Rafe replied, "We'll get it to you."

Already the other members of their family had started out of the courtroom. The press followed them like bloodhounds.

"I don't suppose there's another way out of here," Allie said with a thin smile.

Their attorney shook his head. "I'm afraid we'll have to face them, but only briefly. I've sent my assistant on ahead for the car. Walk straight through, and remember, say *nothing*."

As they came out, Val suddenly appeared. She walked up to Rafe, put her arms around him, and kissed him quickly. It happened so quickly, no one had the opportunity to stop her. She stepped back just as quickly, a self-satisfied look on her beautiful features.

"Hot and fast, Rafe. You always made me burn hot and fast."

The suggestive words were spoken in a voice just loud enough for a member of the press to overhear. The hallway suddenly erupted as the other members of the press smelled blood and closed in for the kill.

Microphones were thrust at Rafe and Allie. "Is that true, Mr. Sloan? Have you been sleeping with her?"

"No comment," the attorney responded before Rafe had a chance to do so.

"What about you, Mrs. Sloan? Was this all a scheme to gain control of the ranch?"

"Mrs. Sloan has no comment on that," the attorney insisted.

"Is this somehow connected to what happened twenty-five years ago?"

Allie shook her head. "No!"

"Isn't it true that your mother was pregnant with her lover's child when she was brutally murdered by your father?"

"My father didn't kill her!" Allie shouted, ignoring the attorney's order to remain silent.

"You were living at the Sloan ranch at the time, isn't that true, Mr. Sloan?"

"Mrs. Sloan, is it true that you came back for revenge on the Sloan family? And married Mr. Sloan as a business arrangement to accomplish just that?"

Allie was trapped between the outside wall of the courtroom and the crowd of reporters that had gathered. Looking past them, she caught a glimpse of Val, who wore a bitterly pleased expression. Deep inside her, Allie felt the old familiar fear and panic begin to build.

She was caught, trapped, with dozens of microphones thrust at her. Then cameras began to go off, the blinding flash of lights, the incessant whirring of automatic cameras that caught every expression, prying, probing, waiting for her composure to crumble, catching it in freeze-frame or on video for the six o'clock news.

The tight knot of fear constricted her throat, and she felt she couldn't breathe. Then she felt someone grab her arm, pulling at her.

In her fragmented thoughts, another memory slipped into place—vivid, crystal-clear, frightening in its intensity.

She was seven years old, standing outside a courtroom very much like the one they'd just left, and she was with her grandparents. There were people everywhere, pushing and shoving to get at her. They towered over her, cameras balanced on their shoulders or at their faces like some strange, distorted creatures. They came at her, the cameras thrust at her face, shouting questions, calling out her name, trying to get her attention.

"Tell us what happened, Allie . . ."

"Did you see your father kill your mother . . . ?"

She turned, trying to find her grandparents, but they had become separated in the crowded hallway. She couldn't find them. And as the cameras clicked, tears rolled down her cheeks, and a traumatized seven-year-old child began to scream.

"Daddy! Where are you? Please, Daddy! Make them go away!"

At that moment, twenty-five years later, Allie felt all the fear and trauma of that recovered memory. At that moment she *was* that frightened seven-year-old child.

"Make them go away," she whispered as tears filled her eyes, and she turned to the wall at her back, trying to escape them.

Rafe pulled her back into the now-empty courtroom, past the judge's platform, and through the door at the back. They emerged into a narrow hallway that connected to the judge's private chambers and several other offices.

"Hey! You can't come back here!" a secretary insisted.

"Where's the back door out of this place?" Rafe demanded, in no mood to argue.

"At the end of the hall, but you can't . . ."

Rafe pulled Allie down the hallway. "I'm getting you out of here." Going through an unmarked door, they emerged into the parking lot at the back of the courthouse. They didn't stop, but kept right on going, across two side streets, until they reached the attorney's office, where Rafe put her in his car.

Seconds later they roared out of the parking lot, swerving sideways briefly as Rafe downshifted hard and sped through the streets of Monterey. They had left Monterey behind, and were on Highway 68 before Allie looked up and realized they weren't headed for the office or Casa Sureno.

"Where are we going?"

"Someplace where we can have some privacy—someplace where we won't be bothered by anyone."

She stared out the window, much as she had that other time, when he took her to Ventana. Then the sunset had been magnificent—brilliant crimson, bright orange, deep purple sliding into midnight blue at the horizon. Today everything was gray under the thick ocean mist.

An hour later they turned off the coast highway at Marin Bay. Mechanically, Allie noted they were only a mile from the cutoff to the ranch road. The Corvette shot up the winding private road, pausing only as Rafe hit the remote for the gated entrance. Then they sped on through to the front entrance of the magnificent multilevel house he had designed, the place where they had first made love.

Allie didn't immediately get out of the car. She sat for a moment as Rafe got out and came around to her side. Her expression was troubled, her eyes haunted by dark shadows and another memory that had clicked reluctantly into place that morning, triggered by the explosive confrontation with the press.

"Sweetheart?" Rafe said gently as he opened the car door and crouched low at the opening. He touched her hand. She was staring straight ahead through the windshield out into the gray oblivion of sky and ocean beyond the house.

"They won't ever let it go, will they? They'll always be there with their cameras and prying questions." At the touch of his hand she turned her tormented gaze to him, her eyes shiny with unshed tears. "I remembered something today."

His hand tightened over hers as she began to explain the memory of the last day of her father's trial. Then she looked up at him as another memory returned. "You weren't there. Everyone else was, but not you."

"I left before the trial was over," he explained. "Don't talk about it now. Come inside. You need to rest."

"Why did you leave?"

His expression shifted slightly, became unreadable, masked. "Everything was pretty unpleasant," he bit off sharply. "There was no reason for me to hang around. I wasn't exactly welcome."

She held on to his hand as they went into the house. It was cold inside, the gray dampness outside seeming to reach in to surround them. Rafe went straight to the fireplace and built a fire. When he finally had it going, he turned to her, brushing her soft, golden hair away from her cheek.

His hand was warm and gentle. "You look tired. Do you want to rest? You can use the bedroom upstairs, where you won't be disturbed."

"You don't disturb me," she said, turning her mouth into the palm of his hand and kissing him.

"I promise to let you rest," he said with a half smile that she ound both endearing and seductive.

Still she shook her head. "I'd rather stay down here." She hought she sensed a bit of irritation as his hand dropped away.

"Suit yourself." He pulled a blanket off the back of the sofa nd handed it to her—the same blanket they'd wrapped around hemselves after making love.

She touched his hand. "I'm sorry."

"What on earth are you sorry for?"

"That this turned into such a mess. I never realized it vould—"

"Quit apologizing," he snapped, then made an obvious ffort not to be angry. "It'll be all right. It will all work out in ne end."

"You seem pretty confident about that."

"I am. I'll make certain it works out. Now, relax. Get some est if you can. I'm going to try to head off the press."

She lay down on the sofa, exhausted.

Rafe reached out to gently cradle her face in his hands. "I'm orry," he said, his mouth very near hers.

"What for?"

"That it had to be this way."

"It will work out. You said so."

Looking down at her, his dark eyes were intense, as if there ere something more he wanted to say. Instead, he kissed her. he kiss was tender, the lightest brush of his lips against hers. hen he headed for the back of the house.

Allie pulled the blanket around her. Terrified of the night-ares she might have, she didn't want to sleep. But the warmth f the room and the remote solitude of the house enveloped er, helping her to relax. She felt safe, protected, here with afe. Surely, as long as he was with her, no monster could get er.

It was dark outside when she awakened at six o'clock. Soft ghts were on in the living room, the fire glowed warm at the earth, and there was a delicious aroma of food being grilled. llie got up and went in search of her husband and that ntalizing aroma.

Finding her way to the kitchen, she saw him standing at the ove. The kitchen and the breakfast area overlooked the back deck that seemed to be suspended in the blackness of the nigh that surrounded them.

''Have a good rest?'' he asked, handing her a glass of wine

''Yes,'' she said, amazed that it was true. She'd been asleep for over five hours.

''How did you keep the press from calling here?'' she asked curiously.

He concentrated on the kebab skewers that lay across the indoor grill. ''I told you I'd take care of it.''

''I hope you didn't have to cut the wires,'' she teased.

He looked up at her sharply. ''Why would you say something like that?''

She shrugged and tried to make light of it. ''I don't know. I just seemed like that might be the only remedy. I know how persistent the press can be.''

He looked up at her then, and smiled, that familiar, seductive smile. ''Well, they can't find you here. No one can.''

They ate in the dining room with candlelight glowing off the windows. The dinner seemed especially delicious because she hadn't eaten all day. He refilled her glass for the third time.

''What are you trying to do, ply me with wine so my defenses will be down?''

''Do you object?'' he asked huskily.

''Not at all. But I thought we might try to get some work done.''

''I worked while you slept this afternoon.''

''Well, you'll have to do a little more work. I want to go over the changes the new draftsman made the past couple of days. He's almost through.''

Rafe capitulated. ''Okay. We'll drink the rest of the win *while* we work.''

After dinner she helped him clear the dishes. Then he took her on a tour of the house, something he'd neglected to d during their brief time there before. It was obvious that he' designed the house himself. His touch was imprinted on it, i the intriguing combination of smooth glass, rough stone, warm wood, and cool tile.

Allie was familiar with the second level. Rafe's bedroom was there, along with the master bath, steam room, an whirlpool spa all overlooking the Pacific.

A guest room and bath were on the third level, with a sundeck guaranteeing guests their privacy. Impulsively, Allie picked up the telephone as they were leaving the top level of the house. She frowned slightly at the silence on the other end.

When he said that he'd taken care of the problem of harassing phone calls from the press, she assumed that he would leave the answering machine on. She told herself it was silly to be upset, but she couldn't help feeling that same swell of panic she'd experienced two nights earlier at Casa Sureno when she discovered both phone lines were dead.

She decided to ask him about it as they went downstairs and he put more wood on the fire. "About the phones . . ."

He looked up. "What about them?"

"They don't seem to be working." For some reason she found herself lying. "I thought I'd call Inez to ask her to come back to the house tomorrow."

His gaze was dark and intense. "This was the only way to be sure you wouldn't be bothered by phone calls." Then he smiled. "Why don't we get to work? I'd like to see those plans."

She knew he was humoring her. He hadn't seemed at all eager to work when she mentioned it at dinner.

"I'll just bring in more wood from the deck." He turned and went out onto the deck.

Allie looked around for the tube of plans she'd thrown into the trunk of the car that morning. She didn't see them, and realized they must still be in the trunk of the Corvette.

She knew Rafe always kept the trunk locked. She went into his office and found his keys on the desk. Curious about what he had been working on during her nap that afternoon, she went to the drafting table. There were several sheets of paper lying across the top. She frowned slightly as she turned them back sheet by sheet.

She knew she was still a little tired, but as far as she could see, these were all old plans—the original set of master plans that he'd first had drawn up. Nothing on any of them had been changed, and there were no new overleaf sketches to indicate that he had been working at all.

Why would he say that he'd been working all afternoon if he hadn't? Her frown deepened as Allie picked up his keys. She intended to ask him about it when they sat down to go over the changes.

Outside, Allie went to the Corvette. Just as she suspected, the trunk was locked. She unlocked it and lifted the lid. Light from the exterior house lights glinted dully off the chrome tube of plans she'd put in there earlier. Lifting it out, she noticed that Rafe had thrown one of his jackets into the bottom of the trunk.

He wasn't careless about his clothes. Yet the lightweight leather jacket had been carelessly thrown inside next to several badly stained rags. With the thought of taking it inside, she took the jacket out of the trunk and laid it over her arm. As she did, something fell out of one of the pockets, and made a clinking sound as it fell onto the aggregate driveway at her feet.

It had fallen just behind the back tire, in the shadow of the car. She bent down to pick it up, and her fingers closed over cool metal. As she examined it in the driveway light, her fear tightened into a hard little knot that rapidly expanded until it pressed against her lungs, making it impossible to draw a deep breath.

Horrified, she stared down at the gleaming metal wire cutters that had fallen from Rafe's jacket pocket.

35

SHE HEARD RAFE CALL to her, then saw him as he appeared at the end of the deck.

"It's cold out here. What are you doing, sweetheart?" he asked.

Her gaze locked with his as she held his jacket in one hand, and the wire cutters in the other.

"I took care of it . . ."

"They knew their way around . . . Someone in the family."

"Be careful who you trust, Mrs. Sloan."

"Allie?"

"It was you!" she exhaled on a terrified breath, wanting desperately not to believe what seemed so obvious.

"What are you talking about?"

She slowly began to back around the rear of the car as she stared up at him.

He called out to her again. "What are you talking about? Allie!"

She heard the urgency in his voice, saw him running along the deck toward the stairs.

"Be careful who you trust."

As Allie watched the man she could no longer trust, all she

could think of was the mind-numbing terror of that night at Casa Sureno as she fled through the darkened house, pursued by someone who wanted to kill her.

Other memories flashed through her stunned mind—the trip to Sacramento that Rafe had insisted was so critical; Inez telling both of them she needed that night off; his decision to drive back that night; the fire road that few people knew about, making it so easy for him to come and go unnoticed; his intimate knowledge of the house; and finally, the wire cutters.

Allie knew she had to get out of there. She had to get away, or she was going to die.

When he reached the bottom of the stairs, only a few yards away from her, he called out again, urgency becoming anger in the sharp edge of his voice.

She dropped the jacket and the wire cutters as she ran for the driver's door. All over again she experienced the oppressive panic that had gripped her in the water when she had felt herself being dragged down by her sodden garments and thought she was going to drown.

She grabbed the door handle, yanked it open, then threw herself inside, locking the doors after her. Fumbling as she tried desperately to get the key into the ignition, she didn't look up, she didn't dare, or she would have been terrified by the sight of him coming at her.

She finally thrust the key into the ignition, twisted it violently, and the car roared to life. Then she jammed the gearshift into reverse. Without thinking, going purely on instinct, she stomped down on the accelerator.

The Corvette dug out, tires squealing, as she jerked the wheel hard to the left. The car spun crazily in a half circle and she slammed on the brakes. Then she shifted to first gear and put her foot to the floor. The tires squealed and there was a sensation of being out of control as it fishtailed.

Straightening the wheel, she let up on the accelerator slightly, then felt the traction catch as she sped down the driveway at a dangerous speed.

Rafe cursed as he ran toward the Corvette. He caught up to her as she backed it around, swerving dangerously out of control. He tried to grab for the passenger door handle. As he did, he caught a brief glimpse of Allie. She was utterly terrified—of him.

Then she floored the accelerator and the car shot down the driveway. The floodlights glinted off something shiny beside his leather jacket. He bent and picked it up—the wire cutters.

How the hell had she found them? He swore again and sprinted for the carport. He had to stop her.

In between the lights that ran the length of the driveway, the surface all but disappeared around winding curves. It was only after Allie had gone several hundred yards that she remembered to turn on the headlights, several hundred more before she dared to look in the rearview mirror. The lights from the house were a fast-disappearing blur.

When she looked again, two of those lights were brighter than the others, zigzagging along the winding driveway behind her—Rafe was following in the jeep.

Her hands were slippery on the steering wheel, and her leg trembled on the clutch as she downshifted at the next curve. The wheel slid through her fingers, she grabbed at it, then overcorrected. The car went sideways a few feet.

She downshifted again, willing strength into her numb hands and legs. Another two hundred yards and the gate came into view. He had closed it behind them as they came in. Now Allie depressed the remote control for the gate, determined to drive right through it if it didn't open quickly enough.

"Open! Dammit, open!" She pounded the wheel as she was forced to reduce her speed to let the gate open. When it cleared enough for her to drive through, she downshifted and sped out onto the highway, heading north on the coast highway.

It had been foggy all day. Now the fog was worse, seeping over the edges of the cliffs up onto the coast road. She could see no more than fifty feet ahead of her in some places, less than twenty in others.

She drove dangerously, her one thought to put distance between herself and those trailing lights. But she couldn't help remembering Rafe's comment, as they'd driven to Ventana, about all the cars that had gone over the edge of the cliffs around there.

After she left the gate, she had glanced in the rearview mirror and seen only darkness. Now, when she looked again, she saw lights and she pressed the accelerator farther to the floor.

The numbers of the car phone glowed back at her from the center console. Allie jerked the receiver off the unit, trying desperately to punch in 911 and keep her eyes on the road at the same time. Listening intently for the responding ring, she heard only a series of beeps as the call failed to go through. She realized that on the twisting coastal highway this far from Monterey, she must be out of range of the cellular signal. On this stretch of coast, the phone was useless.

''My house is remote . . . No one will bother us . . .''

Tears streamed down her cheeks and blurred her eyes. It had been so easy for him to lure her out there. She had trusted him, had needed to believe in him, because . . . she had fallen in love with him.

Allie wiped the tears that streamed down her cheeks, obscuring her vision even more than the fog was doing.

''Your mother was used and thrown away. You're being used, and then you'll be thrown away too.''

She began to cry uncontrollably, and swerved around another corner at a reckless speed, losing sight of the road markers, drifting over the centerline.

A wall of light suddenly came at her. Allie jerked the wheel, bringing the Corvette back into her own lane as the oncoming car sped past. She braked hard, the roadster going sideways in the road and drifting onto the opposite shoulder.

For long, wasted moments she sat there, her forehead resting on her arms crossed over the crown of the steering wheel, sobbing as she struggled to drag deep gulps of air into her lungs.

She had stalled the car on the extreme edge of the road, the left front tire up over a slight embankment. Looking out the window, she realized where she was—the sheer dropoff that she'd seen days earlier. She'd very nearly driven over the edge.

Though she couldn't see them in this dense fog, she knew that below were the cars that had plunged off the road and gone over the embankment, their rusting skeletons exposed at low tide. The drop was so steep that it was impossible to retrieve the wrecked cars, and so they had simply been left there, a stark reminder of the dangerous highway curves.

She knew Rafe was somewhere behind her on the coastal highway.

"The jeep may be old and ugly, but it will outrun just about anything. And you can't beat it for sheer brute strength."

With a small strangled cry she imagined him ramming the back of the Corvette, forcing her over the edge. It would all be so simple—a tragic accident on the coast road, like so many others.

Frantically, she tried to restart the car. The engine finally caught and she carefully backed away from the edge of the embankment. Then she cut across to the northbound lane. But she knew that eventually she had to get off the highway and to a phone. She nervously watched the road behind as well as the road in front.

How far had she come from the turnoff at Marin Bay? Two miles, five, more? The fog almost completely obscured it, but somehow she found the cutoff road to the ranch. She turned hard to the right, the wheels losing traction briefly as they left pavement for dirt and gravel.

She thought of turning off the headlights so that she couldn't be seen from the highway, but it was too dangerous. Instead, she barreled on ahead, praying the main gate was open, or else she would lose precious more seconds stopping to open it. Seeing that it was open, she sighed with relief, then sped on through, hoping desperately Miguel and his wife were at the hacienda.

She tried to recall how far the hacienda was from the main road, but her mind refused to think beyond the basic mechanical functions of keeping the car centered over the dirt road. Gravel spit up from beneath the tires and spattered the undercarriage. Behind her, dust curled up beneath the wheels and churned with the swirling fog.

Was he still following her? Had he seen her turn off the highway? Or had he driven past?

She glanced briefly in the rearview mirror and let out a strangled sob at the sight of headlights on the ranch road behind her.

The Corvette wasn't meant to be driven at such speeds over dirt roads. It bucked over unexpected rises in the road and bottomed out where the road dipped away suddenly, but Allie didn't slow down. Finally the ranch came into sight and Allie's heart leapt with hope.

The light that glowed at the barn across the wide yard and the outside lights at the hacienda were a welcoming beacon. Allie brought the car to a skidding stop and ran up the wide flagstone walk to the front door.

She pounded on the thick oak door. "Miguel! Let me in!"

There was no answer. The hacienda was frighteningly silent. Frantically, Allie called out again, beating her fists against the stout door. Still there was no answer. Before she realized what she was doing, she ran back down the steps to the adobe slumpstone pillars that stood at each side of the steps.

Counting the stones from the inside corner, she pried a loose one out. Her fingers closed around the key that had lain hidden there since she was seven years old.

"I'll put it here for you, Allie," her mother had said. *"If you ever need to get into the house when no one's here, the key will be there."*

"I remembered," she whispered as she retrieved the key and ran back to the front door. Quickly unlocking it, she pushed it open and ran inside.

"Miguel!" she called out again as she stood in the middle of the hallway near the stairs.

With a sinking, sick feeling in her stomach, she realized that no one was there, and Rafe was on the road behind her. Driving her fingers frantically back through her hair, she forced herself to think. She had to get to a phone, but where was it?

She felt along the wall, her fingers finding the push-button switch. When she pressed it, lights came on down the length of the hallway. For just a moment she had feared they wouldn't come on.

With the reassurance of those soft lights in old, ornate fixtures, she felt her panic subside slightly. She tried to remember if she'd seen a phone in one of the rooms on her previous visit, but she'd been so upset by old memories that she hadn't noticed.

"Think!" she whispered desperately to herself, trying to keep the terrifying childhood memories of the house at bay.

There used to be several phones. She remembered one in the

kitchen at the far end of the house, but had no idea if it was still there. There had also been a phone in the den.

Even as she thought of it, Allie felt herself taking backward steps, her gaze going briefly to that darkened doorway, then darting away as she grabbed the newel post at the stairs for support. Then her gaze cut up those stairs and she remembered there had been a phone in her parents' bedroom.

The upstairs held no hidden terror for her. As a child, she'd found it a place of safety and refuge. Allie ran up the stairs to the top landing, then turned toward her parents' old bedroom. She hesitated briefly at the door, then opened it.

Quickly finding the light switch at the bedside lamp, she turned it on. There was that momentary jolt as light pooled softly on the furnishings and across the soft wood floor. How many times had she come running into this room as a child, searching for her mother? Playing dress-up in her mother's elegant gowns before the antique cheval mirror, laughingly playing the game.

"Mirror, mirror, on the wall . . ."

Why were those happy memories so strong now, when she was scared to death?

Allie blocked out her memories as she ran to the phone and picked it up. She almost wept when she heard the dial tone at the other end of the rotary phone. Frantically, she dialed 911. The emergency operator quickly answered and Allie struggled to remain calm as she spoke. "I'm at the Sloan ranch—" She broke off as she heard shouting downstairs.

"Allie? Where are you?"

The receiver dropped from her numb fingers.

Then she heard Rafe's voice again from the front of the house as he angrily called out to her.

The frightened child in her wanted to hide, to reach someplace safe, where he couldn't find her. But somewhere in the rational part of her mind she realized that if she stayed upstairs, she would be trapped. She had to get out of there.

She flicked off the light at the bedside table, plunging the bedroom into darkness, and for just a moment she experienced again the terror of that night when she had heard shouting and ran to her parents' bedroom, only to discover that they weren't there.

With all her strength she refused to think of it. She heard him again at the front door and realized that she'd left the door unlocked. She forced herself to move, but she was stiff and slow as the old fears made her legs weak and unresponsive. As an adult she now knew what waited at the bottom of the stairs.

Gathering her strength at the doorway, she forced herself to go to the landing, then down the stairs, listening for the sounds that would reveal Rafe's whereabouts in the house. She had to get out before he found her. It was her only chance.

At the bottom landing she felt as if she would collapse. She grasped the newel post for support, clinging to it like a frightened child.

She heard shouting, much closer now, and in tiny fragments those old memories became reality once more. She cringed against the post, trying desperately to block out the horrible nightmare sounds.

When she saw the mirror at the far wall, she stopped, frozen. She was once again a child, standing in the hallway, staring fixedly at the mirror. But this time the image in the mirror wasn't that of a monster. This time Allie could clearly make out the face of the person bending over her mother's body—Rafe.

The memory of that reflection wavered and was replaced by a new one as Rafe stood staring at her. This reflection didn't come from inside the den, but from the hallway behind her. She whirled around, all the terror of that night colliding with the fear of the present.

"Allie! Sweetheart, please!" He held his hand out to her as he slowly walked toward her. "There's nothing to be frightened of. Please don't run away."

"It was you!" she whispered increduously, tears streaming down her cheeks. "You were here that night."

His expression was stark, his eyes dark and intense. Instead of denying it, he said, "I was afraid you would remember. I prayed that you wouldn't."

"Rafe was crazy about her . . ."

Hysteria bubbled in her throat. "You were with my mother in the den that night! I *saw* you!"

"Allie, please! You've got to believe me." His voice was

hoarse with agony. "Your mother was already dead when I found her."

"No!" She shook her head. "I saw you bending over her. That was what you were afraid I would remember. When Mac left me those shares in the ranch, you couldn't allow it to happen when you had been denied so much.

"My God!" she whispered, her heart breaking. "I loved you."

"Then believe in that love, Allie." He came toward her then, moving quickly. "You've got to believe me! I didn't kill your mother and I'm not trying to kill you!"

If she ran down the hallway, she thought, he would very likely catch her before she got to the back of the house. There was only one chance to get out, and it lay through the double doors on the other side of the den.

Now that she was certain she had discovered the truth that had been hidden in her memory for so long, neither the mirror nor the room held the same terror for her. The real terror was in the hallway with her.

She glanced briefly back over her shoulder as she ran into the den. As she turned, she collided with someone directly in her path beside her father's desk.

Hands grasped her arms, holding on tightly. As Allie recovered, she looked at the person holding on to her.

"Charlotte!" Relief poured through her. "Thank God!" she cried hysterically. She glanced back over her shoulder, the fear starting all over again as Rafe followed her into the den.

"We've got to get out of here! I've remembered everything!"

"Have you?"

With those first words, it was as if something else jolted into place inside Allie. Not so much a memory, but a vague, growing awareness.

"Yes . . ." she answered hesitantly, for the first time noticing that the lights were now on in the den just as they had been that night.

"Charlotte, what are you doing here?"

Charlotte smiled faintly. "I followed you, of course."

Behind her, Rafe stopped just inside the doorway. He looked

from Allie to Charlotte in confusion, then called out to Allie. But she stood frozen, caught between them.

It all happened in a fraction of a second. Out of the darkened corners of her mind, fragments of memory slipped back into place. She heard again thc shouting and arguing.

Rafe called out to her, "Allie, you've got to believe me. The wire cutters don't mean anything. I always carry them in my car, for emergency repairs."

Allie shook her head, clasping her hands over her ears, trying to block out the memory of that argument, the horrible shouting that reached out from her dreams.

"I would never hurt you," he said desperately. "I swear it." Then his voice softened. "I love you. Trust me—trust your own heart." He held his hand out to her.

Those old memories had shattered her, unraveling the very fiber of who she thought she was. But they had also betrayed her, refusing to reveal all the secrets of that night. She had to rely on instinct.

From the beginning he'd asked her to trust him, and she had. Now he was asking her to trust her feelings for him.

"I can't," she cried softly.

"Yes, you can. They're real, Allie. Not some dim memory. Trust your feelings."

She felt as if she were already dying inside. Her feelings for him were so intense, so deeply a part of her. She hesitated, torn by the powerful struggle between her heart and her memory. Then, giving into instinct, wanting desperately to believe him, she slowly reached out to him.

She was stopped by Charlotte's cold words. "You're just like her, you know."

Slowly, Allie turned to face her.

Charlotte went on in a voice made ugly by bitterness. "She ruined everything, too, making my husband fall in love with her. Just like that woman made my father fall in love with her."

At the mention of his mother, Rafe turned his gaze from Allie to Charlotte. She was mad, he thought. Completely mad. He wondered why no one had seen it before.

Her face was contorted with fury. "You always ruin

everything . . . you women who take away what matters to me."

As she spoke, her hands went to a small statue sitting on the edge of the desk. Grabbing it in one hand, she raised it above her, threatening Allie.

Shock and terror collided as Allie saw the clawlike hands clutching the statue. The long, perfectly manicured nails glistened bright crimson, like blood. They were the same monster hands from the shadows of a child's hidden memory.

"It was *you,*" she breathed. "*You* killed my mother."

Charlotte's eyes seemed to glaze over and her mouth trembled. "I had to. She would have made David leave me, just like that woman made my father leave my mother and me."

Charlotte's expression hardened. "I can't let you take away all that's left."

She lunged toward Allie. Before she could strike the first blow, Rafe had crossed the room and gripped her thin wrist in his strong hand.

"Stop it, Charlotte! It's over!"

Charlotte screamed sounds of madness and rage as she fought against Rafe. He held her away from Allie, twisting down hard on her arm. But Charlotte had the strength of madness. Pulling away from Rafe, she ran out of the room.

Rafe started to go after her, but Allie stopped him. "Rafe, please, don't leave me."

He went to her, pulling her into his arms. His hands moved over her possessively, reassuring himself that she was all right.

Outside, they heard the sound of a car start up, then race away down the driveway.

"Rafe . . ." Allie whispered helplessly.

"Shh, sweetheart, it's all right now, everything's all right." He pulled her closer, drew her hard against him.

"I trusted you," she said, clinging to him.

"I know." He gently rocked her in his arms, trying to reassure her and give her strength, even as she gave it to him simply by being alive.

The police arrived a few minutes later. It took an hour for Allie to calm down enough to give a coherent account of what had just happened—and what had happened twenty-five years earlier. Rafe sat next to her the whole time, holding her hand, murmuring words of reassurance.

The patrolman had immediately put out an APB for Charlotte. But as Rafe and Allie were going out to the car, a call came in over the radio in the patrol car. Another patrol car had seen Charlotte's car, which was traveling much too fast for the foggy conditions. On a particularly dangerous section of Highway 1, she'd gone off a cliff.

Epilogue

HE ONLY WAY TO *remember is to go back.*

Allie had gone back, and she had remembered. All the pieces f broken dreams, the nightmare images and fragmented emories, had finally been put into place. She had always elieved that if she knew the truth, no matter what it was, she ould face it. Well, she had faced it, and now that she was free f the shadows of the past, she could begin to live for the iture.

Rafe explained to her that when he found Barbara that night, e assumed Alan had killed her in a fit of jealous rage. When lan was arrested and tried for Barbara's murder, Rafe fled, errified that he might be asked to testify against Alan, for hom he still felt a profound loyalty.

Allie had always believed in her parents and their love for ach other. In many ways, the ache of loss was sharper if omehow sweeter in knowing that she had been right to believe them, to believe in herself, and in her husband.

Now she slowly came down the hallway from the kitchen, here she'd been helping Miguel's wife, Cathy, prepare ipper. It was one of those magnificent winter days where inshine warmed everything, teasing everyone into believing iat it couldn't possibly be winter.

Outside, the sky was a magnificent crystal blue. There had been no fog for weeks. Inside, she hesitated slightly at the sight of the hall mirror. Her heart beat a little faster with old remnants of fear, but she quickly brought it back under control. Tentatively touching the glass, she forced herself to look unafraid at the reflection of the open doorway into the den across the hall.

"Mirror, mirror, on the wall . . ." she whispered. And out of her memory came her mother's soft voice, asking, *"Who is the fairest one of all?"*

Allie's smile was tinged with sadness and profound love as she whispered back to her mother, "You're the fairest one of all, Mommy."

Then she saw her husband's reflection as he came down the stairs. There were no lingering twinges of fear, no moments of uncertainty.

"Are you ready, sweetheart?" he asked, taking her into his arms.

Allie pulled closer, holding tightly to him. She loved the way he could be so gentle and caring with her, but she also loved the rough urgency she felt in him when he held her, as if he were afraid she might disappear.

He'd arranged for a wedding reception, since they'd never had any formal celebration of their marriage. The thought had crossed her mind that a small, intimate gathering with friends might go a long way toward convincing the judge their marriage was real. But more important, she and Rafe wanted to reaffirm their vows to each other.

After her brush with death, Allie realized that she very much wanted to have a baby—Rafe's baby. It would be an affirmation of life, and she found she very much wanted to hold on to life as hard as she could. They hadn't discussed it yet, but he had once told her that the reason he'd never had a family was that he wanted to be able to give his children a solid family foundation that included both a mother and father.

There were no guarantees in anything, but she truly believed that because of the losses they had both experienced, they would try doubly hard to be good parents.

She kissed him long and slow, bringing her body full against his in a way that suggested all over again why they had been ate getting downstairs that morning as their guests had started o arrive.

She had come out several days earlier with Inez to supervise he cleaning of the hacienda, and to banish the last of the ghosts rom the night Charlotte died. Allie wanted to live there—it vas something that felt right. Instinctively, she knew she vanted to raise her family there.

Rafe drove out in the evenings. He spent the last two days ielping get things ready. The previous afternoon he had ridden out with the vaqueros on horseback to the southern range, as he iad when he was a rebellious youth, perhaps exorcising the last of his own demons.

He had suggested that they close the den off, thinking that he would prefer it. Allie recalled what Mac had once said, that he hacienda was a living history of the Sloan family.

It was a place of marriages, births, and deaths. It defined vho they were, and symbolized the survival of the Sloans and Aarins. Allie persuaded Rafe that the den should remain as it vas, with a few minor changes.

The reception he'd planned was to be a traditional old Californio celebration. Musicians had been brought in from Aonterey, and a side of beef turned at the barbecue. Long ables had been set up in the center courtyard and decorated vith brightly colored cloths taken from chests at Casa Sureno. anterns had been strung along the heavy timbered overhang. Out in the pastures, descendents of Ben Sloan's brown and vhite Virginia cattle grazed while vaqueros rode in the lazy fternoon.

If she blocked out the Mercedes, pickup trucks, and rental ars that had brought their guests out from Monterey, Allie new that El Sureno would look very much as it had when Elena Marin had married Ben Sloan.

Ben had been an enterprising man. He'd understood that hange was necessary to preserve what he loved. Allie and Rafe also understood that. The development of El Sureno that hey had begun would preserve the heart of the land that they oth loved.

Outside, their guests waited. Julia had flown in from Seattle. he sat at one of the tables with Liz DiMaggio, laughing at omething Liz said.

Miguel, his wife, and their children bustled about setting out the original dinner plates that Elena Marin had purchased for the hacienda.

Inez had come with her daughter and grandson. The little boy hung over the fence at the paddock with the vaqueros, staring longingly at an agile roping pony that was being put through its paces.

The other members of the Sloan family were conspicuous by their absence. Since the party was Rafe's idea, she suspected they hadn't been invited, and knew they wouldn't have come even if they had been.

The lawsuit was still pending, although Rafe was confident it would eventually be dismissed. But they both knew that would never change Gavin's feelings toward his half brother. There were some fences that could never be mended.

At Allie's urging, Rafe had paid off Nicky's gambling debt. Allie reminded him they were, after all, family. But Rafe made it clear this was the only time he would do so. Nicky would either clean up his act, or face the consequences.

Valentina was an entirely different matter. It wouldn't have surprised Allie if she had shown up at the party uninvited. Although the last anyone had heard of her, she was trying to put the scandal of having a murderer for a mother far behind her—as far as the yacht of a Kuwaiti prince, who was also a racing enthusiast, could possibly take her.

Allie had flown up to Seattle and brought her grandmother back to Monterey with her. It took all her persuasiveness to do it.

During that time together on the flight, she explained everything that had happened. Her grandmother found it difficult at first to accept that her son-in-law hadn't killed her daughter after all. Some feelings were hard to let go of, Allie realized. In many ways Anna Wyatt would always hold the Sloan family responsible for her daughter's death.

Her grandmother had also been upset about the marriage until Allie made her understand just how much she and Rafe loved each other.

Now Anna sat alone at the edge of the courtyard, still trying to come to terms with the past.

Allie gently laid a hand on her shoulder as she came up

behind her. "You shouldn't sit alone, Gram." Then she added softly, "You have to let go of the past, Gram. It's too painful to try to hold on to it."

Anna sighed. "I know, Allie. I'm trying."

Gesturing toward Liz, Allie said, "Did you know she was my mother's best friend?" At her grandmother's look of surprise, she went on. "I think you two could share a lot of memories of her. It might help make up for the emptiness of the past twenty-five years."

Anna reached out and took her granddaughter's hand. "The past twenty-five years were never empty. You filled them up with love and joy, for both your grandfather and me."

Her grandmother paused, then said, "When you lose someone you love deeply, you learn truly to value those who are left. And you keep the memories of those who are gone in your heart."

Allie reassured her, "I know Rafe loves me. I know I can trust him."

Anna responded hesitantly, "I hope so . . ."

Allie knew it might take a long time for her grandmother to accept Rafe, but she was confident it would happen eventually.

Rafe joined them. "Miguel has announced that supper will be in exactly one hour. That gives us just enough time." He slipped his hand around hers.

She held on to his warmth and strength as she smiled up at him. "Enough time for what?"

"For the real reason for all of this," he explained. Then he pulled her to her feet. "We have to drive to get there. But first I wanted to give you this." He handed her a small wrapped box that looked suspiciously like a ring box.

Allie looked chagrined. She hadn't gotten him anything. "I think my gift to you will have to be a new paint job on the Corvette after that drive I made across the ranch."

"Come on, sweetheart."

She gave him a perplexed look as he asked everyone to get into their cars and follow them. Then they climbed into the jeep and led the procession away from the hacienda, down the dirt road they had followed months earlier when they had first gone exploring together.

It had all been so new to her then, this vast ranch. It was over one hundred thousand acres and almost twenty miles of pristine coastline, virtually unchanged over the past one hundred fifty years. And except for a small four-mile stretch in the north that encompassed six thousand acres—the new township of El Sureno—it would remain so.

"What are you thinking?" Rafe asked as they churned over the open road, the wind blowing through the open four-wheel-drive vehicle.

She lay back against the headrest and looked up at the sky. "That I would like to be up there," she answered, thinking of the time they had spent in the glider. "So that I can see it all at one time, and know that it really exists." She made an expansive gesture at the surrounding golden hillsides. "So that I know it's safe."

His hand covered hers on the seat beside her. "It exists just as it did for Elena Marin and Ben Sloan. And it's safe. We'll make certain of it."

Then they were driving past the point where the road angled inland toward the east grazing ranges. She realized that they were headed for Elena's Point.

Her guess was confirmed as Rafe slowed the jeep and finally came to a stop at the base of the slope a few hundred yards below the point. They waited for the other cars to arrive.

Then, as everyone got out and stared at the coastal panorama that spread before them, he took her hand. "Ready for a walk?"

She closed her hand around his, guessing that he intended to show their friends and guests the breathtaking view from the top of Elena's Point, the most spectacular vista on the entire ranch, and the place where Elena use to ride as a young woman.

It was a short, easy walk. At the top, near the wedding rock, Allie discovered someone waiting for them as the guests slowly gathered around them. She recognized the priest who had performed the mass for Mac's funeral at the small Church of the Wayfarer in Carmel.

Rafe briefly explained, "Father Peters agreed to perform the ceremony."

Allie was stunned. "What ceremony?"

"The formal Catholic marriage ceremony," Rafe told her.

"Here at the wedding rock, where it all began for Elena." She could only stare at him as her eyes filled with tears. Her grandmother had said once that the true measure of love came when a person gave of himself, not because it was necessary, but because it was given freely.

This gesture, completely unnecessary when they were already legally married, came from the heart.

Rafe took something out of his pocket and unfolded it. It was Elena's black lace mantilla with the tiny pearls at the edge that Allie had worn to the Cascarones Ball.

"We're not in church, so it's not required that you wear it," Rafe explained. "But I wish you would." He reached over and draped it over her shoulder-length hair. Then, taking her hand, he said, "There's something very important that I want to ask you."

She was so overwhelmed, she could respond only with a nod.

"Will you marry me?" he asked in a husky voice.

She felt as if her heart would break. In that brief moment that he asked it, she sensed the need deep inside him that came from the young boy who had been cast off from his parents and family, who had made his way alone in the world, and never asked for anything from anyone. He was asking now.

She smiled. "Not for business, not for the ranch. Just for you. Yes, I'll marry you."

Then they turned to the priest. And there at the wedding rock at Elena's Point on the promontory overlooking the magnificent Pacific Ocean, Father Peters began the wedding ceremony.

When he asked to bless the rings, Allie started to remove the wedding band that Rafe had bought for her in Lake Tahoe. But he reminded her of the gift that he'd given her before they left the hacienda. She quickly unwrapped the small package, and found a black velvet ring box. Inside was a gold ring intricately designed with what appeared to be hands clasped over the crown of the ring. The etched design was of the finest craftsmanship, yet the design in the gold was faintly worn, as if the ring were very old. Rafe took it from her and revealed that it was in fact two rings, one overlaid on top of another simple band, as the tiny clasped hands opened to reveal a single heart underneath. When the hands were once more clasped, the ring represented two hands holding one heart.

"Ben Sloan gave this ring to Elena Marin on their wedding day. I wanted you to have it."

He gave the antique ring to Father Peters, who blessed it. Then he placed the ring on her finger. Beneath a brilliant blue winter sky and the warm sun where it had all begun one hundred fifty years ago, they stood together on that windswept hillside, hands clasped, as the priest intoned the ancient vows binding them together forever.

About the Author

PAMELA SIMPSON is actually the pen name for the writing team of Pamela Wallace and Carla Simpson.

PAMELA WALLACE, a native Californian with a degree from UCLA, worked as an editor and writer for magazines before beginning her career as a novelist and screenwriter. She co-wrote the screenplay for *Witness*, for which she won an Academy Award (the Oscar), a Writer's Guild Award, and the Mystery Writers of America Award (the Edgar).

Three of her novels have been produced as made-for-cable movies for SHOWTIME: *Tears in the Rain; Dreams Lost, Dreams Found;* and *Love with a Perfect Stranger*. She also co-wrote the screenplay for the movie *If the Shoe Fits*.

Her current projects include a mini-series for NBC, a pilot for a series for HBO, and a new novel written with Carla Simpson. She lives with her son, Christopher, in Fresno, California.

CARLA SIMPSON has written nearly a dozen novels, including *Memory and Desire* (a Zebra Special Release), and *Always My Love* (a Pinnacle Super Release). She is the creator of a series of historical mysteries called *California Gold*, coming in 1993 from Zebra. Carla lives in Coarsegold, California with her husband and family.

If you loved MIRROR, MIRROR, don't miss

Fortune's Child

by

Pamela Simpson

"This **exceptionally well-written novel** completely mesmerizes the lucky reader. Ms. Simpson's **wonderfully rich characterizations** delve deeply into a bevy of **fascinating personalities**, while her subtle but **powerful romantic theme** strikes a **tremendously satisfying** emotional chord. **Don't miss this knockout read!**" —*Romantic Times*

She was a woman of ambitious dreams who wasn't afraid to play the games of the rich by their precarious rules. Other women had claimed to be Christina Fortune, missing heiress to one of the world's largest shipping empires. Now this beautiful, self-assured woman had stepped out of the shadows of the past, daring to take what she insisted was hers.

29424-5 $5.99/6.99 in Canada

☐ Please send me a copy of Pamela Simpson's FORTUNE'S CHILD. I am enclosing $ 8.49 ($9.49 in Canada)—including $2.50 to cover postage and handling.
Send check or money order, no cash or C. O. D.'s please.
Mr./ Ms. ____________________
Address ____________________
City/ State/ Zip ____________________
Send order to: Bantam Books, Dept. FN103, 2451 S. Wolf Rd., Des Plaines, IL 60018
Please allow four to six weeks for delivery.
Prices and availability subject to change without notice. FN103 - 5/93

BANTAM DOUBLEDAY DELL
PRESENTS THE

WINNERS CLASSIC SWEEPSTAKES

Dear Bantam Doubleday Dell Reader,

We'd like to say "Thanks" for choosing our books. So we're giving you a chance to enter our Winners Classic Sweepstakes, where you can win a Grand Prize of $25,000.00, or one of over 1,000 other sensational prizes! All prizes are guaranteed to be awarded. Return the Official Entry Form at once! And when you're ready for another great reading experience, we hope you'll keep Bantam Doubleday Dell books at the top of your reading list!

OFFICIAL ENTRY FORM

Yes! Enter me in the Winners Classic Sweepstakes and guarantee my eligibility to be awarded any prize, including the $25,000.00 Grand Prize. Notify me at once if I am declared a winner.

NAME

ADDRESS APT. #

CITY

STATE ZIP

REGISTRATION NUMBER **01995A**

Please mail to: LS-SBA

BANTAM DOUBLEDAY DELL DIRECT, INC.
WINNERS CLASSIC SWEEPSTAKES
PO Box 985, Hicksville, NY 11802-0985

OFFICIAL PRIZE LIST

LS-SBB

GRAND PRIZE: *$25,000.00 CASH!*

FIRST PRIZE: FISHER HOME ENTERTAINMENT CENTER

Including complete integrated audio/video system with 130-watt amplifier, AM/FM stereo tuner, dual cassette deck, CD player, Surround Sound speakers and universal remote control unit.

SECOND PRIZE: TOSHIBA VCR *5 winners!*

Featuring full-function, high-quality 4-Head performance, with 8-event/365-day timer, wireless remote control, and more.

THIRD PRIZE: CONCORD 35MM CAMERA OUTFIT *35 winners!*

Featuring focus-free precision lens, built-in automatic film loading, advance and rewind.

FOURTH PRIZE: BOOK LIGHT *1,000 winners!*

A model of convenience, with a flexible neck that bends in any direction, and a steady clip that holds sure on any surface.

OFFICIAL RULES AND REGULATIONS

No purchase necessary. To enter the sweepstakes follow instructions found elsewhere in this offer. You can also enter the sweepstakes by hand printing your name, address, city, state and zip code on a 3" x 5" piece of paper and mailing it to: Winners Classic Sweepstakes, P.O. Box 785, Gibbstown, NJ 08027. Mail each entry separately. Sweepstakes begins 12/1/91. Entries must be received by 6/1/93. Some presentations of this sweepstakes may feature a deadline for the Early Bird prize. If the offer you receive does, then to be eligible for the Early Bird prize your entry must be received according to the Early Bird date specified. Not responsible for lost, damaged, misdirected, illegible or postage due mail. Mechanically reproduced entries are not eligible. All entries become property of the sponsor and will not be returned.

Prize Selection/Validations: Winners will be selected in random drawings on or about 7/30/93, by Ventura Associates, Inc., an independent judging organization whose decisions are final. Odds of winning are determined by total number of entries received. Circulation of this sweepstakes is estimated not to exceed 200 million. Entrants need not be present to win. All prizes are guaranteed to be awarded and delivered to winners. Winners will be notified by mail and may be required to complete an affidavit of eligibility and release of liability which must be returned within 14 days of date on notification or alternate winners will be selected. Any guest of a trip winner will also be required to execute a release of liability. Any prize notification letter or any prize returned to a participating sponsor, Bantam Doubleday Dell Publishing Group, Inc. its participating divisions or subsidiaries or VENTURA ASSOCIATES, INC. as undeliverable will be awarded to an alternate winner. Prizes are not transferable. No multiple prize winners except for Early Bird Prize, which may be awarded in addition to another prize. No substitution for prizes except as may be necessary due to unavailability in which case a prize of equal or greater value will be awarded. Prizes will be awarded approximately 90 days after the drawing. All taxes, automobile license and registration fees, if applicable, are the sole responsibility of the winners. Entry constitutes permission (except where prohibited) to use winners names and likenesses for publicity purposes without further or other compensation.

Participation: This sweepstakes is open to residents of the United States and Canada, except for the province of Quebec. This sweepstakes is sponsored by Bantam Doubleday Dell Publishing Group, Inc. (BDD), 666 Fifth Avenue, New York, NY 10103. Versions of this sweepstakes with different graphics will be offered in conjunction with various solicitations or promotions by different subsidiaries and divisions of BDD. Employees and their famililes of BDD, its division, subsidiaries, advertising agencies, and VENTURA ASSOCIATES, INC. are not eligible.

Canadian residents, in order to win, must first correctly answer a time limited arithmetical skill testing question. Void in Quebec and wherever prohibited or restricted by law. Subject to all federal, state, local and provincial laws and regulations.

Prizes: The following values for prizes are determined by the manufacturers' suggested retail prices or by what these items are currently known to be selling for at the time this offer was published. Approximate retail values include handling and delivery of prizes. Estimated maximum retail value of prizes: 1 Grand Prize ($27,500 if merchandise or $25,000 Cash); 1 First Prize ($3,000); 5 Second Prizes ($400 ea); 35 Third Prizes ($100 ea); 1,000 Fourth Prizes ($9.00 ea); 1 Early Bird Prize ($5,000); Total approximate maximum retail value is $50,000. Winners will have the option of selecting any prize offered at level won. Automobile winner must have a valid driver's license at the time the car is awarded. Trips are subject to space and departure availability. Certain black-out dates may apply. Travel must be completed within one year from the time the prize is awarded. Minors must be accompanied by an adult. Prizes won by minors will be awarded in the name of parent or legal guardian.

For a list of Major Prize Winners (available after 7/30/93): send a self-addressed, stamped envelope entirely separate from your entry to Winners Classic Sweepstakes Winners, P.O. Box 825, Gibbstown, NJ 08027. Requests must be received by 6/1/93. DO NOT SEND ANY OTHER CORRESPONDENCE TO THIS P.O. BOX.